LADY CATHERINE'S SECRET
SECRETS AND SEDUCTION

SHERIDAN JEANE

A Flowers and Fullerton Book / published by arrangement with the author

Copyright 2014 by Sheridan Jeane
Cover Design by Earthly Charms
ISBN: 978-1-63303-006-0

Produced by Sheridan Jeane
at Flowers and Fullerton, LLC
Cleveland, OH
www.SheridanJeane.com

For my husband Bob,
and for my father,
but especially for my mother,
Winnie Jean Flanegan Ferguson,
who loved this book.

Whenever I look upon its pages,
her love and support shine upon me.
Lady Catherine's Secret will always hold
a special place in my heart.
I miss you, Mom.

BERNINI'S ACADEMY

January, 1853, London

"You're walking like a girl."

Lady Catherine Williams whipped around, scowling at her older brother. Her hood fell back, but even under the flickering glow of the gas lanterns outside the fencing academy, it hardly mattered. The snug white cap she wore kept her hair securely hidden.

"Slouch your shoulders." Charles's critical gaze swept over her. "And lengthen your stride."

She shot him a challenging look and then spit expertly into a pile of icy slush at the edge of the slick cobblestone road.

He closed his eyes and shook his head in mock despair. "Mother would be so proud."

Catherine chuckled. "Spitting would be the least of my problems if Mother could see me now."

She hurried up the stone stairs of Bernini's Academy and into its welcoming light, her brother trailing a step behind her. As she stepped through the doorway, contentment enveloped her. She was finally returning to her true home. She grinned at Charles, overwhelmed by the sheer joy of the moment.

He shot her a quelling glare.

Mr. Winston, a secretary for the academy, sprang to his feet from behind a tall, gleaming front desk.

"Lord Spencer, how good to see you." As always, his unctuous tones made Catherine want to avoid him. "And young Master Gray," he said, turning his gaze toward Catherine, "how wonderful to have you both back in London. If I may say, it's been much too long since we've seen you."

Despite the small, balding man's over-effusive behavior, Catherine had to admit that he was good at his job and kept the place running smoothly. Even so, she could only manage to give him a curt nod.

Winston peered at them through his round, wire-framed spectacles. "I'll let Maestro Bernini know you're here. He'll be quite pleased." He gave a small bow and departed through the office doorway with short, precise footsteps.

"I hate doing this next part," Catherine murmured.

"You'll get no sympathy from me. You can always go home," Charles said. He didn't even pause before heading toward the dressing area. He knew her too well to think she'd actually leave.

Catherine followed closely on Charles's heels and crossed the threshold into a purely male domain no properly-bred young woman should ever lay eyes upon. Her stomach knotted, and she kept her gaze trained on the polished, wood-paneled walls and the tall personal storage boxes. The woodwork gleamed from the regular applications of lemon oil, and its aroma lingered in the air, not quite masking the musky, male scent of perspiration.

Long ago, she'd laid claim to a storage cabinet near the entrance. With Charles by her side to shield her, she snatched up her foil and mask, and then darted back out the door.

"*En garde.*" Charles's traditional parting words trailed behind him as he entered the academy's main salon without a backward glance.

As if she needed a reminder of how much she risked by being here.

Catherine strode into the main room with her chin high. Charles said her disguise would still pass muster, and she trusted him. By design, the pants fit tightly around her calves and were loose around her hips. She'd become a bit rounder in the past year or so, and the carefully crafted clothing helped hide her curves. The doublet, with its heavy padding across her chest and some additional padding she'd sewn around the waist, successfully hid any hints of femininity. The most important part of her disguise came from the careful application of collodion. She used that clever bit of theatrical makeup to create a natural-looking puckered scar that ran from her cheek into her hairline.

She tugged at the snug white skullcap covering her hair, assuring herself that no stray strands had escaped. The other fencers were used to seeing her wear it, and only newcomers looked twice at it these days. Years ago, Charles had let it slip that Gray had suffered a severe burn, leaving his head horribly scarred. The fake scar she created with the collodion supported the story.

Catherine stopped to absorb the feel of the space, letting it soak into her bones. She bounced on her toes and then peered up at the gas chandeliers with their cut-glass shades that always caused the light to sparkle. She inhaled, savoring the various mingled scents of men's colognes—along with that unpleasant faint undertone of perspiration.

She was finally home—in her *true* home.

Catherine set her fencing mask on the floor along one of the walls. She wouldn't need it until they picked up their foils. The crisscrossing strands of wire protected her face from being injured by an accidental slashing motion, but the large, one-inch-wide mesh squares would never be able to deflect a direct thrust. At least she could see clearly through it. Papa had given it to her a number of years ago. He always insisted upon safety and had ensured that both Catherine and Charles were well supplied with the necessary fencing gear.

Smiling faintly to herself, Catherine made a quick perusal of the occupants in the large fencing salon. She spied only two faces she didn't recognize, so she paused to assess the newcomers' fencing abilities as they warmed up with some light sparring. After only a moment, she realized they were friends.

"Pick up the pace, Huntley," one of them called out over the clashing steel that echoed through the room. "Is the hunt for the perfect wife wearing you out? Must be exhausting, trying to find someone *perfectly* proper."

In response, the slightly taller man, Huntley, performed an envelopment, sweeping his friend's blade through a full circle. He lunged forward on his long, muscular legs and scored a point. The other man scowled, clearly annoyed.

Huntley moved gracefully as he whipped his foil through the air. He looked lively enough to Catherine. The muscles in his extended rear leg bunched and moved under his tight-fitting breeches, reminding her of jungle cats she'd seen at the London Zoo. He was like a panther, she decided, as he pulled off his mask, revealing his black hair. But his eyes seemed slightly incongruous with that image. They should have been golden brown rather than a clear, bright blue.

Huntley regarded his friend and raised his left eyebrow so high it disappeared behind a lock of his tousled hair. "I'm here tonight to escape all that, and thank you for bringing it up." He peered at his friend more closely. "What's bothering you? You're testy tonight. I'd hoped some light sparring would improve your mood, but I'm beginning to think the only thing that will knock some sense into you is a thrashing." Huntley slipped on his fencing mask and dropped into an "*en garde*" stance, raising his foil in a salute. "Maybe I can accommodate you." When his friend hesitated, Huntley flicked his foil in a beckoning gesture, inviting the challenge.

His friend responded with a fierce grin, lowered his mask, and raised his foil. In the blink of an eye, they were locked in a brisk, yet friendly, duel.

Both men were skilled, but Catherine's gaze kept drifting to Huntley. His powerful stance and fluid movements through each lunge held her attention. He wasn't just tall—he was quick, his agility belying his size. He would be a formidable opponent.

With an almost palpable intensity, he seemed to notice everything taking place in the room, even as he focused on his fencing match.

Just like a predator.

Huntley's piercing gaze caught hers, and his jaw tightened, clearly aware she had been staring. Catherine instinctively began to smile but quickly stopped herself, turning it into a smirk. Where did she think she was—at a soirée? Her fingers fumbled with the foil as the realization hit: she had nearly flirted with him. How could she have been so careless? She turned away, her face burning with embarrassment.

As she stretched, feeling the tension ease from her lower back, Catherine continued to watch them, casting only the occasional furtive glance over her shoulder, careful not to be caught staring again. Though the two men held back, their attacks lacking force, Huntley's blend of polished technique, strength, and power was still an impressive display. She'd need to watch them both more closely during a real match.

Catherine was so focused on the newcomers that she didn't notice someone slipping up behind her until a sharp tap landed on her shoulder. The unmistakable feel of a foil handle. She spun around, already knowing who it was. Maestro Bernini. Of course. He delighted in sneaking up on his students, though he rarely managed to catch her off guard.

His eyes sparkled at his rare victory. "*Buona sera*, Gray. It's good to see you. Don't you ever grow?" His gravelly voice held an

Italian accent as the words rolled off his tongue. He shook his head and tut-tutted.

Catherine pressed her lips together, pushing aside the flicker of anxiety. Bernini either didn't notice the discomfort he'd stirred in her or simply didn't care. Either way, it was another reminder—she wouldn't be able to pass as Alexander Gray much longer.

"You're no taller than the last time I saw you six months ago." Bernini's brows furrowed together as he glared at her. "*Eat*, boy. We need to increase your reach." He clapped her hard on the back, almost causing her to stumble.

Fortunately, he didn't notice her grimace.

"*Attenzione*. Let's begin, shall we?" Bernini's voice cut through the chatter, commanding immediate attention. They started with basic footwork drills, but it wasn't long before he moved them into more intricate techniques. He prowled the room, offering corrections to each student with his sharp, discerning eye.

He gave Catherine a satisfied nod as he passed, and some of her anxiety dissipated. She hated it when he found fault with her. There was nothing she could do about his earlier criticism except grow taller, and unfortunately, that was well beyond her abilities.

As was typical for the last part of the evening, Bernini demonstrated a more advanced technique for them to learn. Catherine watched him carefully and then slid through the steps of the move, mastering it quickly and earning another nod of approval from the maestro.

She glanced at Huntley in time to see that he, too, earned a similar nod. She hid the small smile of satisfaction. She'd been right. The man was good.

Excitement raced through her when, at last, the best part of the evening arrived. Catherine rolled forward on her toes, anticipation coursing through her as Maestro Bernini began pairing off the students, matching them by size and skill. As usual, she was the exception. Her small stature meant she was often pitted against much larger opponents.

Charles was paired with Huntley, and she felt a wave of mixed relief and annoyance. At least she wouldn't have to face him. Still, it was probably for the best; Huntley distracted her, and that unsettling fact gnawed at her. Then Bernini's voice broke her thoughts as he called her name, pairing her with one of Huntley's friends. A spark of intrigue flickered through her as they approached each other, fencing masks tucked under their arms, each sizing the other up. He was a few inches shorter than Huntley, but at six feet tall, he still towered over her.

He lifted his chin, looking down his nose at her, eyes narrowing as he sized her up. Clearly, he found her lacking.

"Gray, you'll be fencing one of our new guests this evening, the Earl of Wentworth," Bernini announced.

"A boy?" Wentworth sneered, curling his lip.

Bernini's smile turned crafty. "Don't let Gray's size deceive you, my lord. He may be the finest student I've ever trained. His only shortcoming is his height, though I'm certain he'll grow out of it." Bernini chuckled at his own tired joke, one Catherine had long stopped finding amusing. "He may even win the tournament I plan to hold in a few months."

Wentworth gave her a look of renewed interest, cocking an eyebrow. "High praise, indeed, young man. I must say, you don't look like much of a challenge—you barely reach my chin."

Catherine arched an eyebrow in return, feeling the collodion tug on the skin where she'd crafted her fake scar. This should be fun. Nothing pleased her more than being underestimated by a newcomer. She'd relish the chance to surprise him.

But that would have to wait. She fixed her gaze on Bernini. "Maestro, did I hear you correctly? Are you holding a tournament?"

"I didn't mean to reveal that yet." His eyes darted around before he lowered his voice. "I'm planning to hold the first annual Bernini's Cup." He pressed a finger to his lips, signaling secrecy. "I'll explain more at the end of the evening."

Catherine straightened, heart pounding. Bernini believed she could win a fencing tournament? A thrill of excitement coursed through her. Could she really do something so daring? She pictured it—her victory, the white skullcap torn off, revealing to the astonished crowd what a woman could achieve when given the chance. But the imagined faces quickly shifted. Admiration turned to shock, then outrage. Her stomach twisted. If the truth came out—that Lady Catherine had entered the gentlemen's changing room, masquerading as a man—her family would be ruined. She'd be branded a woman of loose morals, shunned by society. The price of a fleeting moment of glory would be too high.

But it *was* a splendid dream.

Though Wentworth angled his body away, Catherine still caught his murmur to Huntley. "After everything I've heard about Bernini's, I expected more of a challenge."

Her fingers tightened around the wire rim of her mask, the metal digging into her skin. If it was a challenge he wanted, she'd make sure he got one.

"Don't be so cocky." Huntley glanced at her, but she avoided his gaze. "I watched him earlier. He's quite good. Fences better than most grown men."

The unexpected praise sent a rush of pride through her. He'd noticed her? She'd been observing him all night, assessing his abilities, but how had she missed that he'd been doing the same?

"That's absurd. He's only a child," Wentworth scoffed, spinning on his heel to face her, his eyes gleaming with anticipation. He tugged his mask into place.

After a traditional salute, Wentworth's first move was a laughably weak advance, clearly meant to insult her. Catherine parried it without effort. He growled, lunging with a loud slap of his foot on the boards, but she merely grinned and danced out of reach. These theatrics wouldn't rattle her.

Wentworth kept testing her, looking for a weakness, but she

stayed guarded. When he deliberately left himself exposed, she didn't take the bait, flicking his foil aside with ease. Her grin widened. His frown deepened. Frustration was beginning to show.

They sparred like this for a while, neither scoring any points, just feeling each other out. One by one, the other fencers finished their matches, gathering around to watch as Catherine and Wentworth remained the only pair still dueling.

Out of the corner of her eye, Catherine caught sight of Huntley, his head tilted as he studied their match. When her foil struck squarely in the center of Wentworth's chest scoring the first point, Huntley joined the others in polite applause.

The moment he was hit, Wentworth jerked his head back in surprise and then glared at her. He let out a huff of frustration and immediately dropped into the *"en garde"* stance to continue the bout.

Catherine saw a brief frisson of tension spark through Wentworth's body. Years of fencing had taught Catherine how to read the subtle shifts in an opponent's mood, and Wentworth's temper had just flared.

"Mind yourself, Wentworth, he's just a boy," Huntley called out.

Catherine's eyes narrowed as she focused on Wentworth, shutting out everything else in the room. Huntley's comment had the opposite effect—throwing fuel on Wentworth's already smoldering temper.

"It's time I taught this boy a *lesson*." Wentworth lunged, clearly hoping to catch her off guard, but his fury made him sloppy. Catherine parried with ease, her foil gliding smoothly along his, deflecting the attack.

The metal of their foils sang as she pushed his blade aside and struck. Her tip found his right shoulder, effortlessly scoring another point. The foil arched as she pressed it into his doublet, leaving no doubt of her hit.

A deep flush crept across Wentworth's face, visible even

through his mask. As she stepped back, his empty hand clenched into a tight fist. Anger was dangerous—it made a fencer unpredictable and careless. And careless was deadly. Catherine could see the tension ripple through the watching crowd, their startled expressions reflecting Wentworth's growing rage. She bit down on her bottom lip, the sharp taste of salt hitting her tongue.

What would he do next?

Thankfully, Maestro Bernini had also noticed the rising tension. He stepped between them, hands raised, cutting off the match before it could escalate further.

"Two points," Bernini announced, his voice firm. "And we are done." He took each of their hands, raising them above his head as he addressed the gathered audience. "Excellent work, gentlemen. I know we usually go to three points, but I'm afraid we must cut this short tonight." He dropped their hands, pausing to flash a salacious grin. "I have a most pressing engagement this evening, so I must ask you all to leave promptly." The twinkle in his eye left little mystery as to the nature of that engagement. Bernini's appetite for women was notorious. "Wentworth, Gray, splendid match. I look forward to your rematch."

Wentworth gave Bernini a curt nod, not even glancing in her direction as he walked away.

The tension drained from Catherine the moment Wentworth turned his back. She almost sagged with relief.

"Before everyone leaves, I have an announcement to make," Bernini said, his voice cutting through the room. He paused, ensuring all eyes were on him. "The first annual Bernini's Fencing Tournament will be held on the second Saturday in March. The winner will receive a modest purse and a traveling trophy." A spark of interest rippled through the crowd as he smiled. "The victor's name will also be engraved on a plaque, and he may keep the trophy until he's beaten in a future tournament. If you wish to enter, speak with Mr. Winston and provide your entry fee."

The room buzzed with murmurs of excitement as students

swarmed Bernini with questions. Catherine, wanting to speak with him as well, knew she wouldn't get close. She'd look like a small dog trying to force its way into a pack of wolves.

Across the room, Wentworth yanked off his mask and locked eyes with her. His glare lingered before he lifted his chin, closing his eyes. A moment later, his shoulders relaxed, his anger evaporating as quickly as it had flared. When he opened his eyes again, they were cool, distant. He gave her a curt nod of acknowledgment before turning on his heel and striding toward the door. He tossed his foil and mask to a servant, leaving behind the other fencers—and the incident—as if it had never happened.

Catherine blinked, watching him go. How had his temper vanished so quickly? Was it an act?

She shifted her gaze to Huntley, looking for his reaction. He seemed relieved. Then, almost as if sensing her eyes on him, his head snapped toward her.

Before she could fully register it, Huntley was already crossing the room, striding directly toward her.

Did he mean to speak with her? Apparently so. She tucked her mask under her arm.

"My compliments to you, Gray," Huntley said, his voice carrying a faint but unmistakable Scottish lilt. "You bested my friend on his first night at Bernini's. He'd planned to show off his finely honed skills, but instead, he found himself beaten by a young pup barely out of clouts." His smile broadened as he handed his equipment to a waiting servant. When he looked back at her, his gaze lingered on the scar that marked her cheek.

Clouts? Catherine didn't know whether to be insulted by his reference to diapering a baby, or laugh it off. "I hope your friend will forgive the affront, as none was intended. Lady Luck favored me tonight. Lord Wentworth is an excellent fencer. I look forward to our next match." She scratched her nose, casting a glance at the empty doorway where Wentworth had exited. How much trouble was that man going to be?

"You seem mature for a boy of your years," Huntley said, drawing her attention back to him. His cool blue eyes focused on her with unsettling intensity, like a hawk sizing up a mouse. "What are you, twelve... fourteen?" His eyes narrowed, sweeping over her, measuring every inch.

The question put her immediately on guard. Perhaps his last comment about clouts *had* been meant to rattle her. She raised an eyebrow, refusing to be baited. "And you, sir? How old are you?"

Bernini, passing by, must have overheard their exchange. He paused, saying, "Lord Huntley, may I introduce our star pupil, young Alexander Gray. Master Gray, you have the honor of meeting the Marquess of Huntley."

Catherine managed not to snort. Barely. So, he was a marquess. No wonder he had that air of superiority. It would probably be wise to show him the appropriate respect, despite his rudeness. "Lord Huntley, the honor is mine," she said, offering a graceful bow before meeting his gaze with calm composure. "How long will we have the pleasure of your company in London? I look forward to many more matches with your friend."

"I plan to stay for the season. Lord Wentworth and I have several interests in town, and I've a project that will demand much of my time."

"Yes," Catherine nodded. "I believe I heard something about your 'project.' You're in search of a bride, am I correct?" The question felt like poking a hornet's nest with a stick.

Huntley raised a brow. "You are remarkably well-informed for a lad your age." His eyes narrowed. "I plan to be back at the academy next week. Will I see you then?"

She glanced away. "I try to come often, but I don't have a set schedule."

"Yes, yes," Bernini cut in, frowning slightly. "The boy would improve much faster if he came more frequently." It was a familiar point of contention between them. "I don't know how he expects to do well in the tournament in two months' time if he doesn't work harder."

The words stung, especially since he'd recently said she had a good chance of winning. Had he changed his mind that quickly? "I haven't decided if I'll take part yet," she replied.

Bernini shot her a sharp look, then grinned. "Playing coy, *ragazzo*? I know you. You won't be able to resist the challenge."

Huntley's gaze flicked toward the door, and Catherine noticed Wentworth, already cloaked and glaring impatiently. Huntley gave him a nod before turning back to them. "Maestro Bernini, Mr. Gray," he said, "I bid you both a good evening. I look forward to our paths crossing again." He took a step toward the door, then paused and turned back to Catherine. In a low voice, he added, "I hope Wentworth's temper didn't offend you. He's quick to anger but just as quick to forgive. He might indulge in a bit of posturing, but he's an honorable man. I've never had a truer friend." With a brief nod, Lord Huntley left to join his companion.

Catherine watched him for a moment, frowning as she tried to decipher his message. Was he trying to reassure her? Underscore his loyalty to Wentworth? Or perhaps he simply wanted to paint his friend in a better light.

She gathered her things and met her brother near the main doors. "I didn't get to see your match with Lord Huntley," she said. "How did you do?"

He grimaced. "Badly." She opened her mouth to speak, but he held up a hand to stop her. "Don't ask." He turned and headed into the foyer.

Catherine hurried to keep pace. "Wait," she said, grabbing his forearm and pulling him aside. "What do you think about the tournament? Should we enter?"

He shrugged one shoulder. "Why? I don't stand a chance, and even if you win, what would you do with the trophy? Hide it in the stables?"

She jutted out her chin. "Maybe. But first, I'll have to win it. Where to put a trophy is the least of my concerns."

He shrugged. "Enter, if you want. I'll help you get here. It'll probably be during the day, so I can help you slip out of the house."

Catherine gave his solid forearm a squeeze in thanks and then crossed the foyer to Mr. Winston's desk. It took less than five minutes to complete the entry form and pay the fee.

She was going to win that tournament.

2

A RIDE THROUGH LONDON

As Catherine headed home, a cool breeze ruffled her horse's mane. She longed to pull off her sweaty white skullcap and let the wind fli through her hair, but she knew better than to take such a foolish risk.

She tilted her head back, gazing up at the stars as her horse followed the familiar path through the slushy streets of London. The sound of metal horseshoes echoed off the nearby town-houses, clattering against the paving stones.

"See anything interesting up there?" Charles teased.

His tone pulled her from her thoughts, and she glanced at him, catching his contented grin. The lamplight flickered in his soft brown eyes—so much like her own. She smiled back, unable to resist. Charles didn't often let his guard down, but when they rode together on these late-night excursions, something in him loosened.

She understood why so many women tripped over their feet when the young viscount asked them to dance. As children, she and Charles had often practiced intricate quadrille steps in front of their mother when they'd visited Kensington House. She never knew that the moment she left them to practice alone, they'd dash to the special cabinet to pull out Father's fencing gear. In her mind, dancing and fencing were forever linked.

"When do you return to Oxford?" she asked. The question had weighed on her for weeks, but after their evening at Bernini's, his spirits seemed lifted. Maybe now, he'd be willing to give her a real answer. She saw him tense, then ease back into the rhythm of his mount's stride.

"Soon, I hope," he muttered, his gaze shifting away.

"I know something's wrong, Charles. Maybe if we talked—"

He cut her off with a sharp glance, his eyes glittering in the dim light. "I *want* to tell you. Truly, I do. But Mother forbade it. She's afraid your delicate sensibilities will be... shattered." His voice dripped with sarcasm.

"My sensibilities? Ha! Mother would be scandalized by half the things I've overheard at Bernini's. Men speak freely when they believe no women are around. Wait... if Mother thinks it would shock me, then it must be a matter of a girl."

He let out a long sigh. "This is exactly why I've avoided the subject. You always know what I'm thinking."

"What happened? Did you dally with the wrong sort of girl?"

"Watch your tongue, Cat. You know me better than that."

"Yes, but I do like to goad you." And it usually worked.

He relaxed slightly at her teasing. "Well, stop it, or I won't divulge anything else. And whatever I *do* tell you stays between us."

She pretended to lock her lips with an invisible key, widening her eyes to appear even more trustworthy.

He snorted with laughter. "Fine. I'll tell you. It's my own fault, really. I was too trusting. I met a young lady who pretended to be smitten with me, but she was actually interested in someone else —an acquaintance of mine. They kept their relationship a secret because she feared her father wouldn't approve."

"Did you fall in love with her? Did she break your heart?"

Catherine scowled. How dare someone take advantage of her brother's good nature?

"No, no. Nothing like that. No hearts were broken, but her father *did* want to break open my head."

"What!"

He chuckled. "She used me to distract her father from the man she truly loved—a fellow with a less-than-stellar reputation. She spread a rumor that she and I were sharing a 'secret love.'" He grimaced.

"That's despicable."

"She thought I'd be the perfect dupe since I was, as she put it" —he switched to a falsetto—"'a hard-working young man in line for a prestigious title.' After they ran off to Gretna Green, her father came looking for me. He threatened to have me horse-whipped if I didn't return his darling girl. Obviously, I had no idea where she was, and things turned ugly until he realized I must be telling the truth since I wasn't in Gretna Green. He was furious. I'm lucky he didn't hit me. The truth will come out eventually, but for now, the gossip in Oxford is rampant. Her father might still expect me to help solve his problems. You see, the girl..."

Catherine's breath hitched. "What happened to her?"

"This is the part Mother doesn't want you to know." He stopped. Catherine knew better than to push. Either he would tell her or he wouldn't, and no amount of pleading would change his mind, so she let the silence stretch between them.

The residential area surrounding Bernini's fell away behind them, and they entered a business district. Most of the store-fronts were shuttered for the night. Once the shops closed, a different world awoke, full of shadowy figures and whispered deals.

Passing a pub, a door burst open, releasing a gust of raucous laughter that faded when the door swung shut again. Gaslights illuminated scattered clumps of night-dwellers in vignettes as they passed by. Here, a man stumbled out of a tavern; there, a woman leaned against a lamppost. Catherine blushed. She knew why the painted woman lingered there. Mother would be appalled if she knew some of the things Catherine had seen.

"The girl is ruined, Catherine," Charles said at last. "The scoundrel didn't marry her. He vanished. When her father tried to track him down, he discovered the man had faked his credentials and letters of introduction."

Catherine's jaw dropped. "That's horrible. What will happen to her?"

"I don't know for sure. Mother and Father thought it best for me to stay away from Oxford this term, especially since her father is a professor. It doesn't help that I share the same first name as the scoundrel, which has caused more confusion about my involvement. They hope by next term the rumors will die down enough for me to return to my studies."

Despite her brother's cavalier attitude, Catherine could tell he was worried. "If there's anything I can do to help, simply ask. You know that, don't you?"

"I know. Brothers in arms, right, Gray?"

As they rode on, passing another woman on the street, Catherine couldn't help but wonder. This one was younger, certainly younger than Catherine's twenty years, but her face was hard, with no girlishness remaining. How had she come to be here? Could she have been like that girl from Oxford? The man who had seduced and ruined her had likely walked away unscathed, while the girl paid the price. It infuriated Catherine— the unequal rules her gender endured.

Catherine chafed against the unequal rules her gender endured. At least she'd been able to find a way to subvert them, even if she had to hide it from her mother and the rest of the outside world. If she were to be discovered, she'd be ruined just the same. Society would never approve of a young woman entering a men's dressing area, or of her spending time with men with no proper chaperone.

Up ahead, a horse jolted out of an alley, pulling a nearly empty wagon onto the street. Catherine and Charles swerved to avoid it. The sharp scent of spilled ale and raw pine boards told her it was a delivery wagon dropping off barrels at a pub. Perhaps the smell of fresh pine accounted for its presence so late at night. It had probably undergone repairs and been delayed.

They rode another twenty minutes before reaching their home. The stately old houses of their wealthy neighborhood loomed ahead, far larger than most newer ones in London, and Kensington House was one of the most imposing. As Charles headed toward the stables, Catherine moved to the shadows, riding alongside the house, keeping to the softer, snow-patched grass next to the gravel carriage path. With the full moon shining down, she wished her warm, black cloak could also make her invisible.

While she lingered in the gloom, Charles opened the stable door. Billy, their twelve-year-old stable boy, dozed near the entrance but snapped awake at the sound. As usual, he'd waited for her rather than retiring to the rooms above the stalls.

"Good evening, m'lord," Billy said to Charles.

Catherine slipped in behind her brother. The sweet scent of hay already awaiting their horses in their stalls greeted her as she entered the stables, and it tickled her nose. The smell mingled with the scents of saddle oil and leather that seemed to permeate the boards of the building.

"Good evening to you too, m'lady. I'll take care of Wildfire for you." Despite having been asleep moments before, Billy looked alert and ready, even at this late hour.

"Thank you, Billy."

He hurried about his work, removing the saddle and bridle from her mount while Charles performed the same tasks for his own horse.

While Billy unsaddled her horse, Catherine rubbed Wildfire's neck. Her father had given him to her three years ago. When she wore her black cloak while riding him, they blended into the night. Trust Papa to think of such details. At least she didn't have to hide her fencing from him. Only Mother opposed it. But Father had never been a conformist, much to Mother's despair.

Catherine pulled a carrot from her pocket. Wildfire snapped off the end with his teeth, then took the rest in two quick bites. His velvety lips tickled her palm as he finished the last piece.

While Billy tended to Wildfire, Catherine set to work on her disguise. She unlocked the trunk she kept in the stables, retrieving fresh clothes. First, she slipped on her wraparound overdress—a design of her own creation that allowed her to transform without help. Petticoats were sewn into the skirt, providing the fashionable bell shape.

Next, she peeled off the false scar, scraping at it with her fingernail until she could pull it away. Finally, she removed the snug white skullcap and smoothed her flattened hair into something passable, though far from perfect. A glance in the small mirror she'd hung in the stable confirmed it. She wiped away the last traces of the scar.

Her transformation was complete. Alexander Gray disappeared, leaving behind only Lady Catherine Williams. Albeit an unkempt, unfashionable version.

With a tattered scrap of grayish cloth, Catherine wiped the black dust from Wildfire's head, uncovering the hidden white blaze, thus removing his disguise as well.

Billy threw a blanket over Wildfire's back. "He's all done, miss —I mean, m'lady." His face flushed as he corrected himself—still adjusting to her new title.

Her elevated status as an earl's daughter weighed heavily upon her, and Billy's small blunder served to remind her of her new responsibilities, new constraints. After the deaths of her uncle and grandfather, her father's title had shifted—first to viscount and then to earl—and with it, her own title had changed from Miss Williams to Lady Catherine. She now commanded a "my lady" instead of a simple "miss." The entire convoluted mess was a bother, but Mother insisted they all adapt to their elevated roles within society.

Catherine hated it all. She much preferred being the daughter of a military officer. The role had been far less demanding.

"I'll put him in his stall for the night, m'lady," Billy said, leading Wildfire away.

At the back entrance to the house, Charles caught her arm. "Remember—you don't know anything about what happened in Oxford. Mother can't know I told you."

"You can trust me, Charles. I'm very good at keeping secrets."

3

HUNTLEY AT HOME

Late the following morning, Daniel strode into his rented townhouse and headed straight for his study. Without breaking stride, he shrugged out of his jacket and handed it to Madson, his valet. "This has a loose button. Can you have it repaired in ten minutes? I have another appointment soon."

"Yes, my lord. I'll take care of it immediately."

Daniel frowned at the ruddy-faced man for saying "my lord," but didn't correct him. He'd tried to convince Madson to be less formal for years, but the man insisted on using the honorific, even when they were alone. The constant "my lord"-ing grated on Daniel, especially coming from Madson's lips. After all, they used to be friends, running through the village and getting into scrapes. Yet, despite their shared past, Madson now insisted on maintaining the proper decorum.

"I put several more invitations on your desk," Madson said, nodding toward the stack.

"More? Doesn't anyone in this town do anything besides throw parties?"

"I wouldn't know, my lord. I'm sure there are other types of entertainment. Perhaps I can look into it for you." His brow furrowed in mock concern.

"Blast it, no. It was a rhetorical question," Daniel said, waving him away with a grin. It was an ongoing joke between them. When Daniel's grumbling became excessive, Madson always pretended to take him literally.

Madson sniffed and left the room, a smile twitching at the corners of his mouth.

Daniel scooped up the stack of invitations and tapped them against his leg as he crossed the room. He sank onto the dark-green sofa, relaxing into the cushions.

He eyed the stack of envelopes, thumbing through them with mild disinterest. Some he immediately tossed aside. He hadn't been in London long, but he could already identify which events were worth attending and which were a waste of time. A card party among elderly matrons certainly wouldn't help him find a wife. He propped the more appealing invitations against his stomach.

The pile shrank after the obvious rejections, but still... He shook his head, bemused by how many remained. Fingering each envelope, he wished one of them could offer him the answer he sought—should he attend, or not?

Or, more precisely, would he find a wife if he did?

He tipped his head back against the sofa, closing his eyes and rubbing them. He'd put off finding a wife for as long as possible, perhaps too long. Rebuilding his estate in Scotland had taken priority. The people there had been desperate for stability. He could still picture the fallow fields and untended timberlands that had languished under his father's neglect. What a wretched waste.

A robust economy had once flourished on the Huntley estates, both from fishing and shipbuilding, but under his father's stewardship, everything had been left to decay. Roads crumbled, bridges weakened, and the economy withered. There had been so much waste, such blatant disregard for what had once been a beautiful, productive estate. It had taken every ounce of Daniel's determination—and money—to begin restoring it all.

Daniel arched his back, tucked his hand into his pocket, and pulled out his timepiece. He flopped back against the sofa and stared down at the familiar object. He always kept it with him, along with the knife that was currently tucked away in his boot. He ran his thumb over the warm, smooth cover of the pocket watch.

In an odd, backward sort of gesture, Thomas Latimer, his father's former butler, had given Daniel the watch upon his retirement, and Daniel had repaid the gesture by ensuring Thomas would live comfortably for the rest of his days. Thomas had cared more about Daniel's future than his own father ever had. It was Thomas who had convinced the old Lord Huntley to send Daniel to Eton, rather than allowing him to run wild with the local village boys.

Daniel carried the heavy pocket watch as a fitting reminder of the value of time. Every second needed to count. His widowed father had squandered his, withdrawing in a self-imposed exile as the world around him crumbled. But time had marched on without him, and when Daniel had inherited, there'd been a time for recovery and a time for rebuilding. Now was the time for planning his legacy.

He clenched a fist around his timepiece. His talisman. Taking an exemplary wife and producing heirs would ensure the hard work he'd done wouldn't go to waste. The perfect woman was here in London somewhere—someone who could hold her own in society, maintain a household beyond reproach, and raise strong, resilient children.

He slipped the watch back into his pocket and turned his attention to the invitations again.

Last night had been his first break from the wife hunt in weeks. He'd needed the respite, especially after Lady Lydia's tiresome "Help me, there's something in my eye" ploy. It was fortunate he hadn't stepped closer to assist, or it might have looked like they were embracing when her parents "unexpectedly" burst into the room. Their timing had been too perfect to be anything but planned. Lord Larchmont was a cunning man. It had come to Daniel's attention that he'd been making inquiries about Daniel's finances, likely hoping to arrange a match for his daughter. The whole scene had reeked of manipulation.

Daniel continued sifting through the invitations until one caught his eye. He plucked it from the stack and strode to his desk to check his calendar. Yes, he'd already accepted this one—dinner at Lady Wilmot's home tonight.

He'd been in London long enough to know that an invitation from Lady Wilmot practically guaranteed an enjoyable evening. It was also blessedly free of the Larchmonts, since Lady Wilmot openly disliked them. It would be a welcome change. The Larchmonts seemed to pop up at every event he attended, almost as though they were following him. He wondered briefly if someone really had been following him home from Bernini's tonight — someone who worked for the Larchmont's. But no, that would be ludicrous.

Lady Wilmot's small, selective guest list always favored good conversation over rank or status. This latest note mentioned that Wentworth would be attending, along with several interesting young women. Single women.

That sounded promising.

Last night, his mercurial friend hadn't been at his best. He'd made a fool of himself, badgering that boy, Gray, and looking like a complete ass in the process. The evening at Bernini's hadn't managed to ease Daniel's tension. The constant search for a wife was wearing on him, leaving him irritable and on edge. When he'd mentioned the strange feeling of being followed, Wentworth had mocked him relentlessly.

Once they returned to the townhouse, Daniel had snapped at Wentworth when he wouldn't stop complaining about Gray.

Fortunately, his friend had changed his tone after that and behaved more genially.

Daniel frowned at his crowded calendar. With all the late nights he'd been spending trolling for a bride, he'd found it difficult to accomplish any actual work. He needed to make a choice soon. Perhaps he should end the search now, settle for Lydia despite her manipulations, and clear his schedule.

He sighed. When would he meet a quiet, intelligent woman—someone above reproach, content to live far from London, and equally content with an absent husband? He'd plucked a few wallflowers, pulling one onto the dance floor and chatting with another, thinking that such solitary women might thrive in the environment he envisioned for his wife. But none had met his criteria.

He rifled through the remaining invitations, letting his thoughts wander. Every proper young lady he'd encountered thus far seemed to have the same personality. Not one stood out as exceptional, nor had any stirred even the slightest attraction in him. But that didn't matter. He wasn't looking for love, just a wife. Affection wasn't part of the equation.

He glanced at the clock. "Madson!" he shouted. "Where are you?"

His valet appeared with a light step, holding Daniel's jacket. "You bellowed, sir? I'm right here. The button's fixed."

Daniel ignored the playful "bellowed" comment and shrugged into the jacket. As he adjusted the cuffs to show just the right amount of white, Madson gave a nod of approval.

"I need you to send responses to these," Daniel said, gesturing to the piles on his desk. "The small stack are the events I'll attend. Send my regrets to the others." The regrets pile was more than triple the size of the acceptances. "Make a note of the ones I'll attend in my calendar."

Madson nodded, efficiently organizing the piles. He handled

most of Huntley's personal correspondence, a common enough task for a valet employed by a bachelor.

"I have business meetings today, and then a meeting at the Ambridge Club with one of my managers. I'll be back in time to dress for dinner. Wentworth will stop by to collect me, so the coachman can have the night off."

Daniel turned to leave, his long strides eating up the floor, but he paused and glanced over his shoulder. "If I'm running late, offer Wentworth a drink. He was quite put out last time when none was offered. Let's make sure the evening starts off well."

4

MARCHING ORDERS

Catherine overslept the morning after her night at Bernini's academy, waking up famished. Now that she was back in London, she hoped to slip into the Kensington House ballroom and run through some fencing drills. Stretching to touch her toes, she felt the stiffness in her legs from last night's exertions. It was the price she paid for her extended break from fencing.

Her stomach growled, urging her into action. Unfortunately, Mother would disapprove if she rushed through her morning toilette, so she dressed with care. She selected a blue day dress, and Simpson, her lady's maid, helped her into it. Catherine forced herself to sit still while Simpson arranged her hair. As soon as she was finished, Catherine hurried downstairs to the breakfast room, where she found Charles at one end of the table. Judging by his full plate, he'd only just arrived.

Catherine eyed his plate hungrily as she slid into the chair beside him. "Has Mother been downstairs yet?"

"Yes, m'lady," Percy, their butler, said as he placed Catherine's meal before her. "She breakfasted about an hour ago and is now in the morning room. She plans to speak with you when you're finished to plan your day together."

Catherine's mood sank. Her plans for fencing would have to wait. Mother would dictate their day, and Catherine would be expected to follow without question. "Thank you, Percy," she said, as he bowed slightly and left the room.

Suppressing a yawn, Catherine noticed Charles grinning at her. "Why on earth would you be so tired this morning?"

She stared at him blankly until she realized he was referring to their fencing session last night. They'd long agreed that the topic was strictly off-limits. "You mean because we only just arrived yesterday?" she replied icily. "It was a long journey."

"You know that's not what I meant. We're alone, Catherine..." Charles paused as her eyes widened in alarm. He turned to see the door opening behind him, but it was only their younger sister, Sarah. He shot Catherine an apologetic look and mouthed, "Sorry."

Sarah rushed to the table and sat next to Catherine, her gaze fixed on the food. "Good-morning-Catherine-you-slept-late!-Can-I-have-a-bite-of-your-ham?" The words tumbled out in a breathless rush.

Catherine laughed and offered Sarah a bite of ham from her fork. "I'll have Percy bring you a plate. Will this be your second breakfast?" She rang the bell, and Percy promptly returned. "Sarah needs her second breakfast," she said with a wink.

Percy nodded and returned almost immediately with another plate of food.

"Percy, you're astonishingly prompt. Are you clairvoyant?" Charles asked, sounding genuinely surprised.

A small smile appeared on Percy's normally stoic face. "The cook saw Miss Sarah returning from the stables and took the liberty."

"They know me well, don't they?" Sarah grinned as she began cutting her ham.

"You have an impressive appetite for a thirteen-year-old," Charles said, shaking his head. "You'll end up plump if you aren't careful."

"Ha! Not with her constant activity. She never stops," Catherine said, plucking a bit of straw from Sarah's hair. "Like a wind-up toy that never tires."

Sarah rolled her eyes and swatted Catherine's hand away. Without pausing to swallow, she launched into a breathless report of her morning's observations.

"Did you know Princess had kittens? And Lord Whatsis is bullying the other cats! He's a blackguard! I saw him attack Mister Flitwitty this morning, and I had to throw a bucket of water at him. Billy laughed at me! He thought it was hilarious!"

"Maybe it was," Catherine suggested with a smile. "Billy works in the stables; he's probably seen plenty of cat-fights. It was likely just a bit of amusement to him."

Sarah pouted. "Why do you always take *his* side? *I'm* your sister." Her expression turned mischievous. "He was telling me about a different sort of diversion last night. Something *you* provided." She gave Catherine a sly wink.

Catherine's cheeks flushed as Charles and Sarah exchanged grins. "I don't appreciate the casual way you both mention my..." She glanced around the empty room, "my interest." Her voice dropped to a sharp whisper. "Perhaps I need to be clearer. You can never allude to it. If word got out, it wouldn't just ruin me—it would ruin our entire family."

She glanced at the closed doors. "We have new servants in the house. How can you be certain they're trustworthy? For all you know, someone could be listening at the door even now, or Mother could walk in and overhear something that might allow her to piece together small clues. I beg you, for all our sakes, don't try to bait me or tease me. You're playing with fire!"

Her siblings had the grace to look chastened.

"I should know better," Charles said, looking down at his

plate. "After what I've been through with rumors, I should be more careful."

"I'm sorry, too," Sarah said. "Can I make it up to you? We could go riding in the park together."

The child was incorrigible. Catherine raised an eyebrow. "And how is that making it up to me? You always ask me to go riding."

Sarah's eyes widened and her cheeks flushed, a sure sign she'd been caught. "But you always have fun when we ride."

"Fine, you little minx. Tomorrow, then."

Sarah grinned triumphantly and bit into a slice of toast.

Catherine relaxed, knowing they hadn't meant to put her at risk. She could never stay angry with them for long. Forgiveness came easily to her.

"I need to take my leave," Charles said, rising from his chair.

At that moment, their mother entered. "Good morning, children," she said with her usual commanding air. "I'm surprised to catch all of you here before you scattered to the winds. Charles," she added, fixing him with a sharp look, "I thought you were meeting with your father's lawyers this morning."

"I was just leaving," Charles said, leaning down to brush her cheek in an approximation of a kiss. At five-foot-five, their mother was only an inch shorter than Catherine, but Charles seemed to tower over her. "I'll be home later to change before dinner."

"Very well. I hope your day goes smoothly," she replied distractedly, already focusing on Sarah as Charles left. "Sarah, your governess will return from holiday this afternoon. Be sure you're dressed appropriately when you greet her. Your sister and I will be out making social calls."

"Yes, Mama," Sarah replied dutifully. "I'm looking forward to seeing her."

Mother gave her an approving nod before turning to Catherine. "You look lovely this morning," she said, her tone pleased.

"That shade of blue suits you. I hope you'll wear it for our calls today."

So much for fencing. Catherine swallowed her disappointment, knowing better than to show any sign of it. Mother had the demeanor of an army general, a product of years spent with Papa in India while he was in the military. Like a general, she expected her orders to be followed without question. "I've arranged for the carriage at half-past two. I trust you'll be ready by then?"

Though worded as a question, Catherine knew it was a command. She nodded in agreement.

Sarah stood from the table. "May I be excused?"

Mother nodded. "Try not to muss your dress," she said as Sarah scampered away.

Catherine rose as well, but Mother gestured for her to stay. Once Sarah's footsteps faded, Mother stepped closer. "Now that we're back in London, our primary goal is to find you an appropriate match. We'll attend every social function that offers visibility and attracts eligible bachelors. Your father's new title of Earl of Kensington will overshadow any concerns about his past involvement in trade. You'll have your pick of suitors. Not just any man will do, of course, but I'm certain you'll be able to choose someone suitable who has status and connections." Mother continued talking, laying out her campaign with near-military precision. "If everything proceeds according to plan, we should secure an engagement for you within two months."

Catherine stiffened. "Two months!" she blurted, her voice rising in panic. The tournament was in two months, and she needed time to prepare. How would she manage both?

Mother's eyes narrowed. "This is your second season, but with your father's elevated status, securing a match should be straightforward. I expect your full cooperation."

Catherine nodded mutely, her heart sinking. She had long learned to dread the moments when her mother's enthusiasm ignited for one of her "projects." Now that all that energy was directed at finding her a husband, Catherine knew it would consume their lives. The mere thought of the endless balls, soirees, social calls, and dinner parties her mother would insist on attending left her feeling drained before it even began.

Satisfied, Mother continued. "The first step is a round of social calls this afternoon. We must reestablish our presence. I know it will be tiring, but it's necessary. Meet me in my office at a quarter past two."

Catherine pressed her lips into a forced smile and nodded.

5

PAYING CALLS

Years ago, Catherine had mastered the art of crafting what she liked to think of as her "social mask." It wasn't a physical object, but an invisible shield she donned whenever she faced the outside world—or more crucially, her mother. Mother's relentless insistence on decorum had shaped that mask, and Catherine's years of secret fencing had tempered it into something as strong as steel. Rarely did she allow any errant emotions to escape past it.

At precisely a quarter past two, Catherine slid her mask firmly into place and entered her mother's office. "Good afternoon," she said pleasantly, ensuring her mother saw only the poised, proper young woman she expected. Catherine's eyes caught the glint of a silver object in her mother's hand. "What's that?"

"Do you like it? It's my new calling card case," her mother replied, handing it over. "The cover is engraved with Prince Albert's new Balmoral Castle."

Catherine held the case, her fingers tracing the intricate lines of the engraving.

"The castle won't be finished for a few years, but this is based on the architect's drawings. Isn't it lovely?" her mother asked, a rare softness in her tone.

Catherine nodded, though her thoughts were far from the castle. Victoria refused to give her husband control of her kingdom by naming him king, preferring to keep Great Britain's reins firmly in her own hands. Unfortunately, Catherine wouldn't have a similar option once she married. It was a bitter pill to swallow, and Mother's plan to swiftly betroth her had sent a knot of dread to her stomach, a knot that tightened with every passing day. The idea of losing what few freedoms she possessed terrified her. Ever since Mother had unveiled her plan, the tangled knot had been shooting out little tendrils of self-doubt.

Rules. Her entire life was governed by them—rules of etiquette, behavior, and marriage—all designed by others. They boxed her in, leaving her with a narrow set of choices. And now, with her new status as the daughter of an earl, the expectations felt even more suffocating.

She handed the case back and watched as her mother meticulously placed a stack of freshly printed calling cards inside. Her mother handed one to her: white embossed cardstock with "Lady Kensington" on top and "Lady Catherine Williams" beneath it in elegant, understated type. She moved closer to her mother's desk to examine the other two boxes of cards. One set had "Lady Kensington" printed on them for when she made calls alone, and the other set was for Papa. His were printed on plain, flat card stock, but the other two sets had a slight gloss. All so proper. All so rigidly controlled by society's invisible hand.

Catherine picked up one of her father's plain cards and ran her fingers over his name. "Have you heard anything from Papa?"

"Not since his last letter a few days ago. He hopes to be back in time for the Norfolk Ball."

Catherine nodded. The ball was still a month away. Papa was hardly ever home anymore, with his business ventures and work for the queen pulling him in so many directions. She wished he'd return. His presence always softened Mother's sharp edges.

"Now, we're ready," Mother said briskly, tucking the card case into her reticule before sweeping out the door.

They set off promptly at half past two, arriving at the Wilmot residence, as was tradition, for their first social call of the season. As the carriage rolled to a stop, Catherine perched on the edge of her seat, her fingers curling around the leather strap for balance. Lady Wilmot's daughter, Elizabeth, was one of her closest friends, and seeing her again was one of the few bright spots in an otherwise dreary schedule.

Lady Wilmot welcomed them warmly into her sunlit morning room. "It's wonderful to see you both. Welcome back to London." The pale-yellow curtains, pulled back to let in the bright winter sunlight, filled the room with a crisp, clear light.

Mother, already alight with anticipation, wasted no time in diving into conversation. "You must catch us up on all the latest happenings. I'm particularly curious about this season's eligible bachelors."

Catherine inwardly groaned, casting a glance at Elizabeth. They shared a knowing look as Catherine guided her friend to a quieter corner of the room, away from their mothers' inevitable discussion about marriage prospects.

Catherine tried to ignore her mother's voice from across the room as she and Elizabeth settled in, but it was difficult. Fortunately, the sofa she'd chosen was positioned so that a tea tray and a bouquet of pink roses partially blocked them from view.

Elizabeth's vivacious green eyes flashed with exuberance. She leaned in, her voice conspiratorial. "Lord Stansbury is back in town, as is Sir Anthony Watters. Didn't they both offer for your hand last year?"

Catherine frowned. "Yes, but I never seriously considered either of them. Watters shifts his affections so frequently that one can hardly keep track of where his heart lies from one week to the next. And as for Stansbury, his fondness for gambling borders on the excessive, and I suspect his interest in me was more for my dowry than my company. I do hope there are more agreeable gentlemen in town this season."

Elizabeth scooted forward on the sofa with such vigor that her soft, black curls bounced around her face. "They're all new to me, since this is officially my first season. Last year's was cut short before I'd barely begun, so I've decided not to count it." She'd been called away from London when her aunt had fallen ill, and Elizabeth had remained by her side throughout her decline.

"I always loved hearing your impressions during that month you were here. Your ability to assess a person's character is uncanny. I must confess, I'll need your advice." Catherine often marveled at Elizabeth's sharp intuition, which bordered on clair-voyance. She wondered, not for the first time, how she had managed to conceal her passion for fencing all these years. Perhaps it was simply too far-fetched for even Elizabeth to suspect.

"My advice? About what?" Elizabeth asked, curious.

"Mother is determined to marry me off quickly. She's like a general planning a siege, and I almost pity the man she chooses as her target."

"You know I'll do anything to help." Elizabeth squeezed her hand briefly before casting a glance toward their mothers.

Catherine peered around the bouquet of roses and caught her mother watching her with a contemplative gleam in her eye. "She's going to be difficult," Catherine muttered. "So, out with it. We haven't much time, and I need your insights before we make a dozen more calls."

Elizabeth tapped her finger against her chin. "Let's see... there's Monsieur LeCompte, that charming Frenchman we met in the fall. I believe he's quite wealthy, though he has no title. He's also a notorious flirt. Everything he says seems designed to curl one's toes. I heard a rumor that a jealous husband shot him after catching him in a rather indelicate situation with his wife. It all happened around the time of that big jewel theft."

Catherine raised her eyebrows. "I remember him from Lady Cecilia's wedding breakfast. Somehow, I doubt Mother would deem him a suitable match. Surely, you can offer a better suggestion than that."

"A pair of rather handsome Scottish lords have arrived, though there seems to be some scandal attached to the one seeking a wife. I've yet to uncover all the particulars, but rest assured, I'm working on it. His companion, I believe, only accompanies him for moral support and has no interest in finding a bride." A coy smile danced across Elizabeth's lips. "It seems our dear nemesis, Lady Lydia, has set her sights on the one in search of a match. I've heard rumors he's quite wealthy, though he has unfortunately tarnished his reputation by dabbling in trade."

Catherine stiffened, her smile faltering. Had Elizabeth really just said that so casually?

Elizabeth paled, her hand flying to her mouth. "Oh, Catherine, I'm truly sorry. I didn't mean to offend. I was simply being thoughtless, caught up in—"

Catherine's jaw tightened, and she waved her words aside with a sharp, controlled motion. "It's a common enough attitude, I suppose, but I won't apologize for Papa's choices. He never expected to inherit the earldom, and without his efforts in trade, we would still be facing an empty estate and debtors at the door. I don't need anyone's approval for the hard work that saved us."

Elizabeth's expression grew stricken, her eyes wide with distress. "But that's never been how I felt," she rushed to explain. "I hope you know that. I let the gossip sweep me up and didn't think how it would sound to you. It won't happen again, I promise."

For a moment, Catherine remained stiff, the sting of the insult lingering despite Elizabeth's contrition. But she sighed softly, knowing her friend's heart. People often spoke without thinking. She reached out, her tension easing as she patted Elizabeth's hand. "I understand. We've always been close, and I know your heart. Don't dwell on it. Now, tell me more of your impressions."

Elizabeth squeezed her hand in return before sliding forward on the settee to pour tea. Catherine noticed the bright smile Elizabeth forced wavered slightly, but she held it in place, clearly making a valiant effort to restore the intimacy broken by her careless words. "Shall I tell you what happened at the musicale?" Elizabeth asked.

Catherine nodded.

"I wish you'd been there," Elizabeth said, sipping her tea. "The evening's highlight was watching Lady Larchmont all but shove Lydia into the Scotsman's arms. He had the good grace not to look irritated, though he did manage to slip away early. She was quite put out."

"Who? Lady Larchmont or her daughter?"

"Ha! Both. Lydia's clearly set her cap for him."

"The gentleman had better be cautious. Lady Larchmont can weave quite the web." Catherine took a sip from her own teacup before setting it down. "Speaking of webs, how is Lydia's sister, Cynthia? Her mother managed a coup with that marriage. I thought the man was a confirmed bachelor." Catherine hadn't been able to attend the summer wedding, since they'd still been in mourning. "I haven't seen Cynthia in ages. Is she happy?"

The playful light in Elizabeth's eyes dimmed as her hand tightened around her teacup. "I saw her recently, with her husband." She set the delicate china aside with an uncharacteristically noisy clatter, then quickly straightened it, a flush of embarrassment rising to her cheeks. Glancing at Catherine, she hesitated before lowering her gaze to her tightly clenched hands. "All is not well with Cynthia, and I'm truly worried. I've heard she's been unusually clumsy since the wedding, and at the musicale, she walked with a noticeable limp. I've also seen bruises on her arms, though she insists she's fallen. But it's happening far too often. What's more, she seems to have developed a certain... aversion to her husband. They're rarely seen together in public now."

Catherine made a small sound of dismay, drawing Elizabeth's gaze. Her friend's troubled expression spoke volumes about the depth of her concern. Poor Cynthia wasn't in the marriage of her dreams, but of her nightmares. "What of her parents? Can't they intervene, do something to help her?"

"I'm not sure. She's still with him, so if they've tried to intervene, it hasn't made much difference. Once married, her husband holds all the power. From what I hear, he's intent on having an heir, but I can't imagine how that will happen with all these 'accidents' she's suffered."

A growing sense of injustice swelled within Catherine. Of course, her own father would never expect her to remain bound to such a brute, but Lord Larchmont clearly held a vastly different view of propriety and matrimonial duty. How could he turn his back on his own daughter so easily?

"Now it seems they're eager to marry off Lydia as well," Catherine remarked. "For her sake, I hope they're more discerning this time." She might not care for the girl, but that didn't mean she wished her ill.

Catherine glanced at her mother. She knew that her mother would never knowingly choose such an unsuitable man as a husband. But how well could anyone truly know another person's character? After all, Catherine herself had concealed her secret identity for ten years. Cynthia's husband had clearly managed to hide his true nature just as skillfully. Catherine had never heard a whisper of suspicion about him until now. Given the tales she'd overheard at Bernini's from the men, he must have been exceptionally discreet.

Across the room, Lady Wilmot raised her voice slightly and leaned forward, peering around the large bouquet of pink roses. "Catherine, I informed your mother that I've sent an invitation for dinner this evening. I know it's rather short notice, but I do hope you can both attend."

"Oh, yes, please do," Elizabeth chimed in, her mop of black curls bouncing with enthusiasm as she nodded.

Mother smiled graciously. "Of course, we'll come. How delightful. Your evenings are always so entertaining, my dear. You manage to invite the most interesting guests." Mother stood to leave. Apparently, her infallible internal clock had informed her that the proper duration for a social call had elapsed. "We really must be on our way."

They made their goodbyes, and before long, they were back in the carriage, setting off for the next of their afternoon calls.

The disturbing news about Cynthia clung to Catherine, refusing to let her mind settle. What if she married a man who isolated her, dictating her every move, far from the freedoms of London? Worse, what if she could never fence again? The thought sent a ripple of cold dread through her. Her heart beat faster. What if she ended up just like Cynthia?

Her breath caught at the realization. What if she shared not just Cynthia's restrictions but her fate—trapped in a nightmare, unseen and unheard, with no escape?

The carriage jolted as a wheel struck a broken patch of road, sending a tremor through the frame. Catherine glanced out the window where she spotted a man seated on the bench of a delivery cart, stuck in the very same rut. He lashed out with his whip, cursing as the horse strained against the cart's weight, trying in vain to break free from the torment. The helpless creature flinched beneath the blows, tethered to its burden with no escape—just as Cynthia seemed bound to her cruel husband. A cold shudder coursed through Catherine as the scene vanished behind them.

"Mother, promise me you'll be more careful than Lord and Lady Larchmont were when they chose Cynthia's husband. I've heard she's suffered quite a few injuries since her marriage."

Mother, who had been absently staring out the window, jerked her head around, frowning. "And you believe her husband to be at fault? That's absurd. He's no common brute—he comes from a distinguished family."

"Distinguished or not, it doesn't preclude a man from being cruel..." Catherine began, but faltered under the weight of her mother's deepening scowl.

"You know better than to repeat such slander. There's never been the slightest hint of that kind of talk about him."

"Until now." Catherine's chin lifted in quiet defiance.

Mother continued to frown, unmoved. "I disagree. I would have heard something before now. Rest assured, things like that have a way of getting out." Her expression softened as she added, "I understand why a tale like this might unsettle you, especially while we search for a husband. But rest assured, we would never marry you to such a man." She gave Catherine's hand a perfunctory pat, withdrawing it quickly, her mouth tightening into a thin line as she turned back to the window. "Still, if Cynthia truly is unwell, that's most troubling. Poor girl," she murmured, almost to herself.

Catherine studied her mother, waiting for something more—an acknowledgment, a deeper concern—but was met with silence.

Again.

Her mother's knack for dismissing anything that didn't fit her worldview was almost staggering. The notion that Cynthia, despite her parents' careful selection, could be married to an abusive cur simply didn't fit into her tidy vision of society.

Catherine straightened, her eyes shifting to the bleak, gray winter sky outside. A quiet resolve filled her, hardening into determination. Let Mother fixate on her grand plans for a wedding in two months; Catherine had her own goal. The fencing tournament was what truly mattered. That victory, at least, would be hers alone. No one—not even a future husband—could take it from her.

It was the one part of her life she still had control over. And she intended to keep it that way.

❧ *6* ❧

THE AMBRIDGE CLUB

Daniel and Wentworth sat comfortably in the Ambridge Club's open salon, positioned just far enough from one of the grand fireplaces to feel its warmth without being roasted. Having grown up in a drafty, crumbling mansion in Scotland, Daniel doubted he'd ever adjust to the overheated rooms of London.

"My brother introduced me to an interesting man recently," Wentworth began, leaning back in his chair with a contemplative expression. "John Sharp. Someone told me he's an influence peddler—whatever that means."

"That's just a jealous man's way of saying Sharp knows how to piece together a business deal," Daniel replied. "He has a talent for finding the right people and persuading them to work in harmony. I've run into him at a few events, and he recently approached me with an intriguing proposition."

Loud laughter erupted from a group of men at the far end of the salon, drawing an irritated glare from Wentworth. He shifted slightly, his attention fixed on the offenders, among whom was Lord Larchmont, seated in his usual spot by the fireplace, surrounded by his sycophants.

"Are you going to pursue it?" Wentworth asked, his tone distracted as he surveyed the group of men.

Daniel followed his gaze, noting the disdain on Wentworth's face. "I haven't decided yet. I'm still looking into Sharp's background, but he has a reputation for being fair. We're both outsiders, in a sense, though I've at least got a title to shield me. Sharp lacks that privilege."

Wentworth returned his gaze to Daniel, nodding. "I've heard he has an unlimited supply of patience—something I can't claim for myself." His eyes narrowed as he glanced at Larchmont once more. "Do you think Sharp can be trusted?"

"That's what I'm trying to determine. So far, he seems pragmatic, with a keen sense of the bigger picture," Daniel replied, drumming his fingers idly on the armrest. "His pragmatism might be useful. Sometimes patience is the only way to navigate the whims of men with power."

Wentworth gave a wry smile, his fingers tapping the arms of his chair. "If only patience would solve the problems my brother throws my way." He sighed. "These days, Frederick seems to see Russian spies behind every lamppost, and he's roping me into his schemes to confirm his suspicions."

Daniel raised an eyebrow. "Is he always so inclined toward paranoia?"

"Oh, it's not just paranoia. He's convinced himself there's a conspiracy brewing, and I seem to be his chosen sounding board," Wentworth replied, a note of irritation creeping into his voice. "The more shocked I am by his ideas, the more enchanted he becomes. I always hoped his espionage fixation would be temporary, but it seems he's only become more enamored with uncovering schemes and thwarting them."

He paused, looking as if he were choosing his next words carefully. "It's troubling, really. Frederick's not content with small, harmless escapades, the way he was as a boy. He's determined to uncover plots that might shake the throne, and each time he drags me along, I can't shake the feeling he's pulling me further down with him."

Daniel watched him, sensing the weight of Wentworth's words. A chill ran through him, his instincts stirring uneasily. "You're not exactly thrilled about being swept up in it, I take it?"

"No, but he's my brother, and saying no to him is harder than it should be," Wentworth replied, rubbing his temples as though trying to dispel the tension gathering there. "I'm reluctant to get any more entangled in this mess. The last thing I need is to be caught up in something that jeopardizes not just my own life but others' too."

Daniel nodded, the unease settling heavier in his gut. He could sense that this wasn't just another bothersome request from Frederick—it felt more ominous, like a shadow creeping into Wentworth's life. "Well, if it's any comfort, a distraction now and then might serve you well. And if anyone can handle Frederick, it's you. Besides, maybe keeping an eye on him will prevent his schemes from turning into something more dangerous."

Wentworth offered a thin smile. "Let's hope you're right."

A footman approached, bearing a silver tray with a note in the center and gave it a cautious glance. "Who do you reckon that's for—me or you?"

"I'd wager it's yours. No one knows I'm here," Wentworth replied casually, but when the footman stopped at his side, his eyebrows shot up in surprise. With a frown, he took the note, and glanced at the writing, his expression darkening.

"It seems someone does know you're here," Daniel said, his brow raised.

"My brother, of course," Wentworth muttered. "He has a knack for finding me at the most inconvenient times." He tucked the letter into his coat pocket, his voice laced with resignation. "Please excuse me. Frederick's demands wait for no man."

"Nothing too serious, I hope?" Daniel asked, though he suspected the answer.

"Let's hope not," Wentworth replied, rising from his chair. "Frederick's obsession with these supposed Russian threats is consuming him. He keeps dragging me deeper into it—he needs a voice of reason, but I fear it may already be too late."

Daniel watched him go, a prickle of foreboding dancing along his spine. *Wentworth might think he's keeping Frederick grounded,* he mused, *but from where I'm sitting, it looks like Frederick is pulling him into a current neither of them can control.*

He sat back, a flicker of anger burning through his unease. Wentworth deserved a better fate than to be dragged along by his brother's whims. As his friend disappeared into the hallway, Daniel knew he would keep a wary eye on Frederick's influence—no matter how hard Wentworth tried to downplay it.

Turning back to his work, Daniel retrieved the folder of papers he'd set aside, intending to pick up where he'd left off. However, a sudden burst of laughter from across the room shattered his focus. Apparently Lord Larchmont, seated among his circle of sycophants, was being amusing.

Daniel's gaze lingered on him for a moment. The earl, draped in an impeccably tailored coat that flattered his tall, slender frame, looked every bit the aristocrat. His dark hair was touched with just the right amount of silver at the temples, and his patrician features were marred only by an overly long nose. It was a face that commanded attention—one well-versed in holding court.

It was clear from the way the other men deferred to Lord Larchmont that he commanded their respect. His power stemmed not from raw charisma but from his deep entrenchment in the social fabric of London. Years of building connections had woven him into the very weft and weave of society, a man whose influence extended far beyond the room.

Another gentleman entered, his gaze skimming over Daniel as though he were invisible—a subtle snub Daniel had grown accustomed to. He could occupy the same space as these men, but more often than not, he was treated as though he didn't exist. The newcomer joined the group surrounding the earl, whose eyes briefly flicked up. When Larchmont's gaze landed on Daniel, however, he didn't dismiss him like the others. Instead, the earl rose from his chair and crossed the room, a broad smile curving his lips.

"Lord Huntley. It's a pleasure to see you," Larchmont greeted him warmly. His gaze shifted briefly to the business papers spread across Daniel's lap, and for a fleeting moment, a shadow of distaste crossed his face, vanishing as quickly as it had appeared. He ignored the papers as though they were beneath notice, as though they bore the taint of something unclean.

And in this society, they were. No respectable peer would be seen openly engaging in the business of earning money. That particular stain on Daniel's reputation kept many of the more esteemed gentlemen at arm's length.

But not Lord Larchmont.

Rumor had it the earl's finances were in disarray. He'd already married off his eldest daughter, though the union hadn't yielded the benefits he'd hoped for. Hence his growing interest in Daniel.

"Care to join us?" Larchmont offered smoothly. "I've just received a new shipment of cigars, and I was about to share them."

Daniel couldn't help but wonder if the cigars were part of the consignment that had recently passed through his warehouse. Some had already been dispatched to customers. "That's very generous," he replied, rising to his feet. "I understand you have a reputation for acquiring only the best."

Across the room, several pairs of eyes turned their way, expressions carefully guarded. Daniel could almost feel the ripple of surprise at seeing him converse so easily with Lord Larchmont.

"I recognize quality when I see it, even when others may lack the discernment," Larchmont added, casting a glance toward his companions. "Most are content to follow another's lead."

"I've observed the same," Daniel replied, a slight smile tugging at his lips.

As they neared the group, Larchmont's tone became more casual, though he avoided Daniel's gaze as he asked, "I hear you're in search of another estate near London. What happened to the one you were considering? It sounded like an ideal opportunity."

"The owner had an unexpected change of heart," Daniel said, keeping his tone measured. "It was rather peculiar. We were on the verge of finalizing everything when he abruptly withdrew, offering no explanation."

"That is peculiar." A faint twitch appeared at the corner of Lord Larchmont's mouth, barely noticeable but telling.

"I'm back to searching for the perfect residence."

Larchmont smiled. "If you'd like, I could assist. Perhaps a word from me might encourage the owner to reconsider."

"I doubt it would do much good. He seemed quite resolute," Daniel replied, though he couldn't miss the underlying implication of Larchmont's offer.

"No trouble at all, my boy," Larchmont said with an indulgent wave.

As they approached the others, Larchmont introduced Daniel around. Men who ordinarily would have kept their distance were now forced to acknowledge him, offering polite smiles, their respect for Larchmont outweighing any disdain they held for Daniel.

Daniel selected a cigar from Larchmont's well-stocked humidor, biting off the end and spitting it into the fireplace with casual ease. Out of the corner of his eye, he saw Larchmont pull back the cigar cutter he had been extending, slipping it into his pocket with barely concealed surprise. Daniel inwardly cursed the lapse in etiquette. If he truly intended to be accepted among these men, he would need to pay closer attention to the finer points of their social customs.

He would learn to blend in. Of that, he had no doubt. After

all, he'd survived by his wits among the street urchins of Edinburgh at the tender age of twelve.

How much more of a challenge could London society pose for
a grown man?

❧ 7 ❧

A MEASURE OF WHISKEY

Daniel sat in his drawing room, papers scattered across the desk—business he hadn't been able to complete at the Ambridge Club. Just five more minutes, and he'd be done. But the front bell rang, breaking the quiet, and Wentworth's voice soon echoed through the hall. With a resigned sigh, Daniel swept the documents into a leather satchel, his thoughts lingering on the task he'd have to finish in the morning.

A long shadow stretched across the doorway as Wentworth strolled in, unhurried.

"You're early," Daniel said, casting an irritated glance at his friend's casual saunter.

"You don't sound pleased about it," Wentworth replied, pausing mid-step. "Shall I leave and return at a more convenient hour?"

"No, no," Daniel waved him off, shaking his head with a small sigh. "That was a poor welcome. Stay, have a drink." He crossed to the side table, raising a decanter of Glenfarclas like an olive branch. "Your favorite."

Without waiting for a response, Daniel poured the amber liquid into a tumbler and handed it to Wentworth, who accepted it with a nod. He inhaled the rich, smoky scent of the Scotch before taking a slow, appreciative sip. A faint smile touched his lips.

"Content?" Daniel asked.

"Quite. You should join me—you're wound tighter than a clock."

Daniel poured himself a measure, staring into the swirling liquid as the firelight danced within it, casting shifting reflections. For a fleeting moment, he fancied he could read some deeper meaning in the patterns, as though the glass were an oracle's bowl. But it was just whiskey, and he felt the tension clinging to him as tightly as before. With a decisive motion, he tossed back the drink, savoring the burn as it traced a warm path down his throat.

"I'm making no headway with my plan," he admitted.

"Ah, yes. Your absurd plan."

Daniel shifted, uncomfortable under the scrutiny of Wentworth's amused gaze. "It's hard enough finding a woman with a sterling reputation willing to attach herself to someone as... unorthodox as I am. 'Eccentric is one of the kinder descriptions I've overheard. 'Bourgeois' and 'unbalanced' have also been tossed around."

"Stop it." Wentworth's scowl deepened. "With your title, you outrank nearly everyone—only dukes and royalty surpass you. No one would dare snub you openly."

"Not openly," Daniel replied, his voice hardening. "But behind closed doors? They're under no such obligation to be polite. My shipping ventures are beneath them, my mother's common birth a stain, and the whispers of my father's madness? That makes me beyond redemption in their eyes." He tossed back the whiskey in a swift motion, savoring the bitter warmth as it surged through him. "The irony is, the very things that bring me the most satisfaction—my investments, my business acumen—are precisely what condemns me in their eyes."

Wentworth leaned back, watching him closely. "Then why

care what they think? Isn't your goal simply to find a suitable wife who'll give you an heir? Why complicate it by demanding that she and her family meet society's narrow standards? Can't you see the hypocrisy in that?"

Daniel thumped his glass down on the sideboard, the sound echoing through the quiet room. He seized the decanter, splashing whiskey into his tumbler with little care. "I know I'm no saint, Wentworth, but I'll be damned if I put my children through the same hell I endured." He met Wentworth's gaze with a fierce glare. "You, of all people, know what it was like for me at Eton. You were there. How can you even ask?"

Wentworth's expression softened. "You're still carrying that, aren't you?"

"Carrying it?" Daniel's voice was rough. "It's part of me. Every humiliating reminder, every whispered insult... they've stayed with me. I grew up in the shadow of a man who barely existed. My mother died giving birth to me, and my father—he buried himself in grief, leaving me to fend for myself. I won't forgive him for it. For abandoning me."

A long silence fell between them, the air thick with unspoken words. Finally, Wentworth broke it, his tone gentle but resolute. "You aren't your father, Daniel. You're not some hermit shunning the world, pushing people away. I met him once, and I saw enough to know—he was weak, selfish. The only thing you share with him is a title."

Daniel's mouth twisted into a bitter smile. "That's easy for you to say. You weren't left to fend for yourself, learning life's harshest lessons from servants and street thieves. His neglect shaped me as much as any inheritance could have."

Wentworth watched him for a long moment before he replied. "You're right. I didn't grow up in your shoes, but that doesn't make your scars any more indelible than mine or anyone else's. You've created a life from those ashes, a future. You're trying to rewrite your past, but that time is gone. You have the chance to live fully, not in fear of becoming a man you despise."

Daniel turned, crossing to the fireplace. "Perhaps. But can I trust myself to be anything more?" Staring into the flames, his voice grew quieter. "My mother's death left a void my father never recovered from." He shook his head, a hint of sadness darkening his gaze. "I've always wondered if that's what love does—leaves you shattered and hollowed out. If so, I want none of it."

Lifting his glass, he took a sip of the smoky whiskey, ruminating on the tragedy love could bring to a man's life. He never wanted to be tangled up in that sentiment. His father hadn't always been a recluse. The servants whispered that when Lady Huntley died, so did the old lord's spirit. Every creak in the floorboards, every chill draft sweeping through the house, was attributed to Lady Huntley's ghost, wandering aimlessly, weeping for what had been lost.

His grip tightened on the glass as memories from those first months at Eton flooded back, raw and uninvited. The isolation, the cruelty—it had almost broken him. He'd begun to believe the taunts, that he was tainted, unworthy. Worse still were the things he'd done, choices that had left scars he could never hope to erase. How could he ever atone for them?

The dogs of melancholy had nipped at his heels relentlessly, pushing him into a corner. He'd tasted despair, but he'd always feared his father's bitterness was far deeper—a gnawing emptiness that had driven him into the bottom of a bottle, leaving him a hollowed shell of a man. What if Daniel was already on that same path? What if his regrets, festering over time, would one day drag him into the same darkness?

"That's exactly why I need a woman above reproach. Someone like Lady Larchmont," he said at last, his tone firm with conviction. "Someone who knows society's rules, someone who can raise my children in a stable, respectable home. I can't be content living on the fringes forever, watching as others judge me for my past. My children won't suffer for my choices. Whoever I marry must understand that."

Wentworth sighed, setting down his glass. "You're building quite a cage for yourself." He softened his tone, reaching out to place a hand on Daniel's shoulder. "But your child will live his own life. You're giving yourself far too much credit if you think your influence will dictate his every choice. Whether he's a rebel, a scholar, or something in between, his nature will carve its own path."

He paused, then gestured toward himself with a wry smile. "Take me. Do you think my parents aimed to raise a contradiction? I remember my father as fearless—the kind of man who'd stake his reputation on his word, who'd throw himself into the fire for those he loved. But the older I get, the more I wonder if the man I remember was ever real, or simply a memory molded by my own desires."

Daniel met his gaze, something akin to relief flickering across his face. He nodded, a tension he hadn't realized he held beginning to ease.

"Of course, I'd do anything for friends or family," Wentworth added, almost as an afterthought.

Daniel leaned back, offering him a rare, faint smile. "Then perhaps you're doomed as well."

Wentworth chuckled softly, lifting his glass in a silent toast. "Perhaps. Though Frederick's work keeps me tangled in a web I'd rather avoid." His tone grew darker. "Today, he roped me into yet another scheme—a supposed Russian conspiracy. He's so eager to win favor with the Queen, but he's playing a dangerous game, one that could easily lead to ruin for us both."

Daniel raised an eyebrow, intrigued despite himself. "So he's taking greater risks?"

"Precisely," Wentworth replied, his tone edged with frustration. "And he's dragging me along for the ride. One day, he'll go too far, and I've a nagging sense I'll be the one paying the price."

Daniel's gaze sharpened, sympathy mingling with concern. "It sounds as though Frederick's ambition may ensnare you even deeper than you realize."

Wentworth kept his eyes fixed on the fire, his expression tense. "That's precisely my fear. So long as he's determined to impress those in power, I doubt I'll ever be free of this madness. I wonder how much longer I'll be his shadow, caught up in one dangerous pursuit after another." He sighed again, his tone resigned. "He's desperate to uncover something grand—something to prove himself worthy. But I can't shake the feeling he's playing a dangerous game. One day, he'll push too far, and we'll all pay the price."

Daniel placed a hand on his shoulder, a rare show of affection. "If it's any comfort, I think you're doing the right thing. Keeping an eye on him might be the only way to keep his schemes in check."

Wentworth managed a thin smile. "Let's hope you're right." He fell silent, staring into the flames for a long moment, before rising and making his way to the door.

As Daniel watched him go, a prickle of foreboding crept over him. His friend was treading close to the edge, and if Frederick misstepped, Wentworth would fall with him. *Helping one's brother is one thing; sacrificing oneself is quite another.*

❧ 8 ❧

WHAT THE WIND BLEW IN

Catherine felt a deep sense of satisfaction as she hurried back to her bedroom after spending a stolen hour running through fencing drills in the Kensington House ballroom. She was supposed to have been resting. It would have been more fun if she'd had a sparring partner, but even working alone helped improve her skills. Every muscle felt limber and relaxed, but now she needed to prepare for dinner at Lady Wilmot's.

She chose a low-necked gown of pale rose chiffon, and Simpson helped her into it, taking care not to tear the delicate, gossamer fabric. Simpson fastened the small hooks down the back of the bodice and then worked the clasp on a pink-and-white cameo necklace. She arranged Catherine's hair so that masses of chestnut waves tumbled down her back and wisps of soft curls framed her face. Simpson tucked an errant lock of hair in place with a hairpin and carefully surveyed her work before nodding her approval to Catherine's reflection.

Catherine glanced at the mantel clock in her bedroom. "It's time." She picked up her reticule and hurried down the stairs to join her mother, slipping her imagined social mask in place.

"Darling, you look absolutely stunning," her mother said with a warm smile from the bottom of the stairs.

"I expect you and I will make quite the sensation when we enter the room." Mother reached out, brushing a small bit of lint from Catherine's shoulder before meticulously checking for any other stray fibers. "Look at us. You in that lovely rose, and I, of course, providing the 'foliage.' We'll be a rose garden."

With a faint smile, Catherine nodded. Tonight, she wouldn't let Mother's obsession with perfection or admiration bother her. She clasped her dark rose mantle, tugged on her gloves, and followed her mother out to the waiting carriage.

The gusting wind didn't penetrate the warmth of the carriage on their short trip to Lady Wilmot's home. They arrived just as another carriage pulled away, and Catherine hurried inside after the other guests, hastened by the brisk wind. The breeze followed them through the door, sending the previous arrivals scurrying into the drawing room. After they removed their mantles, Lady Kensington discreetly tucked a few windswept strands of Catherine's hair back into place.

Mother's sudden attempt at grooming Catherine struck her as odd. Normally, she never fussed with Catherine's appearance in public—such behavior, Mother believed, was entirely gauche. Was this just another sign of her relentless determination to secure Catherine an exemplary husband, or was something else at play?

As they entered the drawing room, Catherine glanced around, searching for clues that might explain her mother's heightened attention to detail, but nothing seemed out of the ordinary.

Another gust of wind swept through the foyer, heralding the arrival of new guests. Catherine instinctively turned to see who had come in.

Standing in the doorway were Lord Huntley and Lord Wentworth.

Her heart lurched in surprise. She spun around quickly, turning her back to the men.

Blast!

She'd always been careful to avoid anyone she knew from the fencing club. That's why she traveled so far to Bernini's Academy —most preferred to practice closer to home and socialize within their usual circles. Keeping clear of acquaintances had been easy enough. But if Huntley and Wentworth joined *her* social sphere, evading them would become far more challenging.

Given her limited options at a dinner party, Catherine resigned herself to trying to avoid Huntley and Wentworth as best she could.

Elizabeth crossed the room, a knowing smile on her face. "Tonight should be interesting," she said. "Mother's new French chef is a bit of a tyrant, but his food is divine. I've actually had dreams about his chocolate torte." Her eyes took on a dreamy, faraway look.

Catherine grinned at her friend's enthusiasm. "You and your desserts. I swear you talk about them more than you do about people."

"Why shouldn't I? Cakes are reliable; people aren't."

From across the room, Lady Wilmot beckoned them with a graceful motion, and Catherine smiled in acknowledgment. Linking arms, she and Elizabeth wove through the crowd.

"Look," Elizabeth murmured, her voice full of mischief. "There's Monsieur LeCompte."

Catherine followed Elizabeth's gaze, spotting the elegant man with his arm draped casually above the fireplace mantel. His pose accentuated his lean frame, though the entire display struck her as far too contrived. "He is preening," she whispered into Elizabeth's ear.

"He has a talent for it. The 'fireplace drape' appears to be his favorite pose," Elizabeth whispered back. They exchanged discreet smiles.

As they approached Lady Wilmot, the man she was speaking with turned his head just enough for Catherine to recognize his profile. Lord Huntley? How had he managed to cross the room so swiftly?

Catherine slowed her step, but Elizabeth, apparently unaware, continued to pull her forward. Huntley turned fully towards them, his gaze settling on Catherine just as she faltered.

One eyebrow lifted in mild amusement.

Blast the man. Heat rose to her cheeks beneath the weight of his critical gaze. That stumble did her no favors, but the less she reminded him of the effortlessly athletic Alexander Gray, the better. She might have missed the chance to avoid him, but perhaps confronting him head-on was the wiser course. She forced herself to believe she remained in place by choice, not because of Elizabeth's light grip still holding her arm.

"Ah, Catherine, I'm so pleased that you and your mother could join us this evening," said Lady Wilmot, her voice warm. "You look lovely. That color suits you perfectly."

Judging by the number of compliments she'd already received this evening, Catherine wondered if she should wear pink more often—or perhaps avoid it entirely if she wished to avoid marriage as long as possible.

Lady Wilmot turned to Lord Huntley with a gracious smile. "You've already met my daughter, Lady Elizabeth Greville," she said, nodding toward Elizabeth, "but I don't believe you've been formally introduced to her dear friend." Her gaze fell upon Catherine. "Lord Huntley, may I present Lady Catherine Williams. Lady Catherine, this is Daniel Kennedy, the Marquess of Huntley. Lord Huntley, I believe that you may have been acquainted with Lady Catherine's late grandfather, the Earl of Kensington."

Lord Huntley offered a polite bow. "Lady Catherine, it is a pleasure to make your acquaintance. I can see a resemblance to your grandfather—particularly in the eyes."

Catherine extended her hand, and he took it gently. His eyes widened slightly in surprise. "You possess quite a firm grip for someone so delicate in appearance," he remarked, arching an eyebrow.

In that moment of déjà vu, Catherine felt like a mouse caught beneath the predatory gaze of a hawk. The sensation was unnervingly familiar, far too reminiscent of their encounter the previous night. She could only hope Lord Huntley was not drawing the same unsettling connection.

But what could she do?

But what could she do? Struck by sudden inspiration, Catherine fluttered her lashes and let her posture wilt, hoping to appear quite unlike the brash, bold boy he'd encountered the night before. She couldn't overdo it, not with Lady Wilmot and Elizabeth standing nearby, but a stammering, bashful young woman might throw off any suspicions he harbored.

"I, uh, I... needlepoint," she blurted, her voice flustered and wavering under his penetrating gaze. "Perhaps that explains the strength of my grip. Do you enjoy needlepoint, Lord Huntley?" She gasped softly, her fingertips flying to her lips. "I mean... that is to say, do you enjoy looking at needlepoint?"

His intense expression flickered, first with confusion and then amusement as her staged "panic" became clear to him.

Catherine cast Lady Wilmot a pleading glance, silently begging for assistance in escaping this self-made mire of awkwardness. Thankfully, Lady Wilmot stepped in gracefully, providing Catherine with the rescue she sought.

"Look over there, my dear. Your mother seems to be searching for you. I just saw her scanning the crowd. Why don't you go join her?" Lady Wilmot's hand lightly touched Lord Huntley's arm, directing him toward the fireplace. "Lord Huntley, have you had the pleasure of meeting Monsieur Francois LeCompte? I believe you share a particular interest—he's quite the accomplished fencer."

Catherine glanced across the room, where her mother was deep in conversation with her friends and clearly not searching for her. Grateful for the timely intervention, she gave Lady Wilmot a look of silent appreciation and, without meeting Elizabeth's eyes, made her way toward her mother.

She glanced back briefly, twiddling her fingers in a playful farewell to Lord Huntley.

That should do it.

❧ *9* ❧

SHE SAUNTERED?

Huntley watched as Lady Catherine sauntered away from him.

Saunter. Yes, that was the only word for it. Her movement across the room held a new confidence, entirely different from the girl who'd tripped over her own feet and blushed in his presence just moments earlier. He furrowed his brow, pondering the sudden shift. It was as though she'd slipped into a different skin altogether. How intriguing.

He did enjoy a good puzzle. And Lady Catherine, it seemed, had just presented herself as one.

Lady Wilmot led him toward another gentleman, but he soon managed to extricate himself from the conversation. He'd come to meet marriageable ladies, not to be quizzed by a gossip-monger.

Tonight, however, events refused to proceed as planned. He found himself pinned down by yet another gentleman who professed a dislike for "trade," while spending an inordinate amount of time prying into Daniel's shipping business.

He noted with some pleasure that Lady Wilmot's gracious home included a piano in the adjoining room. He began to devise a plan to tempt Wentworth into an impromptu concert after dinner. The man loved to sing, and it always lifted his spirits. Daniel would try anything to stop Wentworth from disparaging his plan to find a wife.

He smiled at Lady Wilmot's approach.

"Lord Huntley, would you escort me to the dining room? I have a special spot reserved for you at my right, and I'm looking forward to a lively chat."

He kept his smile in place as he offered his arm to the lady. So much for speaking to someone marriageable over dinner.

❧ 10 ❧

SANTA LUCIA

Catherine nearly heaved a sigh of relief when she discovered that Lord Huntley would be seated to the right of Lady Wilmot, far from her own position mid-table. Instead, she found herself opposite the incorrigible Monsieur LeCompte.

"Last night, I was speaking with Lord Watters at the opera," LeCompte said. "Are you acquainted with him?" At her brief nod, he smiled. "He is such a droll young man. He has become quite enchanted with their newest soprano. Someone should warn that young man to guard his heart more carefully. Sopranos can be terribly difficult, *non*? For them, everything is about their dedication to their craft. Too often they view members of society as troublesome, but necessary, nuisances. He must not let himself become too attached to the young woman. *N'est-ce pas?*"

If he only knew. Watters already had a reputation for falling in love in an instant and then falling out of love just as quickly. She paused as she tried to find something positive to say about him and latched onto her favorite attribute. "He's a kind man," she stated with confidence, "but I don't believe he'll bother the soprano for long. It is unfortunate, but he's become known for his quixotic attachments to various young ladies."

LeCompte's eyes lit up at this news. Clearly, he enjoyed learning about the foibles of other gentlemen. "How is it that a young lady such as you would come to know these things?"

"He has never been circumspect when mentioning his most recent enthrallment with whichever soprano or ballerina has caught his eye. It would be difficult to remain unaware of his interests."

LeCompte looked slightly deflated, and Catherine realized that, for him, it was not as interesting to know about something already common knowledge. Apparently, he preferred discussing secrets and more scandalous things.

Catherine was amazed by LeCompte's detailed knowledge of the shortcomings of so many members of society, considering that he'd only been in town for a few months. Thankfully, he didn't include her brother among his litany of scandals.

Throughout dinner, she cast an occasional glance down the table, but Lord Huntley seemed engrossed in his conversation with Lady Wilmot. When she looked once again, she caught him observing her. Catherine's stomach clenched.

Why would he stare at her in such an assessing manner?

She quickly glanced back at LeCompte and tittered in a silly way at something mildly amusing he said. When she surreptitiously glanced back at the marquess, she saw that his attention had returned to Lady Wilmot.

"*Le marquis* is said to be searching for a bride," LeCompte said.

The comment startled her, and she couldn't think of anything innocuous to say. "Is he?" she finally remarked. LeCompte must have noticed her glance down the table at Huntley and drawn the wrong conclusion.

LeCompte watched Lord Huntley openly for a moment before sipping his wine. "Is it true he has a checkered past? His father is said to have been quite mad. Apparently, he forgot he even had a son, which left the boy all but orphaned, since his mother died in childbirth. The household servants raised him, which probably accounts for his rough manners." He narrowed his eyes as he gazed down the table at Huntley. "At least the man has money. It may be difficult for him to find a bride, despite his wealth. Rumors of bad blood have a way of keeping brides at bay. Nobody wants to risk having a grandchild who suffers from melancholy." He clicked his tongue. "At least he has the Midas touch. It's said every business endeavor he pursues is fruitful."

"I hadn't heard about his parents. That's quite sad. Such a childhood must have been difficult for him." She glanced back down the table at Huntley, noting his perfect posture and graceful movements. Why would LeCompte say he had rough manners? Huntley certainly looked the consummate gentleman, despite his purported neglected upbringing. One would never guess his childhood had been grimmer than most. What must it have been like to have no family to care for you? Mother dead, father mad? Had he been alone, or had there been siblings?

Catherine pulled herself up short with a sort of mental shake. What was she doing, imagining Lord Huntley's childhood? Was she mad?

Well, perhaps "mad" was a poor choice of words when contemplating Huntley, but really, she shouldn't be mooning over the man. She needed to avoid him.

Throughout the remainder of the meal, Catherine tossed a few surreptitious glances down the table, but she never caught Huntley looking at her again. Still, the man's presence presented an enormous risk. She needed to convince Mother to leave early.

As she rose to exit the dining room after dinner, she glanced back one last time and was surprised to see Lord Huntley's gaze upon her again. She scurried through the doorway, eager to put some distance between them.

Catherine joined her mother, Elizabeth, and the other ladies in the drawing room. Not all of the gentlemen seemed inclined to linger over glasses of port, and a few of them soon began to return to the drawing room as well.

"There's Lady Cecilia," Elizabeth said with a warm smile, giving her a wave. Lady Cecilia returned the gesture but made no move to join them.

"Her mother's jewels were stolen right before that big auction last fall," Catherine reminded her mother.

"I'd nearly forgotten. Were they ever recovered?" her mother asked.

"Yes, but not without complications," Catherine replied. "There was an accusation made against her fiancé—now her husband—which caused quite the scandal. Lady Cecilia stood by him, though, believing in his innocence."

"Such devotion," her mother murmured. "And was she right?"

Elizabeth's curls bounced as she nodded. "Absolutely. The truth came out, and they were able to marry after all."

"We should speak with her," Catherine suggested.

"I was hoping you'd say that," Elizabeth replied with a smile.

As they made their way toward Lady Cecilia and Mr. Montlake, Catherine cast a quick glance back at the dining room. Thankfully, there was still no sign of Lord Huntley.

Lady Cecilia's face brightened as they approached. "Lady Elizabeth, it's so lovely to see you. Thank you for inviting us this evening."

Mr. Montlake nodded in agreement. "We're most grateful."

Elizabeth waved a hand. "It was all my mother's doing, but I'm delighted you could come. How are you finding your new home in Maidenhead?"

"Oh, we've settled in beautifully. Though, I must admit, London's charms still call to us," Cecilia said warmly. "And your help with those introductions has been invaluable. We couldn't have managed without you."

Catherine smiled and slipped her gloved hand through Elizabeth's arm. "You couldn't ask for a better friend or ally."

Before Catherine could say more, two gentlemen joined them. "Mr. Montlake," one of them said. "I was hoping I'd get a chance to speak with you."

Catherine's mother took that moment to pull her to one side for a private word. "You seemed to be having a pleasant conversation with Monsieur LeCompte," her mother observed. "I noticed you laughing. He must have been quite entertaining."

"Yes, but you should be careful of him," she replied, keeping her voice low. "He's a rumor-monger and seems to enjoy sharing everything he knows." Catherine smiled as she remembered some of the more colorful stories he had shared.

"Hmmm... thank you for the warning, dear." Mother had a calculating gleam in her eye. "I think, however, that I might try to engage him in conversation. I need to keep abreast of the most recent gossip."

Catherine looked at her curiously for a moment, and then realization dawned on her. Of course. Mother wanted to know if any rumors regarding Charles had reached London.

"I don't see LeCompte," Mother said. She peered around the room, trying to spot the Frenchman. She suddenly stiffened. When Catherine followed her gaze, her stomach fell. She was looking directly at the marquess.

She dreaded the wily look in her mother's eyes.

"There he is," Mother's voice came out in a sharp whisper.

"There who is?"

"The marquess. Come with me."

"But Mother, I can't simply approach him."

"Why ever not?" Mother's sharp gaze pinned her in place. "What's the matter?"

"I... I made a fool of myself earlier when we met. I can't face him again."

"Nonsense. Stiffen your spine." Without waiting for further protest, Mother looped her arm through Catherine's, marching her determinedly across the room toward Huntley. "You must correct that impression immediately."

Trepidation fluttered in Catherine's chest as she was steered forward. What was it about him that unsettled her so? Was it simply the element of danger he represented?

His eyes swept the room, missing nothing, including her hesitant approach. Beneath that cool exterior, she sensed a fire, something intense that simmered beneath his calm restraint.

As they came to a stop before him, Catherine averted her gaze, not wanting to witness the amusement she was sure would spark in his eyes at her discomfort.

"Lord Huntley, did you enjoy the dinner?" Lady Kensington asked. "I found the chocolate torte especially delightful."

Catherine dared a glance at him. His thick black hair, a bit too long, curled around his ears, and his sharp blue eyes flicked to hers for a moment before shifting away with what appeared to be boredom.

"Yes, it was quite good," he replied, though Catherine felt he was far more attuned to her than his casual response suggested. His focus remained on her mother. "Lady Wilmot certainly knows how to host a fine meal."

The crowd in the drawing room had begun to thin, many guests making their way into the adjoining music room. Huntley watched them with a thoughtful expression, then turned abruptly to her.

"Lady Catherine, I've heard that you are an accomplished pianist, and I notice the piano in the next room is sitting idle. It would be a great pleasure if you would consider performing." His intense gaze met hers, unexpectedly entreating. "Perhaps you might allow me to assist in selecting a piece for you to play?"

Startled by his request, Catherine wasn't entirely sure if she'd nodded her assent before he took hold of her elbow. Swept toward Lady Wilmot's piano, she hurried to match his purposeful strides. He offered no opportunity to protest, forging ahead with determined intent. Perhaps *this* was what LeCompte meant by Huntley's rough manners.

The whole situation baffled her. What was his motive? How had he known she could play? Had he been asking about her? Gathering information?

Glancing over her shoulder, she caught sight of her mother's pleased expression, eyebrows raised in approval. A silent encouragement—perhaps more than that.

Once Mother set her sights on something, she was relentless, like a bulldog with a bone. A sinking feeling crept over Catherine as realization hit: her mother must be considering a match with Lord Huntley. Why *him*, of all people?

This can't be happening.

The music room felt noticeably warmer than the drawing room. Catherine noted the glowing embers in the fireplace, assuming the servants had built it up to combat the chill from the gusts of wind that swept through the house earlier. She tried to convince herself that the heat radiating through her body was purely external, not the result of the man gently clasping her arm, his fingers curled around her bare skin, lingering in the crook of her elbow.

She willed herself to relax, but the tension simmering inside wasn't so easily dispelled.

Sliding onto the piano bench, Catherine kept her back straight as she meticulously arranged her full skirts. Lord Huntley sat beside her, just a little too close for comfort. The forced intimacy with the very man she was trying to avoid made her heart race.

Taking a deep breath— as deep as her corset allowed—she released it slowly, letting a small measure of tension slip away.

Huntley, already rifling through a stack of music he'd gathered from the table next to the piano, glanced at her. "What would you prefer, Lady Catherine? Do you have a favorite piece?" His voice was low, intimate. She caught the faint scent of brandy on his breath.

She would have much preferred for him to leave her in peace, but of course, she couldn't say that. "You should choose, my lord," she replied formally. "I'm familiar with most of Lady Wilmot's selections, having had the privilege of playing here on several occasions." Her fingers toyed nervously with a stray tendril of her hair. Normally, she found it easier to converse with men when she adhered to the formal rules of social interaction.

So why wasn't that helping her now? The irony of relying on the very formalities she had been rebelling against earlier was not lost on her.

"I've developed quite a fondness for *Santa Lucia*," he said, pulling the music from the stack. "I only wish I had a voice to do it justice, but sadly, my talents lie elsewhere."

His smile turned seductive, sending an unwelcome ripple down her spine, and Catherine had to force herself to look away.

Much too dangerous.

He grinned, clearly aware of the effect he was having. The wretched man knew he'd rattled her. "Perhaps Lord Wentworth might be tempted to join us once he hears the opening notes. Let's see if he finds you as... enticing."

As his eyes met hers with a rakish glint, she placed the music on the stand, suppressing a small shiver of excitement. There was no doubt his double-entendre had been intentional. To her own surprise, she found herself beginning to enjoy Huntley's attention, despite how unsettling he could be. He certainly hadn't recognized her as Gray. Perhaps she could indulge in a bit of light flirtation.

Dipping her chin, she allowed a small smile to grace her lips. "This is one of my favorites as well. Let's see if I can tempt your friend to sing," she emphasized playfully.

His smile deepened as Catherine placed her fingers on the smooth ivory keys and quickly ran through a scale before beginning to play. She intentionally bumped her arm against his side in an attempt to make him move.

Really, he's such a large man.

Obligingly, he leaned slightly away and bent close, murmuring softly near her ear, "May I assist as your page-turner?" His breath stirred a loose strand of hair near her neck.

Catherine gave a small smile of assent. The moment she played the opening notes of *Santa Lucia*, Lord Wentworth's head lifted from the crowd, his eyes searching until they settled upon Huntley. Without delay, he made his way toward the piano.

"Lady Catherine," Huntley said with smooth courtesy, "allow me to introduce an old friend, the Earl of Wentworth."

Her stomach tightened as she glanced up to find Wentworth observing her with keen interest. Did he recognize her? Quickly, she lowered her gaze, unwilling to meet his eyes. Now she found herself contending with both Huntley, the panther, and this new complication, Wentworth.

An anxious thought flitted through her mind. What if being together in this setting sparked a memory? What if one of them realized who she truly was?

Focus. You can manage this.

Catherine straightened her posture, unwilling to yield to the rising tension within. While still playing, she inclined her head in a graceful acknowledgment.

"You've selected one of my favorite pieces. Might I accompany you with a song?" Wentworth leaned in slightly, his tone light and cheerful. "I must confess," he continued in a candid manner, "it becomes quite difficult for me to resist joining in whenever I hear this melody."

Despite her initial unease, Catherine felt a small measure of it dissolve under Wentworth's charm. How could this man, so composed and amiable, be the same tempestuous figure she had faced the previous night? Perhaps he was both— a man driven by strong passions, equally at ease in a ballroom as he was in the heat of a fencing match.

"Certainly, Lord Wentworth," she responded, pausing her fingers on the keys. "I shall begin again." As she struck the opening notes, Lord Huntley dutifully turned back the first page.

The moment Wentworth began to sing, his rich tenor voice filled the room with such strength and brilliance that it left Catherine astonished. The sheer power of his performance brought the room to an immediate hush, every guest pausing to listen in rapt attention.

> "Sul mare luccica l'astro d'argento.
> Placida è l'onda, prospero è il vento."

Guests from the drawing room gradually made their way into the music room, drawn by the impromptu performance. Catherine had learned this song years ago, so typically, she would have had no need to rely on the sheet music. But with Huntley seated so closely beside her, she found herself having to concentrate more than usual.

Wentworth's vibrant tenor resonated through the room, yet despite her best efforts, Catherine's focus wavered. She allowed herself a brief smile—if it weren't for her "helpful" page turner, she wouldn't require one at all. Each time Huntley leaned in to turn a page, she caught a whiff of his cologne, the woodsy scent bringing to mind the forest surrounding her parents' country estate.

> Venite all'agile barchetta mia,
> Santa Lucia! Santa Lucia!"

The room burst into applause as the final notes drifted away.

"Wentworth, *c'est très magnifique*. You transported me straight to Venice!" LeCompte exclaimed, clapping with enthusiasm as the guests crowded around the piano, offering their praises.

With so many people gathered, the air grew heavy and stifling. Lord Huntley's presence alone radiated warmth like a blacksmith's forge, and with the added heat from the fireplace and the press of the crowd, Catherine felt a wave of lightheadedness. She attempted to draw a deep breath, but the tight lacing of her corset made it impossible to fill her lungs fully. Had she rested earlier instead of fencing, she might not have been so overwhelmed now. She picked up a sheet of music and fanned herself subtly, but Huntley's watchful gaze caught the movement.

He studied her face. "Shall we take a turn about the room for some air?" he offered, his tone quiet and attentive.

She gave him a tight nod. If she didn't escape the stifling heat soon, she feared she might embarrass herself by fainting. The fashionable restrictions of her corset were especially unforgiving. Once, as a girl, the thought of wearing such a garment had thrilled her, but the excitement quickly turned to disdain. Now, the only times she was free from its oppressive confines were at night in bed or when she donned her disguise as Alexander Gray.

As she stood, she realized how many of Wentworth's admirers were gathered in a tight knot around the piano. How would she make her way through the impenetrable mass?

Huntley tucked her hand into the crook of his arm and moved forward, forcing his way into the throng. The large man cleared a path with ease as the crowd readily parted for him.

An absurd image popped into her mind, and a grin tugged at her lips. Perhaps she was more lightheaded than she'd realized, for the smile lingered as they finally broke free of the crowd.

The marquess glanced over his shoulder. "You look rather pleased, Lady Catherine. Would you care to enlighten me as to why?"

"It was nothing, merely a foolish thought."

"Then you must share it. I have a particular fondness for foolish thoughts."

"I find that hard to believe. But since you insist... as you cut through the crowd, I couldn't help but picture you as a grand ship plowing through the waves, leaving a wake of startled partygoers in your path."

He raised an amused eyebrow. "Ah, yes, I know that thought well. I've had the same one on occasion. Am I truly so fearsome a vessel?"

Yes, she thought, but instead searched for a more suitable reply.

He nodded at her hesitation, dramatically sighing. "Just as I feared. It seems I'll spend my life with people fleeing before me, intimidated by my very presence. If only they knew I'm nothing more than a harmless kitten."

"More of a panther, I'd say," she quipped before flushing with embarrassment.

His surprise quickly turned to amusement, a grin spreading across his face as he looked down at her. "And here I was, hoping to set you at ease. It seems you've already figured me out."

Their eyes locked, and for a brief moment, it was as if he could read her thoughts. Catherine quickly broke the gaze. "I'm not sure I've figured you out just yet, my lord, but I've learned enough to be... cautious."

It was only then she realized they had left the drawing room and were standing at the threshold of the library. She had been so absorbed in their banter that she hadn't noticed where he was leading her.

"Oh, I'm not sure we should—" she began, trying to withdraw her hand from his arm, hesitating at the thought of entering a secluded room with a man.

He merely smiled, his grip gentle yet firm as he kept her hand tucked in the crook of his elbow, guiding her forward. "You have nothing to fear, Lady Catherine. I assure you, this panther won't attack—if that's what has you looking so flustered." His crooked smile was undeniably disarming. "Of course, if you prefer, we can invite your mother to join us. Though I had rather hoped to take a moment to admire Lord Wilmot's fine library..." His voice trailed off, giving her the choice.

Her mother? Really? He'd tossed down that gauntlet with infuriating ease. Catherine glanced at the open door of the library. Through it, she could still see the swaying backs of guests gathered around the piano in the music room. Someone new had begun to play, and as she stood there debating, Lord Wentworth's tenor voice soared to a high note.

Lord Huntley's challenge still rang in her ears.

She wasn't used to feeling uncertain. His not-so-subtle dare caused an automatic response—she straightened her shoulders, chin lifting as she met his unfathomable blue eyes. "My mother is quite enjoying the music. I'd hate to interrupt her. I think we'll manage to avoid scandal as long as we keep the door open."

With a satisfied nod, Huntley released her hand and moved to examine the collection. He let out a low whistle. "Impressive. Perhaps you could help me find a particular book? Lady Wilmot mentioned that you're well acquainted with the library."

They'd discussed her? When? Over dinner? She pushed the thought aside. "Certainly. What are you looking for?"

With the familiar subject of books at hand, her lingering trepidation vanished. Her grandfather and the late Lord Wilmot had been close friends, and she had spent many contented hours in this haven of leather-bound volumes. Now, Catherine felt more secure, standing on firmer ground as she guided him through the collection.

"I've been searching for works by the orators of ancient Rome. I've read a great deal of Cicero, and I heard that Lord Wilmot had amassed quite the collection of his writings. Lady Wilmot invited me to explore it further when we spoke over dinner."

"Lord Wilmot was immensely proud of that part of his

library," Catherine replied. "He was always pleased to find others who shared his interest in Cicero." Mentally shrugging, she abandoned her attempt to feign empty headedness around Huntley. "The volumes you're after are just over here, to the right of the door." She guided him toward the bookshelves, pointing out the section of interest.

Huntley let out a low whistle of admiration. "What a remarkable collection." He stepped forward, scanning the leather-bound spines. "I don't believe I've ever seen one quite this extensive. Does it include Cicero's letters to Atticus?"

"Yes," she said, a note of pride entering her voice. "In fact, you have your pick of translations." She could feel his gaze follow her as she moved toward the corner of the room, where a library ladder rested against a polished brass rail. With practiced ease, she wheeled the ladder into place beside the shelves she intended to access. Catherine then gathered her skirts to avoid entangling them and ascended the narrow rungs to reach the higher volumes.

She recalled that Cicero's letters were stored on the second shelf from the top. When she spotted a volume containing his correspondence with his wife, Terentia, she knew her memory had served her well. From there, it was simply a matter of locating the letters to his closest friend, Titus Pomponius Atticus.

"Ah, here they are. Sixteen volumes in total. Do you have a particular one in mind?" she asked, dropping her handful of skirts as she reached for the first volume. With a small smile of triumph, she plucked it from the shelf and glanced down at Lord Huntley.

His hand rested on the ladder to steady it, and to her dismay, she realized that in reaching for the book, her skirt had ridden up, catching on a rung just above where she stood.

Her stocking-clad ankle was now mere inches from his bare hand.

When his eyes followed hers to the cause of her embarrassment, he froze. For a brief moment, both of them remained perfectly still, the proximity of her ankle to his hand not lost on either.

Huntley appeared startled, and he instinctively stepped back, releasing his grip on the ladder.

Embarrassed, Catherine reflexively jerked her leg back, trying to conceal it beneath her skirts. But in doing so, her leather sole slipped across the smooth wooden rung, and she lost her balance. Her fingers slipped free, and she tumbled backward, the floor rushing up to meet her.

Just as suddenly, she found herself caught, her fall broken by Lord Huntley's strong arms as they encircled her.

"Oh, my," was all she could manage as he cradled her in his arms.

Lord Huntley looked momentarily surprised, his gaze locking with hers, before a lopsided smile tugged at the corner of his mouth. He shifted his hold, drawing her more securely against his chest.

His palm pressed firmly against her ribs, just above her waist, and as his knuckles brushed the soft underside of her breast, she gasped, her eyes widening as they met his once again.

"Don't worry. I have you," he murmured, his voice low and steady.

The panther has captured the mouse.

She stared into his eyes, and for a fleeting moment, it felt as though a veil had lifted, offering her a glimpse into his very soul. His lips parted slightly, and her gaze fell to his mouth, her own lips parting in response.

A sudden, undeniable longing bloomed within her, an unfamiliar hunger that took root as she found herself utterly captivated by him.

He bent his head, pulling her closer, until their lips hovered a mere breath apart. Catherine exhaled shakily and closed her eyes.

Their kiss was tentative at first, a delicate touch of lips, but a shiver coursed through her as she inhaled the intoxicating woodsy scent that clung to him, enveloping her senses.

Huntley kissed her with increasing fervor, his tongue tracing the curve of her lower lip before gently parting her mouth. He released her legs, and she slid down his body, her petticoats softening the descent as his hand lingered at the small of her back. He pulled her flush against him as her feet found the floor, the heat of his touch radiating through the fabric.

Catherine's breath quickened, her entire body alive with a deep, yearning desire. A searing warmth spread through her, threatening to consume her entirely. Without thought, her hands found their way into his thick hair, pulling him closer as she surrendered fully to the kiss.

The sudden clatter of footsteps in the hallway jolted her back to reality. Startled, she drew back, her heart racing. How long had the music been silent?

Her eyes flew open in panic, and she withdrew her hands from Huntley's hair, stepping back quickly. He was already smoothing his disheveled locks, straightening his coat with a practiced grace. Catherine hurried to adjust her rumpled skirts, giving them a quick twitch. Fortunately, her hair remained untouched, though she could only hope her face didn't betray what had just transpired.

His gaze swept over her from head to toe, assessing her appearance. Satisfied, he gave her a curt nod. Yet, her stomach tightened with unease, the weight of what had occurred still heavy between them.

"We have a much larger music selection in our library," Lady Wilmot's voice preceded her through the doorway. "An extensive collection of opera librettos... or *libretti*, if you prefer."

Huntley cast a quick, conspiratorial wink at Catherine before lunging forward to shove the library ladder aside, sending it clattering noisily along the brass rails.

"Lady Catherine, are you hurt?" he called out, his voice deliberately loud. The sudden flurry of footsteps rushing toward the library made it clear his diversion had worked. As the footsteps neared, he shot her a steadying look, his raised brow silently urging her to play along.

Catherine, catching on, gave a quick nod and responded with exaggerated uncertainty, "Oh, I'm not sure!" She feigned fluster, which wasn't difficult under the circumstances. When she turned, she found her mother and a few other guests frozen at the doorway, aghast at discovering her alone with Huntley.

"I slipped on the ladder while retrieving a book," Catherine explained, snatching the volume from the floor and hastily handing it to Huntley, all the while carefully avoiding his gaze.

Her mother, clearly suspicious, intercepted the book with a sharp glance at Huntley, her eyes narrowing as though seeking to uncover the truth. Before she could examine it too closely, M. LeCompte stepped forward and snatched the volume from her hands with a flourish. A devilish gleam sparkled in his eyes, and Catherine's heart sank. He appeared ready to stir up scandal—or perhaps even craft one from nothing.

"A book, *oui*? And just which book did you feel compelled to retrieve?" LeCompte's voice oozed curiosity.

"Cicero," Catherine and Huntley responded in unison.

LeCompte inspected the title with evident disappointment, his features falling as the pair's answer proved accurate. "How dreary," he muttered, handing it back to her mother with a dismissive flick of his wrist. "I would have thought you'd choose something a touch more engaging, *ma chère*."

"It isn't for me. It's for Lord Huntley," Catherine replied evenly.

Her mother's eyes flicked to the marquess, studying him with a sharp gaze, though his expression remained unreadable. Huntley received the book with a polite smile, outwardly attentive to Lady Kensington, though Catherine could feel the quiet intensity of his focus still lingering on her.

"How very kind of you," Lady Wilmot interjected, sweeping into the exchange with her usual ease. "I had intended to bring Lord Huntley here myself after dinner, but Lord Wentworth's magnificent voice quite distracted me." She laughed, a musical trill, before stepping smoothly between Catherine and Huntley.

"You're such a good girl, showing him Lord Wilmot's collection," Lady Wilmot added, taking Catherine's hand and patting it with maternal affection. "He was so proud of these books. I remember how he and your grandfather would talk for hours about them. You're the perfect person to help Lord Huntley find just what he needs."

Catherine's discomfort deepened under the weight of their scrutiny. She shifted her stance, and as she placed weight on her right foot, she feigned a wince.

Her mother, ever watchful, immediately noticed. "Are you injured?"

"I'm sure I'm fine. "I must have landed poorly when I fell," she lied—with only a twinge of remorse.

She shifted again, testing the imaginary injury, and added another small wince for effect.

Her mother frowned. "I'd rather not take any chances. We'll leave straight away so you can rest. With a poultice, you should be fit by morning."

"That's probably for the best," Catherine agreed, allowing relief to color her tone. "I promised Sarah I'd take her for a ride in the park tomorrow. She'll never forgive me if I don't keep my word."

TEMPTATION

Daniel watched as Lady Catherine limped away. Odd that he hadn't noticed before how her gown displayed her shoulders in such a fetching manner. They seemed more muscular than soft—an unusual but intriguing contradiction. Could her devotion to needlework account for it? It hardly seemed strenuous enough to explain such fine form. There were, of course, other parts of her equally as striking...

He tore his gaze away from her, not wanting to be caught staring.

Dammit. He ought to have known better than to kiss her—especially after the near catastrophe with Lady Lydia only the other evening. Tonight felt like an echo of those events, yet while the scene with Lady Lydia had been staged by her and her parents, tonight's interlude had been entirely accidental.

Well, not entirely accidental. He had been fully aware of the risk when he led her to the library. But there was something about Lady Catherine that stirred in him a desire to take chances. His behavior had been reckless, and he knew it. If there'd been any hint of scandal, her prospects for a good match would have been ruined, and he refused to have that on his conscience. If necessary, he'd fulfill his duty and protect her name.

It had been foolish to take such a risk, especially with someone he hardly knew.

Daniel claimed a comfortable chair and relaxed in a casual sprawl, ostensibly leafing through the volume of Cicero's letters. But his concentration faltered. The sensation of Lady Catherine's lips against his lingered, an undeniable distraction.

Behind him, Lord Wentworth's voice cut through the air. "Lady Wilmot, I cannot seem to find the opera I'm searching for in your collection."

"If it's a newer one, then perhaps you never will. I haven't added to the collection since my husband's passing."

Lady Catherine was certainly a tempting morsel. What was it about her?

"That would explain it," Wentworth sighed. "I was hoping to find Verdi's *Rigoletto*."

"That's quite new, isn't it? Wasn't there some scandal associated with it?" Lady Wilmot sounded unsure.

Daniel's mind still drifted back to Lady Catherine, trying to make sense of the magnetic pull she had over him. She had seemed no different from other young women at first, but now, , but there was something more to her. As though she were playing a part.

"Yes, *mais oui*," LeCompte interjected. "The censors in France took issue with it. The opera is based on a play by Victor Hugo, which was banned because it was thought to insult King Louis-Philippe."

"I thought it was about King Francis I," Wentworth mused.

"It was meant to be, but Hugo's allusions were too transparent. The censors saw right through them," LeCompte explained, shaking his head, though whether in disdain for the censorship or Hugo's daring was unclear.

"I recall hearing about that play—*Le roi s'amuse,* was it?" Lady

Wilmot's brow furrowed in concentration. "I can understand why our French neighbors might have been embarrassed. After years of exile, King Louis-Philippe had a difficult reign. The censors must have been overly cautious. Of course, King Francis was something of a rake. Then again," she added with a twinkle in her eye, "our own Henry VIII wasn't much better. Did the censors eventually relent?"

"Not exactly." Wentworth continued to leaf through the collection of operas. "Verdi shifted the setting from France to Italy and changed the characters' names to get around the censorship. It was finally performed in Venice just over a year ago."

LeCompte's eyes gleamed. "I was fortunate enough to attend one of those performances in Venice. It was *spectaculaire*." He made a graceful gesture with his hand. "And it will soon be performed at Covent Garden."

"Here? In London?" Lady Wilmot's excitement was palpable. "I must attend its debut. Surely, it will be a highlight of the season."

Daniel allowed himself to relax, relieved that the conversation had veered away from him and Lady Catherine. Their brief interlude had been interrupted at just the right moment, before things could escalate further. And upon reflection, it was likely for the best. If they hadn't been interrupted, he wasn't sure he would have had the will to pull away.

Why did he find Lady Catherine so blasted tempting? Was it because she was a puzzle to him? Her response to his kiss had been the most surprising part of the evening.

At first she'd reacted as any innocent would, but when he'd deepened the kiss, her passion had emerged. The feel of her, pliant and responsive in his arms, had been more of a temptation than he could resist.

He'd been reckless. Foolish.

Was she suitable for him? Could she meet his exacting standards? Possibly. Was she above reproach? The kiss, admittedly, had been a lapse in judgment, but the situation had been unusual. He couldn't fault her for that. After all, he'd given in to the moment as well. In fact, having a passionate wife could be a pleasant bonus. One he hadn't anticipated.

Daniel shifted uncomfortably in his chair as he forced his thoughts back to the present and away from the tempting Lady Catherine.

Daniel shifted uncomfortably in his chair, forcing his thoughts back to the present. They were still discussing that opera? He stifled a sigh. Yes, *Rigoletto*.

All things considered, the evening had turned out well. He had escaped Lady Lydia, Wentworth had entertained the guests admirably, and he had even met a potential candidate for the role of Lady Huntley.

His thoughts drifted back to Lady Catherine. She had mentioned a ride in the park tomorrow. Perhaps he could arrange a "chance" encounter there. And with her sister acting as chaperone, it would lend the encounter just enough propriety to be respectable.

❧ 12 ❧

A RIDE IN THE PARK

The moment they arrived home, Mother summoned Mrs. Evans, their housekeeper.

Though the woman had retired for the night, she arrived promptly, accustomed to being called upon at all hours. Over the years, they had come to rely on her gift with poultices and home remedies.

Catherine reclined on her bed, lying atop the covers. Simpson had already helped her change into her nightclothes, and now she leaned against the headboard, her "injured" foot propped on a pillow. Her mother hovered near the window, waiting anxiously for Mrs. Evans.

When Mrs. Evans entered, her tired eyes were full of concern. She moved swiftly to Catherine's bedside and ran her fingers along the girl's ankle, her brow furrowing as she examined it. Her expression shifted as she cast a sharp, knowing glance at Catherine, her lips pressing into a thin line of disapproval.

Catherine flushed. "I... I slipped off the ladder in Lord Wilmot's library," she explained quickly. "I must have twisted it when I landed, but it feels much better already."

"And why were you on the ladder during a dinner party?" Mrs. Evans's gaze bored into hers, pinning her in place.

"I was helping the marquess find a book," Catherine murmured, her gaze slipping away. Mrs. Evans had a way of seeing too much in her eyes.

Mrs. Evans's eyes gleamed with understanding. She patted Catherine's leg before standing. "I'll fix you up right quick. A poultice will have you good as new by morning."

"You're certain?" her mother asked, still worried. "We have that musical soirée tomorrow evening, and knowing our hosts, Catherine will be on her feet for quite some time."

"Quite certain, my lady. My poultice will work wonders." She bustled out of the room.

Catherine sank back against the pillows with a sigh of relief. Mrs. Evans was impossible to fool, but she was loyal and could be trusted to keep her secrets. She undoubtedly suspected that something more had happened in the library, but she would never speak of it. Servants were often the source of scandalous tales, passing gossip from house to house, but Mrs. Evans would never betray her.

She had even kept Catherine's fencing expeditions a secret from Mother.

Mrs. Evans returned shortly with a bowl of poultice, a few crisp cabbage leaves, and a length of gauze. Catherine could tell by the slight limp in the woman's gait that her hip was bothering her, and a twinge of guilt stabbed at her. Mrs. Evans shouldn't have to suffer for her folly.

The housekeeper sat on the edge of the bed and set the bowl beside Catherine's knee.

"That smells good enough to eat."

Mrs. Evans returned the smile. "Almost. It's grated potato and mugwort, with a tincture of peach to reduce the swelling. The peach is probably what's whetted your appetite." She spread the messy concoction over Catherine's ankle, then layered a cabbage leaf on top and wrapped it securely with gauze.

"There you are, my lady. You'll be right as rain by morning." She glanced toward Lady Kensington before leaning closer to Catherine, her voice a whisper. "Mugwort can also bring prophetic dreams. Just rub a little of the poultice between your eyebrows before sleep."

Catherine blinked, taken aback, as Mrs. Evans as she cleared her items from the bed. The woman was full of surprises.

Once alone, Catherine turned off her bedside lamp and slid under the covers.

Blast Lord Huntley and his nimble hands, his devilish lips. How could she return to Bernini's now, after facing him as both Lady Catherine and Alexander Gray?

The man was far too bold... far too maddening.

She'd simply avoid him. That shouldn't be too difficult. London was large enough for that, surely.

The pleasant scent of peaches filled the room. For a moment, she considered Mrs. Evans's suggestion to rub some of the poultice between her brows but dismissed it. The last thing she needed tonight was a prophetic dream. What if Huntley pursued her there as well?

❧

As Catherine and her sister rode into the expansive park, she noted many familiar faces among the friends and neighbors also enjoying the fine weather. The clear skies and warmer air had lured out nearly the entire neighborhood.

"It's been far too long since we've ridden together," Catherine said, glancing at her sister. "I'm glad you convinced me to come."

Sarah shot her a teasing smile. "If I didn't, you'd spend all your days with mother paying calls. Someone has to remind you there's a world out here."

Catherine laughed. "You're not wrong."

With the trees bare of leaves, the bright sunlight filtered through the branches, warming her. Her broad-brimmed hat, with its delicate veil trailing down the back of her neck, shielded her eyes from the sun's glare. The bridle paths had begun to dry, but patches of mud lingered here and there. Catherine guided her horse carefully to avoid any splashes that might mar her skirts. Even in the grayish-black of her fitted jacket and full skirt, the mud would still show.

As she relaxed into the rhythm and sway of her mount, her thoughts kept returning to last night. Lord Huntley had become a problem—one she needed to address. The most troubling part was her own annoying tendency to dwell on the man— or, more particularly, on his tantalizing taste and the feel of his lips.

She'd been kissed before, of course. In the gardens at the Norfolk Ball last year, she'd endured the fumbling advances of Lord Watters when he'd proclaimed his undying love. His kisses had been nice, or at least, not unpleasant, but they left her unmoved.

His undying love had died a quick death within the span of a week, allowing him to move on to his next object of affection.

Last night had been a wholly different experience. It was hard to believe both incidents could even be called "a kiss." The sensations had overwhelmed her—Huntley had caught her entirely off guard.

The scoundrel.

Even now, thinking about that kiss made something melt inside her.

She recalled the Oxford girl Charles had told her about—the one who'd run off to Gretna Green. Had she felt this way? Was this why she'd taken such reckless chances?

Catherine shook herself. No, this couldn't continue. Lord Huntley posed too great a danger, with a foot in both of her lives.

He needed to be kept at a distance, far from the fragile balance she was trying to maintain.

As she and Sarah rode through the park, Catherine struggled with the whirl of thoughts inside her. Most riders stayed on the main path that circled the park, eager to be seen and to exchange pleasantries. Catherine, however, had no taste for idle chatter today. Preferring solitude, she led her sister off the main circuit and down a quieter path into the woods.

Soon, they came to a fork in the road. Slowing their horses to a walk, Catherine tugged at the reins, guiding them along the less-traveled route that wound up a rocky hillside. It had always been one of her favorite paths, though she hadn't ventured here in months. She urged Wildfire up the small incline toward where the trail curved around a jagged outcropping of rock.

How she wished she could ride astride, rather than this tiresome sidesaddle. Her right leg was locked in place by the fixed pommel, while her left tucked under the lower leaping horn, leaving her with only her hands to control Wildfire. At least her left foot rested in a proper stirrup, unlike the loose right one. And poor Wildfire—he had to compensate for her weight being off-center on his left.

Just over fifty years ago, Catherine the Great of Russia had ridden astride, even insisting the women of her court do the same. Too bad Queen Victoria didn't share that sentiment.

As Catherine rounded the corner, the steady rhythm of Bibbles's hoofbeats faltered, followed by the unmistakable sound of a stumble. Catherine glanced back just in time to see a blur of petticoats.

Sarah shrieked as she toppled from her horse, hitting the ground with a painful thud. The impact forced a grunt from her, and Bibbles, now spooked, bolted up the hill. The riderless horse charged past Catherine on the narrow path, his broad flank grazing her legs. Perched precariously on her sidesaddle, she teetered, grabbing Wildfire's mane for balance.

Startled by the commotion, Wildfire clamped down on the bit, instinct urging him to flee. Catherine pulled hard at the reins, muscles straining as she fought to keep control of the powerful animal. Her precarious position—legs to one side—made the task all the more dangerous. Had she been riding astride, she could have clamped her knees and kept her seat with ease.

By the time Bibbles disappeared around the bend, Wildfire was still skittish, dancing with nervous energy. Catherine didn't wait. She spun him around and hurried back down the path, leaping from the saddle as soon as she reached her sister, keeping a firm hold on the reins.

Heart pounding, she knelt beside Sarah, her corset biting into her waist as her breath came in shallow gasps. A strange ringing filled her ears as she stared down at her sister. Sarah lay face down in the leaves, her hair spilled from its pins in a halo of loose brown curls. The sight of her lying so still sent a jolt of terror through Catherine, fear constricting her throat.

In a terrifying tableau, Sarah lay sprawled face down in a pile of leaves, her hair tumbling free from its pins to form a halo of loose brown curls. The stillness of her body seized Catherine's heart with icy fear.

"Sarah?" Catherine's voice trembled as she placed a hand on her sister's shoulder and gently turned her over. "Sarah!"

Her breath caught at the sight of blood trickling from Sarah's hairline. Pulse racing, she patted her sister's cheek, desperation rising as she waited for any sign of movement.

But Sarah remained still.

Catherine's gaze darted up and down the empty trail, but there was no one in sight. Her breath came in ragged gasps as she took Sarah's limp hand in hers, rubbing it frantically between her palms.

"Sarah, please! Wake up!"

When her sister's eyelashes fluttered, relief flooded Catherine, air rushing from her lungs in a shaky exhale.

Sarah moaned softly, pulling her hand from Catherine's grasp as she struggled to sit up.

"Ow!" Sarah winced, clutching her head. She pulled her hand away and stared at the red smear on her glove. "There's blood... I think I'm hurt!" Panic edged her voice. "Catherine, I'm bleeding!"

"Stay calm, darling," Catherine urged, her voice steady despite her racing heart. "Lie still for just a moment." She gently patted Sarah's shoulder. "Do you hurt anywhere else?"

"No... well, yes... I think I hurt my ankle." Sarah's eyes welled with tears.

"I'll find help," Catherine said, keeping her tone as calm as possible. "Bibbles ran off, but I'll get you home." She gave Sarah's shoulder a reassuring squeeze. "Just wait here. I'll be right back."

Sarah's chin trembled as she fought to keep her fear in check. Catherine's heart ached, but she knew she had no choice but to leave her side. Mounting a horse sidesaddle required two grooms or at least one and a mounting block. There was nothing nearby for her to stand on. Besides, she couldn't possibly lift Sarah onto Wildfire by herself.

Standing, Catherine grabbed Wildfire's reins, steadying the horse as she led him up the path in search of a rock to climb onto. Just then, the sound of approaching hoofbeats reached her ears— rapid and growing louder.

She quickly turned, pulling Wildfire across the trail to shield Sarah from the oncoming rider. Judging by the intensity of the pounding hooves, the horse was moving at a fast clip.

Catherine tightened her grip on Wildfire's bridle, making sure he wouldn't startle. The hoofbeats thundered closer, and she realized there were two horses approaching.

"Help!" she shouted, her voice ringing with urgency. "Please, help us!"

The horses slowed, and a man's voice called out, "Are you hurt?"

Catherine took a shaky step forward as the rider came into view, rounding the promontory with Bibbles in tow.

13

EYES THE COLOR OF
SCOTCH WHISKEY

D aniel's stomach twisted as he rounded the corner of the trail, heart pounding at the sight before him. Lady Catherine stood there, blocking the path with her horse, her shoulders tense yet steady. Relief washed over him—she appeared unharmed. The instant he'd heard her call for help, he'd feared the worst, her voice slicing through the air and driving him forward with a single, unrelenting thought: get to her.

"Lord Huntley?" Her voice held a note of uncertainty as she took a step to the side, allowing him a clear view of what lay behind her.

The moment Daniel saw the crumpled figure on the path, he leaped from his horse. Although he'd planned an "accidental" encounter with Catherine, the urgency of the situation made him grateful to be here now. Of course, it also had something to do with the fact that he'd seen her take this path and had circled around to the other end, planning to meet her halfway. When he'd recognized her voice calling for help, dread had tightened in his chest.

"What happened?"

"My sister, Sarah, took a bad fall from her horse and hit her head.

She was unconscious for a moment, but she's awake now," Catherine explained, still looking as if she couldn't quite believe he was there. Her hands were clenched, but her calm demeanor was remarkable.

Daniel furrowed his brow as he crouched down beside Sarah. The metallic tang of blood stung his nostrils. He removed his riding gloves and gently moved aside Sarah's hair to inspect the wound. A lump had already formed on her forehead, and blood trickled down toward her ear.

"The good news is that it's a small cut, only about half an inch long."

He pulled a fresh white handkerchief from his pocket, tucking it into Lady Sarah's hand to press against her head. He glanced up at Catherine, noticing her remarkable calm. No hysterics, no hand-wringing.

He turned back to Sarah. "Hold this firmly against the wound. I know there's a lot of blood, but head wounds bleed profusely. It should stop soon. Are you hurt anywhere else?"

Sarah gave him a wide-eyed stare, and Daniel wondered how hard she'd hit her head. Could she be addled?

When she didn't respond, Catherine answered for her. "She mentioned her ankle hurts. Perhaps she twisted it in the stirrup when she fell." Catherine crouched beside her sister and rested a hand on Sarah's laced-up boot.

"You can't say ankle in front of a man," Sarah whispered loudly, casting a look at her sister. "It's not proper."

Catherine grinned. "Well, I just did, and nothing terrible happened, did it?"

Sarah glared, then turned her gaze to Daniel. "The fixed pommel was bothering me, so I lifted my... my *limb* out of it to rest it on top. Just then, Bibbles stumbled, and I slipped off." She lifted her head from the ground to glance at her feet, her chin trembling. "It isn't broken, is it?"

"I can't tell, but it's best to keep your boot on until we get you home. I'd don't want to disturb your *limb* any more than necessary."

She nodded her approval at his plan— or was it at his proper use of the term "limb"?

The horses shifted restlessly, and Daniel became acutely aware of the cold earth beneath his knee. If they didn't move Sarah soon, she'd be chilled to the bone.

Sarah pulled the cloth from her head and examined it. "So much blood," she murmured, her tone shaky. The tears welling in her eyes began to spill, mingling with the blood on her face.

"That's normal for head wounds," he reassured her again, though he exchanged a worried glance with Catherine, wondering how severe that blow had been. "It isn't as bad as it looks. Keep the cloth pressed against it. Let's see if we can get you up on your horse and get you home."

He stood and extended a hand to Sarah, helping her to her feet. She stumbled and clung to his sleeve for balance. Wrapping an arm around her waist, Daniel steadied her.

"My head is spinning," she whispered.

"I don't think you'll be able to ride your horse home." He considered their options. "Why don't you ride with me on my horse? I can help steady you, and your sister can bring your horse."

"Bibbles," Sarah interjected.

Daniel blinked. "Bibbles?" It sounded like an expletive. Had the girl struck her head harder than he thought? She seemed befuddled.

"My horse's name is Bibbles," she clarified, sounding slightly annoyed.

"Ah!" He chuckled in relief, pleased to learn she wasn't spouting gibberish. "A fitting name. Bibbles sounds like a friendly sort."

"Oh, he is."

"Good. Your sister can lead Bibbles, and you'll ride with me on Rajah."

"Rajah? Like a king?" Sarah asked as he guided her toward his horse.

"Yes, precisely. You're a clever girl." Gently, he lifted her onto Rajah, careful not to jostle her ankle. "My Rajah has a king-like disposition, and I'm sure he'll be proud to carry a princess such as yourself." With Sarah's skirts trailing over the horse's rear, it appeared as though Rajah wore a dress.

Daniel suppressed a smile as he handed Muggle's reins to Sarah. "Keep a firm grip and hold on to these. Play the groom while I help your sister onto her sidesaddle." He waited for her to nod before turning to Catherine and her horse.

He stooped down and laced his fingers together so Catherine could step into them. He avoided looking at her small foot as she placed it in his hands. The last thing he needed was a repeat of last night's incident. Though recreating the moment when her ankle had been bared and she fell into his arms might be enjoyable, it was not ideal with Sarah watching.

Once he was back in the saddle, with Lady Sarah's arms wrapped around his waist, she announced, "I know about Rajahs because Papa was in the army. We lived in India for years. In fact, Catherine, Charles, and I were all born there."

"Really? How unusual." He glanced curiously at Catherine, noting her tight-lipped expression. Was she embarrassed by her unusual childhood, or simply tired of her sister's chatter?

"Papa sold his commission when he became Grandfather's heir. He'll probably never take us back to India. It's so unfair."

"Hmm." The girl was full of information. Perhaps that accounted for the sour expression on Catherine's face.

"Catherine doesn't like to talk about India," Sarah added, "but Charles mentions it often. That's where he first learned to fence."

"We don't live far," Catherine interrupted, clearly eager to change the subject.

Daniel grinned. As an only child, he'd never suffered through the tribulations of having a younger sibling, but he'd witnessed Wentworth in similar situations. Lady Sarah was precocious... and particularly chatty.

"Look at the way Rajah holds his head up high," Sarah remarked. She leaned to one side to look at the horse, prompting Daniel to sweep an arm behind her to keep her balanced. "He's so handsome, and he looks proud and regal, just like a king. See?" she said as she released one of her arms on his waist to point. "He's twitching his ears because he knows I'm talking about him. I'm surprised Prince Albert doesn't ride him. I'm sure he'd love Rajah."

"Prince Albert would certainly admire Rajah, but I'd hate to give him up. Should I hide him away in Scotland for safekeeping?"

Sarah giggled, then winced. "Don't make me laugh—my head hurts."

Daniel exchanged amused glances with Lady Catherine.

The route to Lady Catherine's home took them directly past Daniel's townhouse. As they approached it, he noticed one of his servants, Driscol, sweeping the front steps.

Driscol marked their approach, returned to his task, and then glanced back to stare at them. He dropped his broom with a clatter and rushed toward them. "Lord Huntley, may I be of assistance?" He trotted alongside them, his eyes full of concern as he took in the blood on Lady Sarah's face.

"You're just the man I hoped to see. I'm escorting this young woman home. Please send someone to Kensington House immediately to inform them that Lady Sarah has taken a small spill from her horse. I'll have her home shortly."

"I'll do it myself, my lord," he said, with a small bow of his head. He trotted around the side of the house toward the rear stables.

Lady Catherine's frowned. "I hope he doesn't alarm them," she said.

"Driscol is a reliable fellow. I'm sure he'll deliver the message without causing any panic."

Lady Catherine's expression softened at his reassurance. As they continued riding, she glanced over her shoulder, her curiosity clearly piqued. Her eyes lingered on his elegant townhouse. "Am I to assume that is your residence, Lord Huntley?" she asked, her tone betraying a hint of intrigue as she studied the building.

"Yes, for now." He gave a small shrug. "I'm leasing it. I hope to buy something larger. This place doesn't allow me to entertain many guests, but it has the advantage of being conveniently located."

"Do you plan to spend more time here in London?" Lady Catherine shifted in her saddle, her eyes fixed on the road ahead as if avoiding his gaze on purpose.

Did his answer mattered to her?

Driscol overtook them on horseback, cantering ahead to deliver the message. The young man's efficiency pleased Daniel, and he reflected on the decision to offer him a position as footman—one that had clearly paid off. Driscol's family had always been reliable, and he'd been pleased to offer him a position as footman. The young man had no interest in following his father into shipbuilding, often expressing his desire to come to London.

Huntley turned his attention back to Lady Catherine, observing her carefully through hooded eyes. "I plan to stay in London for the next few months," he said.

He caught the faintest twitch of her mouth, though she said nothing. So, it *did* matter to her. But in what way? And why?

"I have a couple of reasons for frequenting London," he continued, keeping a close eye on her reaction. How much gossip about him had reached her ears? "Over the past few years, I've developed several business interests in the region, which require my presence. And, if I'm honest, I've come to enjoy my time here. London has become something of a second home. This is the first year I've truly taken advantage of society's entertainments. My title has been helpful in making me more welcome, despite my lowly business interests." His mouth tightened into a thin line.

"Yes, many gentlemen shy away from business, thinking it beneath them," she said. Then she rushed to add, "But not in my family. Papa takes a keen interest in shipping, and he encourages my brother, Lord Spencer, to be involved as well."

Daniel's eyebrows lifted slightly in surprise. He had forgotten about the new Earl of Kensington's involvement in trade. It had kept the man on the fringes of society until just recently, when he'd inherited his grandfather's title.

He frowned. Was Lady Catherine something of an outsider as well?

"I'm glad you like London," Lady Sarah piped up from her perch behind him. "It's one of my favorite places. Catherine loves it too, don't you, Catherine? Perhaps you'll find a house near ours, and we could be neighbors." She bounced a little in the saddle, her voice taking on a singsong tone. "Wouldn't that be wonderful, Catherine? I'm sure you'd love having such a handsome man as Lord Huntley next door."

Catherine visibly stiffened, her sister's teasing hitting its mark. "Yes, wonderful," she said dryly, casting a quelling look at Sarah. With a sigh of exasperation, she turned her attention back to the road ahead.

Daniel studied her profile as they rode in silence. Fetching, certainly. Kind and intelligent, without a doubt. But as much as he admired her, an uneasy realization settled over him. Lady Catherine didn't meet his most fundamental requirement for a wife. He'd chosen to ignore it, yet her family's involvement in trade placed her just outside the circle of impeccable respectability he needed. He wasn't proud of the thought, especially since he held himself to a different standard, but he couldn't shake it. He needed someone more like Lady Lydia—proper, well-placed, and above reproach.

The decision left a hollow ache in his chest, one he hadn't expected.

"Tell me more about Bibbles," he said, twisting in his saddle to glance back at Lady Sarah. "He seems like a fine horse."

Lady Sarah eagerly took the bait, launching into joyful descriptions of Bibbles and his stable companions—Lord What-sis, Princess, and Flitwhitty, the stable cats—each introduced with delightful enthusiasm.

Daniel stole a glance at Lady Catherine, who shot him a look of silent gratitude for distracting her sister. He smiled back, dipping his head in acknowledgment.

When they reached Kensington House, two women stood at the entrance—one in a gray dress with a white apron, the other in a plain black gown with a white collar. The housekeeper and governess, no doubt. The women fussed over Lady Sarah the moment she dismounted, assisting her up the stairs with a flurry of concern over ice packs and poultices.

Lady Sarah would be well cared for—perhaps overly so. The front door clicked shut behind them.

And then Daniel found himself standing alone with Lady Catherine.

"Thank you for your help, Lord Huntley," she said, her gaze fixed on her hands as she absentmindedly tugged at her leather riding gloves.

As she nervously licked her lips, Daniel found he couldn't look away. The memory of last night, and the feel of her lips against his, suddenly crashed upon him as though it had only happened moments ago.

He could almost hear an echo of the soft moan that had escaped her lips.

"You were our savior today," she murmured, her voice low sending an involuntary tremor down his spine. When she lifted her chin, the sunlight fell across her face, illuminating eyes the color of rich Scotch whiskey. "I truly don't know what we would have done without you."

Daniel forced himself to tear his gaze away, suddenly too aware of how captivated he was by her mouth. "Assuredly, Lady Catherine, the pleasure was all mine." His voice came out huskier than he intended.

Her cheeks flushed at the unintended implication in his words, and he mentally cursed himself for his clumsiness. He hadn't meant to flirt—especially since he had no intention of pursuing her further. He needed to stop this before it went any further.

"Good day, Lord Huntley." Flustered, Lady Catherine turned on her heel and hurried into the house.

Despite her quick departure, a small smile tugged at his lips.He really ought to examine the whiskey collection at the Ambridge Club. Which one, exactly, matched the color of her eyes?

Then he shook his head. No, he needed to stop this train of thought entirely. Dwelling on her wouldn't help. Intriguing as she was, a future with her was impossible. His children would already have enough challenges without two parents leading entirely unconventional lives.

Still, he couldn't help wondering if her eyes were closer to the shade of Glenfarclas.

14

GANESHA

During the following week, Catherine grew increasingly restless. In the past, Mother's busy schedule of afternoon calls provided ample opportunity for Catherine to fence without risk of being detected, but this week had been different. With Mother's new plan for securing a quick engagement, she had insisted Catherine accompany her every afternoon. That meant Catherine had only been able to steal a few scattered moments to practice. Tonight's weekly excursion to Bernini's Academy couldn't come soon enough.

She glanced out the window and grimaced at the thick fog that had descended upon the city. Would it lift before she needed to leave tonight?

Catherine loved their converted ballroom. When they had first returned from India, Grandfather had allowed Papa to install a couple of cabinets in the seldom-used space, along with a number of large wall mirrors. Everything looked perfectly elegant. No one would guess that the cabinets held fencing supplies.

When Mother was home, Catherine normally resisted succumbing to the temptation the room presented. But today, her restlessness spurred her on, and she decided to risk escaping to the ballroom, if only for a short time. Once inside, she approached one of Papa's cabinets. An artisan in India had created the pair for him, and the doors bore carvings of Ganesha, dancing and holding swords. She couldn't help but smile. Dancing and fencing… Papa knew her so well. She wondered if they were the only two people who understood the significance of the images. She swung open the elaborately decorated door and selected a foil.

Catherine avoided looking in the ballroom's mirrors when she fenced in women's garb. The sight disoriented her. It was difficult to reconcile her thoughts and actions as a fencer with the demure young woman in the reflection. Only when fencing did she allow her fire and passion to emerge.

With a quick flick, she took an *"en garde"* stance. As she worked through some footwork exercises, she relaxed, feeling more limber than she had in days. The tension that had grown in the week since her last trip to Bernini's began to ease.

The sound of the ballroom door opening startled her. Catherine quickly dropped the tip of her foil to her side, hiding its length in the folds of her bell-shaped skirt. She spun toward the door, but when she saw Charles, she relaxed.

"I received your note," he said as he shut the door behind him. "Since the door was unlocked, I gather you were certain I'd come." He turned the key to ensure their privacy.

"Not certain, but hopeful." The exercise had warmed her, dispelling the chill of the day. She flipped her foil out from the folds of her skirts with practiced ease, rolling her shoulders. She beckoned her brother to join her with a flick of her wrist.

He said nothing but turned to the fencing armoire. He plucked a helmet from its depths and tossed it to her, then selected one for himself. "Don't damage my frock coat. I'd rather not change again, and I've an appointment soon." He dipped low in his stance, preparing to spar.

"You aren't going to limber up?" Catherine asked.

"You've only fenced one night in the past five months, whereas I've done so almost daily. This is the best chance I've had in ages to beat you." Charles crossed his sword tip with hers. "*En garde*," he said, lunging abruptly but just barely missing a hit.

Did he truly think she was out of practice? She grinned as she parried and countered with a precise strike that landed on his right shoulder. The button on the tip of the foil prevented it from ripping through the fine fabric.

"Point," said Charles, frustration lacing his voice as he reset his stance. "I thought you'd be slower."

"I may not have fenced while we were at the country house, but I kept up with my training," she said, flicking the foil toward his midriff. "I'll try not to ruin your clothing."

He gave a crooked smile and shrugged out of his frock coat. "I should have known better than to assume. To think I thought you'd be out of condition."

"You should know I'd never let my skills deteriorate. Fencing is my life—or rather, it saved my life." She glanced at the carved Ganesha on the door, then turned to face one of the fencing dummies hanging from the open cabinet. With a steady hand and firm aim, she thrust the foil's tip at the red heart painted on the dummy's chest. Satisfaction gleamed in her eyes as she looked over her shoulder at her brother.

He draped his dark coat over one of the delicate balloon-backed chairs lining the wall. "Actually, it was more hope than assumption," he said, bending the steel of his foil between his hands. "You're right. I should have known. How did you manage it? We've no private fencing parlor at the country house."

She gave him an enigmatic smile as she stepped away from the dummy to face him again. "Weren't you ever curious before now?"

Charles stepped into the *en garde* position. "I knew you wouldn't risk Mother finding you with a foil in hand."

"Certainly not. She'd be livid if she ever knew I still fenced." Catherine brushed aside his feint with ease. "At the country house, I resorted to less conventional methods," she admitted, keeping a careful eye on her brother as he shifted his weight. She could always predict his attacks by the movement of his feet.

Charles raised his foil, and Catherine beat it to the side, executing a graceful combination of feints to drive him back. She withdrew for a moment to avoid his parry and then performed another feint, followed quickly by a lunge.

"Walking on the stones along the brook is excellent practice for my footwork," she explained, demonstrating by taking two quick steps back.

Charles performed a *glise*, sliding the edge of his foil up the edge of Catherine's, causing the lengths of steel to ring in anger, and closed the distance between them. "That explains why you came home soaked last September, just as I was leaving for Oxford," he teased, grinning. "Your waterlogged skirts left a trail of shame through the house."

She advanced swiftly, lunging again. "Are you trying to throw me off? Teasing won't work." She glared at him. "I only fell in once, and you just happened to witness my return. It became much more difficult once the stones became slick with snow." And the ice-cold water had provided a much greater incentive to stay dry.

In a flash, she performed a *fleche*, leaping off her leading foot and scoring a second point on his chest as she passed him at a run.

"Two to nothing. This match is going quickly," Charles remarked, spinning to face her.

"Are you letting me win? I expect a fair fight!" She stamped her foot on the polished parquet floor of the ballroom. "Don't throw the match just to rush off to the Ambridge Club."

"Stop it, Cat. Five months ago, you won every match. You've no reason to think that's changed." He tugged off his face mask and closed the distance between them, anger furrowing his brow.

"Why don't you show a little appreciation? You know I only fence because you and Father love it."

She pulled her head back as if struck, but the sharp retort on her tongue faded when she saw the pain in his eyes. Of course, he was right. "I'm sorry," she said softly, looking down. "I shouldn't have said those things. You've always been supportive."

"Supportive? You wouldn't be Bernini's star pupil if not for me. I forged the letter to get you into the academy. I fence with you at home. I keep the others from discovering your secret."

He took a step back and looked to one side, meeting his own gaze in the mirror. He stared for a moment and then let out a great sigh. With a grimace, he shook his head and stepped closer to her, looking into her eyes. "Don't misunderstand me, Cat, I *am* proud of you. If you were a man, I'm sure you'd come to be known as the best swordsman of your generation."

She removed her mask, leveling her gaze at him. "The best?" She searched for any hint of deceit.

"The best," he said firmly, but added, "Yet it's galling to be beaten again and again by one's little sister." With that, he picked up his coat and silently slipped out of the room.

Despite the sting of regret for causing him pain, a quiet confidence bloomed within her. His words left her with a bittersweet smile. *The best.*

But the moment was fleeting, and she quickly began putting away her gear. She couldn't risk staying too long; Mother might return.

Glancing at her reflection, Catherine was momentarily taken aback. In her current frame of mind, she had expected to see the boy, Alexander Gray, staring back at her. Instead, she saw Lady Catherine, triumph shining in her eyes. The juxtaposition of the boy's expression on the woman's face felt foreign. It had been many years since she had split her life in two, disentangling the threads that made up her being. Seeing them spliced together now left her momentarily disoriented.

She could barely recall a time when the threads of her life had been united. Back in India, when they were children, Papa had taught Charles to fence. At seven, Charles had been the pet of the regiment, strutting about in his miniature uniform. The colonel's son was praised and applauded by all the soldiers. Even though she was only four, Catherine had mimicked the moves she saw her brother learning. Mother scolded her, but Papa just grinned and patted her head.

Then Catherine fell ill. Beside himself with worry, Papa was convinced she suffered from the same ailment that had plagued both his sister, Isabella, and his older brother, Richard. Isabella had died as a child, and although Richard grew to manhood and married, he never truly flourished. He had provided no heir, as his wife had died in childbirth along with their child.

Everything changed for Catherine after that. Mother kept her indoors constantly, insisting she rest to regain her strength. Catherine chafed at the restrictions, longing to be with Charles, to ride horses, to partake in the regiment's lively activities— anything but sit and sew and learn needlework.

Despite Mother's coddling, she only grew weaker.

She knew what frightened her parents. It frightened her too. She overheard their whispered conversations. Papa couldn't conceal his grief over poor Aunt Isabella, who had barely had a chance at life before it was taken from her.

Catherine vividly remembered the day Papa announced an upcoming meeting with his commander in Bombay. He wanted the entire family to accompany him. Catherine could tell he was bracing for an argument from Mother, but to everyone's surprise, she agreed.

On their first day in the strange city, they visited an open marketplace, the vibrant heart of Bombay. Stalls were set up in a bustling square surrounded by smooth white buildings, and the air was thick with the smells of spice and adventure. Catherine was overwhelmed by the sights. Exotic birds perched on stands, snakes coiled lazily in baskets, and men played hypnotic tunes on curious instruments. Everywhere she looked, there was food, drink, and bolts of brightly colored silk. But what captured her attention most were the spice vendors, whose fragrant wares announced their presence long before she even approached.

Mother had purchased a bunch of white flowers and, with a rare moment of tenderness, plucked two from the bouquet. She tucked one behind her own ear and then another behind Catherine's, making her feel both special and cherished.

Catherine darted about, trying to take in everything at once, though her small body tired more quickly than she liked. Despite the weariness creeping in, she fought against it, unwilling to slow down. She knew Mother would insist on rest soon, so she tried to avoid drawing attention to herself, slipping toward the cool shade of the white walls while Papa kept a watchful, indulgent eye on her.

It was there, tucked into an alcove, that she stumbled upon the statue of a strange creature. It had the body of a man but the head of an elephant, with four arms holding various objects. Slightly taller than she was, the figure startled her at first. But as she peered closer, examining its curious features, she decided the creature looked friendly. Its unusual face made her smile.

"That's Ganesha, the Remover of Obstacles," Papa said, coming up behind her.

"Ob-stacles?" she repeated, wrinkling her nose.

"Obstacles are the things that prevent you from getting what you want, Cat."

She nodded solemnly, trying to absorb this important information. "Why does he have food piled around him?" she asked, noticing the offerings scattered at the statue's base.

"The people here leave him gifts and ask for his help in removing their obstacles."

Catherine cocked her head to one side, staring into the wise elephant eyes of the statue. After a moment's thought, she reached up and plucked the flower from behind her ear, laying it gently among the other offerings.

"What was that for, Cat?" Papa asked, his voice curious.

She shrugged, uncertain whether Papa would be upset by her gesture. Hesitating, she glanced up at him, but his face showed only interest. "Perhaps he'll help remove the ob-stacle of my illness."

Papa's expression shifted subtly, something unspoken flick-ering in his eyes before he looked away. "Perhaps he will," he murmured. Clearing his throat, he added, "I think your mother is ready to return to our rooms."

The next day, Catherine strolled along the waterfront with Charles and her parents, enjoying the sights and sounds of the bustling city. Papa bought them each a vada pav from a street vendor—her favorite treat. The soft bread enclosed a spicy fried potato, infused with curry, onion, and ginger, and her mouth watered as she took a delighted bite.

But her enjoyment was short-lived. A gull, seizing the moment, swooped down without warning, snatching the food from her hand. Catherine screamed in both fright and pain as the bird's sharp beak slashed her finger, leaving a jagged cut that became hot and swollen later that day.

Mother had already taken a strong dislike to Bombay, and the gull's attack seemed to be the final insult. She complained bitterly about the crowds, the noise, and the filth. So, when Catherine's finger grew worse, Papa took her to see a doctor while Mother and Charles stayed behind in their rooms.

The doctor wasn't English at all but Indian, and Catherine took to him almost instantly. His singsong voice and round, smiling face put her at ease. He beamed at her constantly, telling her what a wonderful girl she was, and then offered her a cup of sweet mango juice and a bowl of figs as a snack.

The doctor handled her infected finger with calm efficiency, applying a soothing poultice as if it were the most routine thing in the world. He handed Papa a small jar of the concoction, instructing him to reapply it the next day.

Catherine sat back in her chair, using her unbandaged hand to pluck figs from the bowl in her lap. She kicked her heels absently against the legs of her chair, not paying much attention to the men—until she realized what they were discussing. Or rather, who.

Her.

The doctor's demeanor shifted as Papa described her lingering ailment. His curiosity deepened, and concern flickered in his eyes as he remarked on Catherine's pale complexion and gaunt features. Papa attributed it to her illness, but the doctor, undeterred, confidently assured them he could help.

Catherine, ever observant, leaned forward, listening closely to their conversation. She knew it wasn't right to eavesdrop, but how else could she learn about her own condition?

Despite Papa's initial skepticism, he eventually agreed to let the doctor examine her. The kind man listened intently to her chest, gently thumping her back and listening for any sounds within. He asked Papa numerous questions about his brother and sister, nodding thoughtfully, then asked more questions, piecing together the family's medical history with great care.

"What this child needs is exercise, *sahib*. By coddling her, you only weaken her further. Over time, this illness will sap more of her energy. The frailty in her heart and lungs can only be stopped if she strengthens them. She requires vigorous activity to regain her health."

Catherine nearly giggled at the way the doctor pronounced "vigorous," quickly covering her mouth. But as the meaning of his words sank in, her smile vanished, and she snapped her head to look at Papa. Even at five, she understood—she didn't have to wither away like poor Aunt Isabella. She didn't have to sit idly by while life passed her by.

"Are you suggesting my daughter begin the Swedish Movement Cure? How am I to find a doctor here in India to guide her through it? Isn't it filled with marching and calisthenics?"

"I'm unfamiliar with this 'Swedish Movement Cure,' *sahib*. But marching doesn't sound like something a child would relish. No, find something she enjoys—perhaps dancing. Try different activities until you discover what captures her interest."

Papa pressed his lips together, nodded in thanks, and paid the doctor.

Later, Catherine whispered her gratitude to Ganesha for removing the obstacle to her health, and then asked him for help with her next challenge.

Mother.

Later that day, Catherine overheard her parents arguing. Mother had refused outright to let Catherine engage in such reckless behavior, fearing it would worsen her condition. But Papa stood firm. He spoke of the "Swedish Movement Cure" gaining traction in Europe and insisted that the Indian doctor's approach aligned with modern ideas about health. He'd already lost one sister to this weakness of the heart and lungs, and he wouldn't risk losing his daughter as well. After much protest, Mother finally relented.

The very next day, before they even left Bombay, Papa placed a foil in Catherine's hand for the first time. She spent the afternoon running through drills with Charles, collapsing into bed that night with an exhaustion that felt satisfying rather than oppressive.

The length of metal had felt solid in her hand, its strength seeping into her. She could feel herself becoming strong and resilient, just like her foil. That night, she hadn't wanted to part with it, even as Mother insisted it wasn't proper to sleep with such a thing. Reluctantly, she placed it on the floor beside her bed, where it rested within reach.

When they returned to the regiment, Papa trained her alongside Charles. Giddy with excitement, Catherine took on her first fencing lessons, facing Papa with her own foil. The men of the regiment held varying opinions about her new activity, but none dared voice their objections to the colonel directly. The women, on the other hand, made no such efforts to conceal their disapproval. They were united in their disdain for this bizarre notion of "exercise."

Mother never accepted it, even when Catherine's health steadily improved. Upon their return to England to visit family, Mother declared an end to fencing once and for all. No one in England could ever learn of such an inappropriate childhood pastime. Catherine would take dancing lessons, like a proper English girl.

That was when Papa conceived the idea of transforming the ballroom into a fencing salon. It marked the beginning of Catherine's dual life. She learned to don the mask she would wear for the next fifteen years, playing the role of the perfect daughter when Mother was near, and revealing her true self—a fencer—when it was just her and Papa.

As Catherine entered the drawing room that afternoon, the cheery fire and the spicy scent of carnations struck her as oddly false. They seemed in stark contrast to the bleak, wintry landscape outside the window. Vases brimming with mixed bouquets created an almost unsettling illusion of summer.

Lady Wilmot and her daughter, Lady Elizabeth, were the first visitors to arrive. Catherine's spirits lifted when she saw her friend, and soon they were settled comfortably, sharing a private moment. Catherine poured the tea while Elizabeth selected a small biscuit from the carefully arranged assortment on the tiered tray.

"Lady Lydia has a man in her sights," Elizabeth announced, pulling her teacup closer with a hint of mischief in her tone. "I think she's closing in."

"Really?" Catherine raised an eyebrow. "What makes you say that?"

Elizabeth arched an eyebrow. "I'm surprised you haven't noticed." She added a cube of sugar to her tea with the graceful precision of a practiced hand. "She and her mother flit from one event to the next, only staying long enough to determine whether he's present. If not, they dash off, hoping to find him elsewhere." She stirred her tea quietly, the spoon never once clinking against the delicate porcelain.

"That explains why I've barely seen her these past few nights," Catherine said, pulling back in surprise. "But to pursue him so openly? I can't imagine Lady Lydia being quite that bold. How does the gentleman feel about this... attention?"

"Well, considering she has to track him down each evening, I'd say he isn't exactly forthcoming with his plans," Elizabeth mused. "But he doesn't avoid her once she finds him, so it's hard to tell what he truly thinks."

Catherine leaned in, curiosity piqued. "And who is this elusive man?"

Elizabeth's smile turned secretive. "I thought you would have guessed by now, especially since you already know him." She watched Catherine closely for a reaction.

Puzzled, Catherine shook her head, her mind sifting through possibilities. She had spared little thought for Lady Lydia's interests and was at a loss as to who had caught her eye.

"Speak of the devil," Elizabeth murmured under her breath.

Catherine glanced toward the entrance just in time to see a new group of visitors entering the drawing room, with Lady Lydia leading the way.

Spotting them seated together, Lydia swept across the room with the poise of a stage actress making her entrance. She selected one of the small, delicate chairs opposite the settee and sank gracefully into it, arranging her full skirts in an artful pool around her feet. Pale blond ringlets framed her face in carefully calculated perfection.

"Good afternoon, ladies," she said, her tone light as she addressed them both.

"Welcome, Lady Lydia," Catherine replied, waiting for her to settle. "How kind of you to call on such a dreary day."

"I just mentioned to Lady Catherine that I saw you briefly at the soirée last night," Elizabeth interjected. "I'm sorry you weren't able to stay longer. It really was a delightful evening."

Lydia gave a small, dismissive sniff and turned her head with a practiced air of disdain. "Yes, well, the guest list wasn't as exclusive as I had hoped. There were certain individuals I prefer to avoid."

Catherine nearly choked on her tea. Lydia's sharp tongue was infamous, and her unfiltered comments kept people walking on eggshells around her, ever cautious not to draw her ire.

Elizabeth's eyes widened, her voice adopting an appropriately shocked tone. "How dreadful for you."

Lydia smiled slyly, clearly satisfied with the effect her words had produced. "Yes, it *has* been quite the ordeal," she sighed dramatically, casting a pitiful glance toward the ceiling.

"Has someone in particular offended you?" Elizabeth leaned forward, her keen interest evident. "It must be serious for you to go to such lengths to avoid them."

"Oh, I couldn't possibly name names. That would be much too indiscreet." Lydia fluttered her handkerchief in a delicate display before pressing it dramatically to her lips, as though stifling a surge of emotion. Was that an actual tear glistening in her eye?

Catherine gently patted Lydia's other hand, playing her part in the performance. She knew full well she had become a supporting character in one of Lydia's expertly crafted scenes. Lady Lydia thrived on these little theatrics, and Catherine could only hope it wouldn't escalate further.

Lady Wilmot rose gracefully from the settee near the door, gesturing for Elizabeth to follow her as a clear signal that their visit was drawing to a close.

Elizabeth smiled at Lydia in reassurance. "I'm so sorry you've had to endure something so obviously distressing. You must stay strong. I'm sure you're right to avoid this person." Lydia's gaze fell to her lap, and as she feigned vulnerability, Elizabeth shot Catherine a quick look—one filled with amused exasperation. She rolled her eyes ever so slightly as she turned to leave.

Catherine returned the smile, grateful for the brief moment of understanding. Lydia was always ensnared in some personal drama, though things were rarely as dire as she portrayed them. Catherine had long learned not to trust Lydia's confessions completely; they were often carefully curated bits of misinformation, woven to suit whatever narrative she wanted to spin. Yet, as Lydia's theatrics faded, Catherine couldn't help but wonder if there might be more to her stories than mere attention-seeking.

After all, Lydia's sister was married to that brute. His reputation for cruelty wasn't widely known, and when Catherine had once mentioned the bruises seen on Lydia's sister, her mother hadn't believed her. But Catherine hadn't forgotten. Was it possible that some of Lydia's dramatics were not just for show but a way to mask her own family's troubles? Perhaps there were deeper truths hidden behind the carefully crafted performances.

Without Elizabeth to enliven the moment, Lydia's charm dimmed, and the usual theatrics began to feel more like a trial. Lydia always seemed to measure her words, angling for a particular reaction. They briefly chatted about Emperor Napoleon's impending marriage to Eugénie, set for the end of the month, before moving on to the latest fashion trends. Lydia bemoaned that her favorite ball gown only had three flounces when, to be properly current, it needed at least five.

After a short interval, Lady Larchmont stood and beckoned her daughter, signaling the end of their visit.

"Well, if you really must know," Lydia said to Catherine, as if continuing a conversation that hadn't actually taken place, "I've been avoiding Lord Stansbury. He's been making the most disagreeable comments about a gentleman my family favors, and I refuse to stand by and listen to his slander." She stood and crossed the room to join her mother, a satisfied look on her face.

Catherine watched her leave, puzzled. Lydia had clearly intended to drop that particular piece of information, but it didn't align with what Elizabeth had said. Was Lydia truly avoiding Stansbury, or chasing someone else entirely? Or both? Not that Catherine could blame her for avoiding the man.

And in the end, did it really matter?

❧ 15 ☙

A CONTRACT

Daniel tapped his fingers against his desk with more force than necessary. The many late nights he'd been keeping wore on him, and he was relieved they'd soon come to an end.

Lord Larchmont's suggestion made that possible.

The transaction he proposed, which included marrying Lady Lydia, would be for the best. The girl was attractive enough, if a bit sharp-tongued and artificial. She always seemed to be playing a role, but that would change once she was married. Based on her mother's constant hovering, Lydia would likely be a doting mother herself. She came from a noble family, was well-connected, had a solid upbringing, and, most importantly, would be easy to ignore. The perfect wife to raise his children and manage his household.

"Madson!" Daniel shouted.

His valet appeared at the door of the drawing room, his expression tinged with disapproval.

"Blast it. Don't look at me that way. I can shout in my own house if I want to."

"Of course, my lord. As you wish, my lord."

Daniel shot him an annoyed look at the repeated *my lord*ing, but Madson only smirked in return.

Blasted man.

"Perhaps I should consider hiring proper servants," Daniel muttered. He pulled a sheet of paper from his desk and slapped it down with more force than necessary. As he scribbled furiously, he issued instructions without looking up.

"I need you to send Driscol to deliver this message with my regrets. I won't be attending the soiree this evening; it's no longer necessary." He thrust the letter into Madson's hands.

"Yes, my lord." Madson turned to leave.

"Wait. When do you depart for my new estate?"

Madson paused. "We planned to leave shortly, but we can wait until Driscol returns from delivering the message." He hesitated. "Are you certain you don't want me to stay here tonight, my lord?"

Daniel waved dismissively. "I'm a grown man. I can manage on my own for one night." He'd been doing so since he was a child, as Madson well knew.

A few minutes later, Madson reappeared. "Lord Huntley, Lord Wentworth is—" He didn't finish the sentence because Wentworth came barreling into the room.

"What the blazes do you think you're doing?" Wentworth flung his hat and cloak at Madson before storming toward Daniel. "Is it true you're going to marry a Larchmont?"

Daniel bristled. "What's wrong with Lord Larchmont's family? They're well respected."

"Well respected? Lydia has a reputation for having a vicious tongue, her brother-in-law's a brute, and her father's wound so tight I'm surprised he doesn't spring a cog. How could you possibly want to tie yourself to such an uptight, conniving man? Are you deliberately trying to make yourself miserable?"

"Don't be absurd." Daniel stood abruptly. "Lord Larchmont is a respected member of society and has already used his influence to help me. Just this morning, I finalized the purchase of the

Savelle estate outside London. You know how much I wanted that property. I'd given up hope of ever acquiring it, but at Lord Larchmont's urging, the former owner changed his mind. I seized the opportunity before he could back out."

"And that sudden reversal doesn't strike you as suspicious?"

Daniel shot him a stony look. "Lord Larchmont is an influential man. People listen to him. Are you implying something else?"

Wentworth met his gaze. "People fear him. There's a difference. You've made a deal with the devil, Huntley. He only likes you for your title and your rich coffers."

"Well, I only like him for his respectability. Don't worry, I can handle him."

"You're paying far too high a price for this vaunted social acceptance. It's not worth it."

"Enough." Daniel's voice was cold, his gaze locked on his friend. "Tonight, I plan to go to Bernini's to celebrate the purchase of my new estate and the end of my search for a bride. I've earned a night off. I'd like you to join me—provided you stop harping on about Larchmont."

Wentworth's lips pressed into a thin line, but he relented. "Then I'll only say one last thing. Read your marriage contract carefully before you sign, my friend. Larchmont is bound to slip in some nasty clauses."

❧ 16 ❧

A CLOSE CALL... OR TWO

Thick fog blanketing London's streets as Catherine rode to Bernini's Academy, enveloped her in a damp, insensate cocoon. The eerie silence isolated her, turning her thoughts inward. She was excited to finally have the opportunity to fence, irritated with Charles for canceling on her at the last minute, and nervous about braving the London streets alone.

She focused on her irritation, fanning the spark into a flame, hoping to stave off her fear. If it weren't for Charles's thoughtlessness, she wouldn't be alone right now. Not only had he failed to return home for dinner, but he'd also sent a belated note explaining he'd be at the Ambridge Club until late—no excuse, no explanation.

Had he forgotten their plans? Unlikely. It had to be something serious to keep him away. He almost never missed one of their fencing nights. Perhaps that rumor from Oxford had reached London?

But wait, she'd been trying to stay angry with him. She let out a sigh. She simply couldn't do it. She couldn't maintain that level of ire. Instead of irritation, worry crept in.

Worry, and a simmering fear of the dark.

The farther she rode, the fewer travelers she encountered. The unnatural isolation clung to her as the silent streets stretched on. She tightened her thighs, urging her horse into a fast trot. Normally, she disliked passing through the noisier areas, with their pubs and rowdy crowds, but tonight she welcomed the prospect of seeing another face.

The hooting and hollering that burst from the first pub she passed shattered her tension, like pebbles skimming the surface of a still lake. The eerie solitude evaporated as the sounds of life surged around her.

Yet it was fleeting. Soon, the raucous noise faded as she entered the residential area near Bernini's, the silence descending once more. A few times, she thought she heard hoofbeats behind her, but when she paused to listen, she realized she must have heard the echo of Wildfire's hooves. The sound bounced off the buildings and came back to her from odd, disorienting angles.

When the lights of Bernini's Academy finally appeared, she had to resist the urge to canter the rest of the way.

Upon entering the main fencing salon, she found it quieter than usual. Perhaps the oppressive fog had kept some of the others away.

She hesitated at the entrance—just as she had every night for the past week. If Lord Huntley was there, she'd turn around and leave before he noticed her. It was the only prudent thing to do.

Scanning the room, her pulse slowed. He wasn't there.

She felt a pang of... relief? Disappointment? Relief, of course. It had to be relief.

Pull yourself together, and push that man from your thoughts. Of course you don't want to encounter him as Gray.

She gave herself a small shake and focused on the swirl of activity around her. Determined to push thoughts of Huntley from her mind, she moved toward the practice dummies lining the wall to work on her lunges. The rhythm of the men sparring sharpened her senses, and she felt herself falling into the familiar cadence of footwork. Once she found a tempo, she began to center her mind, intent on improving her skills.

Facing down the red heart painted on the dummy's chest, she lunged again and again, driving the tip of her foil into the target with precision. The dummy, ragged from years of use, absorbed each blow. Its densely packed body was pockmarked with scars from its many battles over the years. Each time she made contact, she leaned into the strike, forcing the length of her slim foil to arch. Her thigh muscles began to tremble, but she pushed herself harder, determined to perfect her technique.

But every time a new fencer entered the room, she paused, her concentration shattered.

Focus.

She faced down her practice dummy, staring into its sketchily drawn eyes. Raising her chin in challenge, she pierced the red heart again. When her gaze drifted toward the door once more, frustration boiled over, and she slapped her foil against her thigh. The sting of metal startled her, and she stifled a yelp.

One of the fencers caught her eye and grinned. She returned the grin with a sheepish shrug.

A subtle shift rippled through the room. The low hum of clanging steel quieted as everyone glanced toward the entrance. Catherine followed their gaze.

Maestro Bernini stood in the doorway, his commanding presence drawing all eyes. He was chatting amiably with two men behind him.

Catherine's smile froze.

There they were—the two men she least wanted to see: Huntley and his ever-present companion, Wentworth.

Despite her desire to avoid them, a thrill of excitement coursed through her. It had been a week since Huntley had escorted her home from the park, and she'd secretly hoped to see him again.

But not as Gray.

Heart pounding, she spun around and yanked her fencing mask over her head, the mesh offering scant protection from recognition. Still, it was something, and at that moment, Catherine would clutch at anything that might help.

Indecision rooted her to the spot. She needed to practice for the upcoming tournament, but staying would be reckless. Huntley had a sharp eye—he'd recognize something in her posture, her voice, some tiny detail that would expose her secret.

She pressed her lips into a thin line. She had to leave. There was no other choice.

The decision made, she acted on it. Just as she moved to slip away, Bernini's voice barked across the room. "Gray!"

She froze.

"Good to see you tonight. I have something I want to teach you—a new technique. Let me get everyone started, and then we'll work on it together."

Trapped. She'd have to stay, at least for now.

Sighing, Catherine took a spot at the far end of the row, as far from Huntley and Wentworth as possible. After some warm-up exercises, Bernini approached her.

"I want to demonstrate the *contre-carte* parry. First, you need to use a counter-parry against me, then I will defend using the *contre-carte*."

They began, Bernini's fluid motions easily deflecting her attacks. Catherine raised her eyebrows in appreciation.

She raised her eyebrows.

"Nice, eh? Let me show you."

They stepped through it slowly, and Bernini demonstrated the move again. As she thrust toward his belly, he made a slight bend to his wrist so his foil tilted a little upward. Then he twisted his wrist in that clockwise semicircle she'd noticed, but his arm barely moved. Even so, the tip of her foil never touched her target.

"Now you try. The trick is in the wrist."

They stepped through the move, over and over, until Catherine felt comfortable with it.

"You're making good progress, but keep that circle tight so your opponent doesn't notice."

After several more repetitions, Bernini nodded approvingly. "Take a break, but keep practicing. This will give you an edge in the tournament."

He moved on to coach another fencer, leaving Catherine to catch her breath. She wiped her face with a cloth, careful not to smudge the fake scar that helped disguise her. Bernini had pushed her hard, as usual.

Out of the corner of her eye, she spotted Wentworth approaching, his eyes fixed on her.

"Gray," he said.

She didn't want to engage, but Wentworth wasn't easily ignored. "Good evening, Lord Wentworth."

"I've been watching you. You're good," he said. "But not as good as Bernini thinks."

He'd been watching her? "I keep telling him the same thing," she replied, unwilling to rise to the bait.

Wentworth's jaw tensed at her reply.

"Time to resume our practice, gentlemen," Bernini called out.

Wentworth's jaw tensed. "Perhaps I'll give you a matching scar on your other cheek."

More posturing. She met his gaze, unflinching. She'd faced better fencers than Wentworth. He stepped back, eyeing her one last time before returning to his friend.

He took a couple of steps backward, his eyes boring into Catherine's in a last attempt to intimidate her. Then he spun on his heel and trotted back toward his friend.

As promised, Bernini came back, this time teaching her the *contre-sixte*, a mirror image of the move she'd just learned. As they practiced, Catherine felt her confidence returning.

"You're progressing well," Bernini said. "This new technique should give you an edge in the tournament."

"We'll take a short break before our practice duels." As Bernini stepped away, Catherine's stomach dropped. She remembered her last match with Wentworth. He'd demanded a rematch. That explained his watchful eyes tonight.

Her pulse quickened. A duel with Wentworth would be the surest way to expose herself to Huntley's scrutiny. There was no anonymity here tonight, no crowded room to hide in. Her shoulders slumped as she shook her head, defeated without even raising her foil.

She had to leave, and soon, before everyone began sparring.

As she thought about the match she would be forced to sacrifice, her hand twitched, causing her foil to jump. She could have defeated Wentworth. She was certain of it. She spared a glance at Bernini. What about him? He'd spent so much time training her tonight. He'd be angry.

She had no choice.

When they paused for a brief rest, Catherine sauntered toward the door, trying to look like a person taking a short break rather than a person making a quick escape.

She slipped out, offering her mask to the academy's assistant, Mr. Winston.

"I need to leave early," she said, her voice low. "Please put this away for me."

"Of course, Master Gray," he said, springing to his feet. "I'm pleased to be of service. I hope nothing is amiss."

Just me. I'm a "miss."

"Let Maestro Bernini know that I wasn't feeling well, and give him my apologies." She swung her black cloak over her shoulders.

"Can I get anything for you, sir?"

"Just my mount, if you please."

"I'll send someone immediately." He turned and beckoned one of the young footmen. His barked instructions made Catherine jump in surprise. Was this the same man who oozed those honeyed tones when speaking to the gentry? The boy scurried off toward the stables. When Mr. Winston turned back toward her, his unctuous smile was already pinned back in place.

"I'll wait outside." She put on her hat over the snug white skullcap and pushed through the outer door.

Outside, the sound of dripping water filled the night. Normally, she would have returned to the agreeable warmth of the foyer to wait for her horse, but not tonight. She couldn't risk encountering the marquess. She pulled her heavy, black cloak tighter, longing for the warmth of her horse beneath her.

Moments later, she heard the academy door open.

"I don't see why we need to rush off," Huntley's voice drifted through the fog.

Her heart thudded in her chest. Ducking into the shadows, her black cloak merging with them, she watched as Huntley and Wentworth descended the stairs.

Wentworth stalked past Catherine's hiding spot without noticing her. "The only reason I came tonight was to even the score with Gray." His voice rose as his anger grew. "How dare he leave before our rematch? He was afraid I'd trounce him in front of everyone. Didn't want to be humiliated and ran off."

"Don't be so dramatic," Huntley said. "You've never learned how to lose gracefully."

The clatter of hooves echoed through the fog. A moment later, the stable lad appeared leading Wildfire and two other mounts.

Wentworth scowled at Huntley. "I didn't lose that match with Gray. Bernini ended it. So blast Gray, and blast you! I'm heading to the Ambridge Club!" Wentworth snatched his reins from the stable boy and launched himself onto his saddle. He rushed off into the fog, the hoofbeats fading quickly into the night.

Huntley peered at Catherine's hose as he walked down the

steps toward the stable boy. "I see someone else is leaving early tonight."

He wouldn't recognize Wildfire with his white blaze blackened, would he?

"Yes sir," the boy replied.

Huntley paused a moment, but the boy didn't volunteer any additional information. Huntley turned with a shrug and climbed into Rajah's saddle. Spinning the horse about, Huntley headed off, , his pace more measured than his friend's.

Once he was out of sight, Catherine emerged from the shadows and tossed the stable boy a wry grin of thanks for his discretion, along with a coin. She rode away into the night, her heart still racing.

A SHOUT IN THE NIGHT

Catherine kept Wildfire to a walk, needing to give Huntley enough time to move farther ahead along their shared route. After carefully avoiding him all evening, the last thing she wanted was to overtake him on the way home. Glancing back at Bernini's, she briefly considered returning, but decided against it. Bernini would likely punish her by excluding her from sparring.

As she entered the business district, Catherine figured Huntley must be far enough ahead by now. Urging Wildfire to a faster pace, they transitioned into a trot. The streets were eerily quiet tonight; even the pubs had little traffic. She spotted only one man hurrying along the side of the street, his collar pulled high against the damp air. Her hand instinctively tightened around the hilt of her foil, but the man didn't spare her a glance, his eyes fixed on the slick walkway.

Leaving the business district behind, she entered a quieter residential area. Her tension eased once she realized her home was only ten minutes away.

As she neared an alleyway between two townhouses, a noise reached her—faint but unmistakable. A muffled yell. Catherine's senses sharpened, and she slowed Wildfire to a walk, drawing closer to the alley's entrance.

Her heart thumped in her chest as she paused, staring into the darkness between the buildings. She heard nothing now except the drip of water falling from the eaves. Her fist clenched around the handle of her foil.

"Hello?" She called out, pitching her voice deeper. "Is anyone there?"

Silence.

She waited a moment longer. She *had* heard something. But perhaps it had just been a rat. Lord, how she hated rats. But no, she reasoned. Rats didn't yell.

It must have been her imagination.

She loosened her grip on the steel, shaking her head, ready to move on. But just as she was about to trot away, a scuffling sound echoed through the night, followed by a distinctly human shout: "Get off!"

Catherine's pulse spiked. That was most definitely *not* a rat! Peering down the alley, she caught a glimpse of movement in the shadows.

"Who's there?" she called again. "Do you need help?"

She didn't like this. Her hand returned to her foil, drawing courage from the cold metal as fear twisted in her stomach. She pulled the blade from its sheath and extended it in front of her, heart racing.

What am I doing?

Steeling herself, she urged Wildfire forward into the alley at a trot. As they neared the end, two figures detached from the shadows and bolted, running away from her. They weren't dressed like gentlemen or servants, but in loose, worn work clothes. One clutched a limp cloth sack.

Catherine's anger flared. Thieves. Without thinking, she spurred Wildfire forward to give chase.

The alley dead-ended at a tall iron fence with a narrow gate. In their panic, the men struggled to open the gate further, but it stuck. Glancing over their shoulders, they saw her closing in, yelped in fear, and squeezed through the narrow opening, disappearing into the night.

Frustrated, Catherine reined in her horse. Glaring at the frozen gate, however, she realized her folly. What had she been thinking, chasing after them with only a fencing foil for defense?

Shaking her head, she turned Wildfire back toward the street, cursing her impulsiveness. Perhaps she should have returned to Bernini's after all, where she could have burned off her frustration more safely.

She was so lost in self-recrimination, she almost missed the crumpled figure lying along the wall. It was only the faint glint of something metallic that drew her attention.

Catherine slid from the saddle, her boots landing with a soft thud. A man lay slumped against the wall, his cloak draped over him. Her stomach tightened as she took in the motionless form.

Listening intently, she caught the sound of deep, even breathing. At least he was alive.

But he wasn't moving. She crouched beside him and gently rolled him onto his back, squinting in the dim light to assess his condition. He didn't smell of alcohol, so he wasn't drunk, but he could be injured.

What could she do? Leaving him here wasn't an option; those men could return. And if he was seriously hurt, she couldn't just ride away.

Her mind raced to come up with a plan when she heard the rumble of an approaching carriage.

Catherine acted on instinct, grabbing Wildfire's reins and hurrying back to the street to flag down the coachman. She waved her arms as she emerged through the fog.

"Wha' in the blazes!" the driver shouted, clearly startled. "Stand back! I 'ave a pistol, so ye won't be robbin' me tonight!"

She heard the metallic click of a weapon being cocked, and a squeak of alarm escaped her. "No! Wait! I need your help—someone's been injured. I think thieves attacked him!"

A thumping noise came from within the carriage, followed by an elderly voice. "What is the matter, driver?"

The coachman shouted an explanation through the fog, and the elderly man inside replied, "Let him know I have a pistol as well."

The coachman didn't bother repeating the message, merely shrugged.

After a brief pause, the querulous voice continued. "If the lad seems trustworthy enough, see if you can help. But I won't be opening this door, no matter the circumstance." The thump of the man's cane punctuated his words.

"Perhaps you could help me put him on my horse," Catherine suggested, wondering what on earth she'd do with the man. "He's too large for me to lift alone, and I don't want to leave him here to face another attack."

The coachman eyed her skeptically before sighing. "Aye, you ain't but a lad. Lifting a full-grown man would be tough for ye." He tucked his pistol into his waistband and followed her into the alley. When they stopped next to the crumpled form, the coachman grunted and prodded the man with his foot. "Out cold."

With a grunt, he hoisted the unconscious form over his shoulder. "Bloody 'ell, he's a big 'un." He tossed the man unceremoniously onto Wildfire's back. The man let out a small groan as he landed.

To Catherine's horror, the man began to slide off the horse.

"Hold on!" she called, grabbing one of his wrists as the coachman pressed his shoulder against the man's backside, preventing him from tumbling to the ground.

"Let's get him back to the street," she suggested, trying to sound more confident than she felt. "If we steady him, we can adjust his weight."

Catherine grabbed one of the man's wrists to hold him steady, wondering what she'd been thinking of when she set out on this short-sighted rescue. The sooner she was safely rid of him, the better.

Once they were back on the main road, the coachman managed to shift the man's body into a more stable position on the saddle.

"That should do. Keep your horse to a walk. I'm sorry I can't help ye more, but I've got my own passengers ta get home safely." He tipped his hat before climbing back onto the driver's box and disappearing into the fog.

Catherine looked at the man draped across her saddle, her heart sinking. *No good deed goes unpunished.*

From the quality of his cloak, he didn't appear to be a commoner. Perhaps he had something in his pockets to identify him. If she could figure out who he was, she could return him to his home.

But as she pulled back his cloak, her breath caught. Beneath it, the man wore white fencing pants.

Her stomach dropped.

In a panic, she rushed around to the other side of Wildfire to see the man's face. Gently pulling back the mantle of his cloak, her worst fears were confirmed.

It was Lord Huntley.

"Why, of all people, did it have to be *you?*" she groaned, letting the mantle fall back over his face as she crossed her arms, standing in the cold fog, trying to decide what to do next.

$$\maltese \quad 18 \quad \maltese$$

THE TOWN HOUSE

When Catherine arrived at Lord Huntley's townhouse, it struck her as odd that no light came from inside. Perhaps he wasn't expected home for hours yet.

She tied Wildfire to the post out front and knocked on the glossy black door. After knocking repeatedly for several minutes, no activity stirred within. Frustrated, she stepped back down the shallow steps, craning her neck to peer up at the building. A quick glance up and down the street confirmed she hadn't mistaken the house—this had to be Huntley's. She was certain of it.

Climbing the steps again, she tried the door handle. Locked.

Her snort of frustration was echoed by her horse.

She grinned, patting his neck. "Come on, boy. Let's check around back."

Leading him around the side of the townhouse toward the stables, Catherine hoped to find an open door at the rear of the house. To her relief, the latch of the back door gave way when she tried it, and she pushed it open. The dark interior greeted her with silence.

"Is anyone here?" she called, her voice echoing down the hallway.

No answer.

Pushing the door wider, she spied a gas light fixture just inside the entrance. Feeling around the nearby table, she found a box of safety matches, struck one, and held it to the fixture. A soft *fumf* sound rewarded her, and a gentle glow illuminated the room.

"Hello!" she called again, louder this time. "Is anybody here?"

Still nothing.

Where was his household staff? How was she going to manage to get that enormous man inside?

With a sigh, Catherine stepped back outside and looked up at the unconscious Lord Huntley draped over Wildfire's saddle. The sheer size of him made her consider her options. Could she somehow coax Wildfire inside and simply dump him onto the floor? She glanced at her horse, who snorted as if in response to the ridiculousness of the idea. No, that would definitely be a last resort. She needed to rouse Huntley.

She pulled back the mantle of his cloak and patted his cheek.

Nothing.

She tried again, this time slapping him a bit harder.

"Oh," he groaned, his head jerking up. "What the..."

"You're lying on my horse, Lord Huntley," she said in a gruff, but soothing tone. "You're at the rear entrance of your townhouse. Let me help you down."

He didn't respond, but his weight shifted, and he started sliding off the far side of the saddle. She scurried around, just managing to catch him as his knees buckled.

"Put your arm over my shoulders, and I'll get you inside." He complied, and together they staggered toward the door, though she struggled to support his full weight. "I'm not strong enough to carry you, so please don't faint."

As if asking him not to faint will help.

"Where's my blasted valet?" he mumbled. "Madson!" he called out, louder this time.

She kicked the door shut behind them as they made their way into the dark hallway. "I've been wondering the same thing. Now, where am I supposed to put you?"

After a few more lurching steps, they reached a drawing room. Catherine guided him toward a long sofa, where he collapsed in a heap, somehow managing to stay seated. He rocked forward, pressing his hands against his head and groaned.

"My head feels terrible. Pour me some scotch, will you?"

Catherine glanced around the room, spotting a collection of bottles and glassware on a low table. She couldn't tell which one was the scotch, so she grabbed the one most prominently placed. If scotch was his favorite, it stood to reason that it must be the one most readily available. She poured an inch into a glass.

Lord Huntley blearily reached for the glass, his eyes still closed. He swallowed the amber liquid and immediately clenched his jaw. "That was a mistake," he rasped, coughing. "It burns." He looked at his glass as if it had betrayed him. "Why does my throat feel so raw?"

Catherine lit another gas lamp, the soft light revealing a fire already laid in the hearth. She lit a taper and poked it into the tinder. As the flames took hold, the room warmed with a gentle crackling sound.

"Where is your staff?" she asked, turning back to him. "I see signs of them, but no one seems to be here."

He finally looked at her, confusion clouding his face before comprehension dawned. "Blast, what a mess. I sent the entire staff to my new country house this afternoon. They're preparing it for my arrival tomorrow."

"Your new country house? I thought you were looking for a new house here in the city?" *No! I shouldn't know about that, because he told Lady Catherine, not Gray. Blast!*

"Oh, you heard about that? I didn't know it was common knowledge." He raised a brow, looking puzzled. He stretched out on the sofa, his muscles shifting beneath his snug fencing breeches as he relaxed. "I purchased the Savelle estate. It's fully furnished, but the staff was long gone, so I sent my servants ahead —" he stopped short. "I hope you'll forgive me, but you're Gray, am I correct? The boy from Bernini's?"

"Yes, my lord." Catherine's heart raced. Better to have been recognized as Gray than as Lady Catherine. "You're fortunate to have acquired it," she said, turning her attention to stoking the fire.

"I owe you a debt of gratitude," Huntley murmured, rubbing his temples. "I remember now. I was attacked. They dragged me into an alley. One of them pressed a cloth to my face..."

"A cloth? Were they trying to suffocate you?"

"I don't think so. It smelled... sickly sweet."

Catherine's brow furrowed. "Sickly sweet?" Could they have used a chemical to subdue him? The collodion she used to make her scar was made from a nitrocellulose mixed with ether and alcohol, and it had a sickly sweet odor. "Perhaps they used a chemical to knock you out—an anesthetic, like the doctors have begun using for surgeries. I recall reading that they have a sweet smell. That could explain your raw throat."

Huntley groaned again. "Perhaps..." He sounded listless.

The warmth from the fire filled the room, but the thought of criminals using anesthetics chilled her. She'd read stories of perfectly healthy people dying from those chemicals. She wished she'd paid more attention to the medical articles.

"My head feels a bit clearer, and I think my stomach is starting to improve." With a grunt, he hoisted himself into a sitting position, though he wobbled. "Well, maybe I'm not completely well after all."

He leaned back, shutting his eyes, his face pale and sickly in the dim light.

Catherine was torn. She knew she should leave, but how could she, with no one else around to care for him?

With a sigh of resignation, she came to the only decision she could live with. She'd stay for a while, just to make sure he recovered. She caught herself gazing at his full lips and chided herself. The man wasn't well.

"If you'll excuse me, I need to see to my horse."

He nodded, his eyes still closed. She hurried outside, leading Wildfire along a well-worn path toward the stables.

To her surprise, Rajah, Huntley's horse, stood just outside, having returned on his own. She fumbled around in the darkness, settling both horses into their stalls. She loosened Wildfire's girth and fed them oats before scratching Wildfire between the ears. All the while, her mind raced, considering the odd nature of the attack on Huntley. If the men hadn't wanted to rob him, could they have been trying to kidnap him?

She turned the idea around in her head. Yes, it made sense. Why else would they render him unconscious? They must have wanted to capture him.

Returning to the drawing room, Catherine found Huntley lying with his arm draped across his face. "You're a good chap for helping me," he muttered, his eyes still closed.

"It's no trouble. And I have some good news. Your horse found his way home. I've stabled him for the night."

"What a clever creature," he murmured. "And you, Gray—you must call me Huntley. I owe you my life. If there's ever anything I can do for you, just name it."

"Did they steal anything?"

"No, nothing. My pockets are still full. Strange, don't you think?"

"Very. It makes me think they might've been after you, not your money."

Huntley's eyes snapped open. "Me? Why?"

"Why else would they use chloroform? It's not a typical weapon for a mugging. I've never heard of it being used before, have you?"

He frowned, considering this. "You're right. I should have thought of that myself. You've got a sharp mind."

He closed his eyes again, seeming more unsettled than before. After a moment, his head jerked back up. "Wait. Won't your family worry?"

"As long as I'm home before daybreak, I'll be fine."

I hope.

"I see. Why did you leave Bernini's early? Wentworth was furious when you disappeared."

She shifted uneasily, unable to come up with a convincing answer.

Huntley chuckled softly. "You *were* avoiding him. Trying to save the confrontation for the tournament, I suppose? That's a long wait."

Catherine shrugged, eager to change the subject. "Would you like anything else? I can fetch you something from the kitchen."

"Just a scone," he replied with a sigh. "I think it might settle my stomach."

Catherine nodded, eager for the excuse to escape the tension in the room. "I'll make a pot of tea as well," she said as she beat a hasty retreat.

It took her some time to find the items she needed in the kitchen and boil some water. By the time she returned with the scones and a pot of tea, Huntley had dimmed the gaslight and stretched out on the sofa, his arm draped over his face.

She set the tray down quietly and stifled a yawn. "Shall I pour you some tea?"

"No tea," he murmured, the fencing jacket he wore now partially undone, revealing his chest.

Seeing him lying there, eyes closed, Catherine took the rare opportunity to observe him openly. His broad shoulders and lean frame stirred something in her, and as her gaze lingered on the exposed skin of his chest, she wondered whether it was soft or firm. Her fingers tingled with the urge to touch him, but she forced herself to move away.

Catherine settled into a chair by the fire. She'd only stay a little longer, just to make sure he was all right. As the fire crackled softly in the hearth, her eyelids grew heavy. She watched Huntley breathe deeply, his chest rising and falling rhythmically.

Just a little longer.

DAWN'S EARLY LIGHT

Catherine awoke with a start, not knowing where she was. Her dreams had been vivid, delicious. She could almost feel the lingering touch of Huntley's kiss on her lips.

As the dark room came into focus, the events of the evening flooded back to her.

Her head felt hot and itchy. She had never slept in that blasted head covering before. Rubbing at her scalp did little to relieve the itch. She couldn't remove it until she returned home. She'd already stayed far too long.

Turning toward Huntley, she found him still sprawled on the sofa. The room had grown cold, so she took a moment to build up the fire again, the flickering light casting shadows on his face. Was he alright?

His slow, steady breathing reassured her, but instead of sitting beside him, she knelt stiffly on the floor. Her thighs ached from the exertion of last night's fencing. She brushed his hair from his face, feeling his forehead for any sign of fever. None. His skin was warm but not clammy.

Her hand lingered as she cupped his cheek, the stubble prickling against her palm. Rough, familiar.

What if something terrible had happened to him last night?

Huntley's deep, even breathing continued, and Catherine absentmindedly stroked his face. The rasp of his whiskers against her thumb was oddly soothing. Were the effects of the anesthetic still making him sleep so soundly?

Almost as if in a trance, she leaned down and pressed her lips to his, expecting the same electric jolt she'd felt last week when they had kissed. But nothing.

She sat back on her heels.

How disappointing.

The kiss left her unmoved. How could that be? The kiss felt... empty, like Lord Watters's had. She frowned, gazing at Huntley's strong features, his full lips.

Perhaps she'd done it wrong.

She leaned in again, more deliberately this time, pressing her lips to his once more. And this time, his lips quivered in response. His arm came around her suddenly, pulling her against him as his kiss deepened, quick and fervent. Her eyes widened in shock as she fell against him, unable to pull away in her kneeling position. His tongue slipped into her mouth, and she gasped, startled. Was he even awake?

His hands slid up her back, warm and insistent, but as his fingers grazed the fabric of her head covering, they froze.

His grip tightened, yanking on the covering. Cathcrine's chestnut hair spilled free, and in an instant, Huntley scrambled away from her in shock.

"Gray! What is the meaning of this?" His voice was sharp, laced with confusion.

The horror on his face was unbearable.

He scrubbed at his mouth with the back of his hand, staring at her as if trying to make sense of what had just happened. And then, his eyes widened with realization. "Lady Catherine?" He searched her face, disbelief flashing in his eyes as they took in her loose hair.

"No!" she cried, frantically trying to stuff her hair back into the head covering. She scrambled to her feet. "It's not what you think! I... I—" Her words tangled in her throat, and her chest constricted so tightly she could barely breathe. She had ruined everything. Her chance at the tournament, her carefully guarded secret, her fragile connection with Huntley—all shattered in a single rash moment. The look on his face spoke volumes.

Huntley's hand shot out, capturing her wrist before she could flee.

She pulled against him, but his grip held firm. "Wait," he said, his voice gentler now. "I don't understand. Why would you do this?"

Catherine's heart pounded. "Isn't it obvious? To fence." She shot him a look of frustration. "How else could I manage it?"

"But your family... do they know?"

"Mother doesn't. She would be appalled if she ever found out."

"As would all of society."

Her eyes widened. He wouldn't. He couldn't. "You can't say anything. Please."

His expression softened slightly. "Of course not. I won't breathe a word of it. But... won't you be missed? Surely someone will notice you've been out all night."

Panic rose in her chest as she scrambled to her feet. "I never should have stayed."

"That's my fault," Huntley said, his jaw tightening. "You wouldn't be in this situation if you hadn't saved me."

"It was my choice, my risk," she insisted, standing taller.

"I owe you a debt," he said firmly. "I couldn't live with myself if you suffered any consequences for helping me."

"Don't be foolish," she said, her voice barely above a whisper.

"What if someone finds out you stayed here all night? Your reputation would be destroyed." His expression grew grim with determination. "I can't let that happen."

Catherine opened her mouth to protest, but something else

caught her attention. She could see Huntley's face clearly in the half-light. She suddenly became aware that the room was no longer as dark as it had been moments ago. While they had been talking, the sun had begun to rise.

Her heart leapt into her throat. "I have to go home. Now." Panic gripped her. "Mother will be frantic if she discovers I'm missing." She stumbled toward the door, her legs stiff and clumsy from those lunges she'd practiced. But she quickly recovered and bolted out the door, the rising sun urging her into flight.

20

WHEN THE TRUTH IS KNOWN

Daniel watched the first light of dawn creep into the room, a faint glow softening the harsh edges of the night. It was as if Lady Catherine had taken the darkness with her when she fled. In the light of day, everything seemed altered.

She certainly seemed altered. What a curious, captivating woman. Nothing like anyone he'd ever met. And *nothing* like Lady Lydia. A respectable woman like Lydia would never have done something so scandalous as dressing like a boy to move among men. Of course, Lydia also wouldn't have stopped to save him from an attack.

He chuckled to himself, picturing Lady Lydia trying to navigate the rough streets of London in the dead of night. Unthinkable.

But Lady Catherine? Well, she'd done just that. Not only had she saved him, but she had managed to deceive everyone at Bernini's all this time. His mind flashed to her in those trousers. He hadn't expected to find them so... fetching.

A slow smile tugged at his lips. He had always thought something was off about Gray—the strange head covering, the awkward way the boy held himself. The story about the severe burn had never quite made sense. Now, everything fell into place.

No wonder Gray had avoided them last night at Bernini's. Daniel had been looking forward to watching Gray and Wentworth fence again, but the boy had vanished, leaving him disappointed. He smiled now at the thought of a woman besting his friend.

She wasn't avoiding the match, she was avoiding me.

The realization sent a fresh wave of curiosity through him. Lady Catherine was remarkable. But last night's events had taken a dangerous turn. Why would an unmarried woman risk spending the night in his study? What a reckless, perilous choice. Did she not care for her own reputation? For her family's?

And what of him? If they had been discovered, he would have been honor-bound to marry her. The thought settled uncomfortably in his chest. Did she even understand the risk she had taken? Surely she must have. Gray's reputation at Bernini's was well-established. Catherine must have been sneaking around in this guise for years. She wasn't a fool.

No, she had to have a plan. A way to make it home undetected. Even though she was impetuous, she wasn't simpleminded. He could only hope she'd made it back safely, without raising suspicion.

He exhaled slowly, leaning his head back. Those whiskey-colored eyes... He should have known they were a warning. Hadn't whiskey been his father's downfall? That and love? There was no doubt—those eyes were bound to cause him trouble.

Perhaps they already had.

It was a good thing he hadn't chosen Lady Catherine as a bride. But a shiver of unease ran through him. He just hoped fate wouldn't force them together anyway.

21

FEATHERS

Catherine hunched over Wildfire's mane as he bolted from the alley beside Lord Huntley's town house, startling two men across the way. Their horses shied as she tore past, but she slowed her pace, trying to avoid too much attention. There were more people on the streets than usual this morning. Delivery carts rattled by as servants bustled about their tasks.

Urging Wildfire forward at a brisk but controlled pace, Catherine rushed to make it home before full daylight. She approached the familiar alley near her home, trying to remain unnoticed. A horse and rider crossed her path—did he glance at her? She kept moving.

At the Kensington stables, she jumped down from Wildfire, hoping desperately that Billy had waited up for her.

The stable door creaked open, and Billy's face appeared, pale and strained from exhaustion.

"I was so worried, miss. Didn't know what ta do. Was about to go inside and tell someone 'cause I feared something bad had happened to ya."

"I'm sorry, Billy. I didn't mean to put you in such a position."

She tugged off her white hood and tossed it onto a nearby bench. "I don't have time to explain right now. I have to get inside before Mother notices I'm missing. We'll talk later, I promise." She hurriedly pulled on the overdress of her costume and rushed toward the door, rubbing at the remnants of her fake scar still clinging to her skin.

As she glanced back, she caught sight of Billy's tired, worried face. "I'm really sorry," she repeated, then disappeared through the stable door.

Once inside, she felt painfully exposed. The early-morning sunlight streamed through the windows, casting long shadows through the quiet house. She could hear the household staff already at work, their distant movements making her heart race.

As she crept toward the staircase, Catherine passed the open door of the breakfast room—and froze. Mrs. Evans, the housekeeper, entered from the opposite side, and their eyes met.

Catherine's breath caught. Mrs. Evans's expression flickered between shock and alarm, taking in Catherine's disheveled state. But then, with a sharp shake of her head, the housekeeper's lips pursed, and she waved her toward the stairs.

"Your mother's already up. She'll be down any moment. *Hurry*."

Catherine's heart pounded as she darted up the staircase, every creak and groan of the wood beneath her feet threatening to give her away. Her bedroom was just down the hall, tantalizingly close.

But as she passed Sarah's room, she heard the dreaded sound of her mother's door opening behind her.

"Prepare the dark-green silk for this evening," her mother's voice floated down the hallway.

Of all the blasted luck!

Thinking quickly, Catherine veered to the left and slipped into Sarah's room, closing the door quietly behind her. She leaned against it, her heart thudding in her chest.

"I'm certain I saw the door close," Mother said, her voice growing louder as she approached. "Why would Sarah be stirring so early in the morning? She must be hoping I'll allow her to leave her room today."

Catherine darted across the room and dove into the bed with her sister, scrambling under the covers.

"What—what's going on?" Sarah's groggy voice came from the bed.

"Help me," Catherine whispered. "Mother saw me. She thinks it was you. I just got back from fencing, and I look a mess. If she sees me like this..."

A knock came at the door.

Sarah, now fully awake, leaped into action. "Lie still," she ordered in a hushed voice. She threw the covers over Catherine's head and began fluffing pillows to disguise the lump of her sister's form. The thick feather bed engulfed Catherine, concealing her just as footsteps approached.

Catherine made a small opening in the covers, just large enough to allow her to see Sarah and provide herself with some air.

Sarah darted away from the bed to stand next to her bureau. She was rummaging through a drawer when The door creaked open.

Catherine held her breath, hardly daring to move.

"Sarah, you're awake early. Didn't you hear me knock?" Their mother's voice carried a note of suspicion.

"No, Mother. I must've been yawning." Sarah smiled as she brushed her hair, looking innocent and serene. "I was planning to visit the stables before my lessons. I've been feeling much better, and I thought I'd be the first one up, but then I saw you in the hallway."

Their mother entered, eyeing the room. "I'm glad to hear you're better, darling. I always worry about head injuries. Be careful, won't you?"

Catherine's nose began to tickle. Nothing bad yet, but still... she slid her hand slowly toward her face while keeping an eye on her mother.

Sarah smiled and nodded, brushing her hair again.

Their mother came closer, taking the brush from Sarah's hand. "Let me do it for you. You have such beautiful hair. It reminds me of mine when I was your age. Thick and chestnut, with those lovely auburn streaks..." Her voice softened. "Your father used to call it my crowning glory. I'm much older now, though."

Catherine pinched her nose, forcing the sneeze to subside. There was a wistfulness in their mother's voice, a loneliness Catherine hadn't noticed before. She spoke about their father with longing, brushing Sarah's hair with a distant look in her eyes.

"You're not old. And you're so pretty. Papa thinks so too. I've seen the way he looks at you when he thinks you don't notice him. He likes to watch you."

"Fa! Don't be a silly goose. Your father hardly even notices me." She smiled slightly and resumed brushing Sarah's hair with a faraway look in her eyes. "There was a time, when we were first married, when he looked at me with such–," she stopped abruptly. "Your father is a busy man. He's doing important work for the queen. These past few months have been difficult for him with the death of your grandfather."

Catherine felt a bead of sweat trickle down her forehead. It was hot under the covers, wearing so many layers of clothes. Especially after that mad dash home.

The expression on her mother's face, reflected in the mirror, held her attention. She looked sad. Lonely, even. She'd always said she was happy for their father and didn't mind that he traveled, but it obviously wasn't true.

"Your father takes very good care of us." Abruptly, Mother put down the hairbrush and turned away, hiding her face, but Catherine had the distinct impression that her mother was holding back tears.

A soft rattle at the door broke the silence.

"I've brought your breakfast, Miss Sarah," came the maid's voice.

"How timely, Simpson," Mother said, pinning a smile on her face as she turned to greet the maid. The heavenly scent of hot chocolate and cinnamon scones wafted to her under the covers, causing a pang of hunger to shoot through her.

"Yes, m'lady. Cook sent me up with a tray for... for Miss Sarah."

"Thank you, Simpson," Sarah said. "Please set it by the window."

"I'll leave you to your breakfast," Mother said. "Come speak to me when you're done."

"Yes, Mother."

When the door clicked shut, Catherine exhaled in relief. Sarah stood at the edge of the bed, watching her sister emerge from beneath the blankets, sweaty and disheveled. Catherine could hardly wait to peel herself out of her clothing.

"You're a sight." Sarah shook her head. "If Mother had caught you, she'd have... well, I don't know what she'd have done, but it would have been bad. Very bad." She shook her head disapprovingly. "You can't keep taking these risks. You're going to get caught."

Catherine sank onto the bed, exhaustion catching up with her. "I know," she said softly, rubbing at the remnants of her fake scar. "I've been thinking the same thing."

22

A CLEAR CONSCIENCE

Although Daniel planned to leave for his new country house later that morning, he first needed to know if that little hoyden had managed to return home undetected. If not, he'd do whatever was necessary to help her.

Stopping by her house at this hour was completely out of the question. If she'd made it home safely, an early call from him would raise unnecessary questions. And if she'd been caught sneaking back inside but had talked her way out of trouble, his sudden appearance might only reignite suspicions.

After a moment's consideration, he struck upon the perfect plan. He would seek out Catherine's older brother, Charles. Perhaps he could find the young viscount at the Ambridge Club. He had seen Charles there frequently—in fact, just yesterday morning. With a little luck, the young man would make another appearance today.

Less than half an hour later, Daniel strolled through the doors of the club, handing his hat and overcoat to the porter. The secretary at the front desk was sorting through a stack of papers but looked up at Daniel's approach.

"May I help you, Lord Huntley?"

"Is Lord Spencer expected here this morning?"

"Yes, sir. He has an appointment and should arrive within the next half hour."

Daniel smiled. *Perfect.*

He settled into a comfortable wingback chair near the entrance, positioning it so he could keep an eye on the front door while also enjoying the view from one of the large windows. A light flurry of snow had begun to fall, and pedestrians left dark footprints on the white pavement. A slow but steady stream of gentlemen trickled through the door, stomping their feet and handing over damp hats and cloaks. Fortunately, he didn't have to wait long for Charles to appear.

Watching the young man's face from across the room, Daniel tried to gauge his mood. Charles chatted amiably with an older gentleman, suggesting that nothing was amiss at home. That was a good sign.

Daniel folded the newspaper he'd been pretending to read and made his way toward them. As he approached, he caught the eye of Charles's companion, John Cunningham, who recognized him and nodded in greeting.

Mr. Cunningham shifted his stance slightly—a subtle invitation for Daniel to join them. Just as he'd hoped.

"Huntley," Cunningham exclaimed warmly. "Splendid to see you this morning. Starting the day early, eh?" His round face shook with a chuckle, his goatee trembling. "I suppose if you're here at this hour, London's debutantes were forsaken by you last night."

Charles glanced quizzically at Daniel. Cunningham looked between the two men and asked, "Have you met the Viscount Spencer?"

"Yes," Daniel replied, offering Charles a friendly smile. "Though you may not remember me. We met briefly last week while fencing."

"Ah, that's right." Charles grinned sheepishly. "I knew I recognized you. I must have tried to block that evening from my memory since you trounced me so thoroughly. Are you in London for the Season?"

Daniel nodded, scanning Charles's face for any subtle signs of distress. But there was nothing out of the ordinary—no hint that Catherine's nighttime adventures had caused a stir.

Cunningham turned to Charles with a conspiratorial air. "Lord Huntley has made quite the impact this Season. My wife tells me his name is often on the lips of mothers with marriageable daughters. I'm afraid he's going to leave a trail of disappointed damsels once he selects his bride." He chuckled at his own jest.

Daniel's jaw momentarily tensed. Fortunately, he wouldn't have to endure this type of teasing for much longer. Once he announced his engagement, most of it would disappear.

"I don't envy you that distinction," Cunningham said. "Be careful, sir. Some of these chits can be downright dangerous once they decide to set their sights on you."

"Yes, I've noticed," Daniel replied dryly.

Charles's eyes widened with recognition. "Wait a moment— you were the gentleman who rescued my sister, weren't you?"

Daniel froze. Rescued his sister? But it was the other way around... Catherine had rescued *him*. "I—I don't know—," he began.

"Yes, of course! Sarah hasn't stopped talking about riding home with you on your horse—Rajah, was it?"

Ah, Sarah. Relief mingled with amusement. "Rajah, yes. How is your sister? I trust she's fully recovered from her fall."

Charles laughed, his eyes sparkling with affection. "You can't keep that one down for long. She tried to get back on her horse the very next day, much to her governess's dismay. Mother had her on strict bed rest because of the head injury. Miss Bell was convinced she'd sneak off to the stables the moment her back was turned. But Mother's finally allowing her to resume her normal activities today. I should warn you, though—she seems quite taken with you. If she decides to set her cap at you, you'd best be on guard. I look out for my sisters." Although his tone was casual, Charles pinned him with a pointed look.

Daniel met his gaze and gave a slow nod. He found himself taking a liking to the young man. As an only child, he'd often wondered what it would be like to have siblings. Would his life have been less lonely? Richer? He hoped his own children might be as close as Charles and his sisters obviously were.

Wentworth had come closest to being a brother to him. They'd met at school, and once Wentworth understood the truth of Daniel's home life, he'd never said a word about it—he simply invited Daniel to stay with his family during every school break. Daniel could never repay that kindness. Wentworth might be difficult at times, but beneath the bluster, he had a good heart.

The other boys at Eton hadn't been so welcoming. At every turn, they'd made Daniel aware of his shortcomings. His education had been neglected at home, and he wasn't cultured enough to associate with them. The worst part was that everyone knew his father was insane. That alone would have been enough to make him a social outcast, but the combination of problems had been insurmountable. If not for Wentworth, his life would have been unbearable.

Cunningham interrupted his thoughts. "You've always had a knack for business, Huntley. I've heard about some of your clever dealings."

Daniel snapped back to the present, realizing he'd lost the thread of conversation.

"In fact," Cunningham continued, "I recall a few years back when some fellows tried to outmaneuver you by having you followed, attempting to circumvent your business dealings."

A sly smile curved Daniel's lips. "Ah, yes. They were rather persistent until I caught on to their game. They were spying on me to gather information about my future endeavors, then swooping in to close deals before I could finalize them. It was a simple matter to lead them toward poor investments instead. After they lost a substantial amount of money, they ceased their interference. I never did identify all the members of that group."

"Devilish clever," Cunningham said, his laughter rumbling. "'Hoist with their own petard,' so to speak."

Charles looked puzzled. "Petard?"

Cunningham clapped him on the shoulder. "An explosive device, my boy. Means they were undone by their own schemes. Didn't they teach you any Shakespeare at Oxford?"

Charles chuckled. "Perhaps I missed that lesson."

Cunningham turned back to Daniel. "So, any good investment tips you'd care to share?"

Daniel offered a polite smile. "You've caught me at a rather inopportune moment. I'm currently negotiating an important contract, and my partner insists on exclusivity." Lord Larchmont had been quite adamant about that. Noticing Cunningham's crestfallen expression, he added, "But if you'd like, I'd be happy to inform you when another opportunity arises."

Cunningham brightened. "That's most generous of you, Huntley. I do enjoy a good venture." He hesitated, then lowered his voice slightly. "But I imagine your... partner will keep you occupied. If it's who I think it is, you might find it challenging to extricate yourself from that arrangement. Tread carefully. In the meantime, I'll keep an eye out for other prospects."

Daniel maintained a casual demeanor, though a flicker of unease stirred within him. Did Cunningham suspect his association with Lord Larchmont? "I appreciate the advice. Happy hunting."

As Daniel prepared to take his leave, Charles gave him a friendly nod. Daniel's thoughts drifted back to Catherine. He wondered if he'd mentioned to "Gray" that he'd be away for a couple of weeks. The events of the previous night were still somewhat hazy, but he did recall mentioning that his servants were at his new estate.

At least Catherine wasn't in immediate danger of scandal. He could proceed with his negotiations with Lord Larchmont regarding his potential engagement to Lady Lydia with a clear conscience.

Leaving the club, Daniel descended the steps, pulling on his gloves. As he did, he nearly collided with a stout, balding man who appeared startled and almost slipped on the snow-dusted pavement. The man righted himself with a huff, and Daniel offered a brief nod before continuing on his way.

23
WORN LEATHER SHOES

It was too bloody cold!

The snow melted as it touched the frosty puddles, their edges already beginning to ice over. When the man accidentally stepped into one, an icy, foul liquid seeped through the seams of his worn shoes, soaking into his wool socks. Each step squelched now, the frigid water leeching the warmth from his feet with every miserable step he took down the busy street.

He arrived at the Ambridge Club, only to find the steps slick with a thin layer of ice. Had some fool of a servant washed them this morning? Idiot. Someone could break their neck. He crept up the steps gingerly, his focus on reaching the warmth inside.

As he neared the entrance, a tall gentleman pushed through the door and descended the steps toward him. The man's breath caught in his throat as the gentleman nodded a polite greeting, continuing down the icy steps without a care in the world.

It was the *marquess. Huntley!*

The man stumbled in shock, his feet slipping dangerously on the ice as he gawked. His mouth hung open, frozen in disbelief. *What the devil? Huntley shouldn't be walking around like this! I paid good money to have him taken!*

His mind raced. Had the men he hired even searched Huntley's home last night? Had they botched the entire job?

He spun on his heel, nearly losing his footing as he rushed back down the street, his worn leather soles slipping on the road.

There were two scoundrels he needed to talk to—and they'd better have some damned good answers.

24

A LETTER ARRIVES

After breakfast, Catherine joined her mother and brother in the morning room. Charles had only recently returned from an appointment at his club, and soon their mother would drag Catherine off on a round of afternoon calls. She only hoped for a chance to speak with Charles before they left. She needed his advice.

A young footman entered the room, carrying a letter. Charles glanced up and frowned as he accepted it. After breaking the seal and scanning the contents, his expression shifted.

"It's from Mannerly. I haven't heard from him in at least a month," he said, but as his eyes darted back over the words, his smile vanished. "What on earth?" His brow furrowed as he read the letter again, more slowly this time.

Mother's gaze sharpened. When he finished reading, he handed the letter to her without a word. She scrutinized it, then sighed deeply. "What do you plan to do?"

"What can I do? This is outrageous. I never laid a finger on that—" He stopped, glancing quickly at Catherine.

It must be about that girl from Oxford.

Mother handed the letter back to Charles. "Perhaps a quick

trip to visit your friend in Cheshire would be advisable—an opportunity to remove yourself from the public eye for a time."

"Yes, I think you're right. I'll leave immediately." With a nod, he stood and left the morning room to pack.

"What was that all about?" Catherine asked.

"Nothing to trouble you, dear. Your brother has some personal business to attend to."

When Catherine returned to her bedroom later, she found an envelope resting on her bed.

Sorry I had to leave so suddenly, was all the note said. Charles had also enclosed the letter he'd received.

⚜

Dear C.,

Rumors continue to fly regarding you and that silly twit of a girl, Calliope.

I know you were never involved with her, but that doesn't seem to matter at the moment. The blame is being placed squarely on your shoulders.

These are the facts. Professor Caruthers chased Attwood and his daughter all the way to Gretna Green, only to discover they'd never arrived. He tracked them to a little town, but only his daughter was there. Charles Attwood had abandoned her.

Caruthers tried to track down the blackguard, but he slipped away, leaving no trail behind. I know how distasteful it must be for you to share the same first name with such a man, but I think the similarity in your names has caused a great deal of confusion. I'm sorry to be the bearer of bad tidings, but according to some stories, Attwood even impersonated you.

Apparently, once Attwood had bedded the little idiot, she confessed she had lied about her inheritance. After a great deal of shouting and arguing, he ran off, leaving the inn's bill unpaid and the girl unprotected.

She proves to be a complete bubblehead. Why lie to Attwood to trick him into marriage, ruining herself in the process, only to confess her trickery before the wedding could take place? It defies comprehension.

Her father insists she marry and is casting about for anyone he can drag into his net. It would be best for you to lie low for a while, as I think he will be coming after you next. He is desperate to get the baggage married and holds you partially to blame since her name has been linked with yours. He believes you may have aided Attwood in her seduction.

I suggest you take an extended trip away from London, as I believe Caruthers will look for you there.

Your friend,

M.

POOR CHARLES. NO WONDER HE'D LEFT. CALLIOPE HAD created an enormous mess.

25

A SECRET REVEALED

The man entered the tavern, scanning the dim room for the two former dockworkers he'd hired to capture Huntley. Even at midday, the interior was dark, and it took a few moments for his eyes to adjust. He soon spotted the men seated at a narrow table in the corner. The place was deserted, save for them. Weaving through the haphazardly arranged tables, he joined them.

Without ceremony, he grabbed a chair from a nearby table, dragged it to their booth, and sat. "What happened?" he demanded, leaning in, his voice low but sharp. "Huntley is walking about town as though nothing occurred."

The two burly men exchanged uneasy glances before the smaller of the pair spoke up. "Someone spotted us. We had to run or be caught."

"Bah. You were two against one." His scorn was palpable. "Cowards, both of you. I'm paying you well, and yet you fail to subdue a lone man on a foggy night?"

The larger man shifted, but it was his companion who spoke again. "We might not have captured him, m'lord, but we've something else that could be valuable."

As the smaller man explained what they'd seen at Huntley's town house—and what they'd discovered about Lady Catherine Williams—the man's eyes widened with interest.

"If what you say is true, this changes everything." His mind raced with new possibilities. "Are you certain of your information?" His voice took on a deadly edge. "If you're wrong, you'll ruin everything."

"We're certain, m'lord. We was searchin' Huntley's place when they arrived, and we slipped out while they slept. They never knew we was there. She spent the night with him, no doubt about it. We followed her back the next day, and I swear on my life, it was her. Saw her sneakin' from the stables, changin' out of her disguise."

The man leaned back, considering. "How extraordinary." He smiled slowly. "You may have failed in your original task, but if this proves true, I'll reward you handsomely."

26

A DISMAL WEEK

Later that evening, while attending a ball, Catherine shamelessly eavesdropped, straining to catch any rumors about her fencing. To her relief, there were none. Huntley wasn't in attendance. One guest mentioned he had departed for his new estate outside London, and only then did she feel the knot in her stomach loosen enough to enjoy the evening.

A small seed of satisfaction began to grow within her. In a surprising twist, Huntley had gone from being a potential threat to an unexpected ally. For such a conventional man, she never would have imagined him so understanding of her passion for fencing.

Yet the week dragged on uneventfully, and with Charles still absent, loneliness crept in. She missed him more than she expected. Even more unexpected was the realization that she missed Huntley as well. She'd gone from trying to avoid him at every event to yearning for the cat-and-mouse games they'd played.

A week after that near-disastrous night, her mother scrutinized her over breakfast. "Catherine, dear, perhaps you ought to rest this afternoon. I had hoped that staying home last night would have reinvigorated you as it usually does, but it seems not."

Catherine pressed her lips together, avoiding her mother's gaze. She had stayed in her room, not because she was tired, but because Charles was still away. She hoped he'd return to London soon, or she'd have no hope of winning the tournament. She didn't dare return to Bernini's without him.

"You know I enjoy your company, but I must admit you're looking a trifle overtaxed. You mustn't overreach yourself on my account, dear. You know how I worry about your health. You have dark circles under your eyes."

Catherine felt stretched thin as tissue paper from lack of sleep. She glanced at her mother and gave her a wan smile. "I have a slight headache," she offered, realizing as she spoke that it wasn't a complete fabrication. "Perhaps you're right. I'll take a break from our afternoon calls and rest. That should help me recover before the Duchess of Linsley's dinner this evening."

Mother nodded, satisfied. "An excellent plan." She gestured toward Catherine's plate. "Make sure you eat a good meal. You've been picking at your food lately. I'd hate for you to suffer one of your relapses."

Catherine glanced down at her plate. Nearly all of her *relapses* had been caused by too many late nights at Bernini's and too little sleep. But this time, it was worry gnawing at her. Gritting her teeth, she forced a bite of food past her lips. What if she worried herself into a relapse? Was that even possible? She took another mouthful, then another, until her plate was clean.

Mother departed the table with a pleased smile, convinced she had solved the problem of Catherine's lethargy.

Catherine, however, felt trapped. Trapped in a life of constraints, like a marionette in a Punch and Judy show—always playing the same role, under someone else's control.

At least Punch and Judy got to whack each other, she thought darkly, rather than smile until their cheeks ached.

Wait. Maybe not. Punch and Judy's cheeks *were* frozen in place.

I AM a marionette. The thought chilled her.

Blast them all! Why did everyone in polite society have to behave exactly the same way? Could no one show a shred of individuality?

But maybe the problem wasn't society. Maybe the problem was her. Was it possible?

She tried to reorient her mind and look at the problem from a different angle.

After all, there were many young women in England who were so disdainful of "polite society" that they chose to spurn it. And others who, upon entering society, decided that the constant round of entertainments simply wasn't for them.

She thought of the women of India, draped in bright silk saris with intricate henna designs on their hands. In the western United States, women wore men's trousers and rode horses bareback. And what about Florence Nightingale? She'd turned her back on the frivolity of aristocracy to do something useful. After returning from Europe, she'd taken it upon herself to inspect London's hospitals. This past fall she'd traveled to Edinburgh and Dublin to inspect the hospitals, tireless in her mission to improve healthcare. The woman was unstoppable.

Catherine sighed, her fingers tracing absent patterns on the tablecloth as her thoughts circled back to the same impossible dilemma. Her thoughts circled back to the same impossible dilemma. How could she disappoint her parents? How could she openly defy society? For years, she had quietly rebelled, but now, staring into the face of disaster, she understood what she was risking—not just for herself, but for everyone around her. And instead of the thrill of triumph at breaking the rules, all she felt was shame.

So that left her here.

Stuck.

And miserable.

❧ 27 ❧

AN ABUNDANCE OF ROSES

As Catherine recalled, the Duchess of Linsley had an intense fondness for the colors pink and rose. With that in mind, she chose a cream-colored dress to avoid competing with the duchess's décor. Tonight, she was in the mood to blend in, not stand out.

She clutched her engraved ivory fan while Simpson fastened the clasp of her pearl necklace. An unusually elongated pearl, the focal point of the piece, nestled just above her cleavage.

"Would you like a wrap tonight, m'lady?"

"Yes, thank you, Simpson."

Catherine selected a cream wrap woven with a pattern of roses from the options Simpson held out. When she arrived downstairs, her mother waved a letter in the air.

"Charles says he plans to return in time for the Norfolk Ball."

That was four days away. Perhaps his return meant the problem with the girl in Oxford had been resolved.

Once their carriage pulled to a stop, they scurried through the downpour into the home of Her Grace, The Duchess of Linsley. Lady Linsley's husband had died nearly two decades ago, and her eldest son had been made Duke of Linsley at the age of fifteen.

The duchess enjoyed hosting dinners and other small social gatherings, but her son rarely attended. She reigned supreme, free of any male control.

Catherine envied her.

At thirty-three, the duke traveled extensively and was rumored to be in the United States at present. Even when in London, he avoided his mother's social events.

Perhaps he loathed pink.

Whenever the duchess could convince him to attend, her guest list was always filled with marriageable young women, and she delighted in matchmaking. Catherine was convinced Lady Linsley's persistence had driven the duke to his travels, a situation that suited Her Grace so well, she might have planned it that way.

The rain pounded against the dining room windows, with the heavy pink drapes doing little to diminish the noise. The table was draped in cream linen and set with Lady Linsley's crystal wineglasses, heavy silver, and porcelain charging plates painted with roses that perfectly matched the drapes. The room gleamed in the candlelight, with vases of pink roses filling the sideboards.

Catherine certainly blended in.

Lord Watters escorted her to her seat at the dinner table, and she was immediately enveloped by the soft, fragrant scent of roses. As she glanced across the table, her stomach tightened—she was seated opposite the Earl of Stansbury. It was like discovering a snake in an otherwise charming garden.

His proximity made Catherine shift uncomfortably in her seat. Toward the end of the previous season, Stansbury had asked for permission to court her, citing the potential for a "suitable match." Catherine had promptly rejected his advances. She knew his interest lay in her inheritance, as they had nothing else in common.

"Lovely day today. It's been much too long since I've had the pleasure of your company," he said, his voice oozing with a false familiarity that made her skin crawl.

Catherine forced a polite smile, but that was all she could muster. With the rain still pounding against the windows, she couldn't agree that it had been a "lovely day" or that it had been "too long" since they'd last spoken. Quite the opposite.

Their conversations were always stilted and halting. Perhaps the sort of absurd pleasantry he'd just made was why. Stansbury had a knack for making statements that seemed completely contrary to reality. Though he had feigned acceptance when she refused his offer of marriage last spring, she had since caught him watching her more than once, his interest unmistakable and unnerving.

Lord Watters, another of her former suitors, was seated beside her. Thankfully, he made for a far more agreeable conversationalist. Safer, too.

"Have you been to the opera lately?" she asked, knowing full well that he attended every performance he could.

"Of course. I was at *The Beggar's Opera* just a few nights ago," Watters replied enthusiastically.

"Isn't that the one about pickpockets and highwaymen?"

"And a man who keeps promising marriage to various women. It's quite entertaining, although I doubt a man like that would have a happy ending in real life," Watters replied with a grin.

Catherine smiled, wondering if Lord Watters realized how much he had in common with the opera's protagonist, given his own tendency for frequent declarations of love. Nevertheless, their conversation flowed easily, and she found herself genuinely enjoying his enthusiasm.

In this relaxed state of mind, Catherine glanced up, only to find Lord Stansbury's small, brooding eyes fixed on her. A wave of unease skittered down her spine, and she quickly looked away, unsettled by the intensity of his stare.

As dinner wore on, Stansbury continued to observe her, though more discreetly now. But Catherine still felt his eyes on her, the sensation growing more oppressive with each passing moment. Worse, his gaze repeatedly dropped to the oblong pearl nestled just above her cleavage, and something about the way he looked at her felt disturbingly proprietorial. The mere thought made her skin crawl.

The moment the dessert course concluded, Catherine seized the opportunity to escape to the drawing room.

It was like stepping into a flower shop. The walls were a soft cream, the furniture upholstered in varying shades of pink, and lush bouquets of roses adorned nearly every corner. The pale-pink brocade of the sofa featured a delicate, muted pattern of roses and pale-green foliage. The abundance of florals should have been overwhelming, but instead, it was rather lovely.

As Catherine crossed the room to join Lady Elizabeth, she greeted her with a quick smile.

"Catherine, it's wonderful to see you. Did you enjoy dinner?"

"Yes," she murmured. "But I've had lamb at the last three events I've attended. I must admit, I'm growing a bit tired of it."

"At least it was edible," Elizabeth replied with a knowing smile. "Be thankful you didn't attend Mrs. Hetherington's dinner last night. The meal was dreadful. Poor woman was mortified, and I'm certain she's already searching for new kitchen staff. Count your blessings."

Catherine chuckled, finally relaxing in the presence of her friend's lively mood. "Charles promised to be back in time for the Duke of Norfolk's ball. Will you be attending?"

"Most certainly. I sorely missed it last year. Wasn't that where Lord Watters proposed to you?"

Catherine cleared her throat, suddenly uncomfortable. "Yes. We'd only known each other for a week, and I hadn't realized he held me in such high regard." She glanced around the room, scanning for Lord Watters, but didn't spot him. He must still be lingering with the other gentlemen in the dining room.

"That was bold of him."

Catherine snapped her fan open and raised it to conceal her

grin. "He took me completely by surprise when he asked for my hand. I'm afraid I didn't handle it well and burst out laughing. I disguised it as a fit of coughing, so I don't think he was offended."

"He must have recovered quickly, as he always does," Elizabeth said, her voice playful. "I hear his current enamorada is a soprano."

Catherine shrugged, uninterested in Lord Watters's romantic pursuits. "There must be something more current to discuss. What's the most interesting news you've heard of late?"

"Hmmm..." Elizabeth tapped her chin thoughtfully. "It's hard to choose. Perhaps the fact that Lord Larchmont stopped blocking the sale of that estate Huntley bought, though that isn't very current, is it? He bought it over a week ago." She paused, then continued searching her memory. "Lord Devlin and a few other gentlemen who were visiting Russia are said to be returning soon at the queen's request. And I heard that Stansbury was on the verge of proposing to a young heiress, but now he's no longer seen in her company." Elizabeth's gaze flicked across the room. "I think she turned him down. Oh, and LeCompte may not be in town much longer. Word is, he'll be heading back to France."

That was odd news about Huntley's estate. Why had Larchmont been blocking his purchase?

"Is that why I haven't seen Lord Huntley recently?"

Elizabeth's mouth twitched in amusement. "I assume so."

"I wonder when he'll return." Catherine tried to sound casual, but there was more behind the question. She needed to speak with Huntley. She wanted to look him in the eye and hear him reassure her that he would never reveal her secret. She needed to see his face when he said it—to know if he was lying. And, if she was honest with herself, she simply missed him.

Elizabeth's eyes gleamed with sudden excitement. "I nearly forgot!" she crowed. "How silly of me! I've just heard the most scandalous news. But you must promise to keep it to yourself." She leaned in conspiratorially. "Last night, one of the Gibson girls ran off with a footman. Can you imagine? They're on their way to Gretna Green even now."

"No!" Catherine's eyes widened in shock. "How did you find out?"

"One of their servants told one of our kitchen maids, who passed it on to my personal maid," Elizabeth rattled off with a dismissive wave. "Her parents are trying to keep it quiet, but you know how these things go. It'll never last. There's at least one elopement every season. These girls get the most foolish, romantic ideas in their heads, thinking they can live on love alone. When she's raising his babies without a single servant to her name, she'll have the cold comfort of knowing they had a daring dash to Gretna Green to start their marriage."

"You sound quite harsh. Surely her parents won't cut her off..." Catherine's voice trailed off. But they probably would—at least, publicly.

"Oh, no. Lord Stansbury is headed directly toward us," Elizabeth interrupted, her tone sharpening.

Catherine caught sight of the earl just in time to glance away, barely suppressing a grimace of distaste.

"Good evening, ladies," Stansbury murmured as he joined them, his gaze lingering briefly on Elizabeth. "I believe your mother is looking for you, Lady Elizabeth." His eyes slid away from her and settled immediately on Cathcrine—more precisely, on her chest.

Heat rushed to Catherine's face.

"Oh?" Elizabeth craned her neck, glancing behind Stansbury. "How odd, since she seems quite engrossed in her conversation." The sarcasm in her voice was impossible to miss, though Stansbury either didn't notice or didn't care. His focus had drifted back to the oblong pearl resting just above Catherine's neckline.

Catherine could only hope it was the pearl that had captured his attention. She raised her fan, the soft fluttering helping to shield her flushed face from his prying gaze.

"Would you like me to escort you to her side?" Stansbury's voice held an edge of irritation as he glanced back at Elizabeth.

"That won't be necessary, Lord Stansbury," Elizabeth replied with a huff. "Since I can see my mother quite clearly, I'm confident I can manage the short walk to her." Her icy tone seemed to bounce right off Stansbury, who remained oblivious. Even Elizabeth noticed when he shifted his weight, angling for a better view of Catherine's chest. She rolled her eyes and cast a pitying look at Catherine.

Catherine gave her a slight nod, signaling that she could handle Stansbury.

Elizabeth hesitated for just a moment before sweeping across the room to join her mother.

"Lady Catherine, would you care to take a turn around the room with me?" Lord Stansbury extended his arm, his expression expectant.

Not in the least. She'd spent the entire evening trying to avoid him, and the thought of linking arms with the man made her skin crawl. When she didn't immediately respond, he simply grabbed her hand and tucked it into the crook of his arm, holding it in place.

Catherine tugged, trying to pull free, but he had her hand trapped against his body, and she couldn't disentangle herself without creating a scene.

What an odious man. She could see a faint, grayish layer of grime on the white collar of his shirt—couldn't he have bothered to wear a clean one to a duchess's dinner?

Perhaps if she engaged him in conversation, she could distract him from his blatant ogling. But as she caught the stale scent of dried sweat barely masked by cheap cologne, Catherine's resolve to engage wavered. She turned her face away, trying to suppress a grimace.

Fortuitously, her eyes met Lady Linsley's from across the room. Catherine cast her a pleading look, and the duchess, though in conversation with another guest, gave a subtle nod of understanding. Relief washed over Catherine; her hostess would rescue her soon.

Stansbury cleared his throat, the urgency he'd displayed while separating her from Elizabeth now oddly subdued. It was as though he couldn't quite figure out how to proceed.

He cleared his throat again, his lips parting as if to speak, but no words came. His behavior struck Catherine as decidedly odd. His eyes darted from group to group, scanning the room. It occurred to her that he was waiting for just the right moment—waiting until he was sure no one would overhear.

For the third time, Stansbury cleared his throat.

"Lord Stansbury, are you quite well? Perhaps I should ask someone to bring you a drink," Catherine offered, her voice cool with polite concern.

"You're very kind, but no, I don't require anything." He fell silent again, guiding her toward the far end of the drawing room, away from the other guests. Once they were suitably isolated, he cleared his throat once more, but this time, he finally spoke.

"Lady Catherine, it has come to my attention that a certain woman of my acquaintance has become involved in something she should not, and I fear it may be her undoing." He cast a sidelong glance at her, as if weighing her reaction.

"A delicate situation, then?" she replied, keeping her tone neutral. Why would he confide this in her? Could he possibly be speaking of the Gibson girl? She wondered if that had been the unfortunate young woman he'd been pursuing.

"Yes. Delicate." His tone sharpened, and Catherine could feel his gaze intensify. "This young lady," he stressed the word, "has been engaged in a charade that, if revealed, would bring shame upon her entire family."

The weight of his words settled over her like a chill. Catherine's pulse quickened as she fought to keep her expression impassive. He couldn't possibly know about Gray... could he?

Stansbury's mouth twitched with a hint of satisfaction as he studied her. "I trust you grasp the gravity of the situation," he added, his voice laced with a thinly veiled threat.

His smug tone sent a cold shiver down Catherine's spine. He believed he had the upper hand. But how could he? Stansbury didn't fence, so who could have told him? Unless... Huntley had broken his word.

Her breath came shallow and quick, her lips pressed tight as she forced herself to respond. "I'm not certain I take your meaning, Lord Stansbury. Perhaps you could be more specific." She held his gaze, her chest tight as she waited for his reply, but it became painfully clear that his beady eyes were fixed on her, relishing her discomfort. She forced herself to breathe deeply, willing her pulse to slow.

"I think you know precisely of whom I speak." He savored the moment, dragging it out as if tasting victory. "But I'll say one word, just to be clear." He leaned in, voice dropping to a near whisper. "Fencing."

Catherine's steps faltered, her heart stuttering in her chest before thundering louder, faster. How could he know? It didn't seem possible. Had someone seen her? Had Huntley betrayed her after all? She replayed her recent trips to Bernini's in her mind, trying to remember if she'd noticed anything—anyone—out of place. The fog that clung to the city that night could have concealed anything... or anyone. And she had been so focused on making it home before dawn that morning, she might never have noticed if someone had followed her.

"I... what do you intend to do with this information?" Her voice was tight, almost strangled. The lamb she'd eaten sat like a stone in her stomach, making her feel queasy.

Stansbury's lips curled into a thin smile. "That," he said, pausing to relish the moment, "is entirely up to the young lady in question." His eyes gleamed with satisfaction. "You see, it's my duty—no, my obligation—to help her. Her family name is already tainted, thanks to certain... activities her father engages in. And I hear her brother has left Oxford under suspicious circumstances. If even a whisper of scandal were to reach society's ears, it would ruin her. And not just her—her sister's chances for a respectable match would be dashed as well."

He stopped, letting the weight of his words sink in. "Fortunately for her, I have a solution. A simple plan. I'll offer her my hand in marriage. My good name will shield her from any fallout." He said it with the air of a man who had just gifted her the world, as though his offer was the only lifeline she could possibly hope for.

Marriage? The sheer absurdity of his suggestion jolted her back from the brink of hopelessness. A wave of calm washed over her, grounding her.

"I can see you've puzzled out this solution quite carefully," Catherine said, meeting his gaze evenly. "But how can you be so certain she'll agree to your plan?"

Stansbury's head snapped back, squinting at her in surprise. Her sudden composure clearly unsettled him.

Catherine smirked inwardly. *Odious man.*

"How could she not?" he stammered, his confusion evident. "What other choice does she have?"

"The young lady must already have a plan for a situation such as this, don't you think?" Catherine paused, letting her words settle between them. "You may submit your proposal with her best interests at heart." *Ha. As if that could be true.* "But I doubt she'll choose to accept it. There are other alternatives available to her. And after all, what proof is there that she's involved in any inappropriate behavior?"

She glanced at him from the corner of her eye, knowing full well that he had no solid evidence. It didn't exist. Unless someone caught her "in the act," there was no proof of her secret.

"Nevertheless," he replied slyly, "the arbiters of propriety need no proof for their scandals. The merest hint of impropriety would be enough to ruin her." His smirk returned, triumphant. "She has no alternative but to accept my offer."

What a sniveling little man. Catherine's anger flared. For a moment, she imagined gripping a real sword with a sharp, piercing tip, not a foil, and calling him out right there.

With a surge of indignation, she jerked her arm free from his grasp and took a step back. Loathing flooded her as she seared him with a look of utter scorn.

Stansbury, taken aback, reached for her wrist again. But she snatched it away, tucking her hand behind her back and wiping it discreetly against her dress as if to rid herself of the oily sensation his touch had left behind.

She opened her mouth to retort, but then noticed their hostess, Lady Linsley, gliding toward them with purposeful speed. Clearly, the duchess had observed the scene and was rushing to intervene before things escalated. Catherine welcomed the distraction and turned to Lady Linsley with a grateful smile.

"My dear Lady Catherine," the duchess began in her soft, lilting tone, "I so enjoy hearing you at the piano, but it has been an age since I last had the pleasure. Would you indulge me this evening?"

"It would be my pleasure, Your Grace. Is there anything in particular you'd like to hear?"

"Something light, I think," Lady Linsley replied, her melodic voice a soothing contrast to Stansbury's unpleasant rasp. "Do you know anything from *Rigoletto*? I plan to attend when it opens at Covent Garden, and I would so enjoy hearing that particular piece... is it 'La donna è mobile'?"

"'*La donna è mobile*,' eh?" cackled Stansbury. "*Woman is fickle.* How fitting." He shot Catherine a venomous look, his triumph clear.

Lady Linsley fixed him with a piercing, icy glare. "Then one must assume you missed the irony of the song, since in the opera, it's the duke who is inconstant and fickle, and the woman who gives her life to protect him." She turned her back on him, dismissing his presence entirely as she focused her attention on Catherine.

Catherine's grin spread in delight at the duchess's perfectly delivered retort. It was like watching an expert fencer effortlessly flick aside an amateur's clumsy thrust. Lady Linsley was masterful in the subtleties of social sparring.

"I'm acquainted with the piece," Catherine said, her mood lightened. "Do you have the sheet music?"

"I believe it's still on the music stand," Lady Linsley replied. She took Catherine's arm, gracefully leading her toward the piano while pointedly ignoring Stansbury. "My grandniece was attempting to play it, but she's still young, and it's quite beyond her skill."

As they moved away, Lady Linsley glanced back at the fuming earl, and Catherine couldn't resist following her gaze. Stansbury stood rooted in place, visibly humiliated.

"Watch that one, my dear," Lady Linsley said quietly. "I remember him as a boy, and even then, he was sneaky and self-serving."

"Yes, ma'am," Catherine agreed, her voice soft with respect. "I believe you have the right of it."

28

VILLAINOUS THOUGHTS

Stansbury glowered at Catherine as Lady Linsley escorted her to the piano, seething at the high-handed way the duchess had dismissed him.

What abominable timing.

That Kensington chit was irritatingly self-assured for a woman. It must have been that blasted penchant for fencing. Her pursuit of such a masculine skill had clearly warped her into something unnatural.

The more he thought about it, the more he relished the idea of bringing her to heel. A bit of retraining was all the wench needed. The prospect was rather appealing.

He chuckled to himself, imagining it, until he caught the odd looks from nearby guests. Quickly composing himself, he smirked, recalling the way Catherine had reacted to his mention of "fencing." The shock on her face had confirmed everything.

Wasn't it fortuitous that the very night Huntley had slipped through his fingers, he'd snared Catherine instead?

Perhaps his luck was finally turning. Marrying Catherine would be far simpler—and vastly more enjoyable—than relying on Huntley to generate the funds. He'd never been entirely confident in his ability to bend the marquess to his will. But Catherine? She'd be easy to manipulate. He knew exactly where to strike.

It would only take a few moments alone with her.

His grin widened. His powers of persuasion could be quite convincing with the right incentive.

Or the right amount of force.

Lady Catherine was much more vulnerable than she realized. Much more vulnerable, indeed.

❧ 29 ❧

HOUSE PLANS

"Wentworth!" Daniel shouted, standing in the morning room, frustration evident in his voice. His friend had an uncanny ability to vanish at the most inconvenient times.

"Blast it, I'm right here! Stop shouting; it's a terrible habit."

Daniel spun around to find Wentworth just entering from the garden.

"Where've you been? I've been looking everywhere for you."

"I was admiring your new gardens. Spectacular, but a bit neglected. Your gardeners will have their hands full."

"My staff from town keeps grumbling about the interior. They're eager to return to London this evening. I need to find servants to maintain this estate—that's what I wanted to discuss with you."

"You want my help selecting your staff?" Wentworth looked appalled at the thought.

Daniel laughed. "Perhaps I could turn the whole project over to you."

"I'll certainly finish it quickly. First person who applies gets the job," Wentworth said, plopping onto the chaise lounge. "I'll leave you to sort it all out later."

"Perhaps not, then. I'd rather not have to replace everyone in a month when they inevitably don't work out."

"Then follow my mother's advice: find the best housekeeper and butler available, and let them handle the rest."

"Excellent advice," Daniel said, his expression brightening. "See, you were helpful. That'll save me quite a bit of time. I have representatives from three agencies arriving today to help staff the estate. I'm afraid the meetings might delay my departure for the ball."

"No need for me to stick around, then. Shall I meet you there later this evening?"

"Sounds like a perfect plan."

30

DANCE CARD

"Good evening, m'lady. May I help you dress for the ball?" Simpson's pinched face and tight smile betrayed her anxiety. There wasn't much time left to prepare. Catherine sighed, knowing she was the cause of the delay—she'd hidden herself away, lost in *Jane Eyre* again.

With a grimace, Catherine nodded. The low-cut gown of light-blue satin had a paler blue gauze overlay, and the bodice was adorned with an intricate pattern of freshwater pearls. The fabric slithered against her skin as it slipped down her body.

When she caught sight of herself in the mirror, Catherine paused. The dress made her look like a water nymph, the pearls mimicking waves cresting on a calm blue sea. Yet her pale face startled her. She didn't look like herself. Her expression seemed frozen—like the figurehead on a ship's prow, rather than a nymph.

She didn't want to attend the ball. Charles still hadn't returned home, and her thoughts weighed heavily on her.

Simpson finished fastening the row of tiny buttons up the back of the gown. From the jewelry box atop her dresser, Catherine selected a thick, multi-strand cluster of freshwater pearls and fastened it around her neck. Simpson placed matching pearl clips in Catherine's hair as a final touch.

"I forgot to tell you, m'lady. Lord Spencer returned not long ago," Simpson commented. "He plans to attend the ball this evening with you and Lady Kensington."

Relief swept through Catherine. *Thank goodness, Charles is home.* "That's wonderful news."

Looking in the mirror, Catherine pinched her cheeks to bring out some color. She smiled at her reflection, but the change did little to disguise her weariness. Perhaps she'd finally sleep soundly once she spoke with Charles.

She hurried down the staircase to find her mother and Charles already waiting for her, ready for the ball.

"Welcome home, Charles," she said, lightly kissing his cheek. Dressed in a formal evening coat with a black waistcoat and tie, he looked trim and elegant. His normally unruly hair had been tamed, though Catherine wondered how long it would last before a stray strand broke free.

Their drive to the Duke of Norfolk's home was brief. As they rounded the cobblestone street, the house appeared on a small rise, grand and stately. Unlike the dimly lit houses nearby, the duke's residence sparkled, with thousands of lights glowing from its many windows. Kensington House was large, but it paled in comparison to the ducal mansion.

Carriages lined the street, waiting to drop off passengers, while a group of musicians strolled along the front walkway, entertaining guests as they waited to enter.

Once inside, Catherine and her mother stopped in the ladies' dressing room to divest themselves of their cloaks. They took a moment to check their reflections before rejoining Charles in the main foyer.

"I have your dance programs," Charles said, holding up two small booklets with tasseled cords. He slid one loop onto his mother's wrist, then did the same for Catherine.

As she glanced at the arriving guests, their faces glowing with anticipation, Catherine felt a flicker of excitement. This would surely be one of the most entertaining balls of the season.

The ballroom was crowded, and Catherine stayed close to her family as Charles guided them toward a pair of empty chairs. Their mother settled into one and consulted her dance card.

"Charles, dear, please escort your sister for the first dance. It's a quadrille, and I so enjoy watching you two dance together. It reminds me of when you were children."

As they moved onto the dance floor, Charles leaned down and murmured, "Do you remember how we only danced as long as someone was watching us? The minute we were alone, we'd grab Father's foils and start fencing." His eyes crinkled at the edges as he smiled.

Fencing. The word struck her like a physical blow, and the weight of regret settled over her. She forced it aside, keeping her mask of serenity intact. There was no room for that kind of emotion here, not in this glittering ballroom.

"Yes, I remember," she replied, her voice tight, wishing she'd already confided in him.

Charles shot her a curious look, but they had reached the dance floor, and the music began. As they weaved through the intricate quadrille, Catherine found herself relaxing. The steps were familiar, and her brother, as always, was a flawless partner.

Afterward, Charles escorted her back to her chair, but Catherine's steps faltered when she saw Lord Stansbury and M. LeCompte in conversation with her mother.

Stansbury was the last person she wanted to see sitting in a cozy little cluster with her mother and that rumor-monger LeCompte. She hesitated, considering turning back, but LeCompte spotted her and stood.

"Ah, *mademoiselle*," LeCompte said, springing to his feet to greet her, "how delightful to see you here this evening. I was hoping you would do me the honor of a dance?" He smiled politely, awaiting her reply.

"Of course. It would be my pleasure," Catherine replied, taking the arm he extended to her.

"May I, too, request the pleasure of a dance, Lady Catherine?" interjected Stansbury. He hadn't risen to his feet as quickly as LeCompte, and was in a half-standing, half-bowing position as he spoke. "Perhaps for the first waltz," he suggested, "since you're otherwise engaged for the current dance."

He'd trapped her. Requesting the dance in front of an audience meant she couldn't refuse without causing a scene. Even so, she would have turned him down if LeCompte hadn't been watching. She didn't want to give the Frenchman more reason to be curious about her distaste for Stansbury.

Despite her irritation, she managed a serene smile as she departed with LeCompte. Stansbury's satisfied smirk, visible as she turned, only deepened her frustration.

After the schottische, LeCompte returned her to her mother, where two more gentlemen immediately stepped forward to request dances. Catherine accepted, though her heart wasn't in it. The shadow of Stansbury's impending waltz weighed too heavily.

The ball was a resounding success, with more and more guests arriving. At times, the crush of people was overwhelming, and Catherine noticed many slipping away to quieter rooms or the gardens.

As the time for her dreaded waltz approached, Lord Watters, her current partner, escorted her back to her mother. The ballroom had become so crowded that moving through the throng was a challenge. At one point, the crowd surged, and Catherine's hand slipped from Lord Watters's arm. She tried to regain her grip, but another group pushed between them, and he was gone.

Standing on tiptoe, Catherine searched for her mother or Watters, but she couldn't see over the heads of the people around her. All four walls of the ballroom looked identical, and without the music to guide her, she was completely disoriented.

"Lady Catherine, may I be of assistance?" a man said as he took her elbow. She looked up to see Lord Wentworth. He made a most unlikely savior, but a savior nonetheless.

"Thank you, Lord Wentworth. I'm trying to find my way back to my mother, and I seem to have lost my escort, Lord Watters."

"Careless of him," he said, tucking her hand into his elbow. "Come, I see your mother and brother just ahead."

Mother raised her eyebrows upon seeing Catherine return with a different escort. "What happened to Lord Watters?"

"Lost, I'm afraid," Wentworth quipped. "The ball has become so crowded, I fear he may not surface for hours." He edged in front of the two ladies to protect them from the buffeting crowd.

Wentworth's charming smile even won over her mother, and Catherine found herself looking at him with fresh eyes. Perhaps she had misjudged him.

"I haven't seen you at any events recently, Lord Wentworth. I trust all is well?" Catherine asked.

"Yes, everything is splendid. Lord Huntley acquired a new estate and asked me to assist him with the renovation plans. I only returned to town this afternoon. The Norfolk Ball is touted as one of the premier events of the season, and I didn't want to miss it." A grin brightened his face as he looked around. "I can see from the turnout that it's a huge success." A passing guest stumbled, knocking an elbow into Wentworth's ribs. He grimaced. "Perhaps a bit too successful."

"How wonderful for Lord Huntley. I'm sure it will be quite the showplace." Mother nodded her approval. She did admirably well at feigning ignorance of the news. It had frequently been a topic of conversation at many events they'd attended, and Mother had been quite curious about it.

Wentworth smiled. "Indeed. He plans to add all the modern

conveniences, but it's a daunting task. The place is spectacular, but it will require a great deal of work to provide modern fundamentals. Huntley certainly has his work cut out for him, but he's a determined fellow. I'm certain he'll do a splendid job." He nodded a greeting to someone Catherine couldn't see.

"It certainly sounds like a daunting task," Lady Kensington said.

"It will be a quite the showplace. I imagine it will take at least a year or two for the workmen to complete the improvements. They're tearing into things even as we speak."

"Do you think he'll spend more time in London, then?" Catherine asked before she could stop herself. She flushed when her mother shot her a warning look.

"His absence has been a frequent topic of conversation of late. I'm sure his return to London will put many hearts at ease." Her explanation sounded thin, even to her own ears.

"*En garde*, Lady Catherine," came a familiar voice from behind her.

Startled, she spun around to find Lord Huntley standing at her shoulder. Her pulse quickened under his gaze.

"You startled me, Lord Huntley," she said, her face warming.

"You've embarrassed the young lady, Huntley," Wentworth teased. "Sneaking up on her like that."

Huntley gave a graceful bow of apology, his teasing smile making Catherine's breath catch. "My sincerest apologies, Lady Catherine. Will you forgive me?"

She flipped open her fan and fluttered it as she examined him more closely. Lord Huntley certainly didn't act as though he had a guilty conscience. If he'd been the source of Lord Stansbury's blackmail information, either he didn't realize he'd provided it, or he hid it well. She laughed lightly and snapped her fan closed. "Perhaps we should put a bell around your neck, Lord Huntley."

He tilted his head to one side, as if seriously considering her suggestion, but then shook his head. "No, I don't think so. It would make it much too difficult for me to overhear what others are saying."

"Be careful what you wish for, m'lord. Eavesdroppers seldom hear anything good about themselves," she quipped.

"Ouch! You've scored a direct hit. Are you saying that I'm both an eavesdropper and a scoundrel?" His tone was playful, and she began to relax. "Point to Lady Catherine."

Hearing another fencing reference gave Catherine a brief pause, but she recovered quickly. "A direct hit? I'm surprised to hear you admit to your character flaws so readily. But if the shoe fits..."

He staggered dramatically, as though hit in the chest. "Another point. I seem to be dropping further and further in your estimation, Lady Catherine. You must allow me to recover. Perhaps if we danced, I could regain some measure of your esteem. Would you do me the honor?"

Catherine frowned but quickly masked it with a polite smile. "I regret I'm already engaged for this waltz. Lord Stansbury requested I save it for him, though he has yet to collect me." *And I hope the annoying man will stay away.* "Perhaps, unlike you, he's been unable to locate me in this crush of people."

"What a shame for him. I'm sure he'll be disappointed, but his loss is my gain. I can enjoy your company while you wait for him. You look quite enchanting tonight. Like a mermaid, perhaps." His gaze locked on hers, the intensity of it catching her off guard.

The crowd shifted around them, and as two gentlemen passed through, Catherine realized they were now momentarily separated from the rest of the group. The bodies pressing in on all sides created a sudden, strange intimacy between her and Huntley.

He leaned down, his breath warm against her ear. "I want to reassure you—your secret is safe with me," he murmured. "I owe you an enormous debt of honor. You may well have saved my life, at great personal risk, and if there's ever anything I can do to help you, you need only ask."

Her heart skipped. "You told no one?"

"No one. You're secret is safe with me."

Before she could respond, a sudden jostle from behind sent Catherine stumbling into Huntley. His hands shot out, catching her by the waist and steadying her. His grip was firm, his hands almost spanning her entire waist.

The heat of his touch vibrated through her stays, as though he had plucked a harp string, and the warmth of his palms seared through the layers of fabric, scorching her skin.

Huntley's eyes widened as he, too, reacted to their touch. She felt his fingertips brush against the corset strings running up her back, hidden by the thin fabric of her gown, and shivered at the sensation. The heat of her body mingled with the rose-scented perfume she had applied earlier, the fragrance wrapping around them both. Huntley pulled her closer, and for a fleeting moment, she wanted nothing more than to feel the length of his body pressed against hers.

A passing stranger's elbow jabbed her ribs, abruptly yanking her back to her surroundings. What was she thinking? They were in public, in a crowded room, standing right in front of her mother.

The spell broke, and his hands fell away. She took a step back as the press of the crowd eased, turning her gaze aside in embarrassment.

Catherine caught her mother's keen gaze. Lady Kensington had sharp eyes, and there was no doubt she had witnessed part of what had transpired. Catherine shot her a sheepish look. A faint smile flickered across her mother's face before it was replaced by a more stern expression.

She glanced up at Huntley, tilting her head back to meet his eyes. He surveyed the room, his gaze locking onto something she couldn't see. The corners of his mouth tipped downward.

"It appears your escort has located you after all." He nodded toward Stansbury, who was making his way toward them.

Catherine froze. She'd forgotten all about Stansbury, forgotten the looming threat he posed, her problems momentarily swept aside by her closeness to Huntley. But now, with Stansbury's intense gaze fixed firmly on her, the weight of it all returned. Her stomach churned at the sight of the man.

Instinctively, she took a step back, only to bump into another guest, trapped by the crush of bodies.

Huntley seemed to sense her unease. He shifted his weight, subtly positioning himself between her and the approaching earl, momentarily shielding her from Stansbury's gaze. Her hands, trembling slightly, clutched one another—until she felt the warmth of Huntley's larger hand covering hers.

Startled, she looked up and caught his gaze.

"Is everything all right?" he asked, his voice low and steady.

"Certainly," she lied, swallowing the unease rising in her throat. She could do this. She tamped down the growing trepidation, forcing it to submit to her control. It would be better to get this dance over with and be done with Stansbury. "Lord Stansbury simply isn't an accomplished dancer, and I fear for my toes," she said, her voice light, though the truth of it lingered. "Since the waltz is nearly over, I'd prefer to keep this dance with him. If I don't, he might request another in its place."

Seeing the look of doubt shadow Huntley's face, she offered a reassuring smile, even though she felt anything but. "I'll be fine."

"In that case, may I have the next dance?" Huntley asked, though a deeper note crept into his voice. He hesitated for just a second before continuing, "I wanted to speak to you again. Tonight, I plan to announce..."

"Lady Catherine! Did you forget our dance?" Lord Stansbury's voice cut through Huntley's, his tone brimming with possessiveness. He pushed his way between them, keeping his back to the marquess as though deliberately ignoring his presence. His grip on Catherine's arm tightened as he addressed Huntley over his shoulder.

"The lady is engaged for this waltz, sir."

Before Huntley could respond, Stansbury hustled Catherine toward the dance floor, seizing upon a momentary break in the crowd.

31

A MOUSE!

Catherine nearly stumbled as Lord Stansbury pulled her into the swirl of dancers. She caught her balance just before they slid into place in the circling throng.

"It's most unbecoming for a lady to agree to dance with one gentleman and then jilt him for another. I'd expected better of you." He sounded like a petulant child.

Catherine took a deep breath, counting to three before answering. "Truly, Lord Stansbury?" she asked in a tone as frigid as the winter air outside. "This waltz is more than half-finished. Since you didn't collect me at the start of the dance, I believe *you* owe *me* an apology. I was under no obligation to wait as long as I did for you to appear."

He scowled. "Perhaps I was a bit tardy, Catherine, but you shouldn't have been chatting with another man when you were supposed to be with me." His lower lip jutted out.

"Lord Stansbury," she said, stiffening her back, "I don't recall giving you permission to address me in such an informal manner. I am '*Lady* Catherine.' After the lecture you just gave me concerning etiquette, I'm surprised by your lapse."

His hand tightened on her waist. "I was under the impression that my request for your hand in marriage had altered our relationship," he said through gritted teeth. "Rest assured, *Lady Catherine*, I meant no impertinence. Perhaps you simply need more time to become acquainted with me."

Catherine could hardly believe her ears. "We shouldn't be having this conversation in public, sir. The dance floor is hardly the place." She kept her tone calm, though fury roiled beneath her placid expression. "I made myself clear when you offered for me last year and again the other night. My opinion has not changed, and I would prefer not to discuss it further."

Her words carried finality, but Stansbury wasn't deterred. As they rounded the far end of the floor, a gap opened near the ballroom's entrance. He used the momentum of their steps to swing them out of the dance, barreling through a group of onlookers.

"We need to finish our discussion now, Lady Catherine," he muttered, guiding her toward one of the curtained doorways. His arm stayed clamped around her waist as they crossed into the hallway.

A few lingering guests watched with wide eyes as he propelled her forward.

"Perhaps through here." Stansbury hustled her into a nearby room, the Duke of Norfolk's private study. The fire burned low, casting the room in a warm, intimate glow.

Stansbury kicked the door shut behind them.

"Really, sir, I must insist you release me." Catherine struggled against his hold, pushing against his chest with the flat of her gloved hand. His grip loosened, and she broke free.

"I insist we talk." He stepped closer.

His determined expression was unlike the weak, self-serving man she thought she knew. A chill crept down her spine

Was this the real *Stansbury?*

She took a step back, but it only encouraged him. With a rapacious gleam in his eye, he grabbed her wrist.

"I know about the games girls like you play," he hissed,

pushing her against the wall and twisting her wrist painfully behind her back.

She tried to slap his face with her other hand, but the angle was awkward and her blow was weak. He snatched that hand as well and leaned his full weight against her, pinning her against the wall.

Fury coursed through her, but when she tried to knee him, the layers of her crinolines cushioned the blow.

"You're a tempestuous little minx," he said, his grin obnoxious as he pressed his body against hers. "This will make our marriage all the more pleasurable. I promise you, we'll be engaged before you leave this room."

He slammed his body into hers again, his lips descending toward her in a brutal attempt to claim a kiss. Catherine turned her head, struggling to pull away as she closed her eyes, but his weight trapped her against the wall.

"Stop!" she cried, her voice choked with desperation. This couldn't be happening.

Desperate to get away, Catherine strained against the man's odious touch as she struggled against him. He moaned in her ear as his wet lips trailed down her neck, leaving a slick, odious trail as he licked her.

A growl of frustration escaped her as she shoved at him, but it was no use. The oaf wouldn't budge.

Suddenly, Stansbury's weight vanished. Catherine opened her eyes just as Huntley spun the earl around and smashed his fist into Stansbury's chin. The impact sent him reeling, spinning back toward her.

As the earl staggered forward, Catherine didn't hesitate. She lunged, slamming her shoulder into his stomach with all her strength. He crumpled to the floor, retching as he clutched his belly.

"How *dare* you! You *vile* little man!" Her voice trembled with rage as she stalked toward him, fists clenched. The coward curled into a ball, clutching his stomach.

"You might want to stand back," Huntley said, trying to position himself between her and Stansbury.

Catherine glared at him. "Are you trying to protect him from me?"

Stansbury had begun to rise, but something snapped inside her at the sight. She raised her foot, aiming for his ribs with a fierce kick, but before she could strike, Huntley grabbed her arm and swung her around to face him.

Her fury turned on him next. "Don't touch me. I've had enough of being manhandled tonight."

"Catherine!" her mother cried from the doorway, hand pressed to her chest, eyes wide with shock. Her other hand clutched the door frame for support.

Catherine glanced past her mother to see the horrified expressions of guests gathered in the hallway. With a quick glance over her shoulder, her mother darted into the room, slamming the door behind her.

Huntley circled Stansbury, who remained on the floor, and moved to block the door, leaning against it to prevent anyone from entering.

"Catherine," her mother said again, her voice softer now. "Come here, dearest. Let me look at you. Are you injured?"

Shooting Stansbury a contemptuous glare, Catherine joined her mother. "I'm fine, but the evening is in shambles. This *beast* thought to press his suit after I had already rejected him. Twice."

Stansbury groaned as he struggled into a seated position, then pulled himself to one knee. "A most regrettable incident, for which I sincerely apologize," he panted, stumbling to his feet.

"Save your apologies," Catherine shot back, her voice icy.

"I deeply regret my actions, Lady Kensington," Stansbury began, his tone laced with false contrition. "In my eagerness to press my suit, I fear I may have caused irreparable damage to your daughter's good name, and for that, I am truly remorseful." A smug smile crept across his face. "But, if I may renew my offer of marriage, I believe we can still salvage the situation. Lady Catherine's reputation need not be permanently tainted."

Catherine's jaw dropped as realization struck her like a blow. "This was your plan all along," she hissed. "You horrid snake!" Her fists clenched, and she took a step toward him, barely able to contain her fury.

Her mother's hand shot out, gripping her forearm. "Catherine, let me handle this. You're too overwrought." She glared at Stansbury, her voice tight with contempt. "You should leave this room before my daughter does you any more harm."

Catherine's hands itched for a foil, her muscles tense with the desire to strike him down. She seethed silently, wishing for the satisfaction of skewering him.

"But, my lady," Stansbury said smoothly, "what about the people outside? What shall I tell them?" His smirk was infuriatingly smug.

"Tell them there was an unfortunate accident, and you must leave immediately," her mother said, her voice clipped and authoritative. "The Norfolk Ball is neither the time nor the place for this kind of discussion."

Huntley, who had been silent until now, finally spoke. "Unfortunately, Lady Kensington, I believe this is precisely the time and place. Stansbury has manipulated this scene skillfully, and we must resolve this matter before anyone leaves this room."

Stansbury's eyes narrowed, his tone turning cold. "I'm surprised by your support, Huntley. But rest assured, I can manage this situation without your interference. You may leave us to settle things privately."

"This is absurd." Catherine turned to her mother, her voice rising with frustration. "I refuse—absolutely refuse—to marry that odious man. I don't care if I can never show my face in society again. I've had enough of this farce. I wouldn't have been dancing with him in the first place if I hadn't been trying so hard to be the perfect earl's daughter, following all the rules." Her voice cracked slightly, but she pressed on. "What good is London if I can't even be myself?" *If I can't even fence?*

Tears burned at the corners of her eyes, and she turned away from them all, fighting to maintain her composure. She felt like she'd failed in every possible way, and there was no way back from this.

Her mother's voice was soft but firm, cutting through Catherine's despair. "I'm sorry, Catherine, but too many people saw Stansbury drag you into this room," she said, echoing Catherine's worst fears. "I could hear your scream from the hallway. So could everyone else. Before long, the entire ball will be buzzing with rumors about what happened in here. No family is powerful enough to stop what's coming."

"You must be reasonable, girl," Stansbury said, his voice dripping with false concern as he pounced on her mother's admission. "This is the only solution. And if you never want to return to London, I can arrange that as well."

Catherine's chest tightened. Was this really happening? Her eyes darted toward her mother, silently pleading for help, for some way out of this nightmare.

Huntley pushed away from the door, his calm presence somehow grounding the moment. He took a step toward her. "I'd like to suggest an alternative to you becoming a recluse. Will you hear me out?"

What now? Would he suggest Stansbury cart her off to Gretna Green? Or perhaps some contrived marriage where Papa would bribe the earl into abandoning her at a remote country estate? She shook her head, her frustration boiling over. But before she could voice a sharp retort, her mother's voice cut in, steady and measured.

"I'd appreciate hearing a calm voice amidst this confusion."

Huntley nodded, his gaze never leaving Catherine. "If Lady

Catherine will agree, I'd like to propose a union between the two of us. It offers an alternative to the proposal the earl has made."

Catherine's heart plummeted. *Marriage?* Her knees weakened, and she leaned heavily against the Duke of Norfolk's desk for support. *Was that the only solution anyone could think of?*

Stansbury's eyes flared wide in disbelief before quickly narrowing, his mouth twisting into a sneer. "I see what's happening here," he said, venom seeping into his voice. "It's the marquess who is *truly* taking advantage of this situation. Catherine hardly knows him, yet here he is, seizing the moment." His lips curled into a cruel smile as he straightened, puffing out his chest. "Whereas I've been a guest of her brother's on numerous occasions. In fact," his tone took on a triumphant edge, "we nearly came to an agreement of marriage just last year."

"I asked you to stop calling me Catherine," she insisted, her voice steady despite the turmoil swirling within her. "What does it matter that you know my brother? You have no claim on me. I rejected your proposal a year ago, and I reject it now."

Stansbury's face twisted into a scowl as he turned back to her. "Dearest, surely you see that you *must* accept my proposal. You can't leave this room without making a decision. Too many people know something happened here."

Catherine suddenly became aware of the rising clamor outside the door. The crowd must have doubled since her mother had entered the room. She was trapped.

Stansbury had played his hand masterfully. Had he always been this conniving? She closed her eyes for a moment, trying to clear her head and find a way through the tangled mess.

It all rested on her decision.

What if she simply disappeared? She could go to America. She wasn't afraid of hard work. She could sell her jewelry and fine dresses. If she lived modestly, she could make the money last. And she had skills—she'd make an excellent governess. The more she considered the idea, the more appealing it became. She could finally be free to choose her own path. Men did it all the time—why couldn't she?

Her mind set, she opened her mouth to refuse both offers when her mother's hand clamped down on her arm, pulling her back. Startled, Catherine turned to face her.

Mother gave Huntley a sharp smile. "Thank you, my lord. On behalf of my daughter, she accepts your generous proposal of marriage."

Catherine's jaw dropped. "That's..."

"No!" thundered Stansbury, his face reddening with fury. "I will *not* have it!" His voice quaked with rage. "This is *not* how things were supposed to happen! It's obvious he only wants Catherine for her money. He barely knows the girl. He just wants to use her dowry to rebuild that ruin he calls an estate in Scotland. Everyone knows it's a money pit! If you think I'll stand by while he steals her out from under me, you're sorely mistaken. I'll tell everyone what she and I did in here. All of London will know—"

Catherine barely saw the flash of Huntley's hand as he snatched up the letter opener from the duke's desk. He moved faster than Catherine could track. One second, he stood across the room; the next, he was beside Stansbury, holding the tip of the letter opener against the man's throat.

Huntley's voice trembled with barely controlled fury. "If you ever again try to sully Lady Catherine's name, you'll find that you're not safe in London. Or anywhere in England."

The ice in his words sent a shiver down Catherine's spine.

Stansbury winced in pain as Huntley pressed the dull point of the letter opener against his throat.

The calm look on Huntley's face made his threat all the more terrifying. All the more believable. "I promise I'll hunt you down myself and make you regret every moment of your miserable life. Do I make myself clear?"

All of Stansbury's arrogance and bluster melted under Huntley's controlled fury. His eyes widened in fear, and for a moment, he seemed to forget how to breathe.

"Do I?" Huntley pressed, his voice low and dangerous.

"Yes-s-s-s," Stansbury's susurrated reply was soft, serpentine. The snake.

"The choice is made. If you so much as breathe a word to impugn Catherine, her family, or our engagement, I will do everything in my power to destroy you." Huntley gave him a small shove and stepped back, his voice steady, measured.

A sharp knock broke the silence, and Charles slipped through the door.

His gaze swept the room, taking in the scene—the tension palpable. He frowned, his eyes landing on Catherine. "There are some ugly rumors spreading. What's going on here?"

No one spoke. Catherine's lips parted, but no sound emerged.

Charles shook his head, his frustration evident. "Stansbury looks cowed, Huntley looks furious, and Mother... looks oddly pleased. I'm not sure which of those worries me most."

Catherine just stared, her mind spinning. Where to begin?

Mother recovered first. Her voice smooth, unbothered, she said, "We'll put the rumors to rest soon enough. There was a small misunderstanding, but happily, we're about to announce Catherine's engagement."

Charles's eyebrows shot up as he glanced between Huntley and Stansbury.

"Catherine and Lord Huntley are to be married." Mother's voice was triumphant, as though all had gone according to plan.

Catherine's shock gave way to disbelief. "This is utterly ludicrous. I won't be a part of this charade."

Everyone froze.

Mother, first to recover again, spoke sharply. "Don't be ridiculous. We have no choice. If you don't walk out that door betrothed, our family will have to quit London. Are you so selfish that you'd ruin us all? Even Lord Huntley could face consequences for being here."

Catherine's gaze flicked to Huntley, and her stomach dropped. Her mother's words rang with truth. She looked to Charles for support, but he refused to meet her eyes.

What about her sister? Her brother? How could her family possibly survive a scandal like this? She could already hear the whispers about her being assaulted at a ball. Would Charles be able to keep his troubles in Oxford buried? Sarah's future—her chances for a decent marriage—would be ruined. The entire family would become outcasts, despite Father's title. And what of his business connections? His work for the queen? Could it all be jeopardized by this one night? Then there was Stansbury to consider, as well. He had already proven how far he was willing to go.

As much as she hated to admit it, her mother was right. She couldn't leave this room without a betrothal.

Her shoulders slumped, and she bowed her head. "I'm sorry. You're right. I've been selfish." Her voice was barely a whisper. "Of course, I accept your generous offer, Lord Huntley."

A collective exhale rippled through the room as everyone seemed to relax—everyone except the odious earl.

Stansbury let out a loud, exaggerated "hrumph," but a sharp look from Huntley silenced him.

"Excellent," Mother said with satisfaction. "Now, we must come up with a believable explanation for what happened in here. Many people heard Catherine cry out."

Stansbury, visibly begrudging the situation, rolled his shoulders and spat out, "Lady Catherine was frightened by a mouse, and when she screeched, Lord Huntley rushed in to investigate."

"A mouse?" Charles's voice dripped with disbelief. "My sister 'screeching' over a mouse?" His tone carried a note of mockery. "Did she also call it 'vile'? Because several people mentioned hearing that word quite clearly."

"Yes," Mother and Huntley said in unison, though neither looked particularly convinced. Catherine pressed her lips together, fighting the urge to scoff.

Charles sighed theatrically, throwing his hands up. "Not the most convincing tale, is it? A rat would have been more plausible, given my sister's extreme distaste for them. But I doubt the Duke's staff would appreciate that story circulating. A mouse will have to do. If you all agree to it, who am I to argue?" He turned to Catherine, studying her closely. "Catherine, do you agree to this?"

Her head dipped in a brief nod. "Make it a large mouse," she muttered.

Mother immediately took command of the situation. "Charles, I suggest you and Lord Stansbury leave first. Deflect the worst of the gossip and perhaps hint that there is wonderful news on the horizon."

She turned to Stansbury, her voice firm and precise. "If pressed, you can repeat your mouse story. If anyone questions your abrupt departure from the dance floor, simply say Catherine was feeling faint." She paused, eyes narrowing. "The full support of her family and all parties involved should prevent any rumors from spreading." Her gaze hardened as it locked onto Stansbury. "And I believe you understand the consequences if you deviate from this plan."

He squirmed under her scrutiny, his eyes darting to the letter opener with its green malachite handle, still firmly gripped in Huntley's hand. With a small, reluctant nod, he agreed.

Charles and Stansbury exited, leaving Catherine, Huntley, and Lady Kensington alone for a moment.

"I don't pretend to know all the details of what transpired here tonight," her mother began, "but I must admit, I'm satisfied with the result." She looked between Catherine and Huntley. "You may not realize it now, but the two of you are well-suited. This may not have been the most ideal start, but as the saying goes, 'all's well that ends well.'"

Catherine kept her eyes averted, unable to meet Huntley's gaze.

Mother's voice sharpened. "Now, both of you, we need to look happy. There's an audience waiting."

Catherine let out a resigned sigh. *How is this any different from the rest of her life? Smile. Pretend. Do what's expected.*

Forcing a bright smile onto her face, she accepted the arm Lord Huntley offered her, though the warmth of his touch only added to her confusion. Together, they followed her mother out of the room.

The hallway outside the Duke of Norfolk's study was crowded with guests, all watching their every move with greedy eyes. Some faces held smirks, others seemed shocked, but all were eager for scandal.

Lord Huntley covered her hand with his, the gesture meant to reassure, but it only deepened the knot of dread in Catherine's chest. She smiled up at him, trying her best to look radiantly happy.

What have I gotten myself into?

With the smile still frozen on her face, Catherine followed her mother as they mingled with the guests, each step pulling her deeper into the charade. Her mother wasted no time, stopping to announce the engagement to her closest friends.

Catherine's eyes flickered toward the guests, surreptitiously studying their reactions. At first, their faces were hard, judgmental, lips pressed into thin lines, mouths curving down in disapproval. But as she and Huntley moved through the crowd, and her mother whispered sweet reassurances, their moods shifted. Smiles began to replace the frowns. The change started behind them, spreading like ripples from friends Mother had already spoken to, then sweeping ahead of them.

Soon, it seemed the entire ballroom knew. There was nothing like fresh gossip to shove an old rumor aside.

Catherine stood on her tiptoes, leaning toward Huntley's ear.

"It seems to be working. Thank you." She inhaled the woodsy scent of his cologne, a smell she was slowly becoming familiar with.

Huntley gave her hand a comforting squeeze.

They continued to walk the perimeter of the ballroom, her mother recounting the engagement to yet another friend. Some of the doors leading outside had been opened slightly, letting cool winter air drift in, easing the heat that had built up in the room. The billowing curtains fluttered softly. When Catherine passed a pair of open doors, the cooling breeze was a welcome reprieve, offering a momentary escape from the pressure of it all.

It wasn't until they reached the far side of the ballroom, away from the open doors, that Catherine heard it: the first mouse joke.

Their story had spread.

"'Mouse girl?'" she whispered to her mother, mortified. "I'm now dubbed 'mouse girl'? How humiliating. It's not even clever."

Her mother arched a brow, unimpressed by her daughter's complaints. "Better 'mouse girl' than 'Lady Stansbury,' don't you think?"

Catherine sighed. Trust her mother to keep things in perspective.

Huntley grinned, placing his hand over the one she had tucked into the crook of his arm. "I rather like 'mouse girl.' It's the perfect irony. Rather like calling a cunning fox a 'watchdog.'"

Catherine let out an unladylike snort. "Or calling you a pussy-cat," she quipped, recalling the night at Lady Wilmot's, where he had seemed more like a panther prowling in the shadows.

He smiled down at her, his eyes glinting with amusement. "Aren't you worried that the pussycat might devour the mouse?"

His gaze captured hers, and she felt herself falling into it, like a mouse snared in a trap. She shook her head, trying to snap out of the spell. *How did I get here?* Engaged to this man—so full of strength, passion, and perhaps a little danger.

Could she trust him? Or had he maneuvered the situation to his advantage, forcing her into this betrothal? He was certainly preferable to Stansbury, but this wasn't how she had imagined choosing a husband. How could a solid marriage be built on a foundation of deception?

A shiver ran through her as her thoughts wandered to the kisses they had shared—the first in Lady Wilmot's library, the second in his study. Her eyes drifted to his mouth, perfectly sculpted, and she imagined the feel of his lips on hers. Her breath caught, and her lips parted slightly.

The corner of Huntley's mouth twitched. "All in good time, my little mouse," he murmured, his voice a low promise. "That's a promise."

Catherine's cheeks flamed, and she glanced around in embarrassment, worried someone had overheard. But her mother had drifted away, lost in conversation with friends, leaving her and Huntley in relative isolation.

A commotion rippled through the ballroom, drawing Catherine's attention. She craned her neck, trying to see what had caused the disturbance. "What's happening?" she asked Huntley.

His jaw clenched. "I believe the news of our engagement has just reached Lady Lydia."

Catherine's stomach dropped. "Why would that cause a scene?"

He leaned close, his breath warm against her ear. "Because I've spent the past two weeks negotiating a marriage contract with her father. We were supposed to meet in an hour to sign the papers. Her father planned to announce our engagement tonight at the ball."

Catherine stared at him in horror.

Oblivious to the tension between them, her mother turned to them, a broad smile lighting up her face. "Everything is going beautifully. Just beautifully."

❧ 32 ❧

NEGOTIATIONS

Catherine descended the stairs the following day, her mind set on speaking with her brother. Upon reaching the main hallway, she faltered. The doors to Papa's study were closed.

Those doors were *never* closed.

As she approached, faint murmurs reached her ears. She couldn't make out the words, but the low, familiar cadence of her brother's voice and her mother's more strident tones gave her pause. Another voice joined in, equally recognizable—Lord Huntley. Catherine edged closer, straining to hear. Her name was mentioned, followed by a word she couldn't quite catch. Then, something clearer. "...terms of the settlement," her mother said, firm and decisive.

Catherine's stomach twisted. The realization hit her like a blow: they were inside, hammering out the details of her future— her marriage—without her. She leaned in, desperate for more, but the words dissolved into indistinct murmurs. It didn't matter. The fact they were having this discussion behind closed doors, without her, was enough. She had been shut out.

For a moment, she stood frozen, listening to the quiet hum of voices. Each second deepened the weight of exclusion pressing on her chest.

She stared at the doors, momentarily thwarted. It wasn't the physical barrier that made her hesitate, but the significance of those closed doors. They represented her exclusion, the plans being made for her future without her involvement. That knowledge was utterly demoralizing.

She straightened. She refused to stand out here while the people inside that room planned her life for her. She'd had enough of that last night.

Seizing both doorknobs, she threw the doors wide and swept into the study. Her eyes immediately landed on Mother, seated primly in one of the upholstered chairs. Charles turned, a broad smile already forming as he moved to greet her.

"I want to cancel the engagement," Catherine declared without preamble.

Charles halted mid-step, his smile fading, while Mother's mouth dropped open in silent shock. Lord Huntley, however, merely looked bemused, as if he couldn't comprehend her meaning.

"I... I was forced to make the decision too quickly, and I am not at all certain it was the correct one. Lord Huntley, you and I hardly know one another. I would hate to abuse your good nature. You were most generous in making an offer for me, but I know your heart lies elsewhere."

Huntley exhaled audibly, causing Catherine to falter. His expression was inscrutable, though there was a hint of something —exasperation, perhaps? Or was that amusement?

Mother's eyes narrowed as she cast Huntley a look of sympathy, as if they shared a private disappointment. The knot in Catherine's stomach tightened. How long had her mother been hoping for this union? Had it begun at that dinner with Lady Wilmot? When had her mother pinned her hopes so firmly on Lord Huntley?

Charles, recovering his composure, regarded her thoughtfully. "Has anyone allowed you and Huntley to have a private conversation since the engagement?"

Catherine blinked, startled by the question. Had he not heard her intention to dissolve the arrangement?

"Well then, it's about time you did." He crossed the room to their mother. "Let's step into the hallway and give these two a moment alone together. I'm sure they have things to discuss." He held out his hand to assist Mother as she rose from the sofa.

Catherine cast Mother a pleading look, but she wouldn't even look at Catherine as she left the room.

The last thing she wanted was to be alone with Huntley. She turned her back on him and crossed the room to Papa's large desk, absently organizing his glass paperweights by size and color.

Lord Huntley remained silent.

"Things aren't going the way I expected them to," she ventured. When she glanced up, she spotted Charles and Mother murmuring inaudibly as they paced outside the door.

"But are they going the way you'd prefer?" Huntley asked.

She glanced at him, then returned her attention to the blue paperweight she held. She set it neatly along the edge of Papa's desk, trailing her fingers across the smooth glass. "I realize you feel you owe me a debt of honor, but the sacrifice you've made goes far beyond being commensurate."

"Catherine. May I call you Catherine?"

She paused, considering. He had, in some ways, earned the familiarity. "Of course."

He moved closer, picking up a clear paperweight containing bright-green flecks. Absently, he pressed it into his other palm. "I understand your reticence. We don't quite fit, do we?"

She stilled, watching his hands as he rolled the heavy piece of glass from one hand to the other.

"Unfortunately, I have a problem. When I proposed and you accepted, it set me down a certain path. I might be able to change the trajectory, but certain choices are now closed to me. I'm sure Lord Larchmont would love nothing more than to sue me for breach of contract, but since I never signed anything or made an announcement, he can't. You must understand that I can no longer hope to marry Lady Lydia. Her family is already denying any association with me."

Catherine's mouth went dry. "That can't be. I know Lord Larchmont can be a stickler for propriety, but surely he wouldn't stand in the way of his daughter's happiness."

Huntley's hands stilled as he gazed at her sharply. "I hope you aren't under the misapprehension that my marriage to Lady Lydia was anything other than a business arrangement. They wanted my money, and I wanted her as my wife."

She realized she was gaping at him and snapped her mouth shut. "I was under the impression that she wanted to marry you too. Wasn't she tracking you down at every social event you attended?"

His eyes narrowed. "What? Explain, please."

Catherine's face grew warm. "It was just a rumor, my lord."

"Nevertheless, you should tell me."

She heaved a sigh at her own carelessness. Now she had to explain. "Someone mentioned that if Lady Lydia didn't find you at one engagement, she'd move on to the next—and the next—until she located you."

A look of dawning comprehension swept over him, brightening his expression. "So that's how she did it. I'd wondered." The smile that tugged at the corner of his mouth held a note of respect. "Well done of her. But you're mistaken. She cared nothing for me. She wanted my title. You might find it hard to believe, but some women find the idea of being a marchioness rather appealing."

He was teasing her? Interesting. "And you? Why would you choose to marry her?"

"For her connections and her family's sterling reputation, of course. Her father is an influential man. She's exactly the kind of wife I was searching for—a woman with means, culture, and respectability who is above reproach. I was certain she'd be able to run my estate in Scotland and raise our children so they'd become solid members of society."

Catherine frowned at his list of requirements. "You mention nothing of love or affection. Not even mutual compatibility."

His jaw flexed. "Love is for fools, and affection comes with time." He set down the paperweight with a firm thump. "In some ways, you and I have even more to recommend our match. At least we're starting with a certain level of desire for one another."

Her anger flared at his presumption. "What could possibly have given you that impression?"

He smiled slowly, edging closer as his eyes locked with hers. "From our kisses, little mouse. Where else? You must have liked that first one, because you stole a second one from me while I slept."

Heat rose to her cheeks. "That was simple curiosity. Nothing more. It was an experiment. I suspected that a premeditated kiss would feel different from one that took me by surprise, and I was right. That second kiss had no effect on me."

His eyes smoldered. "That's because it was no true kiss. There was nothing behind it. If you want a real test, you'll have to do it when I'm conscious."

Was he right? Had the kiss left her cold because he'd been asleep? Her gaze slid to his mouth. She remembered how those lips were an intriguing combination of softness and firmness—and now, as she watched, they curled at the corners. She glanced up to find the knowing look in his eyes.

"I think I'll forgo that experience," she said tartly.

His smile deepened. "I can wait."

She scowled at him, refusing to take the bait.

He leaned back against the desk. "The real issue is our engagement. If you renege now, you'll harm more than just your reputation—you'll hurt mine. I can't repair things with Lady Lydia. Breaking off our betrothal was a significant insult, and Lord Larchmont will never forgive me. I need a wife, and finding one has taken too long already. Now that my plans with her are ruined, it's you who owe me a debt."

He was right. She had made it impossible for him to marry Lydia. Catherine's chest tightened. "Surely there is some way out of this. We hardly know one another. How can we marry?"

"Many marriages have started with less." He paused, his gaze resting on her thoughtfully. "I admit, I find you... compelling. It isn't only a sense of duty that drives me to insist on this arrangement." He let the words settle between them before continuing, "I'll grant you one concession if it will make this easier for you to accept. If you can manage to be circumspect, I'll agree to let you continue fencing. It isn't my desire to transform you into someone you're not. That being said, you can never go to Bernini's alone again. I insist you must always be with either me or Charles."

She stopped breathing for a moment. Hope swelled within her, making her skin tingle. "You'll let me fence?" She had to force the words out.

He frowned. "Yes. I said so, didn't I? But I repeat: you must remain circumspect and never go alone."

"I promise." Catherine's smile felt as though it might split her face in two. "The only time I ever had a problem was the one night I went there alone. It's caused me no end of trouble. I've learned my lesson."

"Then we're engaged?"

She hesitated. "You've placed restrictions on my behavior. I have a few conditions of my own."

He pushed away from the desk and stood straight. "This sounds like a negotiation." He moved behind her father's desk and settled into the chair, giving it an exaggerated air of authority. "I always feel more comfortable negotiating from behind a desk," he said, a hint of a smile tugging at the corner of his mouth. He drummed his fingers lightly on the armrests, as if preparing for a grand transaction. "So, what are your terms, my lady?"

"Fidelity. I assume you want it in a wife, and I must insist on it in a husband. If you cannot promise to remain faithful to our vows, then I can't agree to marry you. I won't marry a man who holds me to a different standard than he keeps for himself."

He nodded. "I can accept that condition."

"And you cannot prevent me from fencing as long as I remain circumspect."

"Agreed, with one caveat. You cannot fence if you're carrying our child."

She pulled her head back with a jerk. Their child? Her face turned hot. Why hadn't she thought of that before now? "Of course."

"Any other conditions?"

"You'll give me a fair allowance, allow me to manage the household as I see fit, speak to me in a way befitting a lady, and never intentionally cause me harm." She rubbed the sore spot on her side where Stansbury had bruised her ribs.

His expression darkened as his eyes flicked to her subtle movement. "Are you injured?" He pushed out of the chair and moved around the desk to stand beside her. "Did Stansbury hurt you?"

"It's minor. Just a bruise. I've had worse fencing at Bernini's. Even so, I had the distinct impression that he knew he was hurting me—and liked it." She couldn't suppress the shudder that rippled through her.

Huntley's eyes flashed with anger. "I should call him out."

"No! Don't be ridiculous. That's illegal. Besides, I'm satisfied with how you cowed him last night. I doubt he'll bother me again."

He looked at her levelly, then gave a sharp nod.

She glanced back down at the neatly arranged kaleidoscope of paperweights, unwilling to meet his eyes. "There's one other thing. You never asked me what prompted his attack, and I think you should know."

"I assumed he was after your dowry," he said, frowning. "Was there more to it?"

"He found out about my fencing. He tried to use it to force me to marry him a few nights ago, and when I wouldn't agree, he contrived that scene you saw at the ball."

"What the blazes?" Huntley's eyes widened in shock. "Your secret is already out?"

"Don't worry. He hasn't made it public yet, and I doubt he will, especially since he has no proof." She held Huntley's gaze, her voice softening to soothe his growing tension. "The embarrassing part is that I inadvertently confirmed his suspicions when he tried to blackmail me." Seeing Huntley's frown deepen, she hurried to reassure him, stepping closer. "But your threats—they frightened him, truly. I could see the fear in his eyes. I don't think he'll dare say a word. Without any evidence, who would ever believe him?"

"How did he find out?"

"That's been bothering me, too. He wasn't at the salon the night I went alone, so he must have seen me at some point afterward. I'm usually so careful, but between rescuing you and hurrying home the next morning, I was distracted. The streets were crowded, and I wasn't exactly subtle. I think that's when he must have spotted me—during my mad dash through town."

He sighed heavily. "You wouldn't have had to race through town if you hadn't stayed to watch over me. Add that to the list of debts I owe you."

Catherine bristled. "No more talk of debts. We can't keep tallying debts if we're to be married. We need a partnership, not a balance sheet."

He looked surprised at her words. "Agreed. You make a valid point." He stared at her for a moment, a contemplative expression on his face. "I wasn't raised in a typical household. I'll need to rely on your guidance in matters like these."

She looked at him blankly. "Forgive me. I don't follow you. Matters like what?"

His face reddened. "I refer to the proper behavior between husband and wife. I'm used to managing things on my own or negotiating business deals. My own family life was nonexistent, so I tried to observe successful marriages. The best ones are partnerships. Those where the husband dominates his family tend to be the worst."

She cocked her head to the side. "Is that why you've decided to let me fence?"

He gave a sharp nod. "And why I never initially planned to ask for your hand. I admit, your passion for fencing is troubling, but I firmly believe asking you to give it up would be the greater mistake."

Relief flooded through her. He truly would let her continue fencing. It wasn't just a promise—it was part of his moral code. "Thank you for explaining. It helps me understand you better."

"Then it's settled. We'll marry as quickly as possible. Any more conditions?"

"None." This might not be the marriage of her dreams, but it would allow her to continue doing what she loved most: fencing.

So why wasn't she happier?

33

FOUND

Daniel and Charles eyed one another in Kensington House's elaborate drawing room. Charles stood framed in the large picture window, the sun streaming in behind him, leaving him silhouetted against the light. It should have been the position of power, with the light partially blinding his opponent, but Daniel remained unperturbed. He recognized the power play for what it was and mentally applauded Charles for it, though he wasn't about to yield the advantage.

He strode across the room, putting distance between himself and his adversary in this negotiation. As he'd hoped, Charles followed him, abandoning his position of strength. Like forcing a chess opponent into a bad move.

Daniel paused before the fireplace, and Charles joined him. This maneuver left them as equals, a situation Daniel vastly preferred. After all, the marriage contract negotiations had been going well, so a détente was in order.

"Should we wait for your father's final approval? If I were in his position, I'd want to meet the man who would marry my daughter."

Charles looked away, not meeting his gaze, which surprised Daniel. He cleared his throat but didn't say anything for a moment.

Daniel examined the younger man closely, searching for any signs of deception. "Is there a problem?"

Charles exhaled through his nose. "Only a minor one. I received a note from Father this morning informing me he's been sent to Paris. I'm supposed to break the news to Mother and Catherine, but I haven't had the chance yet. I wanted to tell Mother first, but she rushed off to Lady Wilmot's home before I could. I know she'll be disappointed."

"Who sent your father to Paris?"

Charles shot him an assessing look. "It's interesting that you asked that particular question. Not 'why' or 'when will he return,' but 'who sent him.'"

Daniel offered a slight shrug but kept his gaze fixed on Charles.

Charles seemed to reach a decision. "Queen Victoria needs him to be her representative at Emperor Napoleon's court. She believes he's the perfect man for the task. The moment his ship arrived in port here in England, he had to take the next one back across the Channel. He'll be there for at least a month."

Daniel frowned. "Then I won't be able to meet him before we announce our engagement, probably not even before the wedding. Will he permit you to finalize the marriage contract?"

Charles gave a crisp nod. "I have Father's trust in this. I hope he'll return in time to give Cat away."

Daniel smiled at the nickname. Did his little mouse have claws?

A footman entered briefly to hand Charles a folded note. Without looking up, Charles murmured, "I'll have our lawyers draw up the papers."

He unfolded the note, his eyes scanning the page quickly. His expression shifted, eyes widening in surprise. He took a quick step back, then forward again, clearly energized by whatever news the note contained.

"Please have Lady Catherine come see me at once," Charles said, almost as an afterthought, and the footman quickly departed.

Daniel looked back at Charles, noting the speculative glint in the younger man's eye.

"I've fenced against you," Charles said. "You strike me as someone good in a fight."

Daniel gave a noncommittal shrug. The young man didn't know the half of it. "I prefer to avoid them, but yes, I can hold my own."

Charles grinned. "Then I have a story to tell you, as well as a request to make." He quickly explained his rather bizarre entanglement with an Oxford professor's daughter named Calliope. "It's been a horrendous mess. I keep worrying that a rumor will surface and drag my name through the muck. My best hope is to help the silly girl find Attwood and force him to marry her."

Daniel froze. "Attwood, you say? What's his Christian name?"

"That's part of the problem. He shares my first name, Charles. Charles Attwood."

"Damn. Attwood? Of all people."

"What? Don't tell me you know the man."

"I wish I didn't. He was at Eton with me until he was kicked out for stealing from some of the other students. He made my life miserable before that, accusing me of the thefts. If not for Wentworth providing my alibi, I would have been expelled."

Charles grinned. "Would you like the opportunity to hold him accountable for his crimes? This note is from Mr. Phipps, the man I hired to find him. He says Attwood is here in London."

A slow smile spread across Daniel's face. "That I would. I've heard rumors about him over the years, none of them good. What's your plan?"

Out of the corner of his eye, Daniel saw Catherine pause in the doorway. "Charles? You wanted to speak with me?"

She cast a cautious glance at Daniel. Clearly, she didn't trust him yet. The thought bothered him, and Catherine, noting his expression, frowned as well. He quickly smoothed his features.

"Cat. I'm glad you're here. Read this." Charles thrust the note into her hand.

She quickly skimmed it and then grinned. "So you've found him. Congratulations. But at a dog fight?" She shuddered. "The man truly *is* odious, isn't he?"

Daniel snorted. He might have guessed as much. "Dog fighting was one of his weaknesses."

Catherine shot him a questioning look.

"I knew him at school. He wasn't very pleasant as a boy, either." That was putting it mildly. "Your brother and I were about to devise a plan, but I need to know our goal."

"Calliope needs to find a husband, and quickly," Catherine said without hesitation. "For obvious reasons, I'd prefer it to be Mr. Attwood rather than my brother. We need to find him, bring him here, and hold him until the wedding can take place. After that, her reputation will be intact, and it won't matter what happens to the man. If she'll have him, that is."

"Oh, I have no doubt about that," Charles said. "Even though he's treated her abominably, she still claims to love him." He shook his head. "I'll never understand women."

"Don't be too hard on yourself. I can't understand her either." Catherine grinned. "Or maybe I've simply spent too much time around men, and some of it has rubbed off."

Charles frowned, then shot Daniel a curious look. Daniel was confused until the realization hit him. "I'm already aware of Catherine's unconventional interests."

Charles grinned in surprise and seemed to relax. "Now, that's a relief. I was wondering if she'd break the news to you before you married her." He furrowed his brow. "What do you propose to do about it?"

"About Catherine's unconventional activity?"

Charles nodded.

"Nothing at all. She and I have come to an agreement."

"You aren't going to insist she stop, are you? You can't. She's truly magnificent with a foil."

"I've seen her, and I agree." He glanced at Catherine and noticed her face turning pink with embarrassment. "But enough of that. We need to apprehend Attwood before he leaves that dog fight."

Charles glanced at Daniel and Catherine with an assessing look but didn't comment. "Mr. Phipps is watching him now. We should join him. I'll send Professor Caruthers a message letting him know we've located Attwood. We'll need to take the carriage to bring him back. Daniel, if you can take your horse, I'll ride in the carriage."

"I'd prefer to ride horseback as well. I wouldn't want to share the carriage with Attwood on the return trip," Catherine said.

Daniel shot her a sharp look, but she just lifted her chin. "You can go without me if you like, but I'll only follow. I already know where you're going. I read the letter."

"A lady can't go to a dog fight. It simply isn't done," Daniel snapped.

"Perhaps not, but Alexander Gray can attend. You'll find he's quite useful as a lookout."

Daniel glared at Charles, but the man only shrugged. "She's always been like this. You might as well get used to it. The only family member she's ever tried to hide this side of her personality from is Mother."

"Fine," Daniel said. "You have five minutes to ready yourself, or we're leaving without you."

Catherine's eyes widened in surprise, and without a word, she spun on her heel and ran from the room.

"Did I frighten her away?"

"Not likely," Charles said. "It takes about seven minutes to create that scar. I think she's trying to make every second count."

Daniel pulled his watch from his pocket. "Let's time her," he said, trying to look stern.

34

DOG FIGHTS

Daniel followed the carriage into a seedier section of London, where Mr. Phipps's note said the dog fight was being held. The wider streets narrowed, and well-kept homes and storefronts gave way to places with peeling paint and broken windows. This was a neighborhood where people minded their own business and stayed behind closed doors—a perfect place for a dog fight.

He glanced at Catherine. Her transformation into Gray still amazed him. She wore the same white head covering he'd seen at Bernini's, now topped with a hat. The false scar on her cheek seemed a bit wider and longer than he remembered, probably due to the rush to get ready within the allotted five minutes. She wore clothing typical of a privileged young man—likely Charles's castoffs.

If he hadn't known better, he would have taken her at face value. As it was, he had a difficult time dragging his eyes away from her thighs. He kept casting sidelong glances at her hips as he rode beside her. Well-proportioned, nicely rounded... He mentally shook himself and forced his eyes to turn away.

They headed toward an abandoned warehouse by the river,

following Mr. Phipps's directions. Even though it was winter, the stench was unmistakable. Years of neglect had left the place reeking of dead fish and rotting debris. Madson would have his work cut out for him trying to remove the odor from Daniel's clothes tonight.

As they neared the warehouse, a tall, burly man stepped out from between two buildings and waved them down. The coachman brought Charles's carriage to a halt, and Charles stepped out to shake the man's hand.

Daniel and Catherine dismounted. He almost moved to assist her, catching himself just in time. He'd nearly given her away with that automatic gesture.

"This is Mr. Phipps," Charles said. "I was lucky to make his acquaintance. When word got out I was searching for Attwood, he contacted me. He'd been friends with the man until Attwood took something that belonged to him."

Phipps's eerie smile didn't reach his eyes, and the evil glint in them made Daniel's blood run cold. "I've been wantin' to catch up with Attwood for years. Wouldn't miss this for anythin'."

The coachman stayed with the carriage while the rest of them approached the warehouse on foot. Raucous shouts came from inside. A smaller shed stood some distance away, and from its shadowed interior came the pitiful whines of frightened dogs.

Daniel ground his teeth. This sport sickened him. He paused, wanting to investigate the sound, but Mr. Phipps blocked his path.

The pair locked eyes.

"It's best to stay against the wall," the burly man said.

Daniel hesitated but relented. There would be time to investigate after their task was done. He'd make sure of it.

Phipps and Charles led the way to the warehouse door. Daniel moved so Catherine was directly in front of him, and her floral scent invaded his senses. He murmured in her ear, "You don't smell like a boy."

Her face paled. "I forgot," she whispered. "I usually wear men's cologne, but I was in such a hurry."

"Just don't stand too close to Attwood or Phipps. Even if they notice, they won't guess the real reason." They'd likely assume she'd been visiting a brothel, but there was no need to embarrass her by mentioning it.

Phipps pointed toward some horses tied to a rail near the entrance. "His mount's still here. Looks like the fight's nearly over. I'll go in an' flush him out. He hasn't seen me in years, but I'll bet good money he'll bolt the moment he does. You can grab 'im then."

As Mr. Phipps entered the warehouse, they positioned themselves on either side of the main door—Charles and Catherine on one side, Daniel on the other.

Moments later, the door swung open. Daniel stepped forward, prepared to apprehend Attwood, but when he glimpsed the man's face, he stopped short.

Wrong man.

The slim, wiry stranger scowled at them but didn't confront them, knowing the odds were against him. He found his horse among the others and rode off. Just as he left the yard, the door flew open again. This time, Daniel immediately recognized Attwood. Charles grabbed him by the shoulder, spinning him around to face him.

"Attwood, old friend. How are things at Oxford?" Charles's grim expression belied the friendly tone.

"Lord Spencer. A fan of dog fights? I never would have guessed." Attwood grinned.

"You're coming with us." Catherine's voice, deepened and full of authority, took Daniel by surprise. "There's a certain young lady you've wronged, and it's time to make amends."

Attwood smirked, ignoring her. His gaze stayed on Charles. "Found me out, did you? You're overreaching, my boy. There's nothing you can do."

"We might surprise you," Charles stepped forward, and Attwood stumbled back. "You're coming with us. Now."

Attwood wavered, seeming to shrink for a moment, and Daniel hoped he'd comply. But the man straightened his spine, his years as a bully asserting themselves. "No."

Attwood edged toward the horses, but he didn't get far.

"Wrong answer." Daniel grabbed his shoulder and spun him back around. "You're coming with us, one way or another."

Attwood scowled but showed no sign of surprise. "Let go of me. Now."

He tried to yank his arm free, but Daniel's grip held firm.

"You can't keep me here." Attwood's sneer deepened. "Think I don't remember you? You're the one with the mad father. Couldn't even add two numbers together at Eton. Simpleton then, simpleton now."

He yanked back and swung a fist at Daniel's face.

Daniel ducked and drove a punch into Attwood's gut. When the man doubled over, Daniel followed with a blow to the face.

Attwood crumpled to one knee, clutching his face. "My nose."

The door swung open, and Mr. Phipps hustled out, taking in the scene with a loud guffaw. "Looks like they got the better o' you, Attwood."

"Phipps?" Attwood gasped. "What the blazes are you doing here?"

Phipps grabbed him by the collar and gave him a rough shake. "Stay quiet, you." He turned to Charles. "We best be gone. This match is nearly over, but there's two more short ones to come. They have a couple a' mongrels they picked up to use as bait. They'll set their newer dogs on them to get 'em used to fighting. Should be over quick."

Daniel's jaw clenched at the sound of the terrified whines from the shed. Knowing their fate sickened him. Without a word, he turned and stalked toward it, jaw tight.

He'd seen this before, back when he'd run away and lived on

the streets of Edinburgh. He hadn't understood at the time what would happen to the poor dogs used as bait. The animal's eyes had been terrified yet trusting as the man had led him to his death. Daniel watched, stunned, as it was ripped to pieces, still alive as the other dog ravaged it.

Not again.

He flung open the door of the shed. His eyes adjusted to the darkened space quickly. A lone man inside looked up, eyes wide with bewilderment.

Daniel reached him in two strides, shoving him hard against a support beam. A forearm to the throat left the man gasping for air.

Daniel glanced around, taking in the filth and the two cowering dogs, terrified and whimpering.

The man slumped to the ground as Daniel let him go. He'd be out long enough to get the dogs away.

He should be out for a few minutes. Long enough to get the dogs away.

The ropes around the dogs' necks were tied to a hook in the wall. He took hold of their leads, murmuring softly to calm them.

"Come along, lads," he coaxed. "Let's go for a walk."

At the word "walk," their ears perked up, and they glanced toward the door. The smaller one let out a whine and bounced with excitement.

Realization hit Daniel. These weren't strays. They were pets, stolen for the fights. It made sense—stealing was easier and cheaper than raising them.

Daniel moved to open the door, but it shifted before he touched it. He dropped the leashes and pressed himself against the wall as it opened.

The dogs shrank back, ears pinned.

Daniel grabbed the arm of the person entering, yanking them into the shed.

Catherine shrieked in surprise, and he immediately released her.

"What in blazes are you doing here? I nearly hit you." His voice sounded harsh, even to his own ears. He couldn't tell if she was more terrified of him or the two growling dogs.

Her chin trembled, and his anger dissolved. He pulled her into his arms, pressing her face to his chest.

She murmured something unintelligible into his jacket. He eased away from her so she could tilt her head back and speak to him. "You were taking your time. I was worried about you," she said.

He shook his head in frustration. "You scared me. What if I'd hurt you?"

She surprised him by rising up on her tiptoes, wrapping her hand behind his neck, and pulling his head down for a quick kiss. "We need to stay together."

He couldn't hide his sudden grin. "And you need to curb your impetuous nature. If you keep putting yourself in danger, I'll have to teach you how to wield a knife."

"What do you mean? I don't put myself in dangerous situations."

He cocked an eyebrow. "Don't you? What do you call this? Or the night you rescued me? Or the night of the duke's ball? I dare say, if you'd had a blade with you, things might've gone differently with Stansbury."

She looked away, her expression guarded. He sighed, softening his tone. "I don't mean to criticize. On the contrary—I admire your courage. But that courage can be reckless, and I worry that one day it might cost you more than you're willing to give."

He glanced at her, noting the tension in her shoulders. "We need to hurry. Someone will come soon to collect these dogs."

A round of boos and catcalls erupted from the warehouse.

"I think the fight's ending," Catherine said.

She followed as he led the way across the snow-dusted lot at a run. When they reached the carriage, the two dogs eagerly bounded inside, underscoring their status as pampered pets.

Charles glanced at Huntley through the open door. "Looks like you've brought two escapees to help guard this lout. Is playing the hero a habit?" He glanced at Catherine. "Why don't you both go on ahead. We'll follow at our own pace. Gray needs to be home before Mother returns from her afternoon calls, so hurry." He shut the door, rapped on the ceiling, and the carriage immediately pulled away.

"Let's go," Daniel said, glancing back at the warehouse as the side door swung open. A man trudged toward the empty shed, oblivious to their presence.

"Just in time," Daniel muttered.

35

SURPRISE VISITORS

Catherine slipped in through the rear entrance of Kensington House dressed as Gray while Daniel waited outside for Charles. Once he arrived, the men would escort Mr. Attwood inside.

She hurried toward her bedroom, but just as she reached the foyer, Mrs. Evans came around a corner, spotted her, and stopped dead in her tracks. The woman glanced over her shoulder and then shooed Catherine forward, a look of impending catastrophe in her eyes.

Panicked, Catherine darted up the stairs. As she reached the next floor, she heard her mother's voice in the foyer below. "If anyone calls, let them know I'll be home in approximately one hour," she said to Mrs. Evans.

That had been close. Too close.

Catherine quickly changed back into her day dress, hid the clothing Charles had given her, and wiped all traces of the scar from her face. All the while, she couldn't stop thinking about Daniel. It hurt her to realize he still chafed at their engagement. Why else would he have brought up Stansbury's attack and her other errors in judgment? It must irritate him to be betrothed to someone as impetuous as she was. Someone so unlike the kind of woman he'd hoped to marry. He was right. She had been impetuous when she'd saved him that night—as well as when she'd kissed him.

Twice.

No, more than that. Including her lapse in judgment at the dog fight, it now added up to three times. So many things to regret... but she didn't actually regret any of them. Not a one.

When she reached the foot of the staircase, Percy, their butler, approached carrying a calling card.

"You have a visitor, my lady."

Catherine examined the card but didn't recognize the man's name. She gave Percy a doubtful look. "I'm afraid I don't know the gentleman. Did he ask for me?"

"The gentleman and his daughter insist they need to speak to a family member. They say it is most urgent."

"Shouldn't my mother deal with this?"

"She left to go riding." When Catherine still looked hesitant, he added, "The girl is about your age, and her father claims to be a professor at Oxford."

Catherine's pulse quickened. Oxford. This could only mean one thing: her brother's troubles had followed him here. She glanced toward the closed doors of the drawing room. "Are they inside?"

"Yes, my lady. I hope that is acceptable."

"Of course. I'll see them immediately."

It had to be Calliope and her father. Could they already have received the message from Charles about Attwood? What excellent timing. Charles should be arriving with Attwood any moment now.

She stepped into the drawing room and spotted the pair perched awkwardly on the edge of a sofa. Mother had recently redecorated the room with the intent to impress and intimidate visitors. She would have been gratified to witness its effect on these two.

Professor Caruthers stared in awe at the opulent space. He appeared to be in his late fifties, with a rounded belly and thick, graying sideburns that ran down to his jaw, his chin clean-shaven. His mouth was set in a thin, tense line, and deep grooves were etched in his brow.

Calliope's little pink mouth was slightly agape, her gaze darting around the room, taking in every detail. She'd made an effort to appear sedate, with her pale blond hair parted down the middle and pulled back into a low bun, but small, errant ringlets framed her face. The look seemed too artful to be accidental, and her lips too pink to be natural.

When Mr. Caruthers noticed Catherine, he sprang to his feet, startling his daughter. Calliope turned her vacant blue eyes to see what had caused him to move so abruptly and, seeing Catherine, rose more slowly. She cast her eyes down as if trying to conceal her excitement.

Catherine stepped forward to greet them. "Mr. Caruthers, you wished to speak with me?"

"You?" He looked genuinely startled. "I don't... I mean, I expected..." His face turned bright red as he stumbled to a halt and bowed.

"You expected someone older?" Catherine asked. She smiled to put him at ease. "I understand. I'm sorry, but I'm the only one home at the moment, and I was told you're here on a matter of some urgency."

"Urgent, yes," Professor Caruthers said, "but I can't discuss the matter with an unmarried woman." He glanced at his daughter.

"I understand your reticence," Catherine said, choosing her words with care. "However, I'm aware of your situation." She glanced at Calliope and gave what she hoped was a comforting smile.

The girl blushed, glancing down in obvious discomfort.

"Although I don't know all the particulars, I understand your daughter's fiancé has gone missing, and you fear some misfortune may have befallen him," Catherine said smoothly, shaping the truth to make it sound more... palatable.

Mr. Caruthers's jaw dropped, but he quickly recovered. Clearing his throat, he said, "Yes, that's the gist of things."

"Then you'll be happy to hear that my brother and my fiancé apprehended... ah, retrieved Mr. Attwood. They left about an hour ago to acquire him and should be here shortly."

At this news, a smile transformed Calliope's expression. Her vacant eyes now held a look of excitement. "He's coming here? Now? That's wonderful. He'll be so thrilled to see me."

Catherine froze, taken aback by the girl's enthusiasm. Attwood hadn't seemed "thrilled" to be apprehended. Did she really love him so much that she was blind to his faults? The man had abandoned her at an inn in the middle of the night. That wasn't the kind of thing Catherine could ever forgive.

Giving herself a mental shake, Catherine recovered. "I suppose congratulations will be in order once the two of you are reunited," she said, looking at Calliope with open curiosity. "You'll just need to have the banns read. Your wedding could take place in as little as three weeks."

Catherine heard a commotion at the front entrance and the sound of low voices, followed by barking dogs.

They were back.

"We've already had the banns read in Oxford. We could marry there with no delay." Calliope bounced on her toes, clasping both of Catherine's hands with surprising strength. "All I need is the groom." Her face took on a look of rapture at the prospect of marrying the ne'er-do-well.

Catherine could only stare in stunned disbelief. Was the girl daft? She forced a polite smile, wondering if Calliope's eagerness blinded her to the man's unsavory character.

"That's excellent news," Charles announced from the drawing room door, "because we happen to have your groom right here."

Catherine whirled around to see Daniel and Charles flanking Attwood, holding him firmly by the arms. A trail of blood stained his cravat, and he pressed a red-streaked handkerchief to his nose.

"Charles!" cried Calliope. She darted across the room and threw herself at Attwood, wrapping her arms around his neck. She bumped the hand he was using to press the cloth against his nose, and he yelped in pain.

"It's touching to witness such a joyful reunion," Daniel commented as he released his hold on Attwood and stepped away.

Catherine caught his eye, and they exchanged wry smiles.

"You're hurt." Calliope's mobile face shifted from abject love to concern. "What happened?"

"I... I tripped getting out of the carriage."

Daniel grinned and rubbed his bruised knuckles.

A strangled groan sounded from behind her, and Catherine turned to see Mr. Caruthers, his face rapidly turning purple with fury. His mouth opened and closed as though he struggled to find the words, his fists clenched at his sides. It seemed to take every ounce of his willpower to resist lunging at Attwood.

Daniel stepped forward, smiling as he clapped the professor on the back. "I knew the couple would be happy to be reunited. Now they can marry at once."

Caruthers gave a sharp intake of breath, his eyes narrowing as they flicked from Daniel to Attwood. His jaw clenched so tightly that a muscle leaped beneath his skin, and a vein throbbed visibly at his temple. He took a shuddering breath, his nostrils flaring as he visibly forced himself to swallow the words that threatened to escape. Finally, he managed a stiff nod, though his expression made it clear that agreeing to this was nearly unbearable. "Yes," he bit out, his voice thick with barely controlled fury. "That would be for the best."

Catherine sighed in relief. For a moment, she'd been afraid the professor might refuse to let them marry.

"If we all throw our support behind the union, I believe we can put a stop to any rumors," Charles said. "I suggest we have Mr. Attwood stay here at Kensington House. I can inform everyone that he's been my guest for the past week. We'll say you've been in London preparing for the wedding. Any scandal surrounding Mr. Attwood's disappearance should fade once they're married."

"Yes," Catherine said. "The best way to put an end to a scandal is to pull its teeth. There's no real damage if they marry as planned."

As Mr. Caruthers absorbed their words, the color in his face faded to a healthier shade. He seemed to weigh the offer carefully, his lips pressed tightly together as though holding back objections he knew he could not voice. "'Poor Mr. Attwood,' my foot," he finally muttered. He glared at Charles. "Are you suggesting that Mr. Attwood can be relied upon to fulfill his obligation to my daughter? What if he abandons her again?"

"Ah, yes." Charles folded his hands behind his back, rocking back slightly on his heels and reminding Catherine of their father. "From what I understand, some men develop 'cold feet' as the wedding date approaches, so we've taken that into consideration. Since Mr. Attwood will be our guest at Kensington House, he will receive all the, ah... *support* we can provide." He cocked an eyebrow at Mr. Caruthers. "I personally assure you he'll be present at the wedding. I've already found a man who can serve as his personal assistant." He stressed the word as he raised his eyebrows. "I have no doubt he'll keep a close eye on Attwood and deliver him to the church at the appointed time." His eyes danced merrily.

"A personal assistant?" Mr. Caruthers sputtered, his face purpling again. "You're telling me that Attwood will have a manservant at his beck and call?"

At that moment, Mr. Phipps loomed in the doorway, his broad frame filling the entrance and casting a shadow across the room. Catherine instinctively took a step back, unsettled by the sheer force of his presence. He must have been standing just outside, listening. Tall and burly, he had a coarse, weathered face, and his nose bore the evidence of having been broken more than once. His clothes, though well-cut and clean, looked as if they'd been slept in, lending him a disheveled air that did nothing to soften the menace in his gaze.

"Ah! Here is the man now. May I introduce Mr. Phipps? He knew Mr. Attwood long ago and was most eager to help us locate him. He possesses the perfect qualifications to be of assistance to us." Charles's tone was pleasant enough, but it turned ominous when coupled with the looks of loathing that Phipps and Attwood exchanged.

As Mr. Caruthers examined the alleged manservant, a small smile finally cracked his expression.

"I'll make sure he's at the wedding, sir. You can rely on that," Mr. Phipps said in a menacing tone, glaring at Attwood. "Perhaps you could let me check the room where he'll be staying. I want to make sure it's snug and secure for the *gentleman*." The way he spat out that last word made it sound more like an obscenity.

Daniel stepped forward. "If you'll permit me, perhaps it would be best if Attwood were to stay at my town house. I'm a bachelor and don't have a family to be put out by hosting an unexpected guest. I also wonder if your youngest sister might not be able to resist investigating such an intriguing mystery."

Charles looked startled at first, then gave a decisive nod. "You make a valid point. Good thinking."

Catherine tilted her head as she glanced up at Huntley. That had been astute of him. Of course, Sarah would have been curious. That was her nature. Even though Daniel had only met her the one time, he'd foreseen a problem her entire family had overlooked.

Another idea came to her in a flash. "Charles, perhaps Lady Wilmot and her daughter could be persuaded to assist us in our ruse. If anyone knows how to spread a carefully placed rumor, it's Lady Elizabeth. With their help, I'm sure news of Miss Caruthers's London visit will spread all the way to Oxford within a day or two."

"That's an excellent notion," Charles said. "Well done."

Mr. Phipps leaned against the door frame, guarding the only exit, while Calliope still clung to Attwood. Despite her earlier bravado, she now acted as though he might disappear at the first opportunity.

Daniel stood at Catherine's side, and, with a jolt of surprise, she realized she liked having him there, close enough to touch. When had that happened? When had she gone from avoiding him to wanting him nearby?

She sidled away, her pulse quickening with a mixture of irritation and confusion. She disliked the notion of wanting him close —particularly when she couldn't seem to control the feeling.

Charles placed his hand on the professor's shoulder. "Mr. Caruthers, if you'd be so kind as to join me in the study, I believe we should discuss the conditions of the marriage and present them to Mr. Attwood. I'm sure he'll be amenable to whatever you deem is a fair dowry."

"Dowry?" Mr. Caruthers's eyes bulged, and his head jerked back as though he'd been struck.

"Certainly, a dowry. You'll want to ensure your daughter isn't lacking in basic necessities once she's married." Charles's brow furrowed as if surprised. "It's your duty as her father. You wouldn't want to cut off your nose to spite your face. I'm sure you, as a prudent man, have set aside funds for her over the years."

Caruthers sputtered. "How do I know Attwood won't just take the money and leave her stranded?" He winced, and Catherine followed his gaze, noticing the hurt expression on his daughter's face. Was the girl really that naïve?

"I'm sure we can craft an arrangement that will protect your daughter's funds from any nefarious manipulations. May I suggest setting up a trust with a regular allowance?" Charles gave a wily grin.

As understanding dawned on Caruthers's face, a smile began to take root. His chin lifted, and his shoulders relaxed. The tense, haggard man seemed to transform before Catherine's eyes. When she'd first seen him, she'd thought he was older than her father, but now she could see he was much younger—likely in his early forties.

"Thank you, Lord Spencer," Mr. Caruthers said. "You've been more than kind. I apologize for any misunderstanding regarding your involvement. It didn't take long for me to realize you weren't culpable. Please forgive us for having drawn you into our predicament." He glanced at his daughter, who, to her credit, looked suitably chastened.

Catherine's gaze softened as she watched Charles—a gentleman even to those who scarcely deserved it. Calliope, meanwhile, looked up at him as if oblivious to the scandal she'd nearly caused.

Catherine was well aware that, along with smearing her brother's reputation, Calliope had cost him a term at Oxford. If it had been Catherine's decision, would she have been able to forgive them? At the very least, Charles deserved an apology.

Caruthers nudged his daughter with his elbow, and she glanced up, confused. He jerked his head toward Charles.

"Oh." Comprehension lit her features. "I want to offer my apologies as well." She approached Charles, standing so close her full skirts brushed against his trousers. She gazed up at him beseechingly. "Please don't be angry with me, Lord Spencer. It was terribly wrong of me to use you. I never imagined things would unfold as they did. I only wanted to keep Father from chasing me to Gretna Green. Who could have predicted that dear Attwood would get cold feet?" She shot Attwood an indulgent smile, oblivious to the way Charles rolled his eyes at the comment. She clasped his hand, tilting her face up with a look of unabashed repentance, though Charles only allowed the gesture, a hint of skepticism glinting in his eyes.

"No lasting harm's been done," he replied.

"You're all most kind to help us," Mr. Caruthers said. "I'm an academic, and not accustomed to the ways of society. It appears to me that I'm very fortunate indeed to have your assistance."

"Join me in the study," Charles said. "I already sent for the family solicitor to finalize my sister's marriage contract, and he should be here shortly. He can help us draw up the legal papers regarding your daughter's dowry and inheritance as well." Charles patted Mr. Caruthers's shoulder as he shot Attwood a look of satisfaction. "Yes, I think everything will work out well."

36

ENLISTING HELP

"Just think about it, Elizabeth, the story is so dramatic. Lovers, separated by circumstances, ultimately reunited." Catherine tried to force a tone of joyous rapture, but she couldn't quite manage it.

"Ha! More like, 'worthless suitor gets cold feet and is forced to altar by irate father.'" Elizabeth's green eyes flashed with delight. She sat at her dressing table and picked up an ornate box filled with ribbons and hair ornaments. She poked through it, searching for something.

Catherine tried to suppress the grin, but she failed. "No, no, no!" She said, laughing. "That attitude just won't do. We must immerse ourselves in the spirit of the ruse. We must believe it, act it, make it true, and then everyone else will believe it, too." Sobering, she shot Elizabeth an imploring look. "You *must* help us carry this off. Although it's true that Calliope's future depends on the ruse, I'm more concerned for Charles. If the truth comes out, Charles could be drawn back into it."

"And that's why you need me, you silly goose," Elizabeth said, looking at herself in the mirror and holding a clip decorated with creamy feathers against her hair. "You never were any good at playacting. Just look at you now." She glanced at Catherine's reflection in the mirror. "You're overacting, and anyone with sense will notice. You're terrible at keeping secrets."

A smile flickered across her lips. "I bow to your greater authority. If anyone can get this story to take hold, it's you. You're quite skilled when it comes to matters such as these." She looked at Elizabeth appraisingly in the mirror. "That piece looks lovely. It shows up beautifully against your dark hair."

Smiling in satisfaction, Elizabeth spun around in her seat to face her friend. "Well, you didn't make a bad start with that story, but we must add details. Let's see," she thought for a moment. "I know. We'll say Calliope and I met when my father was searching for a book for his collection, and I was drawn to her bold nature."

"Bold nature?"

"Any girl who would run off to Gretna Green must be bold."

Catherine shrugged. Bold? Perhaps she'd missed that character trait when she'd met Calliope.

"What's her father's field of study at Oxford?"

"You can't guess from his daughter's name?" Catherine chided.

"Hmmm. Calliope was in Greek mythology as the muse of poetry. Which is it, Greek mythology or poetry?

"Greek mythology."

"Oh! That really *is* perfect. How very convenient of him. You know..." Elizabeth paused, thinking further. "It's quite likely that he really *did* know my father. Perhaps we should ask Mr. Caruthers about that before he returns to Oxford. We could include it in our story." She smiled. "I love it when the details come together this way."

"I'll leave those details to you, dear. You're much better at this than I am."

Elizabeth poked around in the box again and pulled out a strand of jewelry. "Can you keep the story straight once I give it to you?"

"Most certainly. This should be fun." Catherine left her seat to stand behind Elizabeth, looking at the mirror for a better view of the necklace her friend held at her throat.

"Calliope needs to stay here with me until the wedding." Elizabeth arched her neck slightly to one side, peering at the cameo necklace. "It will help with the story I'm weaving. And since I'm miffed with you for planning to marry Huntley with such annoying haste, I've decided that Calliope and I will become the very best of friends." She turned her nose up.

Catherine rolled her eyes and let out a long-enduring sigh.

❧

A WEEK LATER, CATHERINE AND ELIZABETH WERE IN HIDING, stealing a few quiet moments together in Lady Wilmot's comfortable morning room. It was a far cry from Mother's more ornate space at Kensington House, and Catherine vastly preferred the homier atmosphere.

Catherine hadn't been able to find many quiet moments alone with Elizabeth since Calliope had moved into Lady Wilmot's house. From what Elizabeth had told her, the girl's visit was beginning to wear thin.

Fortunately, last night Catherine had enjoyed her first night back at Bernini's since that fateful foggy night, and she felt much less tense today. Bernini had pushed her hard, obviously annoyed that she'd been gone so long, but she'd performed well and had earned a reluctant grunt of approval from the man.

Charles had escorted her. Huntley hadn't been there. He'd been avoiding her ever since she'd kissed him in her "impetuous" way in the shed.

Impetuous.

Blast the man.

At least she had both the upcoming tournament and Calliope's situation to distract her from her own upcoming wedding. She did her best to push the annoying man from her mind, focusing instead on the present.

Catherine and Elizabeth sat chatting on the comfortable pale-yellow sofa near the window, enjoying the sunlight streaming in. Lady Wilmot's morning room was beautiful, with soft-yellow patterned drapes and exquisite yellow-gold silk chairs. Calliope burst in, interrupting their conversation.

"The wedding is set for this Saturday in Oxford," Calliope announced. "Father just sent word. Thank you ever so much for helping me and dear Charlie. We're terribly grateful." Calliope flung herself onto the sofa, directly between Catherine and Elizabeth. "You're both absolutely *wonderful* friends." She glanced from one to the other with an adoring gaze. "I don't know what I'd have done without you. I probably would have *died*!" Her head bobbed with emphasis, causing the blond curls around her face to bounce as well. Even her hair was energetic.

Catherine, taken aback by Calliope's exuberance, suppressed a sigh. *Died? Really?* She recalled Elizabeth's assumption that any girl who would run off to Gretna Green would be bold and assertive. Over the course of the past week, they discovered they'd been gravely mistaken. However, she *did* tend to be stubborn in her belief that Mr. Attwood loved her. Perhaps that was a form of assertiveness.

Something Calliope had said finally seeped through Catherine's annoyance.

"Married? On Saturday? But, Calliope, that's marvelous." She exchanged a relieved glance with Elizabeth.

"Yes, isn't it? Lady Wilmot just told me the arrangements have been finalized." An annoyed expression crossed Calliope's face. "Although I don't understand *why* my father had to be so stubborn about having a solicitor draw up the papers," she grumbled. "And in an irrevocable trust, too. My Charlie would *never* fritter away all of my money. He *loves* me. I *do* hope he isn't terribly offended."

Catherine swallowed and stared at the girl in silence. No wonder Charles had referred to her as a simpleton.

"But your mother just gave me the other good news, too," she said, focusing her gaze on Elizabeth. "And *thank* you so *much*. I simply couldn't believe it when she told me that you both would be my bridesmaids," she gushed. "You're too *good* to me."

This was certainly news to Catherine. It meant that she'd be taking the train to Oxford for the weekend.

Elizabeth glanced at Catherine and then beamed at Calliope. "We're only too pleased, Calliope. You'll make a beautiful bride."

SATURDAY MORNING, THE MEMBERS OF THE WEDDING PARTY were settled in three private compartments on a train heading to Oxford. Catherine sat in the rear compartment with Elizabeth and Calliope, while Mother, Charles, and Lady Wilmot rode in the middle one. Huntley guarded Attwood in the compartment at the front of the train car, with the help of Mr. Phipps.

Catherine had her hands full trying to keep Calliope from seeing Attwood. They all wanted to make sure the wedding went smoothly, so they'd decided to keep the couple apart. It would be disastrous if the ceremony didn't take place because they quarreled or because Attwood wheedled Calliope into helping him escape.

Catherine escorted Calliope to locate the ladies' water closet on the train and returned to the compartment, sliding the door closed. She sat next to Elizabeth to wait for Calliope's return, enjoying the few moments of relative silence.

"I thought Calliope was your new best friend," Catherine chided her friend. "Won't you miss her?"

"Oh, stop it. I was just getting caught up in the story I was inventing. This charade has been more exhausting than I anticipated." She leaned her head back against the seat on the train. "I don't know how people manage to keep track of so many lies."

"What truly confounds me is how much the reality of Attwood differs from Calliope's opinion of him." Catherine shook her head in consternation. "No matter what the man does, no one can shake her faith in him. He doesn't deserve it."

Elizabeth gave her a knowing smile. "I wouldn't worry about it if I were you. She's much more aware of his failings than she lets on. At first, I thought she ignored what was being said when people spoke badly of Attwood, but I was wrong. I think she hears everything. She may come across as empty-headed, but there is more to her than she lets on. Attwood will have more to contend with in her than he realizes."

"It sounds as though you two have grown close during the past two weeks," Catherine teased.

Elizabeth wrinkled her nose at her. "Now you're annoying me. Speaking of being close, what about you? Tell me more about Huntley."

Elizabeth's sudden change of subject put Catherine on guard. This must be Elizabeth's way of getting even. "What do you mean?"

"He's still an enigma to me. I've barely spoken to him. I know he's handsome and has a title, but there must be something more to him, or you'd never have agreed to marry the man. Tell me what made you choose him."

The question took Catherine by surprise. She'd kept the real reason for their hasty engagement a secret, and once they'd announced they were planning to marry, no one had bothered to ask her why. "Well, it's a number of things, of course. I find him trustworthy, reliable, supportive, kind...," she stumbled to a stop. Not to mention stubborn and obsessed with propriety. But what about how he made her feel? The annoying man was also exciting, passionate, sensitive, and could make her knees buckle with desire. His kisses could make her lose all sense of time and place.

A look from him from across the room could make her turn to water.

A slow smile spread across Elizabeth's face as she watched Catherine. "So, it's like that, is it?"

"Like what?" Catherine pressed her lips together. Elizabeth couldn't possibly have read her mind, thank goodness.

"It's a love match. I can see it in your face, Catherine. You can't fool me."

A love match? Catherine's eyes grew wide as she met Elizabeth's triumphant gaze. Love? Was she in love with Huntley? How ludicrous. The man didn't even approve of her.

The door opened abruptly, startling Catherine.

Calliope slipped back into the private compartment with an annoyed look on her face. "That man, Mr. Phipps, is it? He refuses to open the compartment door and let me speak to my Charlie!" She plopped onto the seat, settling into a sulk.

"Calliope! You promised you wouldn't try to see him," Catherine admonished. Thinking better of it, she continued on in a more soothing tone. "We'll be arriving shortly, and then you'll be married. Just think of it. You'll spend the rest of your lives together." Exchanging a look with Elizabeth, she added, "Isn't it bad luck for the groom to see the bride before the wedding? You wouldn't want to tempt fate, would you?"

"Tempt the Fates?" Calliope repeated, clearly thinking about the white-robed incarnations of destiny from Greek mythology. The stories must have been drummed into her since childhood, with a professor for a father.

Taking her cue, Elizabeth chimed in, "Yes, I heard the same thing. You want to get your marriage off on the right foot, don't you?" She reached across to where Calliope was sitting in the seat opposite her and patted her hand. "We'll arrive in Oxford shortly. You won't have long to wait."

This immediately pulled Calliope out of her sulk. With unshed tears shining in her eyes, she said, "I certainly wouldn't want to tempt the Fates. They can become quite angry. What would I do without the two of you to guide me?" She gave them a smile. "I'm so lucky you're my friends."

"This really is quite eye-opening," Catherine whispered into Elizabeth's ear as Calliope busied herself looking for a handkerchief in her reticule. "And here I thought you were the queen of drama. I believe you just lost your crown." The corners of her eyes crinkled as she tried to contain her laughter.

"Shush!" scolded Elizabeth, grinning in reply.

37
SPYING ON HUNTLEY

The damp London morning was slow to warm. Certainly not fast enough for Stansbury as he watched Huntley's townhouse. The cold dug its way deep into his bones, causing his left knee to ache. Huntley's daily excursions walking those two dogs and visiting Kensington House had only been a waste of shoe leather so far, as were his daily business meetings. At this rate, winter would pass before anything interesting took place.

Initially, he'd re-engaged the men he'd hired to kidnap Huntley and search his town house. They owed him for bungling that job, so he'd tasked them with following the man. Unfortunately, they'd become annoyingly insistent in their demands for money. Why couldn't they see the bigger picture? He'd be able to pay them handsomely once he married the Kensington girl, but they were too impatient. They insisted upon getting their money immediately, the shortsighted fools. When he'd ultimately had to let them go, he'd taken over the job of following Huntley himself. It was cold, tiring work, spending so much time chasing the man about town.

Just as he was considering getting a drink to warm him, he

spotted movement at Huntley's front door. This was earlier than usual, so perhaps something different would happen today.

He could hope.

Two other gentlemen accompanied Huntley. One was that burly-looking one he'd occasionally seen coming and going. He'd stay for long hours, so Stansbury assumed he was a servant of some sort. He didn't seem like type of man you'd want to cross.

When the burly fellow shoved the third man into a waiting carriage, Stansbury's interest peaked.

He hadn't seen the third man before today. He appeared to be about the same age as Huntley. Although the men clearly weren't friends, the third man didn't appear to want to leave Huntley's town house and enter the carriage. This was all rather odd, and anything odd was interesting.

Stansbury followed them, and was even more surprised when they arrived at the train station. There, they were joined by the Kensington family, the Wilmot family, and another girl whom Stansbury didn't recognize. Lord Spencer joined Huntley's party and the men stood a small distance away from the rest of the group. It appeared that although everyone knew that third man, nobody liked him. It was as though they were all guarding him.

Curious.

When Lord Spencer's servant set off toward the ticket window, Stansbury followed him and eavesdropped to learn their destination. He rushed through purchasing a ticket and scurried on board the train for Oxford moments before it pulled away from the station.

He counted his remaining money.

Blast that Huntley.

If he wanted to set aside enough coin to purchase a return ticket, he'd have barely enough to buy a single meat pie for dinner. His stomach rumbled.

He closed his eyes and leaned his head against the side of the train, resting in the warmth of the passenger car. He stretched out his left leg, easing the ache in his knee and as he thought about that damned marquess.

All Stansbury's problems had become much worse in the past few months. Was Huntley bent upon destroying him? Had he finally uncovered Stansbury's involvement in that ruse to steal his shipping contacts out from under him? It had been an inspired plan to undercut the man before he had a chance to finalize his deals— until Huntley found out. Did the man's vengeance know no bounds? He'd done everything in his power to destroy them. The others had managed to weather the storm, but not Stansbury. Huntley was the root cause of his financial ruin. He'd intentionally tricked Stansbury into making those bad deals. Damn, but Huntley could be vengeful. It wasn't as though Stansbury had done him any lasting harm.

The train rousted Stansbury from his reverie when it stopped with a jolt at the platform in Oxford. Through the window, he could see Huntley's party disembark, so he rushed out to the platform, hiding behind other passengers who were alighting as well.

An older man met Huntley's group and embraced the girl. Was he her father? He was about the right age, and there was a family resemblance.

The group climbed into some waiting carriages which immediately departed the station. Stansbury rushed to hail a hansom cab so he could follow.

There goes more of my money. No meat pie. Blast that Huntley.

Fortunately, the group didn't travel far before they arrived at a little church. As they stepped out of the carriages, Stansbury had his driver pull around the corner out of sight. He managed to enter the church through a back door, and it soon became obvious that a wedding was about to take place.

There were few guests, but Stansbury could still slip unnoticed into a pew at the back of the church. As soon as the wedding party assembled, the ceremony began.

The girl seemed deliriously happy, but not the gent. Once they both recited the words that tied the knot, the burly man seemed disappointed.

I bet he wishes he could have smashed the gent's face in.

Huntley and the others certainly looked satisfied with the result. Why was this wedding between these two nobodies so important?

The wedding party walked to a nearby restaurant. Stansbury followed them inside and ordered tea and toast, earning an annoyed look from the waiter for placing a small order during such a busy time of the day. Stansbury chose a table where he could keep an eye on the wedding party. Huntley's group didn't stay long. Stansbury overheard them make their goodbyes to the newlyweds, and then they hurried off to catch the return train.

The best use of my time might be right here in Oxford. I need to investigate further to see if I can make any use of this mystery.

Stansbury continued watching the newlyweds and their remaining guests, hoping that the trip here hadn't been a waste of time and money. Why would Huntley travel so far something so mundane as this?

A middle-aged couple passed Stansbury as they left the wedding breakfast, and he overheard a snatch of their conversation.

"... appears that the situation is quite respectable now. Caruthers was awfully distraught a month ago," the man said.

"I'm just thankful the poor girl wasn't ruined. When I heard that Mr. Attwood ran off in the night ...." The remainder of the wife's reply was lost as the couple moved out of earshot.

Stansbury grinned with glee. He had two names and enough information so that he could ferret out the rest.

This might prove to be a productive day after all.

❦ 38 ❦

A BIT IMPETUOUS

Catherine stood next to her brother at the platform, deliberately avoiding looking at Huntley. The two of them would be going through the same ceremony in a couple of weeks, and the thought both terrified and thrilled her.

"If it's all the same ta you, sir, I'd like to stay here in Oxford fer the day," said Mr. Phipps. "I've never spent much time outta London."

"Certainly," Charles replied, handing the man his ticket. "Return whenever you like. Attwood is no longer your responsibility now that he's married."

"Much obliged, sir," Mr. Phipps said, tucking it into his pocket. He whistled a merry tune as he strolled down the street.

For the return trip, they all kept their original compartments. Elizabeth and Catherine shared one, and Elizabeth sat quietly reading a book, giving Catherine time to think. Huntley had seemed preoccupied all day. Whenever she'd glanced his way, he appeared lost in thought. She hadn't seen him at any social events lately, either. Now that they were engaged, his focus had returned to his shipping business.

She frowned, staring moodily out the train window and

watching the pastoral landscape rush past. Perhaps she should have married Anthony Watters. But no. That would never have worked. The man couldn't focus on anything for more than a few weeks, and he had never accomplished anything in his life. How could she respect someone with so little ambition?

The thought brought her up short. Did she truly value ambition and hard work? Of course she did. Why else would her goal be to win the fencing tournament?

Catherine glanced up as the compartment door slid open and Lady Wilmot entered. The door banged shut behind her as the train rounded a bend, and Lady Wilmot almost fell into the seat next to Elizabeth as she lost her balance.

"Oh, my!"

"Are you all right?" Elizabeth asked.

"Quite well. Just a bit unsteady." She patted Elizabeth's hand and then smiled at Catherine. "Wasn't the wedding lovely?"

"It was," Catherine agreed. "The best part is that it was uneventful."

"The best part is that Calliope won't be living with us anymore," Elizabeth replied.

Lady Wilmot cleared her throat. "Catherine, your mother wanted a moment alone with Charles, so I hoped this would be a good time for me to have a word with Elizabeth. Would you mind terribly if I asked you to step outside?"

"Of course not. I was just thinking about taking a short walk. This is the perfect opportunity." Catherine stood and smoothed her skirts. As she exited the compartment, she had to grab hold of the door frame as the train swayed, but she quickly righted herself.

The corridor was narrow, and there wasn't much to see. All of the compartment doors were closed, so she headed toward the far end, where there was a door leading to the next car. Perhaps she could look outside and feel the wind. That would be exhilarating.

With the swaying of the car, it was difficult to walk down the corridor, and when the train gave a sudden jerk, she stumbled against the wall and banged her elbow.

The compartment door beside her opened with a snap, startling her. She looked up to find herself face to face with Huntley.

"Lord Huntley. Were you trying to give me a fright?" A thrill of excitement shot through her.

"Call me Daniel," he said. "I prefer it." His eyes seemed to sparkle with pleasure. Because of her? "I heard a noise and thought it might be the steward."

She gave a short, embarrassed laugh. "Trying to walk on a train while it's moving is a lot like being on the ocean. I don't seem to have my sea legs."

He grinned. "May I escort you somewhere? I'd hate for you to fall from a moving train."

"It would be nice to have someone along who could shout 'woman overboard' if the worst happens." She rolled her shoulders in a relaxed shrug. "I'm not actually going anywhere. Lady Wilmot wanted a private moment with her daughter, so I'm pacing."

She suddenly became aware of how alone they were. He seemed very close to her in the narrow hallway. She could smell the faint, woodsy scent that she would always associate with him, and it affected her like an intoxicant.

"In that case, would you like to join me in my compartment? With Attwood and Mr. Phipps gone, I'm on my own. I wish I'd thought to bring something with me to read. As it is, I've become bored with my own company. Perhaps you'd be willing to converse with me for a while."

She glanced down the empty passageway. Could she? A heartbeat later, she found herself gazing into Huntley's eyes.

She really shouldn't.

But she did. As she brushed past him into his compartment, the train gave an extra jolt, and Catherine fell against him. He wrapped his arm around her from behind to keep her from falling.

"I see what you mean." She turned her head to meet his gaze

as he grinned down at her from over her shoulder. "You're all fumble-footed."

One of his arms left her waist and he reached back, sliding the compartment door shut. Then, he wrapped both arms back around her, nuzzling his chin against her neck. "I like it when you fall into my arms," he murmured, gently kissing her neck, tickling her skin with his breath. "It reminds me of the night we officially met at Lady Wilmot's dinner. You tumbled off the ladder and into my arms."

A jolt of heat rushed through Catherine at the memory of that evening and their first intoxicating kiss. She leaned back against Daniel, savoring his firm chest and his arms encircling her waist. He was strong and warm. A woodsy fragrance with hints of leather and silk and something that was uniquely him enveloped her. He pressed his palm against her ribs, just below her breasts, and his heat seared through her stiff corset.

She closed her eyes, allowing the rhythmic beat of the train to synchronize with her own internal cadence. Its pulse filled her with a corresponding tempo that steadily grew stronger. She let out a soft sigh as he nuzzled her neck with gentle kisses.

How was it that this felt so normal? So natural?

"I have a surprise for you," Daniel murmured in her ear. "Would you like to know what it is?"

"A surprise?" Catherine's voice was breathless.

"It's my wedding gift to you. May I give it to you now? In fact, with your permission, I'd like to help you put it on."

Catherine turned in Daniel's arms to face him. "Put it on?" Was it jewelry? It must be jewelry. Perhaps a necklace—that would certainly be traditional. "Of course."

The grin he shot her was a bit too devilish. Perhaps she'd been too hasty in agreeing.

Daniel reached into his pocket, pulled out a long, slim, blue velvet box, and handed it to Catherine.

A jewelry box—a very heavy jewelry box.

She lifted the lid and discovered a small silver knife inside. It had a green malachite handle inset with a small engraved disk. "A knife?" Her jaw dropped in surprise. She also found a brown leather sheath and strap tucked into the box.

No one had ever given her something like this before. Well, Papa had given her a fencing mask, but this was different. This was a weapon of her own—a symbol of an entirely new area of knowledge and expertise, but even more importantly, one representing Daniel's acceptance of her true nature.

"I had it engraved."

Fumbling slightly in her excitement, Catherine removed the smooth, cool object from the box and located the words he'd had engraved on the disk. "*Petite souris*," she said, then grinned at him with delight. "Little mouse. How appropriate. It's perfect."

"I was certain you'd love it, *ma petite souris*. Now, my little mouse will have a sharp bite."

"I do love it."

"Its handle is made of malachite, the same as the letter opener on the Duke of Norfolk's desk." He gave her a wry look.

The letter opener he'd held to Stansbury's throat. "An excellent reminder of the importance of a good blade." She tested the edge with her finger, finding it sharper than she'd expected.

"Can I help you put it on?"

Something in his smile drew her attention. Why was he so intent on this particular question? "But it will hardly go with my dress," she pointed out. "And the strap is much too short to fit around my waist."

Daniel laughed. "That's not where you wear it," he said, his grin deepening as a wicked glint appeared in his eyes. "You wear it —somewhat lower."

Catherine's jaw dropped and her eyes grew wide as she realized that the strap was the perfect size to fit around her thigh. "Lord Huntley. That's hardly appropriate."

He looked crestfallen.

But slowly, a sly smile grew on her face until she was grinning back at him with a similar wicked glint in her eye. He'd earned her trust. He'd proven to her time and again that he valued her.

Perhaps it was time to let him see that having a wife who was a bit impetuous would have its advantages.

39

MALACHITE

A jolt of excitement hit Daniel when he noted that particular gleam in Catherine's eye. He was learning to appreciate that look. As a gentleman, he should release her from her promise, but now that she'd agreed to let him help, he couldn't deny himself. He'd never believed it would come to this. He'd been teasing her.

But she'd turned it back on him.

"Place your foot on the edge of the seat," he said as he pulled the butter-soft leather sheath from the box. "Your right foot, please, since you're right-handed. I chose the softest strap I could find. I didn't want it to chafe you."

Catherine blushed and glanced away as she placed her right boot on the edge of the seat.

He moved up behind her and grabbed the soft folds of her dress, sliding her full skirts up her leg. He was standing a little to the right of her, and his thighs pressed slightly against her hips as he leaned forward.

The loose pantalets Catherine wore fell just below her knees, and he edged the white cotton fabric up, revealing Catherine's soft, creamy white thigh.

Daniel froze for a moment and then slid his hand across her thigh, marveling at its perfection. Her body wasn't as soft as that of most women. Regular horseback riding and fencing had toned it over the years, and her long, smooth thighs reflected her many hours of exercise.

It took all of Daniel's self-control to keep him from stroking her leg.

Forcing himself back to his task, he took a steadying breath and slipped the soft leather strap around Catherine's thigh. He buckled it snuggly in place. A rectangle of lamb's wool directly under the buckle would keep the metal from irritating her skin. He gently slid his finger under the strap to reassure himself that he hadn't over-tightened it. Satisfied, he slipped her knife into its sheath.

His task was done, but he couldn't resist wrapping his other arm around her waist from behind. He flattened his palm against her belly and held her against his chest while his other hand lingered on the soft flesh of her inner thigh.

"Is it comfortable?" he murmured in her ear, barely trusting his voice. The heat of her thigh made his palm grow hot. He hated the thought of breaking that small, intimate contact with her.

When she didn't respond, Daniel realized her eyes were closed. Her blissful expression and rapid breathing told him she was as aroused as he was.

For a moment, he simply held her, becoming attuned to every infinitesimal change taking place in her body. With his hand against her ribs, he could feel her breathing accelerate as her heart rate quickened.

Her growing arousal fueled his own. When she pressed her hips back against his groin, he could't hold back the low moan that escaped his lips.

Did she know what she was doing to him?

The chuga-chuga-chuga sound of the train entwined with his

very soul. He closed his eyes as he let the rhythmic sensation fill him.

He began teasing her inner thigh with his fingertips as he slid his other hand across her breasts. He cupped one, wishing he could bare them, but he didn't dare undress her here in the train car. The corset she wore under her day dress pressed her breasts upward, and he could feel where the stiff corset ended and her soft bosom swelled above. His fingertips brushed against her erect nipple pressing against the thin fabric of her dress. Gently, he teased the small, firm bud, flicking at it with the rough edge of his thumb, and she let out a small gasp, allowing her head to fall back against his shoulder.

His lips quickly found the delicate spot below her ear that was now exposed to him. He savored the taste of her skin, continuing his gentle assault on her neck and breast while his other hand slid up the inside of her thigh, searching for the opening in her split pantalets. He deftly slipped his hand inside, moving unerringly toward the soft mound of curls hiding within. Catherine let out a soft, surprised gasp as his fingers gently cupped her mound. She pulled back from his hand, inadvertently pressing harder against his groin.

"What are you doing?" she murmured, her head popping upright and her eyes opening wide. He continued caressing her breasts, and a moment later her eyes slid closed again.

"Something I think you'll enjoy," Daniel murmured against her neck, nuzzling at the skin beneath her ear. She relaxed, letting him caress her as he tried to both soothe her need and arouse it to greater heights. Her head fell back against his shoulder.

As his fingers touched her inner folds, he discovered the slickness he had been certain he'd find.

Her entire body tensed. "Oh my!" she said, sounding more surprised than anything else.

He turned her sideways and pressed his lips against hers,

drawing her attention to their kiss. She responded tentatively at first, and then with a sudden burst of passion.

With his arm wrapped around her waist to keep her from falling, he used that same hand to hold her skirts up while he continued to stroke her. He pulled his slick finger from inside her and gently began to rub the small nub above her entrance while he simultaneously nibbled on her lower lip, sucking it into his mouth. Catherine's supporting leg began to tremble, and she let out a deep moan.

Daniel pulled her closer, supporting her weight so she wouldn't fall to the floor. He trailed kisses across her lips as he tried to hush her moans. "Shhhh. Be silent, my love," he whispered as he continued to assault her senses. His mouth traced its way to her ear, where he began to nibble on the pink lobe.

She seemed have given herself over entirely to sensation as she panted with frustration at the tension building within her.

A sudden tremor shook her body, followed quickly by another, and Daniel captured her mouth with his, swallowing the sound of her moans of release.

Lord, but she was passionate! He had suspected she would respond this way to him, but the knowledge left him elated. With his arms wrapped tightly around her, he held her close, her spent body resting limply against his. She let out a deep sigh of satisfaction and nuzzled her cheek against his chest.

He pulled her skirts back down, letting them fall gracefully to the floor. Would he ever be able to look at them again without imagining what lay beneath?

She recovered her footing and stepped away, returning to herself. A pang of regret hit him as the moment they'd shared evaporated, leaving a chill where her warmth had been. He ached to pull her back, to hold her just a little longer, but the growing distance in her eyes felt like an insurmountable chasm. He always felt that the brief time after passion receded was precious.

He gazed at her intently, but Catherine looked away. She

stepped back, increasing both the physical and emotional distance between them. She turned and stood with her back to him, one hand resting on the door latch.

"I—I—I don't know what to say," she said, her words barely audible. Her gaze darted to the door, then back to him, torn between the warmth of his gaze and the shadow of shame that crept in, uninvited. "I'm so ashamed. Nothing like that has ever...."

Her words hit him like a physical blow. He hadn't meant for her to feel this way. He'd simply been overwhelmed by her—to the point that he hadn't been able to think straight. Overwhelmed by the sheer temptation of her. "If it was shameful for you, then it was shameful for me as well, and I refuse to accept that. We'll be married soon. There should be no shame between us."

He reached out and took her hand, gently turning her to face him. She didn't want to meet his gaze, so he touched her under the chin. After a moment, she glanced up at him. "Please don't regret what we shared. I'm happy I was able to give you pleasure." He smiled, hoping to tease an answering smile from her.

Someone knocked at the door, and they both jumped.

"Lord Huntley?" Lady Wilmot called through the closed door.

Catherine gasped, stepping back so quickly that she nearly stumbled, her cheeks flushing a delicate pink. Daniel moved to open the door with a swift motion, meeting Lady Wilmot's narrowed gaze as she entered. Her critical eyes swept over the couple, then flicked around the compartment, evidently searching for signs of impropriety.

Daniel kept his expression calm, while Catherine, though composed, held herself with a slight stiffness, a lingering blush giving away her discomfort. Together, they projected a picture of respectability. After all, they had opened the door immediately, and they weren't even seated. What could possibly have happened in such a short time while they were standing?

"Lady Catherine, I'm surprised to find you in here—" Lady Wilmot's gaze locked onto the younger woman, "—with the door closed." Her tone was reproachful.

Catherine looked down, obviously embarrassed.

"That was my fault, Lady Wilmot," Daniel said, giving her his most charming smile. "I asked her to step inside because I wanted a word with her, and I closed the door without thinking."

Her scowl deepened. "You know better, Lord Huntley."

"My apologies, ladies," he said with a nod. "You're quite right. My enthusiasm got the better of me." He gave Lady Wilmot a chagrined smile. "I wanted to give Lady Catherine an engagement gift. I never considered the ramifications of closing the compartment door." His hand slid inside his jacket and pulled out a second identical velvet box.

Catherine gasped in surprise, her hand instinctively sliding to her thigh, clearly checking for the knife strapped there. Daniel smiled at the gesture.

Taking the slim box from his hand, Catherine looked perplexed. She lifted the lid and revealed a silver necklace set with alternating triangles of green-striped malachite and black onyx.

She let out a small gasp, her eyes misting with tears. The necklace had an Egyptian flair, with the triangular stones aligned so that the lower ring of malachite pointed up, while the upper ring of onyx pointed down, perfectly meshing into a dense, fourteen-inch necklace.

Her hands trembled as she lifted the necklace. "It's perfect," she breathed, a smile breaking through the lingering shadows of her embarrassment. Looking up at him, her eyes were full of a new, quiet kind of awe. "Thank you, Daniel. I love it." She made him feel as though she'd just given him an even greater gift.

"I'm glad you like it. It's an unusual piece. One of a kind. Just like you."

Lady Wilmot craned her neck, clearly curious to see what kind of necklace had inspired such delight in Catherine. Her face fell, however, once she caught sight of it. Clearly, she had expected something grander than simple malachite and onyx stones. She shot Huntley a startled look. "Malachite? How... unusual." She clamped her mouth shut.

Daniel caught her eye, and a shared smile passed between them, a silent promise of understanding. She reached for his hand, a brief squeeze to show him that she meant it—she did love it.

"I assure you, Lady Wilmot, that Lord Huntley couldn't have chosen a more perfect gift. I love it."

"Of course, dear," Lady Wilmot said, forcing a cheery smile to cover her faux pas. "It's lovely. And thank you for allowing me to have a few moments alone with Elizabeth. I'm going to return to your mother's compartment now. Would you care to join me, or will you return to Elizabeth?" Clearly, there was no third alternative.

"Thank you, Lady Wilmot. I believe I'll join Elizabeth."

Lady Wilmot stood waiting as Catherine stepped into the corridor, and then followed her out, sliding the door shut behind them.

40

STRIKING A DEAL

Lord Stansbury tailed the newly married couple to a flat in Oxford. The woman seemed jubilant, in stark contrast to the man's subdued demeanor. The pair went inside, and Stansbury tried to resign himself to a lengthy wait in the cold. He supposed Attwood wouldn't linger long. One never knew with a man barely wed, but judging by his posture as he'd walked through the door, he'd likely try to escape his bride at the earliest opportunity. Stansbury sneered at the thought; a fool who thought marriage to a wealthy chit would be easy was precisely the sort of man who deserved his fate.

There weren't many places where Stansbury could easily watch the flat without drawing undue attention, so he wandered from shop to shop on the street below, pretending to browse the wares and casually chatting with shop owners to glean whatever information he could about Attwood. At least the shops were warmer, and he was grateful for any break from the chill.

Everyone he spoke to seemed surprised to hear the flat had been rented after sitting empty for so long, which suggested that Mr. and Mrs. Attwood were new to the area. It was a fairly low-class district, though Stansbury could hardly be surprised.

Attwood had struck him as one of those men who had perhaps enjoyed refinement once but would never quite fit it. Stansbury could read a man's true character through the signs in his dress, his speech, and his demeanor if he cared to pay attention—and Stansbury always paid attention.

As a boy, he had once secretly followed his father to just such an area. The man would often leave the house carrying a wrapped item, only to return hours later, drunk and flush with money. It hadn't taken long for young Stansbury to realize his father had been selling off family heirlooms to pay his gambling debts; that much had been obvious even to a child. Stansbury had wanted to learn where his father went and how the transaction took place, hoping to copy the man if it became necessary. He'd grown tired of going hungry and vowed never to let himself or his fortunes be vulnerable to the same whims.

Now, he entered a pawn shop similar to the one he'd followed his father to all those years ago. He knew how to haggle for the best price, a skill he'd honed through necessity. Many of his family's possessions were scattered around London, in the hands of various pawnbrokers and collectors. Just a few weeks ago, in the home of an acquaintance, he'd recognized a longcase clock that had belonged to his great-grandfather. Its repaired casing had almost completely hidden the scratch his father's knife had left on its front. Though he hadn't minded losing that particular piece —its associations were tainted by far too many unpleasant memories—he hadn't enjoyed seeing it so casually displayed. It spoke to a part of his past he preferred to leave forgotten: too much blood, too much pain, and far too much death.

Today, though, he had few items to offer. He couldn't part with his warm cloak on a day as cold as this one, so he'd be forced to leave his pocket watch behind if he wanted enough cash to buy dinner and a return ticket home. He tried not to let the loss of the watch bother him. Once he was flush again, he could come back to Oxford and collect it. In the meantime, he'd consider this a minor setback—just another pawn in a game he knew well.

The negotiation was fierce. The odious pawnbroker pretended not to recognize the quality of the watch and only began to haggle in earnest when Stansbury followed through on his threat to leave. The man actually trailed him out the door and onto the damp, narrow street, and Stansbury didn't bother to hide his contempt. He knew he'd gained the upper hand, and the pawnbroker knew it too.

Once the transaction was complete, Stansbury walked away with even more money than he'd anticipated. Just as he stepped back into the cold, he caught sight of his quarry. Had he been seconds later, he might have missed the man entirely. Fortunately, his timing was perfect—hadn't everything been working in his favor today?

Attwood strode directly to a nearby pub, and Stansbury ducked in after him. He made a show of taking off his hat and coat in an angry huff, muttering under his breath as he approached the bar near Attwood's seat.

"Whiskey," Attwood told the bartender as he slumped onto a stool, looking as though he planned to settle in for a long stay.

"Certainly, Mr. Attwood," the bartender replied.

"I'll have the same," Stansbury added brusquely, catching the bartender's nod before both glasses were set down. He threw his coin onto the bar and raised his glass in a toast, eyeing Attwood with a smirk. "Here's to a good woman," he muttered darkly. "Just let me know if you ever find one. I never have."

Attwood snorted and tossed back his drink. "I just got married today," he announced, his bottom lip jutting out like a sullen child.

Stansbury raised a brow. "Then you're a fool. You don't sound particularly happy about it."

Attwood shrugged, his gaze fixed on the scarred wooden bar.

"Could be worse. Her father settled a bit of money on her. Just wish it was more." His tone reeked of dissatisfaction.

"Then why'd you marry the girl?"

Attwood gave him a sidelong glance. "You really want to know?"

Stansbury shrugged as though he could take it or leave it, but his expression showed the faintest glimmer of interest.

"Buy me a whiskey, and I'll tell you."

Stansbury let out a huff of disgust. "What, is she keeping you on a tight leash already? No ready cash?" He noted the way Attwood's jaw clenched and suppressed a smile. The man looked as though he'd like to take a swing at him, which only added to Stansbury's amusement.

"Buy me that drink," Attwood repeated, his tone petulant. "Think of it as a wedding gift."

Stansbury flicked a few coins onto the bar, signaling the bartender, and Attwood wasted no time in downing the drink, wiping his mouth with the back of his hand like a common laborer.

"The chit lied to me," he began. "Told me she had a big dowry, so I trotted her off to Gretna Green, quick as I could. Fathers don't usually approve of men like me, so if I wanted to marry her and get that dowry, it was the only way." A smug grin twisted his features. "The stupid girl actually believed I loved her. When we stopped at an inn for the night, she let slip the true amount of her dowry. I couldn't get out of there fast enough. Truth be told, even before then, I was wondering how long I could tolerate her. That mouth of hers never stops. Goes on from sunup to sundown."

Stansbury let out a low chuckle. "So how'd you end up married, then?"

Attwood's grin widened. "Buy me another whiskey, and I'll tell you the rest."

Annoyed at his own curiosity, Stansbury plunked down

another coin, eyeing Attwood with contempt. If given the chance, Attwood would bleed him dry.

Once he'd drained his third glass, Attwood sighed. "Her father's got powerful friends. Tracked me down in London, and now I'm stuck. Not only am I married, but her money's locked up in an irrevocable trust as tight as a miser's fist." He glowered into his glass. "I can't touch it, even if she dies."

Stansbury felt an instinctive wince. An irrevocable trust— every man's nightmare. What had the world come to, with women able to control their money in such a way? "Then why in blazes did you go through with it? Why sign over your rights like that?"

"Those powerful friends I mentioned? They sweetened the pot, so to speak. Doubled her dowry." Attwood's eyes narrowed as if savoring the memory. "Huntley got involved, too. He kept me locked up in his house so I couldn't slip away, 'Not that we don't trust you,'" he said, his tone mocking as he mimicked Huntley's pomposity. "Ha!"

"Huntley?" Stansbury's eyes gleamed as he seized on the name. "The marquess? Scottish fellow?"

"That's the one. You know him?" Attwood looked at him with the first spark of real interest he'd shown.

"Know him? The man's a menace. Puts on airs like he's a saint, but he's a filthy cur." Stansbury could see the appreciation in Attwood's face, as if relishing that someone else shared his disdain. "He destroyed me financially. Ruined me. Stole my fiancée right from under my nose. I'd give anything to see him laid low."

Attwood smirked. "I knew it. That pompous ass! He actually thinks he's above us all. I should have broken his nose when I had the chance."

Stansbury let his words hang in the air, watching Attwood's expression change as the man weighed the possibilities. "Seems we have a common enemy," he continued, extending his hand with a calculating smile. "The enemy of my enemy is my friend, as they say. Stansbury is the name—*the Earl of Stansbury,* to be exact."

Attwood leapt from his stool and gave an awkward bow. "Your lordship," he stammered, eyes wide, "I had no idea—"

"No, you wouldn't. But perhaps we can be of assistance to one another, Mr. ...?"

"Attwood. Charles Attwood at your service, m'lord." The man straightened, his face a mixture of eagerness and deference.

Stansbury hid his satisfaction behind a mild smile, considering the beginnings of what might prove to be a useful alliance. Huntley wouldn't know what hit him.

❧ 41 ❧

REVERBERATIONS

The following day, Daniel sat alone in his study and read the same line of the contract he was reviewing for the fourth time. His mind kept drifting back to those moments he'd spent alone with Catherine on the train. He pushed the papers aside with a frustrated groan. He felt torn, Catherine's memory lingering stubbornly in his mind. Why did it seem she could unravel his every resolve with a single glance, a mere brush of her hand?

He'd been much too careless in that train compartment. What if Lady Wilmot had opened the door just one minute sooner? If they'd been caught, the consequences for her would have been disastrous, and the thought made his stomach churn. Catherine deserved more than to be subject to scandal because he couldn't control himself.

Another week. He sighed, pushing back from his desk and rising to his feet. He'd simply have to exercise self-control. To that end, he'd ensure that he wasn't tempted again. He needed to avoid any situation where he might find himself alone with Catherine. He paced the room to release some of his restless energy.

He forced himself to face the uncomfortable truth—he couldn't simply ignore her impact on him. He would marry her, and yet, he was determined to guard himself against any further lapses in propriety. His life had been ordered and controlled until now. He couldn't let that slip because of desire.

Public meetings would be acceptable, of course—but no more private encounters. As long as their relationship remained public, he was confident he'd able to keep his physical attraction for her under control. The risk came in being alone with her.

He gazed blankly toward the window, and an image of her crystallized in his mind. He could see her face as she gasped in unrestrained passion. He groaned, spinning on his heel, banishing the memory from his thoughts. He needed to stop remembering her on the train. He glanced down at the bulge in his trousers and grimaced.

He reminded himself of Catherine's unsuitability as a wife, hoping that would help cool his ardor. He'd come to London with a plan, and she'd destroyed it with her foolish risks.

No, that wasn't fair. If not for her risks, anything could have happened to him the night he'd been attacked. He owed her an enormous debt, and he intended to repay it. He'd treat her well, and he'd do his best to respect her choices, even when they didn't correspond to his.

He'd always refused to accommodate people who tried to force him into a role he didn't want to play, and he'd be damned if he'd force Catherine into being someone she wasn't. She'd never be a prim and proper wife, and he'd known that before he'd asked for her hand in marriage.

He glanced down at his trousers to ensure that he'd regained control of his own body, and then he headed down the hallway toward the kitchen. He burst through the door, causing the cook to drop a container of flour, spilling it all over the counter.

"Lord Huntley. You startled me," Mrs. Meigs said. "Is there anything I can be getting you?"

He grimaced. Why was he in here? He'd just needed to move, and his legs had automatically carried him here. When he'd been a boy, he'd always sought out the comfort of the kitchens.

He noticed the startled expressions on the faces of the cook and her staff, so he pasted a polite smile on his face. "I'd like a pot of tea sent to my study. And some bread and cheese." He turned on his heel and sped back toward his office. The kitchen hadn't been the comforting retreat he'd needed, and he still felt restless.

His thoughts immediately flew back to Catherine, like homing pigeons. An ideal wife was not in the cards for him. He shook his head. Wentworth had been right. His goal of having the perfect bride had been a foolish dream. It had been conjured by the lonely and isolated child who still hid in his core, but he wasn't that person any longer. He was a man, accountable for his own actions and his own decisions.

Reentering his study, Daniel thought about his moldering old mansion in Scotland. It had never been a home— at least, not for him. He slid his hand into his pocket, fingering the smooth metal of his pocket watch.

As he pictured Catherine in his childhood abode, the scene changed, becoming brighter. The fire and passion she carried within her seemed to bring life to that dismal place. As the image of her standing in those drafty halls bloomed in his mind, he saw something new—a light, where before there'd only been shadows. She would bring a warmth and vibrancy to those stone walls, a liveliness that had never truly existed there. She was the fire he needed—the spark to begin anew, to make the old place into something worthy of a family.

Catherine would be the foundation of his new family, not that tumbling-down eyesore.

As he imagined the old building, its form seemed to undergo a transformation in his mind's eye. It had been sorely neglected by the past two marquesses, but five generations had lived there. It was time to set aside his childhood loathing of the place and recognize the gem that had been hidden there all along.

No man is an island, as John Donne had written so many years ago—words that felt as true now as they had then. His father had tried to create an island of isolation within that house to protect himself from the pain of losing Daniel's mother, but he had ended up losing so much more in the end.

Daniel had realized that by putting off searching for a wife and creating his own life, he'd begun walking down that same path.

In a burst of inspiration, he decided he was finally ready to restore the manse. A sixth generation would call it home, but this time it would different— it would be a place of kindness, warmth, and refuge.

He turned to the shelves behind his desk, searching for the plans he'd tucked away. When he spied the long leather cylinder, he plucked it from the shelf. He pulled the furled papers from within it and laid them out on a nearby table, using paperweights to keep the large drawings from curling back into a tube again. He stared at the heavy piece of glass he held in his hand, recalling the day Catherine had tried to release him from his promise to marry her.

Returning to his desk, he pulled out a sheet of paper and began to write a letter to his estate manager in Scotland, instructing him to begin implementing the plans Daniel had drafted five years ago to restore the main house. The man would be pleased to begin the task. He'd been urging Daniel to take action for years.

He realized with a jolt of surprise that he now had two homes to renovate: his original one in Scotland and his new Savelle estate outside London.

His purpose felt rekindled, and a newfound energy surged within him. He'd rebuild from the ground up, not only in Scotland but here in London, establishing a home—a legacy—for them both.

He'd need a second letter.

"Madson," he shouted. "I have some messages!"

42

A PLAN

"Blast it!" Stansbury crumpled the note he'd just read and tossed it onto the floor of his study, in the general vicinity of the fireplace.

"What's wrong? Bad news?" Attwood drawled. He'd only arrived a few minutes ago, wearing the expensive new clothing his wife had purchased.

"The ship still hasn't arrived. No ship means nothing to sell and no money coming in. And by now, even when it does arrive, it'll be too late. The advantage of being early to market has evaporated. Too many other speculators made the same gamble on the same commodities. Now they'll flood London with the same items I thought would be scarce."

Stansbury kicked the leg of his chair, knocking it over with a loud bang.

Attwood turned his back on Stansbury and examined the bookcase.

Smart man. He's learned when to keep his head down to avoid having it bitten off.

Most of the books that had formerly graced the bookshelves

had been sold, some by Stansbury, but most by his father. Attwood selected a slim volume and leafed through it.

Stansbury turned back to his desk, his hand trembling as he sorted his bills. His creditors were becoming more and more insistent. Three months ago, he'd drained his first investor's funds to cover his most pressing debts, but his other creditors were still clamoring for what he owed them.

Fretting, he shuffled through the papers again, trying to place them in order of priority. Gambling debts, of course, must take precedence. Those were debts of honor, and it would be unseemly not to pay them. The ones that absolutely must be paid were on top, those that could be delayed a week or two came next, and any that could be delayed a bit longer went to the bottom. The remainder he chucked into the wastebasket below his desk.

Unfortunately, the pile that remained was far too large, with those requiring immediate payment making up the bulk of it.

He needed a solution, fast, and he had already begun to consider drastic measures. The old warehouse he'd acquired on the East End could be useful—it was tucked away from prying eyes and empty until that shipment arrived. It might serve him well in the future, a place to plot undisturbed. Stansbury scowled, his thoughts racing. Everything had gone so wrong, yet he could still salvage some dignity, perhaps even orchestrate Huntley's ruin. That, at least, would be satisfying.

Stansbury smacked the stack of bills onto his desk and grabbed the fallen chair, righting it with a clatter.

Attwood whirled at the commotion and cocked an eyebrow.

Stansbury glared at him. "This situation is intolerable. Every-thing has gone wrong." Walking behind the chair, he shook his head. "My streak of bad luck has lasted for over a year now. One business deal after another has withered away, and to make matters worse, each heiress I offered for turned me down. Me! The Earl of Stansbury! My title is one of the oldest in England. It goes back to 1074 when William the Conqueror created it!" His voice thundered in the nearly empty room.

He clenched the back of his chair, his knuckles growing white with the force of his grip. "Women should be *begging* to marry me, if only for my title. Instead, they had the temerity to refuse me."

"Why not marry some rich American heiress? That's what I'd do if I had a title to peddle. At least you'd be able to offer something in exchange for the dowry. I had nothing, and that solicitor Calliope's father forced me to deal with wouldn't let me forget it."

Stansbury bristled. "I refuse to marry someone beneath me. I'd never debase myself by pairing with a lowly American or some upstart from the *middle class*." He said the words as though they were a curse. "I'd rather die." He might have fallen low, but not that low. "No, my wife *must* be the daughter of a peer. Anything less would be intolerable." He shoved at the back of the chair as he stepped away from it, almost causing it to topple over again.

"I can't fault you there. Calliope is unbearable. Her father may have settled a sizable dowry on her, but she still holds the purse strings. It's that damned marriage contract they made me sign. Now I'm forced to ask her for every penny I spend. It's unnatural. A man shouldn't have to degrade himself by begging his wife for money."

"Bah!" Stansbury's voice echoed in the nearly empty study that had once been filled with priceless objects. His grimace deepened as he considered how his current dilemma could have been averted with the influx of some cash. "It's that bastard, Huntley. He's behind all this. First he scuttled my business deals, then my marriage plans. He had no right swooping in and plucking the Kensington chit from my grasp. He's entirely responsible for my current straits. I invested two years in wooing Catherine. I had her in the palm of my hand. She was on the brink of saying yes. I could read it in her eyes. The audacity of that man, interrupting my marriage proposal with one of his own!"

"She's a silly, stupid wench for choosing to accept *Huntley's* proposal," Attwood sneered, fueling Stansbury's anger.

"She'll soon learn he isn't the hero she thinks he is. He's only sniffing around for her money. He might do well in business, but it will take a lot more than he's managed to accumulate to restore that falling down estate in Scotland. Once her gold lines his coffers, he'll find a way to hide her away in that drafty castle of his. Mark my words, he'll be a recluse, just like his father. I'd never treat her that badly." He pinned Attwood with a glare. "A thorn in my side. That's what Huntley is. A thorn in my side."

"Didn't you tell me that every time your business deals go bad, Huntley makes money?" Attwood smirked. "I've heard that the man has King Midas's golden touch."

"And now that damned Midas touch has spilled over into his personal life, destroying all my plans." Stansbury considered taking his anger out on the chair again by kicking it, but thought better of it. He didn't want to break a toe.

"Could there be more behind it than luck? It can't be a coincidence that Huntley always triumphs when you fail, can it?"

The comment brought Stansbury up short. Could Attwood be right? Could Huntley be *intentionally* working against him? Up until now he'd assumed Huntley only caused him misfortune because the man was focused on making money and defeating his rivals. What if it was more than that? What if Huntley had singled him out for reprisal?

That might be the case. The more Stansbury thought about it, the more it made sense. He approached the fireplace, its embers glowing as hotly as his anger toward Huntley. "Maybe he's been working against me for years. Maybe this is his revenge for the fact that I plucked a couple of ripe contracts out from under him." He chuckled. "Did I tell you about that? I was able to swoop in and steal them out from under his nose. I made quite a lot on those deals." He scowled. "But that didn't work for long. I thought that last shipping contract would set me up for years, but it turned out to be a bad one. Dreadful even. It wiped out all my previous earnings. I'm certain Huntley knew— he tricked me into pursuing it, knowing I'd lose everything."

And now the man wanted to claim Catherine.

Catherine. Little Cat. He smiled, thinking about the way the minx had squirmed so deliciously when he'd pressed her against the wall in the duke's study. A girl like that would provide many nights of pleasure, especially when he made her scream like a cat in heat. A wildcat. He'd seen the passion in her eyes. Even now, his body responded to the memory of her writhing against him. Wouldn't she'd be amazing in his bed? Especially once she'd learned how to please him. Teaching her would be an amazing experience as well.

Unfortunately, it was one he'd never have. That cur Huntley had ruined all his careful plans. "That self-righteous ass! He thinks himself so superior."

"Just because he has money, it doesn't make him superior," Attwood said. His tone held a mixture of commiseration and persuasion.

At first, Attwood's comment barely registered with Stansbury, but when he realized the man had echoed his own words, he scowled.

Attwood cocked his head to one side. "It's a shame. The two of you are so similar. Why is it that where he succeeds, you fail?"

"Everything always goes his way, doesn't it? It's because of his grand title and his money. All but the most discerning members of society welcome him with open arms while turning their noses up at me. Too many of the others are ready to sell their daughters off to him. There are even some who ignore the way he flaunts his shipping company. At least I have the decency to be circumspect in my business dealings. I follow the rules. He breaks them. The man is detestable. How is it he's led such a charmed life? Of course, there's his childhood. Did you know Huntley's father was stark raving mad?"

Recently, Stansbury had started trying to bring the man down — discreetly, of course. He didn't want to find himself on the wrong end of a blade. Ever since the Norfolk ball, he'd been spreading rumors that Huntley was overextended and needed cash. When someone repeated the rumor he'd created back to him, he knew it had taken hold. He'd nearly crowed with delight. Maybe now everyone would see what a wastrel man really was.

He cast a sideways glance at Attwood, a thought forming. He might need that warehouse sooner than he'd realized—a place where things could be arranged far from the civilized circles where Huntley and his ilk enjoyed their charmed lives. He hadn't mentioned it to anyone, but in the back of his mind, he'd been tallying what he could use to change his fortunes. And now, with Attwood by his side, perhaps his prospects weren't so dim after all.

"Somehow that doesn't surprise me," Attwood said. "Maybe his rule-breaking is a symptom of his own growing madness. After all, he *did* hold me captive against my will."

Stansbury immediately latched onto the idea. "I hear that as a boy, his father completely ignored him. Forgot he even existed. Could that have sown the seeds of insanity within him? By the time the old marquess finally tipped up his toes, the entire region's economy was in ruins because he hadn't bothered to keep an estate manager." Stansbury shook his head. "I still don't know how Huntley managed to come back from that. How did he build his shipping business when he started at such a disadvantage? He created it from nothing."

"Not from nothing. Didn't you say he had timber to sell?"

"That's right, I did. I'd forgotten that." Stansbury glanced at his sparsely furnished room. He'd had things to sell as well, but only in bits and pieces. "But I still don't understand how he did it. I tried to do the very same things, but everything I touched turned to dust. How is it that things turned out so differently for me?"

Was it better to have a drunken madman as a father, like Huntley, or a drunken gambler? His own father had usually been absent, but when he'd been around, he'd been intoxicated. He'd been a mean drunk, too. At an early age, Stansbury had learned to disappear when Father was home and remain as invisible as possible.

Mother had normally provided a diversion, distracting Father away from him; however, it had never been intentional, but simply a byproduct of her mercurial moods. She'd been an unstable woman. She'd be happy and laughing at one moment, screaming the next. When Father was home, her anger had a focal point, and she directed all of her frustration with her life at the man she held responsible— but when Father was gone, she became despondent, and her focus would shift to her son.

"So his father ignored him and his mother was dead?" Attwood asked.

Stansbury shrugged. He wished he'd had the same benefit. It had been worse with Father away, because then Mother threw things at him. But he could always duck out of the way of flying shoes and teacups. The worst was when she'd lock him away in a room. If not for the servants, she'd probably have forgotten him, leaving him to starve or die of thirst. He was fairly sure that was what had happened to his pet cat. It had disappeared one day after annoying Mother, never to be seen again. He'd always suspected she'd locked it in a trunk and then forgotten about it. He'd never risked caring about an animal again after that.

As a child, he'd learned to avoid his parents because he was better off when they forgot about him. Nannies hadn't been willing to endure the chaos in their household for long, so after the fourth one left, his parents had given up. He'd become so good at remaining invisible that nobody ever bothered with his education until he was about twelve. Around then, Father finally took enough notice to send him away to school.

"I knew Huntley at Eton," Attwood said, interrupting Stansbury's thoughts. "He got me expelled." He plopped down on the sofa and a puff of dust burst from it, drifting in the weak sunlight.

"What? He went to Eton?" Stansbury hadn't attended such a lofty school. Since his education had been neglected for such a long time, he'd been enrolled someplace less demanding, but even so, he'd found himself at an appalling disadvantage. The other boys and the teachers made him feel the fool, always struggling to catch up to where he should have been. When the other boys had free time, Stansbury was either holed up in his stifling room studying or closeted with an annoyed teacher who was trying to teach him things he should have already known.

At first, sensing his weakness, the other boys had teased and bullied him— but they had stopped. He'd *made* them stop. He'd already taken more than his share of abuse at home. He refused to endure it at school as well. He still looked back on that part of his life with a mingled sense of triumph and shame. Nobody had been able to prove he'd started all those fires, but the other boys left him alone after that. It had been an easy matter to sneak into his tormentors' rooms and set fires while the boys were out with friends. He'd gloated over their misfortune in a way that left them with no doubt that he was the culprit. They'd never accused him though, and he'd been able to finish his education in relative peace.

Setting the fires achieved his goal, but at great personal cost. He'd never known he was capable of causing so much pain and damage until he'd unleashed his pent-up anger on those boys. Provoking their fear had proved to be an effective solution, and it had left him feeling powerful. Perhaps he could employ a similar solution with Huntley. He'd love to see that man quake in terror. Anything to bring him down.

"Bollocks! I detest that bloody Huntley!" Stansbury snarled. A warm glow of pleasure filled him as he imagined making Huntley squirm. And Lady Catherine... he'd love seeing her squirm too, but in an entirely different way. "Maybe she can still be mine," he mumbled, half to himself. "I can't simply let her go, not with the money she'd bring to the marriage."

Certainly not with what I know about her secret life. There has to be a way to turn that knowledge to my advantage.

This was one secret he didn't want to share with Attwood. At least, not yet.

"If you could dispose of Huntley, she couldn't marry him. She'd be free to marry you." Attwood said, dripping the poisonous, honeyed words into Stansbury's ear.

Stansbury could see what Attwood was doing, but for once, the man's honeyed words struck a chord. He shot Attwood a skeptical look. He didn't trust the man. He was altogether too smooth and manipulative. He'd begun to wonder why he'd thought it wise to enlist him in his vendetta against Huntley. "Why do you care who I marry?"

"He got me expelled from Eton. He kept me a prisoner. He helped that lot force me to marry a woman I detest. Because of him I'm now kept on a leash like a pet. Isn't that enough? I want to hurt him in every way possible. I want to destroy him. If you can find a way to take Lady Catherine from him, then all the better."

Stansbury mulled over the idea. With Huntley gone, Catherine would have no protector, making his own offer of marriage her only recourse to avoid ruin.

"I like you, Attwood. You have a devious mind. Let's see if we can put our heads together and devise a plan to destroy the marquess. Perhaps we can even arrange circumstances so that we can line our pockets in the process. It would be the ultimate victory to steal both his wealth and his woman." Stansbury chortled with glee. "The perfect revenge—swift, merciless, and deliciously bitter."

43

LESS THAN A WEEK

O n Monday afternoon, less than a week before Catherine's wedding, she and her mother called on Mrs. Tidwell. Apparently, they arrived on the heels of another pair of callers.

The foyer was dim after the bright winter sunlight, and Catherine was momentarily blinded.

"Catherine. What a wonderful surprise." Elizabeth's delighted voice greeted her.

Catherine reached out, fumbling slightly as her eyes adjusted to the dim light, and took Elizabeth's hand. She squeezed it lightly before removing her cloak. She was relieved to have a friend here to break up the monotonous series of afternoon calls.

Elizabeth linked arms with her, and they walked into the drawing room together, followed by their mothers.

"Welcome, ladies," Mrs. Tidwell said. "Lady Catherine. I hope you'll allow me to extend my felicitations on your upcoming marriage."

Catherine murmured her thanks.

Elizabeth pulled her to one side while the three older ladies talked, saying, "Let's take a turn around the room, shall we? I need to speak to you."

Catherine cocked an eyebrow and then looked around the small space pointedly. "Don't tell me you need to stretch your legs. That could be a challenge in here." The small room was bursting with knickknacks and furniture, not leaving much room to maneuver.

"I wanted to ask you about your engagement to Huntley," Elizabeth said in a hushed voice. "Are you happy about it? Are you certain of your decision?"

"What? Of course I'm certain." Catherine said emphatically, causing Mother's gaze to snap toward them. Catherine noted her attention and smiled reassuringly at her.

Unfortunately, they also attracted the attention of some of the other young ladies in the room. Lady Lydia Larchmont and her compatriot, Lady Mary Givvens, were also paying a social call.

"It must be a love match," Lady Lydia said languidly. "Why else would she marry him unless she wanted the title? Everyone knows that his estate in Scotland is a disaster. That ridiculous house he just purchased will consume the entirety of his funds."

Elizabeth's eyes grew wide. "Lydia!"

Lady Mary Givvens snickered. "I heard he was trying to find a bride who could fund the renovations on his estate in Scotland. People are saying he's short on money." Mary and Lydia trained their gazes on Catherine with almost identical narrow, assessing expressions.

Catherine could only stare at her in confusion.

"Oh, Catherine. I'm so sorry. I assumed you knew." Lady Lydia's eyes glittered with false sympathy.

Elizabeth didn't appear surprised by Lydia's accusation. She must have heard the rumor as well. Where on earth had it started?

Then it hit her. Lydia. The woman scorned.

Seeing Lydia's gloating expression, Catherine summoned the

grace and aplomb she'd cultivated over the years. What had Mother always said? *Don't let anyone take the upper hand. Always remain in control.* The same advice applied in fencing. Never allow your opponent to take the higher ground or the upper hand.

She raised her chin, her gaze becoming steely. "Lady Lydia, I'm surprised at you. Although I wouldn't dream of discussing my fiancé's financial situation, the *marquess*," she said, stressing his title, "has been quite forthcoming with me." She refused to allow Lydia to believe she had scored a point. "For you to suggest otherwise is appalling," she continued, her tone sharp. "One might question your motive in spreading such rumors, especially given how upset you were when you learned of our engagement at the Norfolk ball."

The gloating look fled Lady Lydia's eyes, and they narrowed in seething anger. "At least I don't have the misfortune to be engaged to the wastrel. Just wait until he hides you away in Scotland in that moldering old castle." A malicious grin twisted her face. "You'll never see London again. He'll leave you isolated and penniless." Lady Lydia turned with an audible huff, composed her face, and crossed the small room to her mother. Lady Mary scurried after her.

Elizabeth opened her mouth to speak, but Catherine held her hand up to stop her. "There are things between Daniel and me of which you know nothing. Rest assured he is the man for me. I'm perfectly satisfied with our engagement."

"What are you girls whispering about?" Lady Wilmot's imperious voice interrupted them. She glanced at the departing forms of Lydia and Mary and then narrowed a suspicious gaze at Elizabeth and Catherine.

Turning her back on Elizabeth, Catherine gave Lady Wilmot a sharp smile. "We were just discussing wedding plans. There is so much to do, and so little time. My wedding is less than a week away."

LATER THAT DAY, CATHERINE AND HER MOTHER MET IN THE morning room and began sorting through the guest responses for the wedding breakfast. Catherine was surprised when Percy entered at around six o'clock, bearing a gentleman's calling card.

"He instructed me to say that Lord Huntley requested he meet with you, Lady Catherine," said Percy.

"Really?" She glanced at her mother with surprise. "Then, by all means, show him in."

Mother gave her a questioning look, but Catherine merely shrugged.

Percy ushered the man into the room.

"Jonathon Newcomb," he declared, "at your service," and bowed with a deep flourish, which was exaggerated by the long tube he held. It was about thirty inches long and three inches in diameter.

The tall slim man could have been almost any age. Catherine guessed that he was youngish, but his thinning dark blond hair gave him the look of an older man. His pale gray eyes were set in a mild face. His patterned vest was more elaborate than most men wore, but somehow it suited him.

"Lord Huntley has engaged my services to perform improvements at the Savelle estate he purchased outside London," Newcomb said, speaking to Catherine. "When we met this afternoon, he instructed me to consult with you as soon as possible."

"Me? But I haven't even seen the property." Catherine glanced at her mother for some guidance in this unusual situation, but she looked entirely bemused as well.

"It is quite lovely, I assure you," Mr. Newcomb said. "I'm here to learn about your tastes and preferences so I can incorporate them into the overall design."

Mr. Newcomb pulled a pocket watch from his vest and consulted it before snapping it closed and replacing it. "If you have a few minutes to spare, m'lady, I can stay to discuss some details with you, or if you prefer, we can make arrangements to meet at a time more convenient to you."

How intriguing. "I have some time now, Mr. Newcomb. Perhaps you could explain further."

"Of course, of course. Lord Huntley has engaged me to assist with the interior of the house. As you're aware, he's making extensive renovations, both to the manse and to the surrounding environs." He waved his hands vaguely in the air, the tube making his movements all the more dramatic. "There are many different tradesmen involved in the work. The furnishings were included in the purchase, and although there are many excellent pieces, the overall décor is quite dated."

"You said you spoke with him this afternoon?"

"Yes, m'lady. I came directly here. I would have sent a note first, but there was no time. Lord Huntley wants me to complete my plans quickly, since you will be leaving for Scotland soon." He chuckled deeply. "I don't envy you all of the renovations you will face over the upcoming year."

She looked at him quizzically. "All of the renovations? But we'll be in Scotland for months. Won't the majority of them be complete before we return?"

"Here, yes. But the ones in Scotland have yet to begin." At her look of confusion, he asked, "Didn't Lord Huntley inform you? His home in Scotland has fallen into a terrible state of disrepair. All of his efforts have been focused on the lands surrounding the castle, but now he has decided to fully restore the house as well." He eyed her more keenly. "I was operating under the assumption he had discussed it with you. He commented that you played a large part in his decision to rebuild his ancestral home. I truly hope I haven't spoken out of turn."

"He'll be renovating two houses, including his entire estate in Scotland, over the next year?" she said, trying to come to terms with the enormity of the tasks. "Are you quite certain?"

"Well, really just the two houses. He has already put most of his estate plan into place." He paused, and then confided, "I've seen his estate plan, and I must say, your fiancé is a man of vision and forethought. I'm accustomed to working with people who have creative vision, but his goes much beyond my ken. There is a certain brilliance in his thinking that I have seldom encountered."

A flash of fierce pride hit Catherine. *My fiancé.* "Mr. Newcomb, if you could provide me with an overview of the plans today, perhaps we could arrange to meet soon to discuss the details."

"Yes, m'lady. I would like to get a sense of your tastes with regard to color and decor so that when I return, I can offer some alternatives for you to consider. Perhaps some sketches would help."

Mr. Newcomb pulled an end-cap off the long tube and extracted the architectural drawings of the proposed changes to the house outside London. Or rather, the huge mansion outside London, Catherine mentally corrected herself upon seeing the drawings. Mother stood at her shoulder as they listened to Mr. Newcomb describe all of the changes planned.

Catherine quickly grasped the details. She could easily envision the final product based on Newcomb's drawings and descriptions. He recommended altering the main entrance by replacing the current façade with a rounded two-story addition full of windows and light. His exterior drawing made it look like something from a fairy tale. "This is beautiful, Mr. Newcomb. I can see why Lord Huntley chose you."

"Thank you, my lady." He fumbled as he re-rolled the drawings, stuffing them back into the tube. "Unfortunately, I need to be going. Thank you for sharing your preferences. May I return tomorrow to show you my changes? I hope you'll be pleased with them."

"Of course. I look forward to your call." Catherine watched as the slim man hurried from the room. He seemed already preoccupied with his next task, offering only a quick nod as he departed.

"That seems like quite a lot for Huntley to be doing all at once," Mother said. "Between running a business, renovating two large homes, and adjusting to marriage, he won't have much stability in his life. Just imagine the cost." She shot Catherine a worried glance.

"I'm sure everything will be fine."

Mother gave her a chastising look. "Really, Catherine. You should know better. People will talk, especially with a hasty engagement. Try not to say or do anything that would add fuel to the fire."

44

A PROMISE

The next evening, Charles and Catherine were finally able to resume their weekly trek to Bernini's. With the excursion to Oxford upsetting her plans last week, they hadn't been able to go to the academy, so she was anticipating the evening even more keenly than usual.

A rainstorm had passed through London a short time earlier, and now the streets were washed clear of dirt and debris. Spring was coming, and Catherine was convinced she could see small buds developing on the trees in the park near the academy. Surely, those were daffodils popping up from the soil. She was having trouble focusing on what Charles was saying as he recounted some conversation he'd had at the Ambridge Club last night.

"And of course, someone had to mention their concerns about Huntley being a fortune hunter," he said.

That certainly grabbed her attention. "You've heard the rumor, too?" Catherine asked.

"Of course." He glanced around and lowered his voice. "You're *marrying* the man, after all. You didn't think someone would mention it to me? There's no need to worry, though. Your fiancé is financially secure. I had someone investigate both Huntley and Stansbury immediately following the ball."

"You what?" Catherine could only stare at her brother in disbelief.

Charles gave her a cocky half smile. "You thought I was just a pretty face? All looks and no substance?"

Catherine reached out to try to poke him in the ribs, but he leaned away in his saddle, causing his horse to veer away.

"During my investigation, I discovered that while Huntley is financially sound, Stansbury's situation is abysmal."

"Really? Stansbury is doing that badly?" She thought a moment and then nodded. "I shouldn't be surprised. He *did* resort to blackmail. He must have been desperate." A sprinkling of rain began to fall, and Catherine pulled her hat down more firmly.

"Another interesting thing I found: the only people who mentioned Huntley's insolvency were ones who never had any business dealings with him." Charles's hat had a narrow brim, and his cheek gleamed in the streetlights from the droplets of rain. "Unfortunately, that tends to be the majority of the peerage. Everyone who ever dealt with him in business spoke of him in the most glowing of terms. They scoffed at the rumors that he was low on cash. Over the past few years, he's amassed a considerable fortune." He glanced at Catherine, brushing some of the rain from his face. "I checked, and I have yet to come across a single one of his investments that failed to turn a profit. He is either extremely lucky or extremely talented, and you know I'm not much of a believer in luck. It's usually a product of hard work."

"Why do you think this rumor is circulating?"

For a moment, all she heard were the soft sounds of rain and the clattering of horse hooves hitting the cobblestones. "I've been thinking about that. At first I thought it might be a business rival, but the rumor is so obviously false that anyone with any acumen would never have concocted it. It must either be someone who is jealous of his success or someone who sees him as a rival and wants to diminish him in the eyes of society."

Catherine rolled the possibilities around in her head. Lord Larchmont seemed the obvious choice. She immediately dismissed Stansbury. He'd been much too intimidated by Daniel's threats at the Norfolk Ball. Charles made a good point that it might be someone who saw him as a rival. Unfortunately, she didn't know enough about his business to hazard a guess as to whom it might be.

As they entered the main fencing salon a few minutes later, Catherine took a deep breath. She hardly noticed the musty odor of the building after so many years, but she'd know she was in Bernini's even if she were blindfolded.

As Catherine took her place opposite Charles to practice, she glanced around the room, surreptitiously searching for Daniel.

He was nowhere in sight.

She was disappointed, but she shook off the feeling as she slipped her fencing mask into place.

"En garde," Charles reminded her.

She smiled to herself. He took his role as older brother so seriously. "Drills?" she asked.

"Of course."

"Lunge, counterattack?"

"Actually, I'd like to try something different," he said. A crafty smile flickered across his face. "The last time I came here without you, we worked on 'disruption beats.' The idea is to establish a pattern of defense in order to lull your opponent into assuming that you'll continue to use that same defense in that same pattern. Then you alter the force of the beats, thereby disrupting your opponent's defense. Understand?"

"I'm not sure, but I like the sound of it," Catherine said, intrigued. "Step me through it."

"For this drill, one partner needs to perform an advance-attack," he said, specifying a move in which a fencer would move forward, advancing toward his opponent, while initiating the attack. The move quickly closed the distance between the opponents.

"The defender then beats back the attack," Charles continued, referring to a move in which he would hit the side of his opponent's foil, pushing the tip to one side. It could be used in many different situations in fencing, but here, it should cause his opponent to miss the target. "I want you to take the role of the attacker. You need to perform an advance-attack repeatedly for this drill. I'll beat your foil to one side each time."

"I can manage that."

"When you least expect it, I'll execute a disruption beat to score a point against you." He gave her a wicked grin.

Not if she could help it. She cocked one eyebrow at him and dropped into the *en garde* position, immediately launching into an advance-attack and rapidly closing the distance between them.

Charles hit the side of her foil hard, in a beat, throwing it to one side and causing her to miss as he retreated to maintain the distance between them. She immediately moved forward in another advance-attack, and Charles repeated the hard beat against her foil, knocking it aside and retreating. They repeated the same set of moves a third time, with the same result.

As Catherine made a fourth advance-attack, she tensed her arm, preparing for another hard beat against her foil. Since Charles had explained the technique, she kept anticipating it, but she was still surprised when, rather than slapping her foil to the side with another hard beat, he instead feinted high to the inside. Because she'd tensed her arm in anticipation of the expected beat, her parry was too forceful. Charles slipped inside and scored a point.

They both stepped back, and Charles pulled off his face mask, grinning. "Like it?"

"That was splendid. You lulled me into a rhythm and then

changed it, using my own reactions against me." She grinned. "I'll have to remember that."

Charles slid his face mask back on. "Let's run through it a couple more times, and then we can switch roles."

They faced off again, repeating the same drill. This time, as Catherine braced her arm for the anticipated beat against her foil, Charles paused. "There. That's how I knew to try the feint. You tensed your arm."

She relaxed her arm. "You're observant."

"I knew what to look for."

They switched roles and Catherine saw that she could easily see when Charles tensed his muscles. She had been reading every opponent's body language this way for years, so she quickly scored a point against her brother.

Catherine kept glancing toward the entrance whenever another fencer arrived, but Daniel didn't make an appearance. Tonight felt like a counterpoint to the time when she'd come here alone. On that night she'd hoped Daniel would stay away, but tonight the thought of seeing him sent a thrill through her.

After an hour or so had passed, she finally asked Charles, "Are you certain you sent him a message?"

"Of course," he replied, knowing exactly what she meant. "I already told you I did."

Finally, her final sparring match of the evening was upon her, and she turned all of her attention toward defeating her opponent. She moved through the match expertly, sliding her foil inside her partner's defenses with deceptive ease.

At the end of the match, Bernini slapped her on the back. "*Eccellente, ragazzo mio,*" he declared proudly. "You'll be primed and ready for the tournament. It's just a little over a week away."

And her wedding was just days away. Those two critical events were hurtling toward her. With a murmur of thanks, she turned to leave. She pulled off her fencing mask and slipped it under her arm as she looked around the room for Charles. She caught sight of him at the entrance, deep in conversation with another fencer.

She lingered toward the back of the room while she waited for him to finish. As much as she had looked forward to being here this evening, she was exhausted. She hadn't been sleeping well, and the combination of excitement and physical activity had used up the last of her reserves.

Distractedly, she watched some of the other fencers as they gathered their belongings. Most of the others had slipped outside into the night. As a pair left through the front entrance of the academy, another man swept inside.

Daniel.

Catherine immediately became fully alert as he scanned the room. She felt certain he was looking for her. When their eyes locked, she felt an invisible tether tighten between them, drawing them together.

She was vaguely aware that Charles was watching her, too. The moment his friend left, Charles hurried over to stand in front of her, breaking her eye contact with Daniel.

Charles pierced her with an accusing glare. "Gray, you need to show more self-control," he murmured.

"I... I'm sorry," she stuttered softly. "He took me by surprise. I'd given up on seeing him tonight."

As Daniel moved toward them, Bernini caught sight of him and hurried across the room on an intercepting course.

"*Buonasera*, Lord Huntley." The maestro smiled. "It's good to see you, but I'm afraid we've already finished for the evening." He furrowed his brow. "I don't want to make you leave right away after coming so far. If you like, you're welcome to stay until I close. That should be in about fifteen minutes."

"Thank you, Maestro Bernini," he said. "I appreciate the offer. I'd like to stay."

Bernini gave a nod of approval. "If you'll excuse me, I need to speak to Mr. Winston." He hurried away.

Daniel glanced at Charles. "Would you and Gray be willing to stay? There's something I promised to teach him."

Elated, Catherine's nod of agreement came quickly, but Charles hesitated. "Just remember who and where you are," he said finally, speaking more to Catherine than to Daniel.

The last group of fencers left the salon, leaving the three of them alone.

"Does Charles know about my gift?" Daniel asked.

Catherine shook her head. Her face flamed as she remembered the train.

"I gave Catherine a knife as an engagement gift," Daniel said, seemingly oblivious to her embarrassment. "It's for self-defense. I promised to give her lessons."

Charles gave a wry smile. "For most couples, it would be an odd gift, but it suits you both. Go ahead. I'll keep watch by the door."

"Thank you." Catherine took a deep breath and tried not to think about the last time she'd been alone with Daniel on the train.

"First of all, *Gray*," Daniel said, emphasizing the name as though trying to keep her identity at the forefront of his mind, "you must understand that if anyone ever attacks you with a knife, their intent is to kill. Knives aren't used in regular fights. They're too deadly."

Catherine was surprised by the force of his words. She immediately focused more carefully on the lesson.

"A knife has three ways to attack, so it has more in common with a saber than a foil. You can use the tip, the edge, or the hilt, depending on the damage you want to inflict. A foil is a gentleman's weapon, used in a drawn-out fight that follows strict rules of conduct. But a knife is simply a tool to kill and maim. Knife fights are very short and usually end in someone's death— and they aren't forgiving of mistakes."

A chill ran down Catherine's neck. She'd never seen this level of intensity in Daniel before. "How do you know so much about knife fighting?"

He gave her a level gaze. "When I was a boy, my father let me run wild. If I hadn't learned to defend myself with a knife, I'd have been dead many times over before I reached my twelfth birthday."

She swallowed. "You're always such a self-controlled person. I would never have guessed your childhood had been so dangerous."

"I learned to be careful," he said.

She shot him a probing look, hoping he'd elaborate, but he didn't. He slipped his jacket off and pulled two dull wooden knives from its pocket. Wearing only his shirt, he wasn't properly dressed, but the white linen seemed more appropriate in a fencing salon than his jacket had been.

How bad had his childhood been? She'd known his father had been mad, but she'd had no idea Daniel had been in so much danger that he'd needed a knife for protection. Why would the son of a marquess need to defend himself?

"Hold it opposite the way you would a foil. " He pressed the knife into her hand with the end of the hilt toward her thumb and the blade near her pinkie. "With this grip, you'll have more strength in your swing. It also allows you to hide the blade behind your arm while holding the hilt in your fist."

She did as he instructed, concealing the blade behind her lowered arm.

Daniel glanced down at her forearm and gave her an approving nod. "Keep the element of surprise in your favor. People won't expect you to be wielding a knife, so don't give away that advantage too early. If you hold the knife the other way around, with the point jutting out past your thumb, your opponent will see it immediately." He demonstrated the two grips, tossing the knife into the air with an expert flip of his wrist as he altered his hold on the handle.

His ease with the weapon was both impressive and disconcerting.

"If the blade is hidden behind your arm, you can move your hand forward without alerting your opponent. You'll be able to strike him before he anticipates it."

Daniel ran through a few defensive moves to teach her how to avoid certain knife attacks. She was breathing hard by the time they stopped to take a break. Charles, who had been watching from a spot near the entrance, joined them.

"I heard you say you learned knife fighting as a boy," Charles said, "but how did you become such an expert? It doesn't look like something you could learn by trial and error." He watched Daniel intently.

"It's not a 'gentleman's weapon,' is it?" Daniel paused, as if considering his next words. "As I'm sure you're already aware, I had an unconventional childhood. I spent most of my younger years running amok. I often ran away from home, heading for Edinburgh, and hoping that perhaps... well... that perhaps my father would notice me. It never worked." He paused and frowned as he glanced down at the wooden knife in his hand. "Our head stableman— or rather, our only stableman— finally decided that if I was going to run wild, I'd better learn to defend myself." He carefully avoided their eyes and shrugged at this admission, but Catherine could tell that revealing the extent of his father's neglect was painful for him. His stoic gaze revealed nothing, but even so, Catherine could sense his pain.

Daniel cleared his throat. "The most important lesson he taught me was this: the best way to survive a knife fight is to avoid one." He gave Catherine a sharp look. "Remember, if the opportunity to escape presents itself, take it."

Her heart twisted at the thought of a child learning this sort of lesson. He'd left for Eton when he'd been twelve, so all of this knowledge must have been earned when he was still quite small.

"I want to show you one last move before we stop for the

evening. This one is critical if someone comes up behind you and holds a knife to your throat." He smiled at her grimace.

The thought of a knife against her neck made her feel sick to her stomach. Thank goodness the practice knives were made of wood.

"Remember, a blade must be in motion to do real damage. If the edge just presses against your neck, it probably won't do much more than make a shallow cut. The real danger comes when the knife slides across your skin. So, the first and most important thing to do is to immobilize your assailant's hand by gripping it firmly. Since you're a w...," he stopped himself mid-word and coughed.

She frowned at him.

"Since you're so small," he began again, "your attacker won't think you'll pose a threat. That will be to your advantage. The moment he grabs you from behind, grab his hand and forearm with both your hands, immobilizing the knife. This might not work if you were a larger man," he said, glancing at Charles, "since your attacker would see you as a threat and wouldn't allow you to grab his hands, but a smaller person could probably get away with it."

That made sense. Men were constantly underestimating her... both as Gray and as Catherine.

"Next, turn your body in toward your assailant, facing away from the arm holding the knife. He might have an arm around your waist, but this will still work. He'll just think you're squirming. At the same time, you need to stoop down while you grip his knife arm firmly with both of your hands so he can't slice you. Then push the knife into his chest while you duck down and pull your head free."

Catherine gasped. "Push the knife into his chest?"

"Yes," he said firmly. "In a knife fight, it's kill or be killed. I hope you never find yourself in a situation where you need to use this maneuver, but it can save your life if you do it properly. Let's practice it a few times until it feels natural to you."

How could pushing a knife into a man's chest ever feel natural? Her stomach tightened as she suddenly understood how deadly this game really was.

Daniel moved up behind her and wrapped his left hand around her waist while holding his right hand, with the wooden knife, against her throat.

Her tension made her jump in surprise, but then her body seemed to recognize him. His hands wrapped around her in a way that reminded her of their interlude on the train, and her body instantly responded. Her breath caught in her throat, and she could feel the entire length of his body pressed against hers.

"Now, grab my hand with both of yours," Daniel instructed.

She tried to ignore the disturbing sensations in her body. His thighs were warm where they pressed against hers. Without the layers of petticoats to separate them, the sensation overwhelmed her. She nearly trembled at the pressure of his palm against her ribcage and his hot breath against her ear. She could feel the tiny hairs on her neck react to his soft exhalation. Her every sense was heightened.

"Gray?" Daniel prompted when she didn't move.

Startled, she quickly placed her hands on Daniel's forearm, but instead of grabbing him with force, she touched him tentatively.

She could hear Daniel moisten his lips with his tongue and then swallow. He cleared his throat.

"Hold my arm more firmly," he directed, "and then turn toward my chest. Make sure you keep the knife away from your throat as you drop down." His voice didn't sound as strong and confident as it had just a moment ago. It sounded husky. Raw.

Taking a deep, steadying breath, Catherine followed his instructions, but very slowly. As she turned toward him, she paused as her cheek brushed against his chest and she heard his breath catch.

"Control my knife as you turn in toward me, and force the tip into my chest. Use the momentum of your turn to give the thrust more power."

Catherine did as he directed, dancing this dance of death in slow motion, pressing the tip of the dull wooden knife into the white cotton fabric of his shirt while simultaneously ducking down and extricating her head from his hold.

As she stepped back to look at him, she saw that he stood with the tip of his knife pointing at his chest.

Their gazes locked for a moment, and then Daniel looked down at his chest.

"Right in the heart, Gray," he said, and then dropped his hand to his side. He wore a bemused expression. He glanced back at her, and then turned away.

Charles turned away from them suddenly and pretended to see something of interest across the room. He strode toward the intriguing spot, giving them some space.

Silence stretched between them. "Good thing it wasn't real," she finally said, needing to fill the emptiness.

"More real than you know," Daniel murmured.

"Daniel?" she asked, unable to read his expression. She took a quick step closer to him. "Did I hurt you?"

His hand rubbed his chest, and he turned to give her a wry smile. "Not that you'd see. It's just that you surprised me."

She wanted to ask him more, but at that moment, Bernini breezed past Charles and entered the room.

"I'm sorry to have to rush you out the door, but a prior engagement...," Bernini smiled, his eyes glittering. "You know how it is. A lady never likes to be kept waiting, and this one has perfected her pout. I'm afraid if I don't hurry, she'll have the advantage she needs to coerce me into buying an exorbitant gift."

"I'll put away my things." Catherine rushed out of the room as she tried to quash the reverberations of her desire for Daniel. For once, she didn't even hesitate before entering the men's changing room. She simply walked straight in.

Fortunately, it was empty.

She pulled open the cabinet and shoved her foil into the corner with a shaking hand. She paused, breathing hard as she thought about her reaction to Daniel's touch. Thank goodness no one was here to see her fall apart this way. She needed to calm herself. She paused to take a few deep breaths. Once she was certain she could appear normal, she returned to the foyer and collected her cloak and hat from one of the waiting footmen.

By the time she rejoined Daniel and Charles at the door, she had herself back under control. Even so, her brother avoided her gaze.

The three of them exited Bernini's together. A young groom stood waiting with all three of their mounts. They quickly departed.

As soon as they were out of earshot, Charles broke his silence. "There's too much tension between you. Until it's resolved, I don't think it's wise for Gray to be seen with you."

Catherine's stomach clenched. Had her reaction been that obvious? She glanced at Daniel and he frowned back at her.

He gave a sharp nod. "I concur. Perhaps once we're more at ease with each another, the tension will fade."

Charles was right, of course. If anyone had seen them together, it could have been disastrous.

Daniel's saddle creaked as he shifted his weight to look behind him before focusing his attention on them. "There is a reason for the lesson tonight. Both of you should know. I didn't want to tell you until I was certain, but it isn't prudent for me to wait any longer." Daniel let out a frustrated sigh. "I'm worried for you, Catherine. I think someone's been following me, and I'm concerned they could be following you as well."

Catherine's eyes widened in alarm. "Who?"

"I wish I knew. I noticed it over a month ago, not long before I was attacked, but then it stopped. I thought that whoever it was had given up, but now... I'm certain I'm being followed again. That's one of the reasons I was late arriving at Bernini's tonight. I wanted to make sure I didn't lead anyone there."

Catherine looked around, taking in the surrounding buildings and alleyways. Any one of the shadows could conceal someone. Each alcove could provide a potential hiding place, and she knew from experience how dangerous a darkened alley could be. A small shiver ran down her spine. "And that's why you were so intent upon teaching me how to use a knife tonight?"

He gave her a wry smile. "You're an excellent fencer. I knew you'd pick up knife skills quickly enough, and I was right. Now you have some skills to defend yourself if someone tries to hurt you."

A chill grew at Catherine's core, and even the approval shining in Daniel's eyes did nothing to warm her. She had thought everything was fine, but it wasn't. Everything had suddenly changed.

She was afraid.

But not for herself. She was afraid for Daniel. Afraid of losing him. He'd already been attacked once.

He looked at her expectantly, and she realized he'd said something, waiting for her to reply. "I'm sorry, could you repeat that?"

"It would be safer for you," he looked at her pleadingly. "Please, promise me that you won't go to anywhere alone, especially to Bernini's."

"She promises," Charles said. "Right, Cat?"

"Yes, of course." As the words left her lips, a chill ran down her spine.

45

TRUST

Catherine stood still as Simpson lowered the white gown over her head. Her lady's maid then began fastening the long row of tiny buttons up her back. The white silk dress was lavishly embroidered on both the bodice and the full, flounced skirt. The bell-shaped sleeves were full along her upper arms, fitting snugly from elbow to wrist.

Her biggest disappointment today was that Papa couldn't be here. He was still in Paris at Queen Victoria's request. Once Emperor Napoleon had extended a personal invitation to stay, he'd felt obliged to remain there. Papa's letter said that nothing but two royal entreaties could have kept him from her side. She understood he was duty bound to do as asked, but she couldn't help but wonder if she, too, would often find herself left behind by her husband.

As Catherine looked at herself in the mirror, she couldn't help but compare what she saw to the images of Queen Victoria on her wedding day. The queen had married her love, Prince Albert, fifteen years ago and had worn a similar white dress. She'd set the trend for every aristocratic wedding in England, and now most brides wore white. Catherine had always imagined she'd wear a white gown on her wedding day, and as she gazed in the mirror, she knew that everything was correct and proper, just as she'd planned. Unfortunately, that knowledge did nothing to settle her nerves. As she glanced into her own eyes, she couldn't help but wonder if the queen had seen the same flicker of anxiety reflected in her own mirror on her wedding day.

Catherine doubted it. Queen Victoria never seemed nervous. Plus, she had the advantage of feeling confident in her groom's love.

Catherine raised her chin as she shoved her doubts away. After all, this had been her choice. She smiled at her reflection, and seeing the confidence of the woman in the mirror, she felt a sense of calm envelop her.

This was what she wanted, wasn't it? Safety and security with a man she trusted and respected? One who respected her as well? She'd hardly dared hope to find someone who'd allow her to continue fencing. But Daniel not only permitted it—he encouraged it.

Simpson left the room for a moment, and Catherine took the opportunity to strap her knife to her leg, the coolness of the malachite sending a chill rippling through her. She glanced down at the emerald handle, its veined patterns swirling together in deep and pale greens, like winding rivers cutting through a verdant forest. As she admired the intricate marbling against her smooth skin, a vivid image flashed through her mind—Daniel's hands, steady and warm, fastening the strap to her thigh that day on the train. He'd been right. At least there was passion between them.

Catherine tried to push down the niggling anxiety that continued to torment her, reassuring herself that all would be well. Perhaps Daniel would come to love her, but if he did, it would have to be for her true self, not for the mask she presented to the world. He had a mask of his own, one that he'd been wearing for years. He'd let it slip a couple of nights ago and had given her a glimpse of the boy he'd been. No wonder he craved acceptance after being rejected by his own father for so many years.

No more disguises. No more lies— at least, not within their marriage. She took a tremulous breath. He had known her secret when he'd asked for her hand, and he promised she could continue to fence. She planned to hold him to that promise.

Could she trust him? Wasn't that doubt the real source of her anxiety? She'd been hiding for so long, from her mother and so many others, that trusting someone to accept her for herself took a tremendous act of faith.

She needed to trust Daniel, with both her heart and her future. Smoothing her dress with steady hands, she took a deep, calming breath. She was ready. She looked up at her reflection, a final spark of resolve igniting in her eyes.

I can do this.

46

IN THE CHOIR LOFT

Stansbury didn't need to follow them. He knew exactly where to find Huntley and Lady Catherine at half past ten that morning.

The day was crisp and clear, with the smell of spring in the air, and he arrived at the chapel early, as planned. He climbed up the narrow stairs to the choir loft. Of course, he'd received no formal invitation, despite the fact that the wedding would never have taken place if not for him.

He sat silently at the rear of the choir loft, hidden from the guests seated below. As he watched people stream into the large, open chapel, he rocked slowly back and forth, humming to himself. A handful of the guests were joyful supporters of the union, but most were sanctimonious sots, eager to sniff out a scandal and curious about the wedding's haste.

If anyone deserved to be an invited guest, he did. After all, he was the catalyst. Lady Catherine's catalyst, he thought, continuing to sway side to side. Lady Cat's catalyst. Her cat. Lady Cat's cat. He smiled, playing with the words.

But he didn't want the role of catalyst, he remembered, frowning. Still, it was all he had left. He shifted his weight forward on the pew, searching for a more comfortable position for his backside.

Everything had gone from bad to worse when the ship from India had docked a few days ago. He had expressly told each of his four partners that he would manage the unloading of the cargo, but two of them had shown up at the dock. It hadn't taken them long to figure out that they had each invested in the same venture with Stansbury as their "sole" partner.

They'd been furious.

He'd barely escaped his warehouse before the authorities arrived. His two other investors had learned about the ruse more quickly than he'd hoped. Now he couldn't even return home for fear of being arrested. He'd slept in that warehouse last night. That empty warehouse.

Huntley must have played a part in his downfall. Perhaps he'd tipped off the four investors. Yes, that must be it.

Despite his best efforts, Stansbury hadn't been able to spring his trap before the wedding. Huntley had become wilier of late. He seemed to have realized he was being followed, and Stansbury kept losing him.

I should be the one down there marrying Lady Catherine, not that undeserving bastard with the Midas touch. Stansbury's mouth twitched at the injustice of it all. Huntley didn't deserve his Cat.

He leaned forward as Huntley approached the altar. The marquess stood toward the right side of the raised area, watching the main aisle as guests continued to file in. His friend, Lord Wentworth, stood with him, and the two men chatted.

Contemptible bastards, both of them.

Lady Kensington was escorted in by an usher and seated at the front, on the left side of the aisle. The front row on Huntley's side was empty.

Ha.

Stansbury felt a seething sense of satisfaction at discovering his rival was so alone in the world.

Alone. The man deserved to be alone.

But from now on, he'd no longer be alone. He'd have Catherine.

My Catherine.

A minister approached the altar. That must have been the cue for the music to begin, because the organist started to play. As the music swelled, all of the guests stood and turned to look back toward the entrance. From his seat at the back of the balcony, Stansbury had to wait until Catherine had nearly reached the altar before he had a clear view of her.

Charles escorted her down the aisle. Lord Kensington must not have returned in time for the wedding. *Pity,* he thought distractedly. A girl's father really should give her away.

Sunlight streamed in through the stained-glass window above the altar, and the bits of colored glass broke it into a million pieces, scattering the floor in a kaleidoscope of colors. Catherine moved to join Huntley, and when she stepped into the carpet of light, the colors fell upon her pristine white dress as she turned to look at him, bathing her in the riotous display.

The moment she turned that tender gaze toward Huntley, he felt as if she'd snatched his heart out of his chest, then laughed as she tossed it away.

She loves him? How could she love him? She was supposed to love me!

The multicolored shards of light that fell upon the couple made it appear that Catherine was clothed in a shimmering rainbow. Something within Stansbury broke into similar fragments as he listened to her speak the words that bound her to the man with the Midas touch.

Fissures of hatred ripped through him, their heat searing away any tender feelings he might have still harbored for the girl. An eruption of anger burst forth from him, and he was barely able to stop himself from howling his fury.

She didn't deserve happiness, and neither did Huntley. They'd already taken too much from him, and now a dark hunger twisted inside him, urging him to strip everything away from them. This was wrong. *They* were wrong.

A flicker of doubt clawed at the edges of his mind, whispering that perhaps he'd gone too far this time. This plan wasn't merely vengeful; it was complicated and dangerous, even for him. But what choice did he have left? It was a drastic measure, yes—but nothing else would suffice to make them pay. They'd walked through life with impunity, oblivious to the destruction they left in their wake. They deserved to suffer, as he had suffered. A grim smile twisted his mouth. They'd pushed him to this, and now they'd face the consequences.

Stansbury caught the scent of burning candles.

This marriage wasn't blessed. The flames of light licking at her dress must be the devil's work, marking her as Satan's own. She was no angel, sent to earth to save him. She was unholy. Unfit for any man.

Who were they to look so satisfied with themselves? Didn't they realize all of this could be gone in an instant?

How dare she push him away and choose Huntley after leading him on for two years? She was an aberration, with her twisted combination of mannish interests and seductive glances. She wore clothing designed to entice and ensnare, then feigned embarrassment when a man dared to show his interest.

He knew just how to bring her down—how to bring them both down. A slow grin slid across his face. He'd been following them long enough now to know all their routines and many of their plans.

He'd destroy them using their own secrets. He'd be a catalyst indeed. A catalyst in deed.

If I can't have her, no one will.

❦ 47 ❧

WEDDING GIFTS

Catherine was barely aware of the ceremony. One moment, she was nervously awaiting her walk down the aisle; the next, she stood beside her husband, signing the church register. Her vows were a blur. All she could recall were her cold hands, the contentment she felt as she stared into Daniel's eyes, and the warmth of his touch when he slid the gold ring onto her finger.

By the time they arrived at Kensington House for their wedding breakfast, most of the guests had already arrived. She and Daniel greeted each one individually as they passed through the receiving line. Most offered their best wishes and moved on, but a few friends lingered, sharing a moment of familiarity.

Lord Wentworth was one such friend. Catherine had been smiling and making small talk with acquaintances all morning, so it was good to see a more familiar face, even if it was Wentworth's. She knew she should do her best to warm to the man since he was Daniel's oldest and dearest friend, but it wasn't easy. Her first impression of him hadn't been a good one. Today, however, she felt a shift in herself—a quiet willingness to see him in a new light, especially given his loyalty to her husband.

After shaking hands with Daniel, Wentworth turned to her with a warm smile, surprising her with the familiarity in his tone.

"Lady Huntley. I can't begin to tell you how happy I am to address you as such. I feel as though you're my sister now." He raised her gloved hand to his lips and pressed a kiss to it. "Huntley has been like a brother to me for years. If there's ever anything I can do to be of service to you, please don't hesitate to call upon me."

"Why, Lord Wentworth, that's quite generous of you. Thank you," she replied, genuinely touched. She found herself liking his presence more than she had before—he seemed softer, more earnest.

Wentworth inclined his head with a slight bow, then turned back to Huntley with a broad smile. "And you, Huntley. I'm glad you decided to stay in town long enough for the tournament. I signed you up to take part in it, and I won't take no for an answer. I'll meet you at your house next Saturday, and we'll make a day of it."

Catherine glanced at Daniel, but his expression remained carefully neutral as he nodded to his friend. It unsettled her, the way he accepted such an arrangement with hardly a second thought.

Once Wentworth moved on, Catherine leaned closer to Daniel, her voice a low murmur. "I thought you were escorting me to the tournament. I was looking forward to it."

He shrugged, though she caught a flicker of irritation. "Charles will be more than pleased to escort you, I'm sure. It's more fitting, really, since you've always attended Bernini's with him. Besides, last time, we nearly gave ourselves away. This change of plans is probably for the best."

He turned to greet the next guest who approached, effectively ending the discussion.

Her heart sank, a chill creeping in to replace the euphoria that had carried her through the day. His words stung. Yes, his point about Charles made sense, but did her wishes truly matter so little? She hadn't anticipated such a casual dismissal, not after their earlier conversations. Pushing down the sharp edge of disappointment, she reminded herself that it was her wedding day, and perhaps these small compromises were minor in the grander scheme of their journey together.

Wentworth lingered nearby, speaking briefly with another guest before returning to Daniel, a faint frown creasing his brow. "I expected my brother to join us today, but Frederick is otherwise occupied."

Daniel looked at Wentworth with a hint of curiosity. "Your brother's work, I presume?"

"Yes," Wentworth replied, his tone just shy of exasperated. "Frederick always seems to be chasing shadows, and when he's not, I'm left making excuses for him. Today, at least, he hasn't roped me into any of his more dangerous schemes." He shook his head, clearly trying to mask his irritation with forced levity. "Though I suppose that's a relief."

Catherine had never met Frederick, but it was clear from Wentworth's tone that his brother's work complicated his life. She found herself intrigued, her curiosity stirred as Wentworth turned to her again.

"Oh, and I've been asked to pass along a message from the Queen." Wentworth's expression softened. "Her Majesty sent her congratulations, along with apologies for sending Lord Kensington to France. She wanted me to assure you that his absence was necessary, though I'm certain he regrets not being here today."

Catherine felt a warmth in her chest at the mention of the Queen's message. "It's thoughtful of her to send word," she said quietly. Despite everything, it was reassuring to know her father was engaged in something meaningful enough to be recognized. And the Queen's acknowledgment on her wedding day? That was an honor she hadn't expected.

Wentworth inclined his head, offering her a faint smile. "Indeed. Few receive such direct regard. And as for my brother..." He trailed off, looking briefly uneasy before his expression steeled. "His dedication to his work is admirable, but sometimes I fear it may take him places better left undisturbed."

The note of reluctance in his tone struck her, but he said nothing further, and with another polite bow, he moved on.

After the wedding breakfast, it was time to go to her new home. She remembered nibbling on some oysters, cold game, and, of course, Troussant's delicious wedding cake with the sinfully rich buttercream frosting, but she didn't recall much else about the meal. She'd been too distracted by a swirl of thoughts—of Frederick, her father's work, and the secrets she seemed just shy of touching.

As they climbed into the coach, Catherine finally felt as though the world had slowed down enough for her to see what was happening. She was married. For better or for worse. Once she sat down, she tugged off her glove and gazed at the ring on her hand. She was surprised when Daniel's fingers slid over hers.

She raised her hand and rested it against his chest, fingering the ornate cravat pin she had given him as a wedding gift. Daniel's hand followed hers, and their fingers entwined, echoing the gold wire encircling the malachite on his cravat pin, suspending the stone in place.

"Thank you for the gift," he murmured.

"I chose malachite to remind you of your gifts to me."

"It's perfect."

"I'm sorry for your sake your father couldn't be here." He hesitated. "About Wentworth and Frederick—as you may have surmised, Frederick works for the Queen. It's important that you don't discuss this with anyone else. It's delicate business, Catherine."

She met his gaze, steady and assured. "You can count on me. I know how to keep secrets," she replied softly, a hint of a smile touching her lips. Leaning her head back against the seat cushions, she let out a sigh. "It's been quite a day, Lord Huntley. I'm glad my new home is close, and the ride will be short."

He gave a soft smile and wrapped his arm around her. She shifted closer, resting her head against his shoulder, marveling at how well she fit there. His chest rumbled with a contented murmur as he pulled her more firmly against him, the carriage gently swaying as they made their way.

"About that short ride," he said, his lips grazing her forehead. "To show you your wedding gift, we'll need to journey a bit farther —to our new estate outside London."

She lifted her head, surprised, but before she could speak, he gently urged her head back to his shoulder, his fingers tracing her cheek. "It's a bit of a trip. Perhaps you should rest during the drive."

She pulled her head back to look him in the eye. "But you already gave me a gift."

He smiled. "That was your engagement gift. This is your wedding gift."

"Isn't the house empty? I thought it needed a year's worth of repairs." What was he planning?

Daniel shrugged and looked out the window, avoiding her gaze.

Another unilateral decision. She frowned, uneasy with the trend. Should she say something? Take a stand? But this was her wedding day. The last thing she wanted was to argue with him. Perhaps she was being overly sensitive.

Tomorrow. She'd discuss this with him tomorrow.

She didn't speak during the ride out to the new estate. After a short time, her sleepless night and the stress of the day began to catch up with her, and she began to nod off despite herself.

Catherine awoke with a start, feeling lips nuzzling her temple. She gave a lazy smile before she remembered she was annoyed with Daniel, but she couldn't quite remember why.

"We're here," he murmured.

She straightened, lifting her head from his shoulder.

"I have a gift for you, but you need to come inside to see it."

Her new husband had the distinct aura of someone with a great secret, and a smile twitched at the corner of her mouth at his eagerness.

"I do enjoy presents," she admitted. "Will I love this one?"

"Absolutely."

Daniel escorted her inside the enormous front hall of the main house, and his barely restrained excitement had her grinning.

What is he planning?

He led her toward the rear of the house, and she barely had time to register the enormous empty salons, tall ceilings, and ornately carved woodwork as he tugged her along by the hand.

Daniel approached a pair of closed double doors and stopped. He dropped her hand and stood in front of them with his back pressed to them, blocking the entrance. Then he placed his hands behind his back, grasped the doorknobs and watched her with a smile of boyish anticipation as he flung them open.

She stepped into the large empty room and gazed around in delight.

Daniel had given her a fencing salon.

"How do you like it, Catherine?" He tried to sound nonchalant, but she sensed the tension in his body as he waited to hear her answer.

"It's brilliant," she said, smiling broadly. "Absolutely marvelous!"

"This is the main salon, but it has a hidden surprise. Come through here."

He led her back out to the hallway and took her to a second

door, set to the right of the main entrance of the salon. This entrance was less grand. When he threw the door open, she caught a glimpse of a small, feminine sitting room with comfortable sofas and chairs arranged around a small fireplace. Everything was new, and the room still smelled of fresh paint.

He walked into the room and faced her, taking another couple of steps backward.

She stood at the doorway and looked around curiously. "It's a lovely room, but I don't think I've ever seen anything like this at a fencing salon."

Daniel's mouth twitched. "That's because this isn't your normal fencing salon. This room is specifically designed for you, along with the wives and mothers of my fencing students."

"*Your* students?"

"In a manner of speaking. I've decided to open an academy here. I plan to hire a fencing expert soon who can take over much of the instruction."

Catherine reached out and wrapped her fingers around the door frame as she heard a ringing in her ears. What was he saying? She'd thought the salon was for her... not him.

This had been *her* dream. Not his. She'd never voiced it, but it had been hers, nonetheless. She tried to comprehend what was happening. First, he showed her his perfect fencing salon, and then he led her to the feminine drawing room to which she'd now be relegated? Was she supposed to be happy about this? She couldn't even put the question into words, dreading his response.

She cleared her throat, trying to find her voice. She tried to speak, but nothing came out, so she tried again. "I had no idea you wanted to pursue this sort of thing."

"Well, it's not my dream, but I know it's yours."

She gripped the door frame more tightly as the world seemed to shift under her feet. "I'm sorry, Daniel, but I don't understand. If you know this is my dream, then why are you...?"

He held up his hand. "There's more. You haven't seen the best part yet."

He moved toward another door Catherine hadn't noticed. It was partially masked by a folding screen. He gestured her toward it with a wave of his hand. "Go on. The best part's right through there."

The best part? She faltered, not knowing if she could stomach any more surprises. How could her life's dream have been turned upside down this way? She hesitated, afraid of what she might learn. But then she lifted her chin and stepped forward through the concealed door.

Inside, she found a second fencing salon.

She stopped in her tracks and turned to look at him, her face blank. "I still don't understand. What is this?"

"This is Lady Huntley's Fencing Salon, an establishment for all ladies who wish to learn fencing and other forms of self-defense."

Catherine's jaw sagged. "What? What are you saying? You're suggesting that I teach fencing? Openly?" Her entire body suddenly began to tingle, and she realized she'd stopped breathing.

"Whether or not you do it openly will be your decision, but if that's what you want, then yes, you could fence openly as a woman. I have an alternate suggestion, if you'll consider it."

This was all coming at her so quickly that she could barely comprehend what he was telling her. She took a deep breath. "Perhaps if you explain more slowly."

"My idea is that women can come to visit you and sit anonymously in your drawing room. It would all be perfectly respectable. Then each of your students could slip through the side door and join you in your secret academy. That way, you could continue to fence, and teach women how to defend themselves. The women could come and go freely without worrying about what society might think. It's a perfect solution. Look, you even have a ladies' dressing area over here," he said as he gestured toward another door off the fencing salon.

Catherine looked around the room anew, overwhelmed by an enormous welling of both relief and gratitude. He'd considered so many details. The large windows were frosted, keeping prying eyes from seeing into the private space. The curtains that hung over them were pale blue, with darker blue accents, and the walls were bathed in pale cream. A pair of blue-and-cream fencing cabinets flanked the fireplace. A massive white marble fireplace was laid with kindling, ready to be lit.

Large, framed mirrors reflected her every movement.

A feeling of deja vu swept over her as she saw her image reflected in the glass, dressed as she was in her white wedding dress. The color of the clothing perfectly matched that of her fencing attire, and this merging of her feminine aspect with the traditionally masculine environment suddenly crystallized in her mind. The threads of her life twined together once again. The momentary feeling of disorientation fled as she saw Daniel, too, reflected in the mirror, anchoring her to the moment.

"It's lovely. Truly," she said in a voice slightly louder than a whisper. She circled the room as she looked at it. There was a crystal chandelier near the windows, and Catherine could envision herself moving through her regular fencing routine in the space. "Did you have Mr. Newcomb create this?"

He nodded, grinning widely. "I'm glad you like it. I hoped you would. The mantel above the fireplace will be the perfect location for the trophy you'll win next week in Bernini's tournament." Daniel came up behind her and wrapped his arms around her waist. He pressed a kiss against her temple as he held her against his chest. "I'm sorry I won't be able to travel there with you, but I'll be there in spirit."

"But what if I have to compete against you?"

Daniel tossed his head back and laughed. "No. Fencing isn't my passion. It's yours. I'm adequate, but I don't have your drive.

I'm fairly certain I'll be out of the running before we could compete, but if you are truly concerned, I'll make sure Bernini has me fencing someone other than you at the beginning of the tournament so that we won't have a chance of facing one another until the final round."

Catherine turned in his arms to face him. Gazing up at him, she wrapped her arms around his neck. His eyes... she could lose herself in those amazing blue eyes.

"But I still don't understand why you want to open an academy. Fencing is my dream, not yours."

The room darkened briefly. A cloud must have passed in front of the sun. It was as though Daniel's eyes darkened to a deeper shade of blue, and she felt herself falling into them, dipping beneath his surface and tumbling into his depths.

He shrugged. "Whatever I do in life, I like to do the right way. The best way for everyone involved. The right way to be married to you means supporting you as a fencer and allowing you to be who you really are, rather than trying to turn you into someone else."

She closed her eyes, her unshed tears finally slipping free and sliding down her cheeks. How strange to think that just moments ago, she'd believed he'd stolen her dream, made it his own. And now, this gift beyond her imagining. Her eyes fluttered open to meet his gaze.

She pressed her body against his, and her lips parted as he dropped his head closer to hers. He kissed her, his touch warm and tender.

Her fingers crept into his hair, clutching at it and holding him firmly in place as her tongue darted into his mouth. Their kiss tasted of buttercream frosting and her own salty tears.

She wanted to cry out in joy and relief.

At least she'd won his respect. Perhaps love could still come.

Her breath caught in her throat as he ran his hands down her back, bumping his fingers against the many small buttons of her wedding dress. He deftly released each tiny fastening as his lips traced a tender path from her ear to the pulse at her throat.

She opened her eyes for a moment and was startled by the light shining in the frosted windows. Hadn't it been darker just a moment ago? Surely what they were doing belonged in the twilight.

Or on a train?

She almost giggled. But perhaps not. Her eyes fell shut again and she sighed as his mouth caressed her just beneath her earlobe. Small shivers of delight ran through her body.

More than half of her buttons were undone by now, and Daniel paused to pull her dress partway down her shoulders, revealing more skin for his lips to explore. His hands quickly returned to her buttons, making quick work of those that remained while his lips trailed down her neck, moving maddeningly closer to her exposed breasts. She let out a soft moan as she reveled in the sensations he aroused in her.

The buttons were finally undone, and the dress dipped from her shoulders. Daniel reached down to bunch up the skirts and lift the entire wedding gown over her head. She was clothed only in her petticoats, corset, drawers, and shift, and he began to untie the strings holding her petticoats in place. There were four layers of petticoats in all, and once the last of the strings were untied, they fell to the floor, puddling around her feet.

Daniel swept her up in his arms, lifting her from the frothy pool of white undergarments. He carried her through the secret doorway to one of the low sofas in the adjoining drawing room.

Up to that moment, everything had happened so quickly that Catherine hadn't considered what was about to take place. But when she felt the cool upholstery against her bare shoulders, she had a brief flash of apprehension.

Before her nerves could take hold, Daniel settled beside her on the sofa, slipping off her shoes with gentle hands. His coat and cravat were gone, his shirt untucked and slightly rumpled, lending him a relaxed, disarming charm. She barely registered the sight before his hands traced along the satin of her corset, his lips finding hers and banishing every thought but him.

Daniel leaned back on the sofa and pulled her onto his chest as his fingers continued their task of undressing her. He untied the bow securing the corset and then deftly tugged at the tight strings. Once they were loose enough, he pushed her up so that she was sitting astride his hips, giving him access to the long row of hooks running down the front of the device. His fingers made quick work of the hooks, and he threw the corset carelessly across the room.

She'd long been used to being dressed and undressed by her lady's maid. The tugging and pulling on her clothes shouldn't have been new to her, but it was. The frantic need building within her made the sensations different. This merging of the practical and the sensual surprised her, especially when she felt her body respond to his touch.

Now freed from the stiff, confining garment, Catherine felt Daniel's hands glide over her body, only the whisper-thin fabric of her shift separating his touch from her bare skin. He pulled down the soft cotton fabric to expose her breasts and leaned forward to press his lips between them, burying his face in their softness. He brushed his thumbs against her nipples, seemingly transfixed by the way they sprang erect at his touch. As she gazed down at him from astride his lap, his tender and unguarded fascination pulled at her heart.

One of his hands glided past her hip and pulled up her chemise. He slid his hand under it, exposing the waistband of her drawers, where he quickly undid their fastenings.

She gasped as he pushed her to her feet and then stood next to her. He grasped her drawers with both hands and quickly yanked them down before pressing her back down on the sofa. He pulled her drawers off over her feet and tossed them haphazardly across the room as well.

She looked up at him as he stood before her, still clothed. Her shift was bunched around her waist, and his predatory gaze devoured her. It had been a long time since she had felt like his prey, but now his intense focus thrilled her and filled her with an awareness of her own sensual power. She met his eyes and lifted her chin, unwilling to bend to his will. She would meet him as an equal.

"I want to see all of you," he said as he pulled her shift over her head.

"I want to see all of you too," she said, reaching for his waistband. It felt strange to be naked in front of him while he was still clothed, but as she saw the hunger in his eyes, she knew there was power in her nudity.

He smiled and yanked his shirt over his head. He removed the rest of his clothing so quickly that she could only blink with surprise.

Daniel's body was firm and muscular, a light trail of dark hair tracing from his chest downward, narrowing along his abdomen. And below that... she was startled by what she saw. Was that really supposed to fit inside her? She barely had the opportunity to look at him before he was moving back toward her, covering her body with his, bare skin sliding against bare skin.

He stretched out next to her on the sofa, all the time whispering tender endearments. "Beautiful. You're so beautiful, my darling."

His knees bumped against hers. "We're a little crowded here. Let's try a different spot." He wrapped his arms around her and rolled off the low sofa, falling to the rug with her on top of him, cradled against his chest.

"Oof," she said, so surprised by his sudden move that she let out a laugh.

When he rolled over again, taking her with him and pinning

her to the thick, soft Aubusson rug beneath them, her laughter disappeared. He leaned down and began to kiss her again, starting with her lips and then moving lower and lower down her body. His hand slid slowly down to her hip, and he gently nudged her knees apart with his leg as he slid his hand to the intersection of her thighs.

His thumb grazed against her most sensitive spot and she gasped, her arm flailing out until it banged against the sofa. She reached up to clutch the cushion just above her head. He'd found that same spot he'd focused on during the train ride, and her fist tightened on the fabric as his fingers drove her wild. She realized now that he'd been looking for it before. He'd known it was there. He knew more about her body than she did.

His hand dipped lower, and he found her slick warmth as he slipped a finger inside her. The muscles of her inner thighs convulsed, pulling together, but his finger kept moving in and out, drawing forth sensations she had been hungering for since that afternoon on the train. He continued to use his thumb to caress that sensitive little nub as he kept up a rhythm that left her breathless.

She heard herself moan, and Daniel responded as though her sounds were exactly what he'd been waiting to hear. He spread her legs farther apart as he pressed his weight against her hips, and she felt something much larger than his finger press against the opening between her legs.

She pulled back, suddenly nervous. "Maybe you're too big. Are you sure this will work?"

"I think you'll find that we fit together perfectly." His finger slid across that nub once again, making her gasp and arch her back.

Gently, he pressed against her, but something prevented him from entering her. Just before he stopped moving, she felt a tightness— a sort of pressure. He paused, and then thrust firmly against her hips.

She cried out as she felt something pop, and then he was inside her. She froze, afraid to continue. "I was right. It's too big."

"Wait just a moment. That part is already over. Did it hurt?"

She shook her head. "Not exactly, but I felt something give way."

He moved a little against her, as if letting her test the sensation. He began to move slowly again, sliding his length deep inside her. Warmth filled her, taking her breath away as pleasure replaced her momentary anxiety. Her legs wrapped around him, almost of their own accord, and she moved her hips to match his rhythm.

After a moment, he paused. "I'm crushing you on this rug. Let's try something different."

He withdrew, pulled her into a sitting position, and then he reclined on his back, pulling her astride his hips as though she were riding a horse.

"Lift up and lower yourself onto me," he said. He gently directed her with his hands. She rested her palms against his shoulders and used them to balance as she lifted her hips. He guided her onto him as he slid back inside her.

One hand continued its gentle caress of that sensitive nub, and the other held her hip.

"Keep moving—rocking," came his rasping demand.

She immediately complied, rocking forward, then back again, savoring the feel of flesh sliding against flesh.

The sensations building within her sent currents of pleasure rippling through her body. Every nerve ending sang with his touch.

Daniel's fingers continued their tender, circular movements, and Catherine moved her hips in concert, meeting him stroke for stroke. She felt as though her body was a musical instrument and Daniel was pulling a symphony of sensations from her.

Just like the time on the train, Catherine felt something building within her— a grasping need that had her clutching

Daniel's shoulders as gasps escaped her. Suddenly, she shattered, and convulsive waves of pleasure crashed through her. Her body broke into a million pieces as every sane and coherent thought fled. There was only sensation.

Daniel responded with his own shuddering moans, and she felt him thrusting, thrusting, as he arched his back and ground his hips into hers. He seemed to freeze in place for a moment, gasping for air, and then the tension in his body ebbed. He collapsed, pulling her back to the floor with him.

They were both breathing hard. Catherine leaned her forehead down, resting it against his shoulder. She slowly began to return to herself. A languorous feeling took over her body. Daniel must be feeling the same the way, because he slowly stroked her back, moving up and down, before coming to rest and cupping her bottom.

She propped herself up on her arms to look down at him, her hair tumbling loose from its pins and cascading around them both. Gazing into his eyes, a smile crept across her lips as the sudden, profound realization washed over her: she truly, deeply loved this man.

His eyes were closed. She wanted to say the words, to let him know what was swelling in her heart. She shifted, hoping he'd look at her, but he kept his eyes shut. She leaned down, pressing a soft kiss to his lips, and his eyes flew open, catching hers for a fleeting moment before he turned away, his body tense.

"We need to leave before nightfall," he said, rolling to one side and inadvertently spilling her onto the rug. He rose to his feet, putting distance between them as he glanced out the window. "This place will be cold and dark soon."

The sudden chill seemed to seep into her bones, lingering far beyond the physical. "Is something wrong?" she asked, a tremor in her voice.

"Of course not." He helped her to her feet, his gaze averted as he gathered her clothing. "We just need to hurry."

Nodding, she slipped into her shift, the words she'd wanted to say now a silent ache. They dressed in a quiet that felt far too empty.

❧ 48 ❧

RESOLVE

Daniel cast a surreptitious glance at his bride as she struggled back into her clothes, her body twisting as she wriggled into her shift. A sharp stab of possessiveness pierced him, catching him off guard. He cared for his wife more than he'd intended. Far more.

His cock was still hard as he pulled on his trousers. He forced his gaze to the floor, hoping to steady himself. Once hadn't been enough with Catherine, and perhaps a lifetime wouldn't be either. The intensity of his craving for her unsettled him; he'd known passion before, but this? This was something altogether different. He wanted her again, and yet he could feel something dangerous lurking beneath that desire.

He'd been a fool to think he could play with fire and remain unscathed. Encouraging her rebellious nature had been a reckless attempt to keep her from creeping into his heart, yet she was there already, lodged firmly in a way that felt unshakable. He could see, with unsettling clarity, just how deeply he'd miscalculated.

It was supposed to be simple. Marry, beget heirs, and keep his heart firmly shielded. Yet here he was, craving not just the woman in his bed but the woman herself. Her laugh, her wit, even her vexing questions that tore through his carefully constructed defenses. She'd become essential to him in ways he'd never anticipated, and that, he realized, was the true danger.

Not only had he married an entirely unsuitable woman, but he was also in real danger of losing himself to her. And therein lay the madness.

If he wasn't careful—if he didn't control this growing fascination—he'd end up like his father. If she were to die young, as his mother had, would he crumble as well? Would he withdraw until he was nothing more than a shadow, a shell driven mad by grief? The thought hollowed him, and he felt the weight of his father's choices pressing down on him, threatening to drag him along that same path.

Even now, he ached to reach for her, to hold her close, to shield her from every hardship and hurt that life might bring. The realization stopped him cold. This was the damage done already, the shift he'd been too blind to prevent.

He'd allowed her to mean something to him, and now he stood at the edge of a precipice, teetering dangerously. But there was still time to pull back, to save what remained of his heart. He steeled himself and forced a step back, turning away as he tugged on his boots, every movement a deliberate act of detachment.

He'd survived alone for years; there was no reason to change that now. He'd guard his heart, protect his soul, and retreat into the safety of distance.

Yes, he'd created this bind himself, but he could still undo it. The sensible thing was to focus elsewhere, distract himself, drown out these unsettling emotions before they grew into something far worse. He'd go to his study, bury himself in work, and regain control. There was safety there—away from her smile, her touch, her unsettling tenderness.

Without another glance, he walked out of the room, leaving Catherine to follow, vowing to reclaim the equilibrium he'd lost.

49

THE GATHERING STORM

Over the next few days, Daniel wavered in his resolve, convincing himself each night that sharing a bed with Catherine might purge this dangerous obsession from his system. They were living in his townhouse temporarily, waiting until enough of the renovations on the Savelle house had been completed for them to move in. But the effect of their proximity had been quite the opposite.

Each encounter, rather than sating his desires, only left him craving more, sinking him deeper into emotions he had no business indulging. He found himself standing at the connecting door between their bedchambers every evening, hesitating before eventually knocking. And each night, she welcomed him with open arms, making it all the more difficult to resist the pull she had over him.

Now, as dark clouds gathered outside, knitting together in a thick, oppressive gloom, he retreated to his study, hoping the familiar weight of work might ground him. Flashes of lightning splintered through the tall windows, filling the room with pale, fleeting bursts before plunging it back into shadow. He barely noticed, hunched over his desk with a stack of neglected documents spread before him. His pen hovered, ink smudging his fingers, but the words blurred together, dissolving into meaningless shapes as his thoughts strayed.

Each night spent with her had deepened his attachment, even as he'd tried to convince himself it was just a passing infatuation, a momentary weakness he could shake. Instead, he could feel his control slipping, his heart treading on dangerously soft ground. Even now, as he surrounded himself with work, her presence loomed in his mind—more vivid than the inked pages in front of him.

He had retreated here, hoping to escape the ever-growing obsession that tethered him to her, and for a time, it seemed to work. He managed to turn a few pages, to scratch out a few notes, but every so often, he found himself staring out at the storm, his thoughts slipping back to their nights together.

Their bed play had been a revelation. He hadn't anticipated such a fierce, physical need for his wife, nor could he have predicted the ease with which she would transcend the narrowly defined role society had laid out for her. A Victorian wife was expected to be demure—a figure of support, quiet stability within the household. That role had always seemed necessary, even comforting in its predictability, but Catherine was so much more than that. She had quickly become his fencing partner, his eager pupil as he taught her the finer points of knife fighting, and now, his ardent lover.

Catherine unsettled him. Or, rather, it was his own reaction to her that did. The desires she stirred weren't about simple companionship or comfort—those were ideas he had once considered enough for marriage. But with her, everything went deeper. She allowed him to explore realms of pleasure and intimacy he hadn't imagined, revealing sides of herself he'd never expected to find in a wife. His nights with her had become something he anticipated with a fervor that both thrilled and unnerved him.

This connection hadn't been part of the bargain. He hadn't

expected to find himself bound to a wife of such wit and skill, someone who could match his passion and challenge his assumptions. Catherine was quickly becoming essential to him in ways that transcended the narrowly defined role society had laid out for a wife. She was his equal, a true partner in every sense. What was growing between them was irreplaceable—a bond that carried a frightening risk. The deeper he allowed himself to feel, the greater the potential for heartbreak. And yet, he couldn't resist her pull or deny the exhilaration she brought into his life.

This wasn't merely a marriage. It was something altogether more dangerous.

His reaction to her was what unnerved him most. She lingered in his thoughts, her presence so vivid that he could scarcely recall what it felt like to have a moment's peace. He replayed their nights together, imagining what the next might bring, devising ways to bring her greater pleasure, and to fulfill the desires she stirred within him. The intensity of his fixation alarmed him, but he couldn't shake it.

With a sharp exhale, he yanked his gaze from the tempest outside the window, forcing himself back to the task at hand. Stacks of documents awaited his attention, and he'd fallen behind over the past few days. He needed to focus, to regain control. Yet even here, alone in his study, Catherine's presence lingered, refusing to be banished.

The soft creak of the door broke his concentration, and he looked up to see Catherine slipping into the room, a tray balanced in her hands. She moved quietly, her gaze warm as she took in the sight of him, hunched over his work, surrounded by papers. The gentle glow from the fireplace caught the faint shimmer of her hair as she approached, her perfume—a delicate blend of roses and something sweet, almost like vanilla—permeating the room.

"I thought you might need some refreshment," she murmured, crossing the room and setting the tray on the edge of his desk. "You've been in here for hours."

He blinked, startled by her presence, then forced a small smile, though it felt hollow. "I hadn't noticed the time." His gaze fell to the tray. "Is that...?"

"Your favorite. Glenfarclas." She offered him a gentle smile, brushing her hair back with one hand. "I asked Madson to pour it, but then I stole the entire tray he'd prepared so I could bring it to you myself."

Touched by her thoughtfulness, he managed a smile as she handed him the glass of Scotch. He took a slow sip, savoring the warmth as it burned its way down his throat, a brief reprieve from the chill of his worries. Catherine perched on the arm of his chair, her hand coming to rest lightly on his shoulder, the warmth of her touch seeping into him, both calming and arousing him.

"Sometimes, you work so hard, I worry you'll wear yourself thin," she teased, a twinkle in her eye. "Not that I mind swooping in to rescue you now and then."

Daniel let out a low chuckle, the corner of his mouth lifting. "Rescue missions do seem to be a specialty of yours."

She smiled, tilting her head as she looked at him. "Someone has to look after you. Besides, you'd do the same for me, wouldn't you?"

Her words, spoken so easily, sent a pang through him. He wasn't certain he'd ever had anyone in his life willing to care for him this way—so openly, so generously. She didn't hesitate to give herself to him, and that terrified him. Catherine kept the conversation light, talking about her plans for the gardens at their Savelle house, ideas for a folly she wanted to add, the open green she hoped to restore. She leaned closer, resting her head on his shoulder, painting a picture of their future with such easy optimism.

"Just think of it—a few years from now, we'll have little ones running about on the green, playing cricket, pulling at your coat, and sneaking biscuits when they think no one's watching." Her voice was soft, brimming with hope, and Daniel felt something inside him clench.

His hand tightened around his glass, the weight of her words pressing on him. He forced a smile, but there was a flicker of something—fear—beneath it. He placed the glass back on the tray, his gaze distant. "You paint a charming picture, Catherine. But life... it rarely follows such tidy paths."

She tensed slightly, her smile faltering. Daniel felt guilt twist in his chest, sharp and immediate. He'd allowed her to believe they could build this life together, this vision of a future so solid and real. But he knew what lay behind that illusion—his own father's despair, the weight of a love lost and a heart hollowed out by grief. Surely this vision she'd conjured required more than a distant, detached lord of the house. It would require him to be involved in her life—in their children's lives. And that meant putting his heart—his sanity—at risk.

Sensing his unease, Catherine offered him a reassuring smile. "You could be right, of course. We never know what life holds. Dreams change. We adapt. My father was content in his role as a second son and built a life in the military, but now he's an earl. My aunt was a sickly child who died young. And my uncle? Well, he wasn't a strong man either. When I was younger, Mother was convinced I might inherit that weakness."

He felt a chill sweep over him. "Did you ever have cause to worry?"

Catherine brushed a strand of hair behind her ear, laughing lightly. "Oh, not in recent years. The doctor in India told me to take up riding and to keep my body active. That's when I took up fencing. He thought it might help ward off my aunt's fate, and I think I'm doing rather well."

She meant to ease his concerns, but her words only deepened the pit in his stomach. His pulse quickened as the weight of her words settled over him. Life's fragility was no stranger to him—he had known it too keenly. The thought of Catherine slipping away, of losing her to some unknown malady, tightened his throat. He could envision himself following the same self-destructive path as his father, heartbroken, isolated, surrounded by shadows and memories.

Panic gripped him, and without a word, he rose, his movements abrupt. The warmth Catherine brought with her, that quiet sense of calm, felt like a danger now. A tender trap. He had to retreat from it. "Forgive me," he said, his voice tense. "It's been a long day. I think I'll retire early."

Catherine looked up at him, surprised, a small crease of concern forming between her brows. "Are you sure? You look as though you could use some rest—but I'd thought perhaps some company as well." Her suggestion flared between them, hopeful, tempting.

Her smile was warm and playful as she reached for his hand, but he took an involuntary step back, his guilt flaring up. He managed a tight smile, gently pulling his hand from hers. "Thank you, but I've been at this too long tonight. I think I need to be alone."

With that, he turned and walked to the door, feeling her worried gaze following him. As he left her behind, her warmth and light dimming with every step he took, he felt the weight of his choice pressing down on him. He feared he had invited something far too precious into his life—a love he was ill-equipped to keep safe.

But he couldn't bear the thought of losing her, either. As he made his way to his room, the chill of the storm seeping into his bones, he wondered if it was already too late to turn back.

Once in his bedroom, he stood by the window, staring out into the darkness. The storm had mostly passed, leaving only a soft rain pattering against the glass—a gentle, rhythmic reminder of the world outside. He drew the heavy drapes closed, casting the room in darkness, and lay down, his thoughts tangled and restless, eyes fixed on the shadowed ceiling above.

He felt the emptiness of the bed keenly—the absence of warmth beside him a deliberate choice that now felt like a hollow victory. This was the first night he'd slept alone since the wedding, and even now, the temptation to knock on the adjoining door was nearly too much to resist. But that was the problem. He needed to regain control, to step back from Catherine and the reckless attachment growing within him.

At last, he drifted into a fitful sleep, only to find himself standing in a vast, mist-shrouded field. The fog rolled thick and suffocating across the landscape, blurring the world around him, muffling sounds. He looked around, disoriented, then spotted Catherine—a distant figure in her night shift, emerging through the haze. She was walking away, each step carrying her farther from him.

"*Catherine!*" he called, his voice muted, swallowed by the fog.

She hesitated, turning back. Her expression held both sadness and love, piercing him with a longing he couldn't name. He tried to move toward her, but the fog resisted, thick as water, each step heavier than the last. The ground shifted beneath him, conspiring to hold him back, and then he heard the voices—whispers in the mist, barely discernible, chilling.

"She's leaving you, just like your mother did," they murmured, a cold dread seeping into his bones. "You'll be alone again, Daniel... doomed to walk in your father's footsteps."

"No," he muttered, shaking his head, straining against the suffocating fog. "Catherine! Wait!"

She turned once more, her voice distant, almost ethereal. "You must let go of the past, Daniel... or it will drag you down."

Desperate, he reached out, trying to close the gap between them, but the fog thickened, swirling like smoke, swallowing her completely. Panic surged in his chest, and he stumbled forward, shouting her name until she disappeared into the mist, leaving him alone in the gloom.

With a gasp, he jolted awake, sitting upright in bed, his heart pounding. The loss...the deep, wrenching ache...it nearly did him in.

It was just a dream, he told himself. Only a dream. His eyes scanned the room, searching for something familiar, something solid to anchor him to the waking world.

He was alone. No Catherine. His breaths came heavy, and he buried his face in his hands, the chill of the dream clinging to him as though it had seeped into his bones. For a moment, he half-believed she had truly vanished, faded away into the mist. But no —he couldn't bring those fears into the light of day. They had to remain locked away. Acknowledging them would only make them real, give them life.

All he had to do was knock on the connecting door, and Catherine would come, her warmth dispelling the lingering shadows of that cursed dream. But tonight, he'd chosen this soli-tude, retreating behind his own defenses to keep his emotions in check.

Lying back down, he fixed his gaze on the faint, gray light filtering through the gap in the curtains. The night stretched on, each hour bleeding into the next as he waited for dawn, hoping the morning light might finally banish the ghostly remnants of the nightmare.

DANIEL HEARD CATHERINE MOVING ABOUT HER BEDCHAMBER, and when he entered the breakfast room a short time later, she was already seated, pouring herself a cup of tea. She looked up, a smile warm and genuine lighting her face, a stark contrast to the remnants of unease clinging to him.

"Good morning, Daniel," she greeted, her voice gentle. She

glanced out the window, where wisps of fog still lingered. "The storm finally blew past. It's a beautiful morning now, and the fog's already beginning to burn off."

He managed a faint smile, but his thoughts remained heavy. "Yes, it seems the worst has passed."

She studied him, concern flitting across her face. "Did you sleep well? You look as though you've seen a ghost."

He hesitated, casting his gaze out the window. "Well enough," he replied, but the tension in his voice betrayed him. "The storm made it a restless night."

Catherine reached across the table, her hand covering his, her touch warm and grounding. "A walk would be the perfect remedy for that, don't you think?" she suggested, a hopeful note in her voice. "Clear the last of those storm clouds from your mind."

He hesitated, fighting against the distance he'd created, and in that moment, he made a decision. He would allow himself to feel for her, to care—perhaps not as deeply as he feared, but enough to be present, to show her the fondness she deserved. Surely, he could do that without losing himself.

He found himself nodding. "Yes, I think you're right." This was exactly what he needed—an excuse to shake off the lingering shadows of the night.

She brightened, setting her teacup aside and rising to join him. Together, they stepped out into the crisp morning, mist clinging to the cobblestones and swirling around their feet. The cool air bit at his skin, grounding him, while the quiet of the hour absorbed his remaining unease. When Catherine slipped her hand into the crook of his arm, he felt her warmth, calming and steady.

They walked in companionable silence until Catherine began speaking softly, as though not wanting to disturb the peace. "There's an upcoming performance of *Rigoletto* I'd like us to attend," she said, her eyes brightening as she described the music and the drama of the tale. "I can only hope they do it justice."

He glanced at her, catching the enthusiasm in her voice, and a faint smile touched his lips. Her warmth, the sparkle in her eyes, drew him from his darker thoughts, wrapping him in a sense of ease.

She continued, an amused lilt in her voice, "And did you hear? Lady Ainsley wore the most extraordinary hat last Saturday. LeCompte swears it looked like a birdcage." She laughed, the sound delicate, and he found himself chuckling, the absurdity of the image enough to lift his spirits.

They strolled on, falling into a comfortable rhythm. After a while, Catherine's voice softened. "I had a letter from my father. He'll be back in a month and looks forward to meeting you."

He absorbed the weight of her words, grounding him in a reality that was close enough to feel attainable. A month away—a future not so distant, yet without the daunting permanence he'd feared. This much he could manage. As they walked, he became aware of the morning's details—the warmth of her hand, the light scent of her perfume mingling with the damp, earthy smell of the fog. His fears lingered, shadowed and deep, but her presence held them at bay.

With each step, a fragile flicker of hope grew within him. Perhaps he could care for her, even cherish her, without losing himself entirely. They moved down the path together, her arm resting in his, a simple gesture that held a quiet intimacy. Her presence was steady, grounding, a thread of warmth in the morning's chill. And as they strolled through the lingering mist, he realized that, though he might face his doubts again, he was no longer walking this path alone.

50

WAITING FOR WENTWORTH

Only a week into their marriage, and Catherine's excitement for today's tournament was already tangible. She moved around the drawing room with a lightness that seemed to brighten even the dreary weather. Daniel watched her with a quiet smile, charmed by the way her anticipation spilled into small, absent gestures—the quick glances at the clock, the way she fussed with the arrangement of decanters on the side table. He reminded himself to keep his own emotions in check, to see their bond for what it was—companionship, desire, nothing more.

"It's nearly time for you to leave," she remarked, her brow puckering slightly. "Is Wentworth usually punctual?"

"Usually," he replied, a small smile tugging at his lips. "I doubt he'll be late today."

She resumed her pacing, and Daniel watched with a touch of amusement as she moved restlessly about the room, unable to remain still. She drifted from one spot to the next, adjusting the arrangement of his decanters on the side table, aligning them with a careful eye, before moving on to smooth the edge of a nearby curtain. Her need to leave a subtle mark on the space was both endearing and quietly telling.

He enjoyed watching her like this, prowling about the house, making it hers. She'd been like this all day. "Would you like Mr. Newcomb to come over and consult with you about the townhouse?" he asked. "You could have him make a few changes to the space, since we'll still be here for a few more months."

Her face brightened, but she quickly shook her head. "He should focus on the new estate, not waste time here. It hardly seems worth the effort."

"As long as you're happy here."

"I'd be happier if you were taking me to Bernini's today," she said, tilting her head and smiling sweetly as she chided him.

"This is for the best, and you know it. It takes all my self-control not to stare at you when we're in the same room. Once you put on those breeches, I'm doomed. It's a good thing Wentworth hasn't seen us together when you're in disguise. I'm fairly certain he'll see through the ruse if he catches me watching Gray the way I watch you."

She grinned. "You'll need to be careful today."

"That's exactly my point, Lady Huntley. Those fencing pants of yours will be the death of me."

He heard a commotion in the foyer, and a moment later, Wentworth burst into the room unannounced.

"Speak of the devil," Daniel said.

Wentworth stopped short at the sight of Catherine. "Lady Catherine—I mean, Lady Huntley. Wonderful to see you."

"And you, Lord Wentworth. I see you're wearing your regular day clothes. Do you plan to change for the tournament at Bernini's? I believe that's Daniel's plan."

Wentworth nodded. "Yes. I intend to spend the evening celebrating my trophy, and I'd rather not do it in fencing garb."

Her mouth twitched. "Touch wood. Aren't you afraid you're tempting fate? What if Daniel wins? Or that upstart Gray?"

"Don't mention Gray's name to me." Wentworth shot a glance at Daniel. "I thought you were only coming along because I forced you into it by signing you up. Are you hoping you'll bring home the trophy?"

Daniel glanced at Catherine. "I doubt my name will ever be engraved on that trophy. Fencing is merely a pastime for me. I prefer focusing my energies elsewhere."

Turning back, he winked at Catherine as he leaned against the writing desk. A clatter sounded from behind him, and a moment later, something wet touched his hand.

"Blast," he said, straightening to see what he'd done. An overturned ink bottle rolled toward the desk's edge. He snatched it up just in time to keep it from tumbling to the rug, but his sleeve dragged through the purplish-black puddle.

He grimaced at the spreading stain. "I need to change. I'll be right back."

51

PREPARATIONS

A young housemaid hurried in, wiping her hands on her apron. "Pardon me, my lady. Lord Huntley says there's been a spill."

"It's there, on the desk," Catherine replied, gesturing to the dark, spreading blotch.

The maid clucked her tongue and set to work, dabbing at the ink with a cloth.

"It's my fault he knocked it over," Catherine explained to Wentworth, who was watching her with a faint smile. "I've been rearranging things all morning. I remember putting the ink bottle there, but I hadn't considered Daniel's habit of leaning in that exact spot." She paused, unable to suppress a slight smile. "No real harm done, though. At least he didn't get any on his jacket."

Wentworth observed her thoughtfully, a subtle softness in his expression. "You and Daniel complement each other well. I suspect he finds solace in your calm."

She let out a soft laugh, caught between amusement and curiosity. "Are you saying he needs a wife with a knack for managing spills?"

A rare smile touched his lips. "In part, yes. You're forthright and not one to fret over trifles. I've seen how that steadies him."

The maid finished, slipping away quietly and leaving behind the faint scent of lemon polish. Catherine tilted her head at Wentworth, a spark of curiosity flaring. "You speak with such certainty."

"I am certain. You're the right sort of wife for Daniel." He met her gaze, his tone both earnest and assured. "You're different from most women I've met, less given to pretense. I like that about you." He hesitated, as if choosing his words with care. "I told him, time and again, that he'd be miserable with someone like Lady Lydia, but he refused to hear it." He let out a quiet chuckle, shaking his head. "You're a far better match than she could ever have been."

He looked away, almost wistful. "Daniel has spent his life pursuing some impossible standard, as though he's being judged by some invisible tribunal. But you... I believe you may be helping him realize there's more to life than seeking approval. I've seen subtle changes in him since you two first met at Lady Wilmot's, and I suspect that's your influence."

Catherine blinked, momentarily thrown by Wentworth's words. A warmth spread through her, an unexpected swell of pride mingling with something tender. "You came to that conclusion simply because I'm not worried about spilling ink?" Her smile softened, a sense of relief settling over her. In truth, she'd feared she wasn't what Daniel wanted—especially after their wedding day, when she'd felt him slip away, retreating behind a wall he'd suddenly erected. But now, as she thought back over the past week, one of their evenings together took on a different meaning.

They'd been sitting together in the study just the evening before, a low fire crackling in the hearth. The night prior, there'd been a subtle rift between them, a shadow that seemed to linger in the air between their words. But yesterday, something had shifted. Daniel had seemed more open somehow, as though he'd let go of a burden, even if only briefly.

She recalled the way he'd spoken of a new business venture, his mouth curving into a bitter smile as he'd said, "I hope you don't mind my interest in commerce. Most of society does. They'll always see me as the son of a madman, and my unorthodox interests frighten them."

She'd met his eyes, her tone gentle but firm. "Then why live your life to please strangers? You've built something good, something lasting. They may never give you credit, but you don't need their approval. You have friends—family—who see the worth in what you've done. They're the ones who matter." She paused, her gaze steady. "You've created a life that brings you satisfaction, and I admire that."

For a moment, his usual guarded expression had softened. He'd reached across the end table, covering her hand with his own, and held it there—not with passion, but with a quiet, steady warmth. That night, when they'd come together in the bedroom, he'd seemed more at ease, less guarded. At the time, she'd assumed it was simply the natural rhythm of their marriage finding its footing. But now, with Wentworth's words echoing in her mind, she wondered if it had been more than that. Had her words given Daniel a kind of comfort, a reassurance he hadn't realized he needed?

A warmth unfurled in her chest, and she met Wentworth's gaze, a spark of hope kindling where uncertainty had lingered. Perhaps she was good for him, just as Wentworth claimed. Perhaps she had the power to reach the part of Daniel he kept hidden from the world, even from himself.

Wentworth's expression grew thoughtful as he turned, gazing out the window where muted sunlight filtered through the heavy curtains. "You ground him. My brother Frederick... well, he's the opposite. Always charging ahead, always certain he's on the verge of some great revelation, as if daring the world to catch him in the act."

"Frederick?" she asked, catching the undercurrent of tension. She remembered Wentworth's mention of his brother on the day of her wedding, tied somehow to Queen Victoria, and a spark of curiosity flared within her.

"Yes. Frederick has lofty ambitions," Wentworth replied, shaking his head with a faint smile. "The man has never met a shadow he didn't wish to chase down and interrogate. Lately, though..." He trailed off, his smile turning rueful. "Lately, it seems he's running headlong into things best left alone, and I fear he won't listen to me until he's landed himself in trouble he can't talk his way out of. I've tried to keep a distance, but he has a remarkable knack for dragging me along, whether I wish it or not."

Wentworth sighed, as if the absurdity of it all was not lost on him, his fingers absently tracing along the edge of a nearby chair. "Family loyalty, I suppose," he said lightly. "Some of us are cursed to be bound by it more than others. Just when I think I've extracted myself, Frederick manages to reel me back in. So, I suppose I should warn you, Lady Huntley—you'll likely be seeing a bit more of me than either of us planned."

She felt a chill, mingling with amusement at his tone. "It must be exhausting, being so entangled in his... pursuits."

Wentworth raised a brow, his mouth curving in a faint grin. "Exhausting? Perhaps. Maddening, certainly. But it's Frederick, after all. Life would be rather dull without him dashing about, stirring up trouble in the name of 'Her Majesty's service.' And I suppose he's the only brother I've got, so I'll just have to endure his antics."

She reached out instinctively, resting her hand lightly on his arm. "That must be hard, though—being drawn in by someone else's ambitions. I can see why it would wear on you."

Wentworth blinked, a trace of warmth softening his features as if he were surprised by the small gesture. "Thank you, Lady

Huntley. I don't often speak of these things, but somehow, it's easier with you. Perhaps it's your calm—or perhaps the way you handle small storms with such grace."

At that moment, Daniel reappeared in the doorway, his cufflinks glinting in the light. He glanced between them, curiosity flickering across his face. "Are we ready?" he asked, his tone warm, though his eyes held a hint of intrigue.

Wentworth straightened, the shadow in his gaze vanishing as he offered her a final nod. "Indeed, we are."

52

MESSAGE

As Daniel and Wentworth stepped out onto the street, a young boy darted toward them, waving a scrap of white paper. He grabbed hold of Wentworth's pant leg and gave it a tug. "Milord?"

"What's this?" Wentworth looked down at the boy.

The boy thrust out a grubby hand, a crumpled note clutched between his fingers. "Some gen'leman told me to give this to ya," he mumbled, casting nervous glances over his shoulder as if he might be caught at any moment.

"Who?" Wentworth asked, taking the note, his gaze sharp.

The boy shrugged, indifferent. "Din't say."

"What did he look like?" Wentworth called after him, but the boy had already slipped away, darting between two townhouses and disappearing into the shadows before he could answer.

Wentworth tore open the envelope, his brows furrowing.

"Who's it from?" Daniel asked.

Wentworth's mouth twitched in irritation. "I'll give you one guess."

"Frederick," Daniel said, grim resignation in his voice.

"Yes. I detest my brother's ability to track me down. It's... unnerving."

"I suppose it comes with the territory of being a spy. What does he want?"

Wentworth gave a hard smile. "Likely needs me for one of his assignments. He wants me to meet him at the Brass Pig. Do you know it?"

"It's an alehouse not far from Bernini's. We'll pass it on our way."

Wentworth sighed. "Then we can ride together, and you can point it out. But he says to come alone. That probably means it has to do with his work for the queen. You'd best go on to the tournament without me."

"I don't mind waiting for you," Daniel offered.

But Wentworth shook his head. "No need for that. I don't want you missing the event on my account. I've no idea how long this will take—sometimes he just needs a scrap of information, and that only takes a moment. But other times, it's something much more complicated. If he doesn't require my assistance with some damnably intricate task, I'll join you at Bernini's directly."

53

A RUNAWAY CART

As Catherine and Charles followed their familiar route to Bernini's, the business district looked almost unrecognizable in the daylight. When she passed through at night, she only noticed the alehouses and streetwalkers. Now, with the shops open, she spotted a barbershop and a shoe repair shop she'd never seen before. The area felt less threatening in the sunlight.

As they neared the end of the business district, a shout of alarm rang out from up ahead, quickly followed by the rumble of a heavy cart barreling down a side street.

An instant later, the cart careened into the main thoroughfare. The driver frantically tugged on the reins, slowing the horses, but now they were charging straight toward Catherine.

"Charles, look out!" She jerked Wildfire toward the side of the road, her heart pounding.

She looked up just in time to see the wild-eyed horses drag the cart off balance as it took the corner too fast. The heavy cart tipped onto two wheels before toppling over, and the horses shrieked in panic as they were pulled down by the harness.

The cart had barely come to a halt when another pair of

horses surged into the street, pulling a plain black carriage. Fortunately, the driver veered in the opposite direction, avoiding the wreckage. But as the carriage passed, Catherine's breath caught—she recognized the driver. Stansbury.

She hadn't seen the man since that night he'd nearly ruined her. His face, twisted with a smug smile, was etched into her memory. A surge of anger flared, hot and potent, but it brought with it a shiver of fear. She could still feel the press of his body against hers, the terror she'd fought to suppress as he'd tried to claim her for himself.

No. Not now. Not ever again. I won't let him intimidate me.

"That's Stansbury!" she shouted. Through the window, she could just make out a dark-haired man struggling, his hands appearing to be tied. "Who is the man inside the carriage?"

"I didn't see. Are you certain it was Stansbury?"

"I'd recognize him anywhere, especially after what he put me through."

She urged Wildfire forward, skirting the tangled mess of wood, leather, and horses. A crowd was already gathering around the overturned cart, and a few men were trying to calm the injured animals.

She nudged Wildfire forward, but her hands shook slightly as she gripped the reins. The sight of that loathsome Stansbury left her shaken, her heart pounding loud enough to drown out the commotion around her. She forced a deep breath, steadying herself. Wildfire sensed her tension, his muscles rippling beneath her as if preparing for battle.

As Catherine and Charles reached the side street, a rider appeared, slumped unsteadily on his horse.

"Isn't that Lord Wentworth?" Catherine asked, squinting. "He looks awful."

"Is that—blood on his head?" Charles replied.

"Lord Wentworth!" she called.

He looked at her, bleary-eyed, taking a moment to register her identity—or rather, Gray's. He scrubbed a hand across his face, blinking hard to focus.

She exchanged a worried glance with Charles.

"Is there anything we can do to help, Lord Wentworth?" Charles asked. "You appear to be injured."

"Spencer...Gray... Thank God." His voice was faint. "It's Huntley who needs help. Stansbury's kidnapped him." The reins slipped from his hands, but he didn't seem to notice.

Catherine's heart skipped a beat. "I saw Stansbury driving a carriage that way," she said, pointing. "I'm sure someone was inside—it must have been Daniel."

Charles took hold of Wentworth's bridle. "Tell us what happened."

Wentworth rubbed his head, wincing. "Huntley and I were leaving his house when a boy came with a note from my brother." He patted his pocket, frowning. "The note... I can't find it."

"Don't worry about it. What did it say?"

Wentworth stopped searching and let his hands drop. "Frederick wanted me to meet him at the Brass Pig. Huntley rode with me there, then went on to the tournament. But Frederick wasn't there. I think the note was forged. Someone attacked me from behind, and I heard Stansbury say he'd already taken Huntley and had him trussed up in his carriage." He slumped in the saddle, looking ashen. "You have to go after him. Stansbury mentioned a warehouse."

Catherine's heart stopped, a cold wave of fear flooding her veins. *Daniel, taken.* Her mind struggled to process the words. Stansbury had him, tied up and helpless, and she was wasting time standing here. She wouldn't let that man harm him—not now, not ever.

"Which warehouse?" she demanded, her voice fierce, almost a growl. She glanced down the street, hoping to catch a glimpse of the carriage even as her pulse pounded in her ears. But it was already gone.

When Wentworth didn't answer, she clenched her fists. She had to find him. No matter what it took, she would bring Daniel back safely.

"It has to be someplace out of the way," Charles said, thinking aloud. His eyes widened. "I know. Stansbury has a shipping warehouse in the East End. It's isolated enough."

"I know where it is," Catherine said. "Papa pointed it out once."

Wentworth groaned, doubling over and resting his forehead against his horse's neck. "I'm going to be sick," he muttered, retching over the side.

"You need a doctor," Charles said.

"He does. Take him to Bernini's. They'll have a doctor for the tournament," Catherine urged. "I'll check the warehouse. You can follow as soon as he's safe."

Charles set his jaw. "It's too dangerous to go there alone. You should—"

"I should go after him while you help Wentworth. My plan makes sense. You can catch up with me."

"Think about this, Cat. Charging in could do more harm than good."

"I've thought about it long enough, Charles. I can't just stand by. I've seen what Stansbury is capable of, and I won't let him take anything else from me."

"This is insane. I can't let you go alone."

"You have no choice," she said, her eyes blazing. "And you can't stop me."

"Cat?" Wentworth said, sounding bewildered as he tried to focus on her.

She flinched at the sound of her name, spoken with such bleary confusion—a reminder of how vulnerable she truly was in that moment—how much she stood to lose. But she swallowed back her discomfort, focusing on the problem at hand. She couldn't risk Daniel's life.

She turned to Charles, seeing the concern in his eyes, and for a fleeting moment, doubt seized her. What if this was another one of Stansbury's traps? What if, by charging in alone, she only made things worse?

But then her thoughts returned to Daniel. He'd sacrificed everything to protect her from Stansbury. She could feel his arms around her, see the fierce determination in his eyes as he'd promised to keep her safe. No, she couldn't abandon him—not now, not ever. She'd only just realized the depth of her feelings for him, only just started to dream of what their lives could be together. She'd be damned if she let Stansbury rip that future away from them. They had too much to live for, too much ahead of them.

With renewed purpose, she swung herself back onto Wildfire, gripping the reins tightly. Taking a deep breath, she steeled herself. "I have to do this," she whispered, her voice barely audible, but her resolve unwavering. She leaned forward in the saddle, gave Wildfire a quick squeeze with her knees, and the horse sprang forward, muscles coiling with every step.

Their life together was just beginning, and she'd fight for it with everything she had. As the pounding of hooves drowned out the world behind her, she knew there was no turning back.

❧ 54 ❧

THE WAREHOUSE

Catherine tore through the streets toward the East End. Panic clouded her thoughts, thick and sluggish as treacle. All she knew was that she had to save Daniel. What if Stansbury had hurt him—or worse? A shiver ran through her as she imagined him lying dead, his eyes glassy and unseeing.

The long ride allowed her time to force her frantic thoughts into submission, bit by bit. She was moving faster than a carriage could. She'd save Daniel. She had to. The alternative was unthinkable.

But why would Stansbury kidnap him? It couldn't be just because of their marriage. There must be another reason, something she was missing. The attempted kidnapping must have been related. Stansbury was behind it, no doubt. But to what end?

Traveling through the maze of narrow streets in the East End, the pungent stench from the tanneries and docks along the Thames grew stronger, and the narrow streets seemed to close in around her. She was forced to slow down, maneuvering around dockworkers and businessmen who threw irritated glances her way.

At last, she arrived at Stansbury's warehouse. The tall, grim walls loomed overhead, the large wooden doors slightly ajar. She glimpsed the empty courtyard within, and a chill ran down her spine.

She peeked through the doors. Empty. Did that mean they hadn't yet arrived, or worse, that she'd gone to the wrong place? She tied Wildfire to a nearby post, then slipped through the open doors into the large courtyard. She wished she wasn't wearing her white fencing costume. It stood out in stark contrast against the dark doors.

Moving cautiously, she scanned the courtyard, peering into the warehouse as she passed each open doorway. The large building was almost completely deserted, the absence of workers unsettling. Charles was right; this would be the perfect place to bring Daniel.

She slipped into the warehouse itself. In the dim light, she spotted a single chair in the center of the room, a pile of ropes beside it. A chill ran through her. The chair was waiting for Daniel. With the doors closed, no one on the street would hear him yell.

A carriage rumbled to a stop outside the outer gates, and her heart seized. Was it Stansbury? She peeked out the door to find him pushing the gate open wide. He clambered back onto the driver's box and drove the carriage through, pulling it up near a set of doors close to where she hid.

Rage filled her, and a cold realization hit. If Stansbury were alone, she might have a chance to take him down. But where could she hide? The warehouse offered few options.

"Stay there while I shut the gate!" Stansbury's shout dashed her hopes as he jumped to the ground. He had someone with him.

As he closed the heavy double doors, Catherine glanced around the dim warehouse, realizing it wasn't as dark as she'd thought. Thin shafts of light pierced the gloom through cracks between the rough wooden boards, casting faint stripes across the dusty floor.

She glanced again at the chair, suppressing the image of Daniel tied to it. She needed a plan to save him, but the task overwhelmed her. She had her blade, yes, but with only a single lesson in knife fighting, how could she hope to stop Stansbury?

Her confidence waned as she searched the room for anything that might give her an advantage.

Nothing. Along the far wall, she noticed piles of debris and a dark stain on the ground. Rats, she thought with a shudder. Of course, there were rats. This was a riverside warehouse, after all. Mice, she could handle; rats made her skin crawl.

Near the door, a dank pile of discarded sailcloth lay in a heap, reeking of mildew and neglect. It offered scant cover, but with few other options, she shook the cloth out, sending bits of debris and dust flying—thankfully, no rats scurried out. She quickly buried herself under the moldy fabric, wincing as it settled around her, then held her breath, heart pounding in her chest.

The warehouse door swung open, slamming hard enough against the wall to echo through the cavernous space. Catherine tensed as footsteps approached, and then someone stumbled in, his hands bound tightly behind his back. She peeked through a gap in the sailcloth and caught a glimpse of his face.

"I was afraid she might get here first," a voice grated through the warehouse, harsh and tense. It wasn't Stansbury—but *Charles Attwood?* Catherine's stomach twisted. What on earth was happening? Why was Attwood tied up? Had Stansbury kidnapped him too? The whole situation was rapidly becoming more and more bizarre.

Stansbury shut the carriage door. Where was Daniel? Was he still inside?

Stansbury pulled a knife from his boots and cut the ropes binding Attwood's wrists, letting them fall to the ground in a tangled heap. Clearly, Attwood wasn't his prisoner. She was beginning to suspect they were working together.

Catherine slipped her hand inside her fencing jacket and

pulled out her knife. Had it been foresight or dumb luck that had compelled her to bring it along? Neither. She'd wanted it with her because Daniel had given it to her. It had become a talisman. She gripped the handle, holding it so that the blade was tucked behind her forearm, just as Daniel had taught her.

"We had a good lead on her," Stansbury said. "She and her brother should be here any minute, though, charging through the gate. This plan is sure to keep them out of the action."

The two men stood silently for a moment, watching the court-yard gate through the open warehouse door.

"You're certain this will work?" Attwood asked in a tone that suggested this wasn't the first time he'd asked.

"Of course I'm certain," Stansbury snapped. "When I drove away, I made sure to meet her gaze. She recognized me. Now Wentworth's out of the competition, as are Catherine and her brother. Huntley will be so rattled when they don't show at Berni-ni's that he'll be in a panic."

Catherine held her breath, relief washing over her. Daniel was alive. She tried to make sense of the rest, piecing together the strange plan that seemed far more complex than she'd anticipated.

The two men lapsed into silence, and then Attwood broke it once more. "Where'd you get the blunt for the wager?"

Stansbury grunted. "Sold my newest carriage and the bays. Had trouble paying to stable them anyway," he said. "But at twenty-to-one odds, it'll be worth it."

"Worth even kidnapping," Attwood mused. "I put nearly five hundred pounds in myself. A bit of wheedling and a bit of stealing."

"Pounds?" Stansbury sounded surprised. "Well done, man."

"Couldn't pass up a sure thing."

Silence fell again, and Catherine took the chance to peek from under the sailcloth. The men stood framed in the open warehouse door, staring toward the courtyard gates. She tightened her grip on her knife, questions flooding her mind. They must be betting on the fencing match. That was the only explanation that made sense, not that much else did.

She heard a rustling nearby and froze. A rat? Her breath hitched.

Something brushed against her foot, and she instinctively jerked it back, stifling a scream. A gasp escaped, though, and she looked across the room to see both men staring at her hiding place.

She might as well have screamed.

As the men approached, she scrambled to her feet. A mouse scurried out from under the sailcloth and dashed toward the wall. Stansbury's eyes followed it before darting back to her face.

She lifted her knife, letting them see it, but they hardly reacted. Attwood pulled out a larger blade, his expression darkening.

A much larger one.

"Lady Huntley," Stansbury sneered. His gaze raked her body, lingering on her legs and leaving her feeling unclean. "A tempting little slut, don't you agree? It's a wonder Huntley allows her to go out in public, showing off her limbs in such a degrading manner."

His voice held a strange, trembling menace, sending a ripple of fear down her spine. Something was deeply wrong with him, like he was wound too tight, about to explode and send little bits of himself flying at the slightest touch. She watched him warily.

Stansbury rubbed his palms against his thighs, and her stomach churned when she realized he was touching himself in a sick, self-indulgent way, a twisted grin spreading across his face.

When Stansbury saw the direction of her gaze, he grinned at her. "Do you like what you see, Lady Huntley?" he taunted. "Maybe you're hoping for someone who can bend you to his will. Your husband isn't up to the task," he added with a sneer, "but I assure you, I am."

Catherine took a step back, her heart pounding as the men

moved closer. She stepped again, catching her foot on the edge of the sailcloth and stumbling.

"Well done, Lady Catherine. All it took was a mouse to expose you and make you scream."

"I didn't scream," she shot back, her voice shrill with fear.

"Not yet," he replied with a smile. "But you will."

The two men lunged forward, pinning her arms behind her back before she could react. Her knife clattered to the floor as Attwood dragged her to her feet, pressing a cold blade to her throat.

"I'll lock the gates," Stansbury said, striding purposefully away. "We don't want to be interrupted."

Catherine's heart pounded as she struggled against Attwood's grip, her mind racing with desperate thoughts. Daniel and Charles would come. They had to. She only prayed they'd arrive in time.

❧ 55 ❧

BERNINI'S

Daniel spotted John Cunningham among the spectators gathered to watch the tournament, chatting with that Frenchman, Monsieur LeCompte. He made his way across the fencing salon to join them.

"*Bon jour*," LeCompte said.

"Huntley, my man. How good to see you. Congratulations again on your marriage," Cunningham greeted him warmly. "Are you here to support your new brother-in-law, Lord Spencer, or your old friend Wentworth?"

"It's a difficult choice. Fortunately, it's one I won't be forced to make. I'll be taking part in the tournament as well."

LeCompte eyed him. "I thought perhaps you'd withdrawn, seeing as you aren't yet dressed for the event. The odds-makers have you coming in fourth. Seems neither you nor your friends are favorites for the trophy. Gray holds the top spot."

"I'm not surprised," Daniel replied, pride welling within him. "I've watched him. He's quite talented with a foil."

LeCompte pinned him with a sharp gaze, prompting Daniel to shutter his expression, returning LeCompte's look with cool equanimity. That flicker of pride had been a foolish slip.

A commotion near the door drew their attention, but Daniel couldn't see past the throng of spectators.

Moments later, Mr. Winston emerged from the crowd blocking the salon's entrance, his gaze fixed intently on Daniel, urgency clear in his eyes, sending a chill of foreboding through Daniel's spine.

"If you'll excuse me," he murmured, making his way toward Winston near the entrance.

The man sidled close to him. "Your presence is required in Maestro Bernini's office," Winston murmured, turning on his heel and leading the way. The smaller man slipped through the crowd. As Daniel followed, the men blocking his path made way for him, stepping to one side lest they be trampled.

Winston led him around a tall desk and toward a door beyond. As they approached, Daniel heard the murmur of voices from within, Lord Spencer's standing out from the rest. He couldn't make out the words, but the distress in the man's tone was unmistakable, intensifying Daniel's unease.

Stepping into the room, Daniel scanned it quickly. A man lay sprawled on a sofa, with another man in a black coat leaning over him, blocking his face. Charles sat perched on the edge of a wing-backed chair, tense, his gaze fixed on the men by the sofa. He looked up at the sound of Daniel's footsteps, his jaw dropping in astonishment.

"You're here," Charles said. "I didn't believe it when Winston told us. I thought he must have been mistaken."

"Where else would I be?" Daniel replied, his brow furrowing. "What's going on? And where's Gray?"

The doctor moved, revealing the man on the sofa—Wentworth, his face bloodied.

"What happened?" Daniel demanded.

"Someone attacked Wentworth," Charles explained, detailing what had occurred over the past fifteen minutes, including Stansbury's claim to have kidnapped Daniel. "Gray took off on his horse to scout the warehouse."

"Gray's alone?" Daniel's heart skipped a beat even as his mind raced. None of this made sense. Why attack Wentworth? Was it to draw Catherine away? If Stansbury had lied about Daniel's abduction, Catherine might have followed, thinking only of his safety. But why go after her through such a convoluted scheme? Why not just strike directly?

There had to be more to this.

"Is Gray alone?" Daniel repeated, his urgency growing.

Charles nodded.

"Get my horse!" he barked, sending Winston, who had been lingering near the door, scurrying away to do his bidding. "I have to go. I have to save... save Gray."

If he hurried, he might still be in time to stop whatever Stansbury planned. Because whatever it was, it boded ill for his wife.

"I'm coming with you," Charles declared.

"No, I'll be better off on my own." Daniel's eyes scanned the room for a weapon. He needed something more deadly than a fencing foil. Among the gentlemanly weapons on the wall, a pair of dueling pistols caught his eye. He crossed the room in two strides, yanking them down.

"I'm not staying behind," Charles protested, anger simmering in his voice. "We're family. We need to stick together."

The word "family" brought Daniel up short. He glanced at Wentworth, injured on the sofa, realizing he wasn't alone anymore. He had Charles, Catherine, and even young Sarah. Family.

Maestro Bernini entered the room, his gaze moving directly to the weapons in Daniel's hands. "Those are only for display," Bernini said, his voice calm but firm. "I wouldn't trust my life with them. Take my new Colt. And listen to your brother-in-law —don't go charging in alone."

Daniel looked back at Charles, assessing him. Then he nodded.

Bernini opened a desk drawer, pulling out a wooden box. Flipping it open, he revealed a pistol, glistening with fresh gun oil. The sharp scent of metal filled the air as Bernini loaded it.

Charles stepped closer, glancing between Bernini and Daniel. "If you're here, who did Stansbury kidnap? We definitely saw someone inside the carriage."

As Daniel accepted the loaded pistol, his mind whirled. "I don't know. My priority is getting to Gray in time. Stansbury's cunning. I have a feeling this whole scheme is an elaborate trap, perhaps even to isolate her." He hesitated, his mind flashing to Catherine. He'd spoken too freely.

"Her?" Bernini's gaze sharpened.

Damn. "Did I say 'her'? I was thinking of my wife. She's home alone, and I fear she'll hear rumors that I've been taken. I simply want her to know I'm safe."

"I'll send word to her," Bernini said, handing the pistol to Charles with a nod. "But you two must hurry. Find Gray." He hesitated, emotion in his voice. "I couldn't bear to lose that boy."

Daniel nodded, a surge of determination filling him. He turned and tore out of the room with Charles close behind.

He only hoped they wouldn't be too late.

LOCKED IN

Daniel pulled his horse up short outside the gates of Stansbury's warehouse.

"That's her horse," Charles said, pointing. "She's probably already inside."

"Let's look around first," Daniel replied, scanning the area, willing her to appear from a nearby alley. But she didn't. His stomach twisted. She was inside. He was certain of it. That damned impulsive streak of hers would get her killed.

He dismounted, tying Rajah beside her horse. "I'm going after her." He moved toward the large wooden doors leading to the courtyard.

"I'm coming with you," Charles said, dismounting quickly and securing his horse beside Rajah.

Daniel didn't wait. He pushed one of the large doors open a crack, testing it—it wasn't locked. He stepped inside, Charles close behind. The moment he rounded the door and entered the courtyard, he came face-to-face with Stansbury, barely two feet away and holding a key.

Stansbury didn't hesitate. He charged.

Daniel sidestepped, narrowly avoiding him.

Stansbury rammed his shoulder into the door, slamming it shut. He twisted the key in the lock with a sharp click and turned to Daniel, a broad smile spreading across his face as he slipped the key into his waistcoat pocket. "Perfect timing, Huntley. I'm delighted you're here to take part in this afternoon's entertainment."

"Are you mad, Stansbury?" Daniel growled, fists clenched. He cursed himself for not having taken the pistol from Charles. It was useless now, locked away on the other side of that thick brick wall. "What exactly do you think you're doing?"

"Oh, I've plans for you, Huntley," Stansbury sneered. "The great Lord Huntley is about to fall—quite publicly. I'll see to it that everyone knows your famous Midas touch was nothing but a sham, a cover for your underhanded dealings. I know you've been asking questions about me—stirring doubts. It's your fault my partnerships are in ruins. I know it was you who tipped them off about my warehouse that day. And you'll pay, Huntley. You and that wretched wife of yours."

"Where is Catherine?" Daniel demanded, his voice trembling with rage.

Stansbury's face contorted, fury twisting his features. "Your little whore? Why would you even want to claim such an abomination? She prances around, dressed as a man, flaunting her limbs and hindquarters for all to see! She's even dared to enter the gentlemen's changing rooms at Bernini's Academy." He gave a sickening smile, eyes alight with a twisted glee. "She's perverted, and she deserves to be taught a lesson—and so do you."

Daniel's anger boiled over, and he lunged, fists raised, but Stansbury dodged, dancing backward to keep the distance between them.

"Oh, don't be in such a rush, Huntley!" Stansbury's voice echoed through the courtyard, an unsettling singsong edge to it.

"Why not let our audience join us? I'm sure you're eager to see your filthy little wife in her final moments!"

From within the open doorway leading into the warehouse, Daniel caught a flicker of movement. He braced himself as two figures stepped into the light, emerging from the shadows.

❦ 57 ❦

DON'T TRIP

ttwood shoved Catherine into the courtyard, pulling her tight against his chest with a knife pressed firmly to her throat. She squeezed her eyes shut, terror clawing at her. The cold edge of the blade was nothing like the practice knives at the academy.

What if one of them accidentally tripped?

Her eyes flew open. One stumble and she could wind up with her throat slit.

Don't trip. Don't trip.

She scanned the courtyard, searching for Daniel. When she caught sight of him, her knees nearly gave way as relief coursed through her. He was alive.

Attwood shoved her forward, his chest pressed against her back. She arched her body away, revolted by his touch.

Stansbury's gaze landed on her, an oily grin spreading across his face. "Your wife thought she could rescue you. Came to take on the two of us alone. Isn't that precious?" His eyes raked over her with a look that left her feeling dirtied. "She's either stupid or brave. Or both."

I'm a little brave. But mostly I'm very, very stupid.

"Catherine. Did they hurt you?" Daniel's voice cut through her thoughts.

"Not yet," Attwood answered for her. "We thought we'd let you watch that part." He pressed the blade more tightly against her neck, drawing a whimper from her.

"No!" Daniel shouted, taking a step forward.

Stansbury chuckled. "What's wrong? Do you feel weak? Impotent? Do you hate it when someone else is in control?" He leaned down, pulling a knife from his boot. "Let's continue our little gathering inside, shall we? I'd hate for someone on the street to overhear."

Daniel hesitated, his eyes darting between Stansbury and Catherine. Stansbury stepped behind him, shoving him forward with an open palm.

Daniel took a reluctant step, then another. His eyes met hers across the narrowing distance, and he offered her a reassuring smile. Despite her terror, the smallest flicker of courage welled up within her in response.

"Move," Attwood ordered, jerking her backward and pulling her away from Daniel. The blade pressed into her neck, but as she shuffled back, he adjusted his grip, loosening his hold for a brief moment. She sagged against him, taking the opportunity to shift the pressure of the knife away from her skin.

"Are you afraid, Huntley? Your wife is," Attwood sneered. She wondered how Calliope had willingly married such an arrogant brute.

Daniel stepped through the doorway, his tall frame taut with tension. Stansbury followed close behind.

Attwood forced her forward, and as they crossed into the warehouse, he paused just inside. Catherine's eyes took a moment to adjust to the dim light. She could see Daniel a few feet away. He glanced over his shoulder, catching her gaze. In that moment, something unspoken passed between them. He gave her the slightest of nods.

Without warning, Daniel sprang into action, spinning on his heel as his foot shot out in a kick that sent Stansbury's knife clattering across the floor, where it disappeared into the half-light.

Catherine knew what to do. She grasped Attwood's arm, turning toward the knife at her throat, exactly as Daniel had shown her, forcing Attwood to tighten his grip. She ducked down, and the blade drove straight into his chest.

It happened quickly. The move felt eerily like their academy practice—until the knife actually penetrated flesh. Attwood looked down in disbelief, a small cough escaping his lips as his eyes bulged. His fingers clutched the knife handle, and he stumbled back, leaning against the warehouse wall before slowly sliding to the floor, blood bubbling at the corners of his mouth.

She stared down at him, a roaring in her ears. Pinkish foam pooled at his lips, a telltale sign that she'd pierced his lung. Her stomach churned.

I just stabbed a man.

She touched her mouth with icy fingers, stifling a groan. Her gaze flew to Daniel.

He glanced toward her, taking in the tableau. He immediately shifted his position so he faced, forcing Stansbury to turn his back to her.

He caught her look, taking in the scene with swift comprehension. Instantly, he shifted his stance, forcing Stansbury to turn his back on her as he advanced on Daniel, now brandishing a makeshift club.

"I don't have a letter opener at hand tonight, like I did at Norfolk's ball," Daniel taunted, his tone cool. "But I'll improvise."

He pulled the malachite pin she'd given him from his cravat.

Stansbury's laugh was scornful as he eyed the small weapon. "A tiepin? My, aren't you terrifying."

Daniel wrapped his fingers around the pin's malachite head, the long point protruding between his knuckles.

Stansbury swung the club, and Daniel stepped back, retreating

—but Catherine recognized his tactic. He was drawing Stansbury away from her.

The loud banging of fists on the outer gate reached her ears, accompanied by shouts.

Stansbury lunged, swinging his weapon at Daniel's head just as the gate splintered with a resounding crash. She turned toward the noise and saw the doors burst open, pieces of the broken lock clattering to the ground.

Charles led a swarm of men into the courtyard, a makeshift battering ram still cradled in their arms.

Catherine darted to the doorway, waving her arms frantically. "Over here!" she shouted, her voice hoarse. "Stansbury is attacking Daniel!"

58

A CRAVAT PIN

Stansbury swung his club, but Daniel sidestepped, thrusting his fist forward and jamming the pin deep into Stansbury's forearm. He gave it a hard twist before yanking it free.

Stansbury staggered back, clutching his bleeding arm as crimson seeped onto his hand, staining his white cuff red. His face paled, and he wiped his bloody hand on his trousers, no longer looking quite so confident. He shifted the club to his off hand, letting the injured arm hang limply at his side.

He shuffled backward, positioning himself for another attack, but his movements betrayed hesitation. His boot bumped against Attwood's crumpled body, nearly toppling him.

Stansbury glanced down, his eyes widening at the sight of his partner sprawled on the ground with a knife protruding from his chest. Attwood was still alive, barely, blood foaming at his lips as he struggled to breathe. Motes of dust floated in the light streaming through the open door.

"What are you doing just lying there?" Stansbury roared, spittle flying from his lips. "Where's the slut? Did you let her get away?"

Attwood only managed a feeble wheeze.

"You imbecile!" Stansbury lunged toward him, grabbing the knife hilt and yanking, but it wouldn't budge. He braced his boot on Attwood's ribcage for leverage.

For a moment, Daniel froze, stunned by Stansbury's brutal disregard for his companion's agony. But as Stansbury dropped his club to grab the knife with both hands, Daniel broke free from his shock.

He leapt forward, driving his cravat pin into the side of Stansbury's neck. He twisted the pin, tearing flesh as he pulled downward, and a sickening vibration ran through the thin piece of metal.

Stansbury staggered away, the pin still embedded in his neck, wrenching it free from Daniel's grip. He clutched at the wound, his mouth slack with shock. The malachite ball of the pin jutted from between his fingers as blood spurted around it.

Stansbury dropped to his knees, yanking the pin from his neck with a gasp, and more blood gushed from the wound.

Footsteps pounded across the courtyard. Daniel turned to see Catherine and Charles appear in the doorway.

She looked unharmed—thank God. Relief surged through him as he rushed to her, the men on the ground momentarily forgotten.

He reached for her, but a scuffling sound behind him made him spin around. Charles's eyes widened as he raised the pistol, and Daniel turned in time to see Stansbury rising to his feet, the knife from Attwood's chest now clutched in his hand.

The roar of the pistol shot exploded next to Daniel's ear, and he saw a dark bloom of red spread across Stansbury's shoulder. Stansbury stumbled back, crumpling to the floor, where he lay still.

He didn't try to stand again.

As the echoes of the gunshot faded, Daniel's ears rang, his hearing muffled as though stuffed with cotton. Dimly, he became aware of the sound of murmuring voices.

Behind Catherine and Charles, a crowd of dockworkers had gathered, craning their necks and jostling to get a better view of the grim scene in the warehouse.

A sudden urge to escape overwhelmed Daniel. The mingling stench of gunpowder, blood, and another foul odor—one he'd come to associate with death—filled his nostrils.

"Find a surgeon!" he shouted, stepping outside. A man at the back of the crowd turned and hurried toward the broken gates.

Inside, Attwood wheezed for each labored breath, while Stansbury lay deathly still, the rank smell of death emanating from him.

Daniel pulled Catherine further into the courtyard, away from the smell. All he wanted was to sweep her into his arms, but with so many onlookers, he barely dared look at her in her fencing garb.

Moments later, two policemen arrived, pushing through the crowd.

"Move aside! Let us through!" the older officer commanded, and the dockworkers parted to allow them entry.

The officer's gaze settled on Daniel and the others at the center of the crowd, his expression shifting with recognition. "Is this lot causing you trouble, m'lord?"

"No, it's the two men in there," Daniel replied, quickly introducing himself and recounting the kidnapping and rescue. He downplayed 'Gray's' involvement, claiming he had been the one to stab Attwood. He avoided Catherine's gaze, hoping she understood that he wanted to protect her. If the police suspected she had played a major role, they might hold her for questioning. It would be impossible for her to maintain her disguise from a jail cell.

She pressed her lips together but didn't contradict him. When he reached the part of the story where Charles entered, his brother-in-law took over, recounting the tale from there.

A surgeon arrived, shouldering through the crowd with a small black bag. He knelt by the two injured men, examining each one briefly. He turned his back on Stansbury's motionless body and pulled a long tube from his bag, wiping it on his coat before pressing one end to Attwood's wound. He forced the tube into Attwood's chest, and his wheezing eased.

"Lord Huntley," the policeman said, "I'll need you and the other gentlemen to stay until an inspector arrives. We've already sent for one."

Daniel frowned. "What about the boy? He needs to get to a tournament."

The officer shook his head. "Sorry, m'lord. With a death involved, I can't let anyone leave until the inspector has a look. It'll be his decision."

Catherine's face paled. "He's dead?"

The policeman gave her a sympathetic nod. "I'm sorry, son. I thought you knew."

She shook her head. Daniel ached to comfort her.

She shook her head, and Daniel's chest tightened with the urge to comfort her. He glanced around, looking for a quiet place to speak with her in private. His eyes settled on Stansbury's worn carriage.

He turned to the officer. "Would it be alright if we sat in the carriage?"

"What with that Stansbury fellow being dead and all, I don't see as he'll mind," the policeman replied with a shrug. "It's the least he owes you." He turned back to the crowd, corralling the onlookers.

"I'll gather our horses," Charles said, "Mine's down the road at one of the warehouses."

"Is that where you went after Stansbury locked the gate?" Daniel asked.

Charles nodded. "I knew I'd need help, so I found some dockworkers. They suggested using that timber as a battering ram." He gestured to the thick post lying in the courtyard.

"Quick thinking. It did the job," Catherine said, managing a small smile.

Charles looked pleased. "Once we're done here, I'm taking these men out for a well-deserved pint." The group cheered at his promise.

Daniel opened the carriage door, gesturing for Catherine to enter first, but she didn't move.

She gave a slight bow. "My lord?"

Right. *Gray* would wait for his superior.

With a tight nod, Daniel climbed into the rickety carriage, and Catherine quickly joined him.

59

HEART TO HEART

Catherine gazed out the window, transfixed by the scene outside. From this angle, she had a clear view into Stansbury's warehouse and could see the worn sole of the dead man's boot.

Daniel slid his hand over hers, his fingers gently prying open her clenched fist. "How are you holding up?"

She shook her head. "I'm fine." Her voice sounded thin, as if she didn't believe it herself.

"Did they hurt you?" he pressed, his tone gentle but insistent.

Her eyes remained on the scene outside as she watched the doctor wave two men over, directing them to load Stansbury's body onto a stretcher. "I think they meant to, but they didn't get the chance. You arrived right after they discovered my hiding place."

He tightened his grip on her hand. "When I saw Attwood holding that knife to your throat, I wanted to kill him."

Catherine reached over and snapped the window shade closed, blocking out the macabre scene and shielding them from any prying eyes. Light still streamed in from the window facing the courtyard, casting a warm glow across them.

She shifted to face Daniel, but still couldn't meet his eyes. Instead, she looked down, watching as their fingers intertwined. "I know exactly how you felt. When I thought Stansbury had kidnapped you, I wanted to kill him, too."

She'd almost lost him. She tightened her grip on his hand, noting the contrast of her pale skin against his darker tone. A faint tracing of straight, dark hair trailed up the back of his wrist, and she covered it by clasping his hand with both of hers.

Her thumb brushed absently over his, and a shiver ran through her at the thought that if things had gone differently today, it could have been one of them lying on that warehouse floor. She squeezed her eyes shut, and a tear slipped down her cheek.

"I'm so sorry," Daniel said softly.

She looked up, surprised. "It's not your fault. Stansbury was a madman. *Was* a madman," she corrected herself.

"Not just for what happened, but for the tournament, too. I know how much it meant to you."

She blinked. "Blast the tournament, Daniel. I'm just thankful you're alive."

A frown creased his forehead. "But you've prepared for it for so long. You've been working toward this for years. It means everything to you."

"No. *You* mean everything to me." She glanced away, startled by her own words. Admitting her feelings out loud felt even more vulnerable than being naked before him.

When had Daniel become so important?

She finally looked up to meet his gaze, only to find him frowning.

"You hardly know me," he said, almost in disbelief.

She shook her head. "I know you better than you think. I've seen the way you work tirelessly, the sacrifices you made to protect me when Stansbury tried to ruin me. I see your honor, your quick mind. You're a kind, faithful man who's willing to put others before himself."

He shrugged. "Those are small things. You make me sound like a saint, and I'm not. I failed at the one thing that matters most. Protecting you. I didn't recognize the danger Stansbury posed, and I let Attwood hold a knife to your neck. Worst of all…" He hesitated, his voice thick with emotion. "I just killed a man. Again." He turned away, his body rigid with tension as he stared out the far window.

"Again?" she whispered.

The silence stretched between them. Finally, he spoke, his voice low. "When I was twelve. I killed someone." He met her gaze, his expression set, as if expecting her to recoil. "I've only told one other person."

Catherine squeezed his hand. "You were twelve. Only a child. I'm sure you were simply defending yourself." Her words sounded like scant comfort. Her heart raced. What if he'd been in a knife fight back then? "Why don't you tell me what happened?"

He sighed. "It's something you need to know. I told you my father was a recluse. Twice a year his lawyer would travel there to have him sign papers. He saw no one else from outside the estate. Apparently, he had visitors for a year or two after my mother's death, at first to offer condolences and later to try to pull him from his despair, but he sent them all away. Everyone gave up on him. Over time, stories about him grew and became embellished. The locals said he was mad, that our estate was haunted. They even said he'd hidden gold and jewels in the house. Some said it was in his bedroom, and others said it was in my mother's crypt." His lips pressed into a thin line. "Eventually, someone broke into my mother's burial chamber, but the groundskeeper scared them off before any damage was done."

Daniel's lips pressed into a thin line. "The last time I ran away to Edinburgh, our butler, Latimer, brought me back. My father instructed the servants to keep me on the estate. I wasn't even allowed to visit the village. I prowled the house, finally exploring my mother's old rooms. I'd avoided them for years, but I found them just as she'd left them, as if she might return any moment. Her jewels sat on the dresser, her letters and books on the shelves. I spent hours there, trying to know her through the things she'd left behind."

He paused, squeezing her hand. She returned the pressure, and he continued.

"I was surprised to find some of her jewels sitting on her dresser as though she'd only just removed them and hadn't yet put them away. Her rooms seemed filled with her presence, as though she'd just stepped out and would be back at any moment. I began visiting the room daily, staying for hours at a time. I found her books and letters and pored through them, trying to learn something of the mother I'd never known.

"One evening, I saw light under her door. I thought my father had come, seeking the same connection I felt. I went in, only to find a stranger tearing through her things, defiling her room. He'd torn everything apart in his search, and her jewels were no longer on her dressing table.

"I must have made a sound, because he whirled on me, dropping her silver comb into a bag and drawing a knife. I tried to escape, but he was too fast. He held a knife to my throat, demanding to know where the rest of her jewels were. He threatened to kill me and throw my body in the river, saying everyone would believe I'd run away again. I knew he was right." Daniel's jaw tightened. "Something inside me snapped. I wanted him dead."

He looked at her, anguish in his eyes. "I used the same move I taught you, and the knife went in deep. He died instantly."

She touched his cheek gently. "You were defending yourself, Daniel. You weren't to blame."

He shook his head. "I try to tell myself that, but I felt the bloodlust. I wanted him dead, and that's something I'll always carry with me."

"What did you do?" she finally asked. "You were just a boy. Did anyone help you?"

"I knew the problem was too big for me to handle on my own, so I found Latimer, the one person in my life who could solve any problem. And he did. I don't know where he took the body, and Latimer said to forget it ever happened. But how could I?

"Father shipped me off to Eton. I think it must have been Latimer's idea. I'm not sure how he managed that part, but he did. I'll be grateful to him for the rest of my life."

She looked into his tortured soul. "You need to forgive yourself."

"It's hard to forgive a murder," he whispered.

"Not murder. Self-defense. You did what you had to, just like today. Stansbury and Attwood brought this on themselves."

He turned back to her, his expression softening. "When I saw that knife at your throat, I was terrified at the thought of losing you." Daniel gently cupped her cheek in his palm as he gazed into her eyes. "I only just found you."

"And I defended myself exactly the same way you did," she said, placing her hand over his. She ached to pull him close. "Do you hold me responsible for what happened to Attwood?"

"Of course not," he said, pulling his hand away.

"Then how could you hold a twelve-year-old boy responsible?" she asked gently.

He blinked, as if seeing himself for the first time. "I forget that I was just a boy back then."

"You were a boy who grew into a man willing to protect others, even at his own expense." She paused. "That's the man I know."

He searched her face, seeming to find something there. He wrapped his arms around her, pulling her close. "What did I do to deserve someone as perfect as you?"

She smiled. "I'm far from perfect. I'm reckless, impetuous, terribly improper..."

"And I love every improper inch of you."

"What?" she whispered.

"I love you. I only realized it when I thought I'd lose you."

She threw her arms around him. "I love you too. I was terrified when I thought Stansbury had taken you."

He cupped her face, brushing a thumb over her scar. "I haven't kissed *Gray* since that night in my drawing room." He traced his thumb along her cheek. "It's a bit disconcerting."

A knock sounded on the carriage door, and they sprang apart.

"It's me," Charles called. "The inspector is here."

Daniel cracked open the door. "We're ready."

"He says he just has a few questions, then we can all go," Charles said, turning away.

Daniel turned back to her, his eyes smoldering with unspoken promise. "Let's finish this quickly so I can take you home. I want to show you exactly how much I cherish you."

60

SHADOWS AND LIGHT

Afternoon sunlight poured into Catherine's new fencing salon, illuminating every corner of the bright, airy space. Tall windows stretched along one wall, casting light over the polished wooden floors and warming the unused fencing gear meticulously arranged in neat rows along the far wall. On the doors leading into the room, an intricate carving of Ganesha, the elephant-headed deity, stood as a protective symbol. She'd chosen the design as a tribute to her father, who'd always told her that Ganesha was the remover of obstacles. In this new endeavor, she could think of no better blessing.

As she stood by the weapon rack, her fingers lightly brushing over the hilt of a foil, Catherine inhaled the subtle scent of lemon oil lingering from the fresh polish. It was clean and sharp, but missing the layers of a familiar, long-imbued fragrance—one she hadn't even noticed at Bernini's until it was absent. That scent had been a mixture of resin, a faint tang of metal, and the faint musk of exertion, barely hidden beneath the surface. She realized now it was the constant, quiet reminder of the people who had filled those shadowed halls, their presence a part of the air she breathed there. This space, in contrast, felt untouched, its air unmarked by any trace of past lives. Here, she'd created something entirely her own—a space that felt like a bright, open canvas, awaiting the brushstrokes of her ambition.

As she stood there, she thought back to the day Daniel had revealed this space to her—a wedding gift, unexpected and quietly thoughtful, an unmistakable sign that he understood her. He'd seen beyond the pretense of Gray, recognizing that fencing was woven into the fabric of who she was. Since then, they'd spent hours discussing how to outfit the room, choosing each foil, mask, and piece of equipment with care. Now, seeing the salon complete, she felt the thrill of possibility mingled with a newfound sense of ownership, grateful for a partner who had crafted a space where she could step fully into herself.

The door opened, and she looked up to see Daniel entering, a small smile tugging at his lips as he took in the space.

"You've done well here," he said, his voice warm with admiration. "It feels like... a fresh start."

She smiled, a spark of pride flashing in her eyes. "It is," she agreed, gesturing around the room. "And I owe it to you."

He shook his head slightly, crossing the room to join her by the weapon rack. "I may have made space in our home for the possibility, but the reality is all yours."

She let out a soft laugh, reaching out to place a hand on his arm. "Perhaps. But there's more to be done." She hesitated, looking down as she gathered her thoughts. "I want to reach the women who would benefit from this—those who would want to learn but might be afraid of what society would think. I can't risk advertising it openly, and I don't quite know where to start."

He raised an eyebrow, a thoughtful expression crossing his face as he considered her dilemma. "Why not begin with your acquaintances? Host teas, dinners—the gatherings they're already inclined to attend. You know who among them might be open to this." He smiled, his hand covering hers briefly. "Be subtle, and word will spread on its own."

She tilted her head, her gaze thoughtful as she processed his suggestion. "You've given this some thought."

He chuckled. "I'd say it's your influence. And I've had ample time to ponder while you were immersed in your plans." He glanced over his shoulder at the doors, where the carving of Ganesha gleamed softly in the light. "He'll watch over this place, I think."

She followed his gaze, a smile playing on her lips as she observed the familiar figure. "Father once told me that Ganesha removes obstacles. If that's true, then I'll have a powerful ally."

Daniel looked back at her, a glimmer of mischief in his eyes. "Speaking of allies, why not invite Sarah? I'm sure she'd love the chance to join you here."

Catherine's eyes brightened. "I'd love that, and so would Father. But we'll have to keep it hidden from Mother. She'd have a fit if she knew."

A knowing smile crossed his face. Their gazes met, a quiet understanding passing between them. The bright promise of the salon, the familiar warmth of his presence—it all felt like the first step toward something that was finally hers.

Daniel moved through the room, adjusting a few pieces of equipment and clearing a space for their sparring session. His hand brushed over the fencing dummy, its unblemished fabric a stark contrast to the one at Bernini's—a dummy that had seen years of wear, its faded fabric torn, the heart patch frayed and tattered, punctured countless times by foil thrusts. This one, however, stood untouched, almost pristine, its clean lines suggesting a readiness that matched the fresh start this space represented. The quiet afternoon light pooled around them, casting a warm circle that felt like a natural arena, intimate and private.

Catherine stepped closer, her gaze falling to the knife in her hand. She turned it slowly, letting the blade catch the light. Memories surged—a flash of Attwood's desperate eyes, the tension in his wrist as he'd tried to twist free, the shock as the blade struck. Her stomach clenched, the vivid recall of that night settling like a weight in her chest. She forced herself to breathe slowly, steadying her grip as the salon around her brought her back to the present, grounding her in the calm of the space.

It was only Daniel and the quiet, sunlit room, but still, she felt a familiar unease. She'd told herself over and over that she'd had no other choice, that it was Attwood or her, but the memory remained, insistent. Now, the thought of striking a mortal blow, of taking someone's life, even in defense, sent a chill through her.

Daniel watched her for a moment before stepping forward, his posture relaxed, his expression gentle. "You're holding back," he said quietly. "What's on your mind?"

She hesitated, unable to meet his gaze right away. She focused on her stance instead, adjusting her weight on her heels, feeling the solid floor beneath her. "I'm fine," she murmured, then stopped herself. Honesty was all they'd promised each other. "It's just...I want to be able to defend myself without..." She trailed off, the words heavy on her tongue.

"Without needing to take a life," he finished, his tone soft, understanding.

Catherine nodded, feeling the weight of her own fears settle between them. "Yes. I don't want to go through that again. Not if I can help it."

Daniel tilted his head, considering her words. "Then let's try something different. We'll work on close combat. There are ways to disable someone without needing a weapon."

She met his eyes, and for a moment, they shared a silent understanding. She recalled the night he'd told her about his past, the anguish in his voice as he spoke of what he'd done to survive —a choice he'd made as a boy that had left scars no one could see. In that moment, she realized he understood her guilt better than anyone else ever could.

Tentatively, she placed a hand on his arm, her fingers brushing against the warmth of his skin. "Thank you," she said, her voice quiet but steady. "For understanding."

He held her gaze, his hand covering hers, grounding her with his touch. "I know what it is to carry that weight," he replied, his voice steady, an unspoken promise between them that needed no further words.

Without another word, he stepped back and held up his hands, demonstrating a basic stance. "All right then, let's start with some close combat moves," he said, slipping into his familiar role as teacher.

As they practiced, she found herself focusing, not on the memory of that terrible night, but on each calculated movement he showed her. And with each strike, each block, she felt the tight knot of fear loosen, just a little. She wasn't free of it yet, but she was learning, step by step, how to hold her own against the darkness that lingered. And for the first time, she felt the beginning of a peace that didn't depend on the weight of a blade.

As they stepped out of the salon an hour later, Catherine was tired, but her mind kept turning over the movements Daniel had shown her, each stance and block a reminder of her determination to move beyond the fear that had gripped her in that warehouse. The quiet of the hallway enveloped them as they walked through the Savelle house, a blend of new and old at every turn. They'd only taken up residence here a few days ago, and everything was still unfamiliar to her.

They passed one room with recently painted walls, followed by another with yet-to-be-removed wallpaper and ancient window coverings. Throughout, she noted the familiar scent of lemon oil mingling with sharp scent of fresh wood.

Outside the wide windows, the garden was beginning to fade against the autumn landscape, the flower garden containing a scant number of blossoms now. Daniel paused beside her, his gaze softening. "The roses will be magnificent by next spring," he murmured.

She allowed herself a small smile, imagining the two of them walking through those very gardens. For the first time, she could almost believe that a life here—a life they were building together —was real.

They moved through the hallway, past rooms filled with draped furniture and tools, a half-finished collection of spaces that would one day feel like home. Daniel's voice was quiet but resolute. "I heard the news today. It's over. Attwood's been sentenced to prison."

She let out a sigh, feeling the tension melt away. "Finally," she said, though her relief was tinged with a shadow of concern. "But the gossip... it will linger, I suppose."

"It may linger, but not for long," he replied, meeting her gaze with a steady calm. "With Stansbury dead and Attwood behind bars, you're safe. And your secret as Gray—no one else will be able use it against you. Since you're no longer attending Bernini's academy, your risk is virtually nonexistent. Gray is gone. Out to pasture."

He took her hand, his fingers warm and reassuring. She squeezed back, a glint of challenge sparking in her eyes. "Until the next tournament, of course. I've no intention of giving up that trophy."

He grinned, the familiar mischievous glint lighting up his face. "I'd expect nothing less."

They passed by another room, where half-covered furnishings stood ready for their life together, each piece waiting for its next chapter. Catherine stepped through the doorway, fingers grazing the edge of a draped chair, the fabric rough beneath her hand. In one smooth motion, she pulled the cover aside, sending a small cloud of dust into the air. Beneath the cover lay a sturdy armchair with a well-worn seat, its faded upholstery whispering of count-less stories that had unfolded here, each stitch a mark of time.

She took a slow breath, letting her hand linger on the arm of the chair, feeling the potential that lay beneath the layers of dust and fabric. "We're building something here," she murmured, more to herself than to Daniel. "A home filled with life, not secrets. A place where our children can feel free to be themselves, without anyone trying to shape them into something they're not."

She looked over at him, catching the quiet certainty in his eyes. He placed a hand over hers, a reassuring warmth meeting her fingertips. "That's what I want as well," he replied softly, his tone carrying an unspoken promise. Together, they would fill these rooms—not with relics of the past, but with laughter and light, moments of their own making.

They continued down the hallway, the late afternoon sun casting long, promising shadows that stretched ahead, leading them into a future they were only beginning to shape.

Upstairs, Catherine's gaze lingered on the door of the small, attached bedroom beside their master suite. In another household, that room would have been hers alone, a private retreat where tradition would demand she sleep, maintaining the illusion of independence even in marriage. But when they'd moved in just days ago, Daniel had brushed tradition aside, insisting they share a bedroom, regardless of what society might think. Now, the unused suite stood as a quiet testament to the life they'd chosen together—a life built on trust, honesty, and an unspoken defiance of the conventions that had never fit them.

The moment she closed the bedroom door behind them, Catherine removed her white fencing cap to let her hair fall free around her shoulders. She glanced across the room, finding Daniel already at ease, his hands busy with a drawer that he couldn't seem to keep straight. She found herself smiling at the sight. He'd come so far from the guarded man who had once been so focused on propriety. He'd shown her glimpses of his past, shared pieces of himself he might have kept hidden forever. It was a gradual unfolding, but it meant more than he could know.

Noticing her gaze, he closed the drawer and moved to her side, brushing a loose strand of hair behind her ear, his fingers lingering. "You're getting too good with that knife," he murmured, a spark of challenge lighting his eyes. "I might need to find something more challenging for you."

Her lips curved in a small, curious smile. "Oh? And what would you suggest?"

He leaned back, clearly savoring the question. "Maybe archery," he replied, a hint of mischief in his tone. "Or perhaps a rifle? I have a feeling you'd be a natural."

She laughed, the sound unguarded, her mind suddenly filled with visions of the two of them at the range, each contest bringing them closer. His words held a promise of adventure, but under it, she sensed a steady admiration—an unwavering belief in her resilience. This was the essence of their life together: peace intertwined with possibility.

"Or perhaps," she countered, meeting his gaze with a wry smile, "we could choose an activity that doesn't involve weapons."

He grinned, unbothered. "Where's the fun in that?"

She grinned wickedly. "I know exactly where to find the fun."

Daniel took her meaning and rushed over to the window seat, tugging at one of his tight leather boots, the heel stubbornly refusing to budge. At his frustrated sigh, Catherine laughed, watching him struggle. She relented, kneeling beside him and brushing his hands away.

"Shall I call for Madson?" she teased, a smirk playing on her lips. "I hear he's quite skilled at dealing with unruly footwear."

Daniel shot her a mock glare. "You're welcome to, but I rather think you'd enjoy the challenge yourself."

She raised an eyebrow, grasping the boot firmly. "Challenge accepted."

She gave it a sharp tug but was as unsuccessful as he'd been.

"Put your back into it," he urged.

Together, they pulled, their efforts clumsy and out of sync, laughter bubbling up between them. With a final, triumphant yank, the boot slipped free, nearly toppling her into his lap. He caught her shoulders, steadying her as they both dissolved into laughter, his breath warm against her cheek.

She held up the boot with a flourish. "I'd say I'm as good a valet as Madson."

He grinned, clearly delighted. "You might make a show of it, but I'm not convinced. Madson, at least, doesn't send me sprawling."

She tilted her head, a playful glint in her eyes. "Well then, I'll just have to fight him for the privilege."

His response was quick—he pulled her onto his lap, capturing her hand. "Not a chance. I value Madson too much to let you hurt him." He nuzzled her neck, kissing her just beneath her ear.

Settling in, she let herself relax, her fingers still entwined with his. She looked up, a gentle smile playing on her lips. "I have so many plans for us. And for this place."

He gave her hand a squeeze, his tone soft. "Tell me everything."

"Well," she said, her eyes gleaming with excitement, "first, I intend to keep that tournament trophy for the next ten years. You'll have to get used to me being a champion."

He chuckled, drawing her closer. "With me as your sparring partner, I have no doubt you will."

She wrapped her arms around his shoulders, leaning in for a kiss that spoke of everything they'd shared, and all the things yet to come. When she pulled back, her voice softened, hope threading through her words. "And perhaps we could start on a family, too."

His face brightened, his eyes warm with anticipation. "I'll always be happy to help with that. We've been putting in the effort. Surely something will come of it soon."

She pulled him close, her lips brushing his in a slow, tantalizing kiss that left him breathless. "Maybe we simply haven't gotten the details right yet," she murmured. Her fingers undoing his fencing jacket, slipping just beneath the fabric, her touch both light and deliberate. He shivered as her hand moved lower, his pulse quickening.

"You've always been good with your hands," he murmured, his voice thick with warmth. "It's one of the things I admire about you. That and your wicked, wicked tongue."

She smiled, a hint of mischief lighting her eyes. "I could use it now, but you might find it overwhelming."

He chuckled, sliding his hands along her back, pulling her flush against him. "I think I'd enjoy the challenge."

Their laughter mingled as his hands roamed, her touch guiding him with an irresistible pull. She leaned in, her breath warm against his ear. "Then let me surprise you."

As she led him back toward the bed, their kisses deepened, each touch igniting a fire that left no space for anything but them. The air around them thickened with unspoken promises, both of them letting go, their laughter and whispers giving way to the shared rhythm of their embrace.

61 EPILOGUE
HUNTLEY ACADEMY

The following January

Daniel swept the deck of cards off the walnut table, the delicate inlays catching the morning light, and replaced them with a set of drawings he extracted from a long tube. The plans had arrived even sooner than he'd expected.

"Catherine, come here. Mr. Newcomb sent over the design plans for renovating that crumbling old folly in Scotland."

She rose from the pale blue velvet sofa and picked up two glass paperweights—gifts from her father—from the side table, setting them on the drawings to hold them flat. Leaning in to examine the main sketch, she inhaled sharply. "Oh my, look at it. Those Grecian columns are lovely. Calliope would be entranced."

"Who?" Daniel looked at her blankly.

"You know, Mrs. Attwood."

He snorted. "I'd managed to erase her from my memory. Don't go resurrecting her."

She smirked. "I hadn't realized you were so traumatized. Thank goodness you never had to share a train compartment with her. I'm not sure you'd have survived it." She glanced fondly at the two dogs they had rescued, curled up nearby. "At least we were able to save these two."

Daniel reached down to scratch Tremor's side, and the once-fearful dog, now loyal and steady, leaned heavily against his leg. Valor, the larger of the pair, lay contentedly before the fire, his warm coat catching the flickering light as he dozed. "Me? Trapped in a compartment with Calliope? I'm certain one of our lives would have ended."

Catherine leaned over Mr. Newcomb's drawing, her shoulder brushing his as she adjusted the edge of the parchment. "This is perfect. He's even added a spot for a picnic lunch. I know a folly's supposed to be pointless, but I'd prefer to give it purpose." She stretched as she stood up, arching her back gracefully, a motion that made him pause.

"You have a streak of practicality I find quite endearing," he said, reaching for her and pulling her into his arms for a kiss. She melted into him, another quality he found irresistible.

"Speaking of practicality," she murmured, leaning back to meet his gaze, "the repairs to the retaining wall along the road to our house seem to be complete."

"They are. Now you can walk along the top without worrying it'll collapse under you. Just promise me you'll wait until this autumn before you try it again."

"You're terribly demanding, but I still like you."

"Admit it. You love me."

She melted into him once again. "Always."

He grinned, tracing his fingers down her back. "How's your new fencing instructor working out?"

"Diana is wonderful. She's patient enough to work with beginners and skilled enough to teach advanced techniques. She's everything I could have hoped for."

"Is your sister coming by today?"

"Yes, she should be here shortly." Catherine stopped as the

butler entered the room, his polished shoes silent on the Persian rug that stretched the length of the grand drawing room.

"Yes, Jenson?" Daniel asked.

"Lord Wentworth is here, my lord."

"Show him in," Daniel replied. "It's later than I'd realized." He compared the time on his pocket watch to the clock on the mantel.

"And send in some tea," Catherine added, rolling up the plans for the folly and sliding them into the tube. She returned to the pale blue sofa, sat, and adjusted her hoop skirt so it draped just so.

"Yes, my lady," the butler said, disappearing through the double doors.

"We still need to discuss Sarah's lessons," Daniel said, his tone suddenly serious as he adjusted the time on the antique clock on the mantel.

"We will, but not with Wentworth about to walk in," Catherine replied, raising an eyebrow. "He's entirely too clever. He'll catch on."

"Hmmph."

Just then, the door swung open, and Wentworth entered, a tall, slender paper bag in hand. "Happy New Year!" he called, glancing around at the tapestries that adorned the walls, each depicting a scene from mythology.

"Happy New Year," they replied in unison as Daniel crossed the room to stand near Catherine.

Wentworth glanced around. "Where are the garlands, the festive adornments? You've taken down all the Christmas decorations. I'd half expected to see them up until Epiphany."

"We had to," Catherine said with a light laugh. "The pine boughs were shedding everywhere."

Wentworth's gaze flicked toward her, and he smiled. "Country life agrees with you, my lady. You're looking remarkably well."

Daniel smiled too as he settled into a chair, then gestured to the matching one beside him. "I was just saying the very same thing last night. Sit, won't you?"

As Wentworth took his seat, Catherine blushed slightly, but her eyes sparkled. "It must be because I'm so happy."

"It must be," Daniel agreed, his tone brimming with contentment.

Catherine stood, brushing a hand over her skirts. "You'll excuse me, won't you? My sister will be here soon, and I have a few things to prepare."

"Of course, Lady Huntley," Wentworth replied, rising slightly from his seat in acknowledgment.

Daniel caught her hand before she could go. "Remember our agreement: no riding, no climbing walls, and nothing reckless."

She sighed, her lips curving into a soft smile. "I promise," she said, squeezing his hand. With one last smile at both men, she left the room.

When she'd gone, Wentworth arched an eyebrow at Daniel. "You've grown rather protective, haven't you?"

Daniel shrugged. "It comes with marriage," he replied, a touch of humor lacing his voice.

Wentworth gave a thoughtful hum, settling back into his chair as the footman entered with the tea tray, setting it on an intricately carved tea table that had been polished to a high sheen. "I must thank you for your investment advice," he said, adding a lump of sugar to his tea.

Daniel looked up, momentarily puzzled. "What advice?"

"About the bonds," Wentworth clarified. "Your Midas touch didn't disappoint."

Daniel waved a hand dismissively. "I'd nearly forgotten. It went well, then?"

"Very. I was able to reimburse another of my father's unfortunate investors. With each one I clear, it feels like a step closer to putting that sordid business behind me."

"You must be nearing the end of your list."

Wentworth let out a small sigh. "I am, thankfully. It's taken years." He handed the bag to Daniel. "A small token of my gratitude."

"You know that's not necessary," Daniel said, though he accepted the bag with a raised brow.

"It isn't, but it made me happy," Wentworth replied with a grin. "Go on, take it."

Daniel opened the bag and pulled out a bottle of Glenfarclas, a twenty-year-old vintage. He chuckled softly. "You do know me well. I've started keeping this on hand because of you, and now I think I prefer it to anything else."

"Well, I wouldn't expect you to settle for anything less," Wentworth said with a smile. "But I'm afraid I won't be joining you for a glass today."

Daniel glanced at the clock. "Ah, pity. Next time then. More urgent matters await?"

Wentworth leaned back, his expression shifting slightly, a shadow passing across his face. "I received a note from Frederick this morning. He wants to meet me at the Winter Solstice Ball at the Russian Embassy tonight. He promised things would quiet down after last year's fiasco. But here he is—pulling me back in."

Daniel's brow furrowed, his expression turning serious. "Russia again?"

Wentworth let out a weary sigh. "Of course. He has an uncanny knack for courting trouble." He paused, then shook his head. "I thought I'd be free of his schemes by now, but it seems that was wishful thinking."

Daniel's gaze remained steady, a flicker of concern in his eyes. "Take care tonight."

"I always do," Wentworth replied, though his smile didn't quite reach his eyes. "But Frederick? I'm not so sure."

With that, Wentworth gave a brief nod, then turned on his heel. "Until next time," he said over his shoulder as he made his way to the door.

Daniel remained where he stood, watching his friend leave. Though Wentworth's words had been light, the weight of what he'd said lingered in the room. Trouble was indeed brewing, and somehow, Daniel had the sense that this was only the beginning.

Catherine nudged Lady Bennett's feet apart with the toe of her boot, eyeing her stance in the sunlight streaming through tall windows. Sunlight cast long, golden beams across the salon floor, dancing over Lady Bennett's outstretched foot and warming the polished wood. "You need to stand more like a man," she instructed. "Widen your stance, and you'll find much better balance."

A soft voice called from behind, barely louder than the clash of foils echoing in the room. "Catherine?"

Turning, she saw her sister, Sarah, standing nervously at the entrance to the ladies' portion of the fencing salon, clutching her reticule. As she stepped further into the room, Sarah's eyes widened at the sight of so many women focused and poised, their faces catching the sunlight as they moved, shadows shifting and stretching across the floor. "I never imagined so many ladies would come here," she whispered, clearly in awe.

Catherine's face broke into a warm smile. "Welcome! I've been looking forward to this. Let's go to the dressing room, and I'll help you change into your fencing costume."

A small smile appeared on Sarah's lips. "I'll admit I'm a little nervous."

"Don't be. You'll love it," Catherine said, wrapping an arm around her sister's waist and guiding her toward the pretty blue room lined with curtained stalls. Unlike the men's open changing area at Bernini's, Catherine had ensured her students had the privacy she had always wished for. Sunlight filtered through a small window, illuminating delicate dust motes dancing in the air, casting soft shadows onto the blue walls.

"Mother didn't suspect anything, did she?" Catherine asked, amusement flickering in her eyes.

Sarah shook her head, a hint of mischief in her smile. "I told her I was volunteering with the Ladies' Aid Society. She was so pleased she insisted I stay all afternoon. She'd never guess this is what I'm doing."

"Good thinking. Let's get you changed."

As Catherine dismissed the waiting lady's maid with a polite nod, Sarah's gaze drifted to the fencing costume, a mixture of excitement and apprehension on her face as she considered wearing one herself. Catherine stepped forward, undoing the row of buttons down Sarah's back, the fabric slipping away to reveal a pale line of skin, half in shadow.

"Even if you don't fall in love with fencing the way I did, you'll gain confidence and learn to defend yourself. You never know when it might come in handy."

Sarah glanced at the mirror, catching the way the sunlight framed her reflection, her expression growing thoughtful as Catherine loosened the strings on her corset. "I hope I'm never in a situation like the one you were in last March," she said with a shudder. "I'd have been petrified."

Catherine slipped Sarah's dress over her head, the fabric rustling softly. "Trust me, I could go a lifetime without a repeat experience." She offered a small smile, hoping to keep the mood light, though a shadow passed briefly across her eyes.

Sarah's expression grew somber as she held Catherine's gaze in the mirror. "Why did Stansbury and Attwood go to such lengths?"

Catherine took a steadying breath, her voice soft but resolute. "Revenge. Stansbury's hatred for Daniel ran deeper than I ever realized."

"But why so elaborate? Why not just slit his throat and be done with it?" Sarah's bluntness brought a flicker of nausea to

Catherine's stomach, but she pushed it down, glancing at the sunlight warming the floorboards.

"Stansbury wanted more than that. It wasn't enough just to kill him—he wanted to ruin him." Catherine picked up a pair of leggings and handed them to Sarah. "He'd planned to rig the tournament and escape with the winnings."

Hesitating, Sarah pulled the leggings on over her pantalets. "That sounds... unhinged. Didn't he realize he'd ruin himself in the process?"

"He had nothing left to lose. Word had already spread about his shady dealings, and he blamed Daniel for it all, as if he were somehow responsible." Catherine retrieved the fencing jacket and helped Sarah pull it over her shirt. "I was terrified, and I'll always be grateful that Daniel arrived when he did."

Sarah looked up, concern in her eyes. "And Attwood?"

"He's dead now. He died of a lung infection in prison, shortly after he was sentenced," Catherine replied, her tone somber. "Calliope's faring well, at least. She's become quite the respectable widow."

They returned to the fencing salon, where the sunlight had shifted, casting soft afternoon shadows across the room. Sarah paused, her eyes wide as she took in the sight above the fireplace. "Is that it?" she breathed, pulling off her mask.

Catherine followed her gaze and smiled. "The traveling tournament trophy? Yes, it is. I won it last month, and I plan to keep winning so I can keep it here."

Hampstead's name was engraved on it first, with hers directly beneath it. Or rather, Alexander Gray's. It made no difference since they were one and the same. Finally, the threads of her life had merged.

"I'm so proud of you," Sarah said, taking in the trophy and then looking around, surprised by the number of women gathered. "It's incredible. I never imagined so many ladies would come here."

Catherine beamed. "The best part is that our meetings are still a secret. The Ladies' Aid Society cover works beautifully, and it gives us the perfect excuse to gather regularly."

Sarah glanced at her, impressed. "How did you come up with it?"

"It wasn't me," Catherine replied, a warm smile touching her lips. "That was Daniel's idea. He knew we'd need a respectable front, and now our contributions provide the perfect reason for our meetings."

As she spoke, Catherine waved over a tall woman with straight black hair. "Sarah, meet Dianna, our newest instructor. She'll be teaching you today—she's highly skilled."

Sarah's face fell slightly. "But I thought you'd be teaching me."

Catherine smiled, placing a hand on her stomach. "Things have changed... I'm afraid you'll have to wait a little while before I'm fencing again. You're going to be an aunt."

Sarah's eyes widened as she realized the meaning behind Catherine's words. "An aunt?" she breathed, a radiant smile spreading across her face. "Oh, Catherine, that's wonderful news!"

Catherine's own smile softened, a look of contentment lighting up her face. "I think I must be the luckiest woman in the world."

The End

ALSO BY

Historical romances
By Sheridan Jeane
Gambling On a Scoundrel

Secrets and Seduction series:

It Takes a Spy...
Lady Catherine's Secret
Once Upon a Spy
My Lady, My Spy
Along Came a Spy

Also available:
Lady Cecilia Is Cordially Disinvited for Christmas
(only available via Sheridan's VIP club)

View the full Secrets and Seduction series and leave a review

Duke By Dawn (Novella, part of the anthology *Dukes All Night Long*)

The Shadow of the Black Rose - a Victorian-era Romantic Suspense trilogy
Whispers and Spies
The Spy In Disguise
Protect the Prince

Contemporary Romances
By Sheri Tyler
The Way to a Woman's Heart series - the **Coming Home** trilogy
Slow Simmer
Here's the Scoop
From Bitter to Sweet

The Way to a Woman's Heart series - the **Destination Wedding** trilogy
One Cup of Chemistry

Say Cheese!
Kebabs and Kisses

ACKNOWLEDGMENTS

Thank you to my husband Bob and our children for their help, their support, and their understanding. I couldn't have done any of this without you.

I want to thank Kristi Avalon, H.O. Knight, Chloe Flowers, and all the members of the Sunshine Critique Group for everything they did to help make this book a reality. Amanda Sumner did an amazing job copyediting.
I want to thank Ann Marie Stone for her awesome proofreading skills.
I also want to thank my friend Dr. Paul (PJ) Foster for providing information regarding medical care in the 1850s.

I want to express my heartfelt gratitude to my dear friend Eva Costa and honor the memory of her beloved dog. The police suspect her pet was tragically stolen from her fenced yard and forced into a dog fight, much like the fate Catherine and Daniel worked to prevent for the dogs they rescued. I only wish our heroes could have been there to save Eva's cherished companion.

Lastly, I want to thank NEORWA- the Northeast Ohio Romance Writers of America chapter of Romance Writers of America, now Great Lake Fiction Writers. I found you just when I needed you most, and you made my transition from hopeful writer to published author a successful one.

Sheridan Jeane is an award-winning author of historical romantic suspense, weaving stories of intrigue, danger, and slow-burning romance. She also writes lighthearted contemporary romance under the name Sheri Tyler.

She grew up in Huber Heights, a suburb of Dayton, Ohio, and now lives just outside Pittsburgh. Sheridan holds a bachelor's degree in computer science with a minor in English. She co-founded Three Rivers Romance Writers, a former chapter of Romance Writers of America that supported a vibrant local community of romance writers.

When she's not reading or writing, she can be found learning to salsa dance, tumbling downhill on skis, or volunteering with the Child Health Association of Sewickley to support children in need in southwestern Pennsylvania.

www.SheridanJeane.com